Mosaic

Susan X Meagher

MOSAIC
© 2021 BY SUSAN X MEAGHER

THIS TRADE PAPERBACK ORIGINAL IS PUBLISHED BY BRISK PRESS, WAPPINGERS FALLS, NY 12590.

EDITED BY: CATRIONA BENNINGTON
COVER DESIGN AND LAYOUT BY: CAROLYN NORMAN

FIRST PRINTING: MARCH 2021

ISBN-13: 978-1-7343038-1-0

By Susan X Meagher

Novels

Arbor Vitae
All That Matters
Cherry Grove
The Lies That Bind
The Legacy
Doublecrossed
Smooth Sailing
How To Wrangle a Woman
Almost Heaven
The Crush
The Reunion
Inside Out
Out of Whack
Homecoming
The Right Time
Summer of Love
Chef's Special
Fame
Vacationland
Wait For Me
The Keeper's Daughter
Friday Night Flights
Mosaic

Short Story Collection

Girl Meets Girl

Serial Novel

I Found My Heart In San Francisco

Anthologies

Undercover Tales
Outsiders

ACKNOWLEDGMENTS

I have never lived in Pittsburgh, but after having visited it fairly often during my research, I'm confident I could happily do so. It has all of the highlights of a major metropolitan area, but it renders them in a compact space, allowing you to traverse large parts of it by foot. I find myself craving another visit, even though the book is finished, and that's a sure sign the city is a winner.

During my visits, I button-holed a lot of people, asking questions until I could tell they'd had their fill. I found Pittsburgers to be very tolerant of my inquiries, and uniformly helpful. Thanks to all who took the time to orient me and give me your perspective on the place you call home.

Catherine Lane helped me a great deal by reading my first draft and urging me to discard a few story threads that didn't lead anywhere productive. Her suggestions about tightening up various other elements were also spot-on. Having someone care enough to spend many hours reading and discussing a work-in-progress is a gift that I'm immensely thankful for.

Teresa Z helped me out by doing a final reading, and I thank her for catching some things that totally escaped my notice. It's so nice to have someone pull you back from an embarrassing mistake.

While kicking around ideas for a title with some friends, Elaine Garrard suggested Mosaic, and I thought it fit like a glove. Thanks for saving me from sticking with my working title, *It's The Pitts.*

DEDICATION

This book, like everything important to me, is dedicated to my wife Carrie. She's the key ingredient in my writing career, and I'm confident I wouldn't enjoy the process even half as much without her continual, enthusiastic support.

CHAPTER ONE

KELSEY MALIAR PILOTED HER CAR along marginally familiar streets, annoyed with herself for having neither juice in her phone, nor a charging cable within reach. She was sure she would have been able to find this factory in no time at all if her car had GPS, but it had not only been built before GPS was a common option, she'd purposefully bought the most stripped-down model she could find. Expensive options were just unnecessary things that started to feel necessary the minute they broke.

The streets in this once heavily-industrial, now hipster-influenced part of Lawrenceville were not particularly gorgeous, now made even more homely by the dirty snow. They'd been surprised by an early November storm a few days earlier, and the temps had been just cold enough to keep the snowy dregs around, making everything look kind of filthy.

Despite having lived in Pittsburgh her whole life, she was often surprised by little snippets of entire neighborhoods or just individual streets she was sure she'd never traveled on. Sometimes she loved the feeling of discovering something new in a place she thought she knew backwards and forwards. Today that love was entirely missing—all because of a dead phone.

She'd spent a decent amount of time in Lawrenceville, patronizing the Neapolitan pizza joints, craft beer emporiums, and farm-to-table restaurants that made you feel like you'd broken the law by eating an artichoke grown in another state. But the places she'd visited had been in the thirties or forties. Up here in the fifties, the vibe was hipster-adjacent rather than full-on eleven-dollar beers. Ten blocks could be a big difference in Pittsburgh.

Continuing to creep up the street, she briefly thought of what this area would have looked like a hundred years earlier. She wasn't sure if any of her ancestors had ever lived in this specific neighborhood, but Upper Lawrenceville had been filled with her people. Immigrants who only knew how to work hard—for subsistence wages and keep their complaints to themselves. What would her great-grandparents say if they witnessed a couple paying eighteen bucks for a pizza that barely filled them? She laughed at the image, assuming they'd tell the hipsters they were as dumb as rocks.

The address of the factory was stuck to her dash with a sticky note, and she took a look to double-check once she spotted the proper street. They were close to the river here, keeping the streets short. At the end of the block was a nondescript, hulking brick building, probably once some kind of foundry or heavy-manufacturing plant—albeit a small one. Someone had told her that one of the biggest blast furnaces had been in this part of Lawrenceville, and, if that was true, all kinds of smaller businesses would have sprung up to provide tools and dies and other pieces of machinery too inconsequential for the big guys to bother with. Back then, these smaller factories would have been chock-a-block to the modest, two-story homes that still lined the streets. It must have been a noisy, stinking mess, with all kinds of crud spewing out of a factory two feet from your bedroom window. How bad must things have been in Slovakia to make industrial Pittsburgh seem like the promised land?

The faded red brick building sported a loading dock on one side and a tiny parking strip on the other that was full of cars, probably belonging to the workers. This didn't look like the kind of place that customers routinely visited.

Kelsey had to turn around and head back toward Butler to stow her car, then she got out, careful to avoid the broken sidewalk and puddles of slushy mess that the cold sun had created.

When she reached the facade of the building, she saw a spiffy metal sign stating the address and street number, which surprisingly improved the look of the building by a hundred percent. Below the address,

"Pittsburgh's Finest" had been rendered in tile, each foot-tall letter framed in what appeared to be, but probably wasn't, rusted metal. Below that big, blocky, industrial-looking name, a curvy handwriting font that might have been hand-painted on the metal added the legend, "Handcrafted Tile." It was a very nice touch, hinting at Pittsburgh's brawny nature, along with the delicate hand needed to craft unique tile. Whoever had bothered with the time and expense to create the sign for a building that probably got few customers was a nit-picker. Since she loved to pick nits herself, she was feeling good as she approached the front door, absolutely sure of one thing. This stuff was going to be expensive.

Kelsey opened the heavy wooden door with the decorative glass insert, hearing a tinkling bell above her head. The reception area was nearly at the doorway, where a woman wrapped in a heavy sweater along with a wool scarf looped around her neck sat. Kelsey closed the door quickly, saying, "I bet you love it when people stand in the open door for a minute or two, right?"

"If I had a gun…" The woman smiled, and Kelsey did what she always did when she was face-to-face with a pretty woman. She tried to guess her particulars. This specimen woman was super young, early twenties more likely than not. She was probably straight, but to Kelsey's practiced eye, not too straight. The graceful, airy tattoo that sat right under her ear showed she also wasn't too staid. She looked a little arty, too, with a spiky haircut that showed off her angular bone-structure. Her hair was probably brown originally, but had been dyed the silver color that a lot of young women were into at the moment. All in all, her image was easily nice enough to ponder for more than a moment, but business called.

"Hi there," Kelsey said. "I'm from Sedlak Brothers."

The woman gave her a blank, but pleasant look.

"The home improvement store over in Breezy Point?" Kelsey added, still getting nothing. "Anyway, we're kitchen and bath designers. I've got a client who doesn't like any of the tile we currently carry. I thought I might be able to find something here that would impress her."

Now the woman brightened. "If we don't have what you want, we'll make it," she said confidently. "You're talking about a single kitchen?"

"A single house," she clarified. "Kitchen, entry way, four bathrooms, and a fireplace surround. But I'm also open to the idea of putting your samples in our showroom." She tried not to look too full of herself. "I make the decisions on what we carry in the store." Her co-workers weren't crazy about that, but Kelsey was damned happy to be the favorite, and she wasn't about to give up her slot.

The woman looked down at her desk, and Kelsey followed her gaze. When a white light on the multi-line phone dimmed, she pressed a button. "Hi, boss. Do you have a minute to talk to someone about having some tile made?" She nodded a few times. "Uh-huh. I think so." She looked up at Kelsey, studying her for a minute. "Mmm-hmm. Right. We'll be here."

She hung up and smiled brightly. "Summer will be here in a minute."

"I wish," Kelsey said, rubbing her arms to show she was making a joke about the weather. But the woman gave her another blank look, her IQ not seeming to match her striking looks.

Kelsey looked to her right when she heard footsteps coming down the hallway. It was turning out to be a surprisingly good day at the tile store. Summer was aptly named, appearing like a warm splash of sunshine on an otherwise grey day. Kelsey was a little tongue-tied as she looked at her, barely noticing her fair hair and brownish eyes, amazed that someone could throw off so much warmth with just a smile.

"Hi there," she said, extending her hand for a firm shake. "Summer Hayes. What can I do for you?"

"Summer Haze? Cool name. Hippie parents?"

She narrowed her gaze for a moment. "Are you picturing it spelled h-a-z-e?" She nodded, looking thoughtful. "Sadly, it's just the standard h-a-y-e-s, but I might change it. I'd like to make it a little more funky."

"I must be longing for the hazy days of summer. I'm Kelsey Maliar, the lead kitchen designer over at Sedlak Brothers in—"

"Really?" She leaned against the reception area's short wall for a second, then put her hands behind herself and boosted her butt up to sit upon it, her booted feet dangling like a child's. "I tried to get you guys to carry my product line when I was just starting out. Bupkis," she said, flicking her fingers in the air.

"When was that?"

"About…" She closed her eyes slightly. "Ten years ago, give or take. I talked to…a pretty old guy called Junior?"

Kelsey nodded. "John Junior was in charge until about eight years ago."

"He had absolutely no interest in my work." Her smile grew a little brighter. "He told me his customers were looking for cheap and cheerful, and my stuff was neither."

"Kind of harsh. But our management, as well as our clients, have changed in the last few years. We're doing more historic renovations now, and cheap and cheerful doesn't cut it with that crowd."

"You're…" She leaned toward Kelsey slightly as a surprisingly flirty smile made her whole face light up. "Offering what? Do you want to become an authorized retailer after kicking me to the curb when I really needed the work?"

Kelsey rocked back on her heels for a second, then Summer let out a laugh. "Kidding," she said, reaching up to tuck her surprisingly long hair back over her shoulder.

Kelsey watched her closely, now enthralled by the color and texture of her hair, obviously a natural pale blonde. What must it be like to have such a rare color? Probably kind of freaky. Guys must have hit on her relentlessly, which had to be a pain in the butt.

"I assume you have one customer you can't please with your current line-up. I'm right, aren't I."

Once again caught off-guard, Kelsey said, "That's true. But it's a good customer, and if I can find something that strikes me, I really do have the authority to decide to carry your line."

"Hmm…" Summer looked her over, clearly trying to decide if Kelsey merited her time.

She should have kept her mouth shut, but Kelsey found herself rattling on. "If I can make this very particular client happy, she'll be my biggest sale—ever."

Deadpan, Summer said, "God knows I want you both to be happy." She twisted around on the counter to reach the desk, giving Kelsey another chance to check her out. She was dressed professionally, but not formally. Her boots, one of which was way off the ground as she squirmed around trying to pick up what must have been a heavy book, were really cool. Mostly brown leather, with a bit of dark brown suede on the sides. Her mid-brown jeans looked really good with the boots, not to mention how they showed off her butt, which was worth a very long look. But Kelsey sternly reminded herself she was working, not scoping out a woman in a club. She removed her gaze from Summer's butt and limited her appreciation to the forest green blouse decorated with white ivy. She never thought to wear a pressed blouse to work, but this one looked awfully nice.

Those cute boots tapped at the wall as Summer balanced the tri-fold sample book on her thighs. "Take a look at our standard line for this year. Most of these are in stock and ready for delivery."

"I can stop you right there," Kelsey said, not bothering to even take a peek. "My client wants something she can't get anywhere else, and I do mean *any*where."

"Really?" Summer raised an eyebrow, which was a particularly nice one. Not too thick, and several shades darker than her hair. "Does your client have any idea of what she'll have to pay for true custom tile?"

"She might. But I can guarantee there isn't a number that will be too large. Her goal seems to be to spend more money on renovating her house than any of her neighbors."

Summer slapped the heavy book closed. "Come into my office, Kelsey. I'll put everything on hold to nab a custom job." As they started to walk, Summer turned back to the reception desk to say, "Hold my calls, Chelsea."

"All of them?"

Summer laughed softly. "Just ones about jobs smaller than this one."

Summer was truly too busy to spend time talking to a rando off the street. But this rando was probably gay, definitely cute, and seemed like fun. One of the biggest perks of owning your own business was being able to have fun when the opportunity arose, and Summer tried to indulge herself whenever possible. Of course, the bills needed to be paid, and if Kelsey had just wanted to buy stock tiles she'd be sitting in the lounge looking at their sample books by now.

Pittsburgh's Finest did a lot of custom work, but most of that was for institutional or commercial settings. Residential customers were just getting on the bandwagon of making a unique, lasting addition to their homes, something future generations could admire. In her biased opinion, a custom fireplace surround or an entryway floor was the best way to leave your mark. Granted, it was an expensive mark, but quality had never been cheap.

She let Kelsey pass in front of her when they reached the office. "Can I get you a coffee? Tea? We've got a huge selection."

Kelsey pulled one of the chairs out and sat, then looked up with a thoughtful expression. "I'd actually love a cup of tea. Do you have Irish Breakfast? That's my favorite."

"Do I have Irish Breakfast," Summer said, rolling her eyes. "This is the big leagues. I'll be back in a flash."

Their break room was at the end of the hall, and Summer smiled to herself when two of her glazers jumped up and made for the exit to the production area the minute she entered. She checked the clock, seeing it was ten forty. The floor supervisor usually called for breaks at ten and three, so the glazers had been dawdling. But she wouldn't say anything unless it became chronic. Some days you truly needed to chill with a friend.

It took a while to get everything in order, then she added a few butter cookies to the tray and carried it back to her office.

When she entered, Kelsey gawped at her like she'd carved a swan out of ice. "You made a pot of tea?"

"It's easier than carrying hot liquid in a cardboard box. I've tried."

"No," she said, smiling gently. "I've just never had anyone make a whole pot for me. I usually get a teabag, along with lukewarm water in a mug."

Summer set the tray on a small round table between the chairs and sat down. "This is a first class concern, Kelsey." She laughed a little. "I was going to use your last name to sound more stilted, but I've forgotten it already."

"Maliar."

"Mmm." She poured the tea into a cup, then offered it to Kelsey. "Help yourself to your add-ins." While she poured her own, she said, "Is your name Ukrainian?"

"Slovak. Actually, it should be Maliarova, but once we got to America we stopped feminizing it."

"I'm not second-guessing you, but Maliarova has a better rhythm. It's not too late to change, you know. Tell you what. I'll change mine to Haze, and we can go to City Hall to file the paperwork together."

Kelsey took the teasing well, smiling and nodding like she was going to get right on that project. After stirring her milk in she took a sip. "Oh, boy, that's good. My grandmother would love this, rest her soul. She complained constantly about not being able to get a good cup of tea in America."

"Are Slovaks big tea drinkers?"

"Actually, I don't know any real Slovaks. From Slovakia, I mean. So I can't guess their affinity for tea. I'm talking about my maternal grandmother. First-generation Irish American, and tea-addict."

"Ahh. Never argue with an addict." Reaching across her desk, Summer pulled her tablet over and opened it to the photos of the custom tiles they'd done in the last few years. "Ready to look at some of our work?"

"Absolutely."

Summer homed in on some of her favorites, tiles they'd done for a patron lounge at Heinz Hall. "I love these," she said. "Every instrument in the orchestra is represented, jet black on a pure white background." She let her stylus hover over the outline of a clarinet. "This shows the level of detail we can create."

"I can see each key," Kelsey said quietly.

"It looks fantastic in the room, but the important thing is that this was exactly what they were looking for. It reflects the orchestra's essence, right?"

"Right." She touched the edge of the tablet. "Mind if I page through?"

"Go right ahead. You'll see it's mostly commercial, but there are a few residential installations in there. People love our tiles for the craftsman-style homes they've been snapping up."

"That's exactly what my clients have," Kelsey said, leaning over to really study the tiles as she flipped through.

Summer was watching to see what interested her, but she wasn't focusing as closely as she should have been. It wasn't every day, or every month, that a nice looking lesbian popped into her office.

She wasn't even sure how she knew Kelsey was gay, but she would have eaten her rainbow flag if she wasn't. It was hard to tell a lot about a person in November, when everyone wore a fluffy down coat, but Kelsey had shrugged out of hers while Summer had been brewing tea, revealing enough of herself to keep Summer busy for a minute.

First, she checked Kelsey's left hand, pleased to see no wedding ring. Same-sex marriage had been awesome for many reasons, but a small side benefit was that you could cross a woman off your list quickly if she wore a ring.

Kelsey's dark hair had a little wave to it, and it looked really nice against her red sweater. She took good care of her nails, which Summer appreciated, but she kept them the lesbian-approved length, long enough to show she didn't bite them, short enough to not injure a partner.

Now that they were sitting close to one another, she could see that Kelsey's legs were a little longer than her own, confirming her guess that she was a bit taller. So far, there wasn't a thing about her that made Summer dread having to work with her, and there were quite a few things that made her consider asking her out once their business was settled. That would be a first, but after running her business for ten years, she didn't mind taking a few risks.

"Pardon?" Summer said when she realized she'd been daydreaming.

"I asked about color. I assume you can do just about anything?"

"Oh, sure. Anything your fertile imagination can come up with. But nearly everyone wants something in green, rust, tan, or a muted orange. If the house is filled with oak, natural, earthy colors look best."

Kelsey let out a sigh. "My client wants to update the house, which means she's going to paint most of the wood."

Summer had to clench her hands into fists to stop herself from grabbing Kelsey and shaking her. After making sure she could control her voice, she said, "They're painting the *original* wood? Pristine oak that's been unmolested for over a hundred years?"

"Uh-huh." She looked down, thankfully showing the shame she should have been filled with. "I just do the technical layout of the kitchen and baths. My client's interior designer is the one who has convinced her to go with mostly white walls, with royal blue and slate gray accents. No unfinished wood."

"Philistine," Summer grumbled. "If I wasn't saving for an upcoming trip to Portugal, I'd turn this job down. But I could really use a nice, big boost to my vacation fund, so I'll throw away my strongly held beliefs for a few bucks." She let out a wry laugh. "I guess it's not as bad as cutting down the rain forest, but I wish to hell there was a law that prevented people from screwing up historic homes."

"I do too. I really tried to talk the home owner into keeping at least the dining room original, but she's even going to take out the built-in breakfront. I assume they'll sell that for a bag of cash."

"Or chop it up and throw it into a landfill," Summer said, her voice taking on a dark tone. She took the tablet back, slugged the rest of her tea down, and got up to return to her side of the desk. "I assume your client will want some ostentatious family crest they make up on the fly?"

"I don't think they have one of those, but..." She paused and swallowed noticeably. "She's mentioned including her dogs in some way. I've been hoping she means just their initials or something..."

Summer picked up her stylus and started to draw, coming up with what she thought was a pretty good representation of a Cavalier King Charles spaniel. "Something like this?"

"How did you know?"

"They're hugely popular right now. Some super-famous influencer must have a couple of them."

Kelsey rested her head on the edge of the desk and thumped it softly against the wood. "Sometimes I can't stand the people who make it possible to pay my rent."

"Roger that. But I'm sure people one or two rungs below us on the income distribution graph think we suck too."

"Most likely." She sat up straight and settled her hair. "So, you can go modern on the tiles?"

"We can honestly do just about anything, Kelsey. I've done tiles that look like leather, or wood, or metal. Just advise your client that having a custom color isn't much more expensive than our standard ones. It's when we have to paint dogs' faces on them that the price skyrockets."

"I'll talk to her designer. I don't like his esthetic, but he understands how to rein a budget in if he needs to." She revealed a wry smile. "So far, my client is trusting him to keep an eye on costs. Have you ever heard anything stupider?"

Summer laughed, glad to hear that Kelsey seemed to have a good grip on reality. "That's like having a pastry chef as your dietician, but I'm constantly surprised at how cavalier people are about blowing wads of money."

"I'm not sure what the opposite of cavalier is, but that's where I am when it comes to spending money."

"That's because you work for a living." She started to stand. "Even though your client sounds like a dope, I hope we can do business together."

Kelsey stood and extended her hand. "I do too, even if the only thing I get out of this is a tour of your shop. I'm fascinated by tile."

"Are you then?" Summer spent a moment giving Kelsey as long a glance as she could manage without seeming rude. The fact that Kelsey stood stock-still, with only her smile growing wider showed that she didn't mind another woman checking her out—albeit politely. After looking at the clock and realizing she wouldn't be ruining her day to blow a little time, Summer said, "Let's go take a look right now. We don't get many visitors, but my crew seems to like it when I boast about them."

"Now? Right now?" She also took a look at her watch, seeming to be wrestling with her conscience about spending more time away from the office. "What the heck? I don't have anything scheduled for an hour."

"If you're going to play hooky, you might as well be doing something interesting. And if you like tile…"

⊛

Summer led the way down the hall, then she pushed open a heavy fire door, revealing the production floor.

"Damn! Do you make all of the tile in the world?"

"Some days it feels like it, but we're probably about a tenth of a percent of the U.S. market."

"Wow," Kelsey said, letting her gaze slowly move across the room. The building itself was two stories, and she'd assumed that the company was spread out over two floors. But this part of the building was a single floor, with a double-height ceiling. Tall windows ringed three sides, probably original, with thin muntins creating so many panes she didn't bother counting them. Another set of windows was just about head-height, and they opened to let in a fresh breeze. But even the cold air coming in didn't cool the space down much. A series of kilns along the back wall were probably all cranking, allowing the workers to get away with wearing tank tops and T-shirts in November.

There were three loading doors at the far end, and they were currently closed. But Kelsey could see how handy they'd be, allowing a truck to pull right into the building to be loaded up with boxes.

Even with all of the fresh air, the place still smelled of clay, which was surprisingly appealing. Of course, since clay was mostly earth, it should have smelled good.

"Don't you love that smell?" Summer said, looking supremely happy. "If I'm in a bad mood, I come in here first thing and just walk around smelling the place. It always makes me feel better."

"I can see that," Kelsey said. "But haven't I read that clay's dangerous?"

Summer smiled, with a sparkle to her eyes that let Kelsey know she was going to say something smart-alecky. "I don't know you well enough to know what you've read, but we've got more industrial-caliber air cleaners than OHSA requires. Plus...we have the floor washed every night. That keeps us from walking on pieces that have dropped to the floor and hardened. It's the dust that's dangerous."

Something wet nudged her hand and Kelsey yanked it back to grasp it before looking down to see a skinny black dog with just one brown eye peering up at her, grinning. "I almost wet my pants!"

Summer squatted down and let the dog lick her face. "Did Tuffy scare you? He wouldn't hurt a fly."

"He only scared me because I wasn't expecting a dog in a factory. My mind started spinning, trying to think of what had a big enough tongue to reach my hand."

Summer's smirk made Kelsey think she was going to say something racy, but she contained herself. When she stood, she pointed across the room at a burly guy in a sleeveless T-shirt. "See that guy with the black beard and the clay residue up to his elbows? He rescued Tuffy when he was a pup. That was just after they removed his eye."

"Aww. Poor puppy."

"I'm sure Tuffy would prefer having two eyes, but he's got a good life. Henry was worried about leaving him alone when he was getting used to his new perspective, so we took a vote and unanimously agreed he could bring him to work until he wasn't running into walls." She stood up and scratched the dog's shiny black coat. "That was seven years ago, and he thinks he works here now."

"I had no idea this small building contained so many employees. They're everywhere."

"And they're all trying to figure out who you are," Summer said quietly. "Like I said, we don't get many visitors."

Kelsey started to count, but Summer saved her the trouble. "I've got twenty, and I might want to hire another, even though my crew isn't in favor of that."

"Do you take votes on everything?"

"God, no! But we're a little short every day, and seriously short once in a while. I asked the finishers if they wanted a small raise or more help, and they all wanted the dough." She shrugged. "I'm willing to try that, but I can't afford to get behind. This isn't a democracy."

Kelsey turned in a circle to check everything out. "I see lots of machines and things I can't name."

"I'll introduce you around a bit."

"Great."

"Hey, Paco," Summer said, walking over to a guy and putting her hand on his shoulder after he'd set a big block of clay down. "How many did you cut today?"

He was a short, stocky guy who looked like he'd win a wrestling match against all-comers. Short, bristly hair, golden-tanned skin and dark, alert eyes. "Well, I didn't get started hand-cutting until I finished that other job." He scratched at his head with his clay-flecked fingers.

"I've got about a hundred on the drying racks. But don't worry. I'll finish by tomorrow."

"I'm not worried," Summer said. "I'm just checking to make sure we're on schedule."

"You know I'd tell you if we weren't," he said, with his voice dropping down into a deeper tone.

"I'm just trying to look like I'm in charge," she said, laughing a little. "I want to show off in front of a client."

"Ohh." He threw his head back and laughed, with his round belly jiggling when he did. "Why didn't you say so? I can play stupid."

"You'd fail at that, buddy. We'll just watch you for a minute, then mosey around and take a look at the project."

"You picked a good time. Today, we're artists."

He settled the big, square block in front of himself, picked up a wire, and sliced through the clay quickly. Then he placed the piece into a hand-powered roller. After cranking the wheel a few times, he took the slab over to a sheet of plaster drywall and laid it down gently. After slapping a pattern onto it, he had two tiles in the blink of an eye.

"That might not look difficult," Summer said. "But getting the clay just the right thickness time and again takes practice. Not to mention how much concentration it takes to do it very quickly." She clapped him on the back and led Kelsey over to the next table, where four women were seated. Each of them had an assortment of tools at hand, and each was working on a large tile, transferring an image onto the still-wet clay.

"The job we're doing is for twenty hand-painted tiles," Summer said. "We need a raven, a sparrow, a woodpecker and an oriole. Five times each. Kamina, Fimi, Azucena, and Noelia are crafting those designs into the clay while it's still green."

"Looks gray to me…"

"That means nearly wet," Summer said. She leaned over one of the women and murmured appreciatively. "Fantastic job, Kamina. The raven's eye looks like it might blink."

Kamina turned slightly and smiled, her teeth looking blindingly white against her dark skin. When she spoke, a charming French accent came through. "Each one is a little better," she said, before looking down again. She seemed like she was embarrassed about admitting her work was good, but it really was.

"They're beautiful," Kelsey said. "Did each of you create the image you're working from?"

"With help," Kamina said, casting her dark eyes at Summer.

"I've been doing this longer," Summer said, "but no one needs much help. Just a little change in perspective or a highlight fleshed out a bit." She laughed. "It's more that I can't stand not to have my hands on nearly everything."

"She's a very good artist," Kamina said soberly. "She teaches me so much."

"It goes both ways," Summer said, giving her a gentle pat on the back.

She led Kelsey over to another area, where a thin, wiry guy was applying glaze to a rack full of tiles.

"These will go into the kiln before we leave tonight," Summer said. "Armando is a masterful glazer. Fast and precise."

"How many kilns do you have?"

"Six now, but I'm thinking about buying another. They're always cranking away." She fanned herself with a piece of cardboard. "That's why it's tropical in here, even on the coldest day. I save thousands on heating, but I get my punishment in the summer when I have to run industrial fans to keep us from passing out."

Kelsey looked at her watch again. "I could honestly stay here all day, but I'd better get going."

"I was just going to launch into my lesson on how to make a good glaze. Consider yourself lucky."

They started for the door, but Tuffy raced back to sniff the bottoms of Kelsey's shoes before Henry called to him. He turned and ran right back, with his long, spindly legs flying.

"It hardly seems like a business in here," Kelsey said, turning to gaze at the space before they exited. "With the music playing and everyone chatting, it's like an art class."

"You wouldn't say that if you were sitting on a stool painting tile all day, but I'll agree that we get along well. That's probably because almost everyone is a referral."

"Referrals from other employees?"

"Right. I've got a brother/sister combo, two sets of cousins, and three women from the same village in Burundi. People only refer good workers when they have to sit right next to them."

"That's probably true, but I'd have to say our company's a much better place to work since Junior retired. A Sedlak is still in charge, but there isn't a younger generation itching for the older one to get out of the way. Now we've got one boss, and his kids are young. I hope to be retired by the time they're poking their noses into things."

Summer nodded. "I've got siblings, but none of them work here. The referral model only works if the people trust each other to pull their weight."

They walked back to Summer's office, and as Kelsey picked up her coat, she said, "I'd love to know more about your business. Would you like to…" She paused for just a moment, trying to create a little build-up. "Have a drink some evening?"

"A drink, huh?" Summer placed her hands on her desk, peering at Kelsey until she started to feel uncomfortable. "Your business isn't tied to my agreeing, is it?"

"Of course not!" She could feel the color drain from her cheeks. "You're the only custom tile maker I've found who'll even consider doing a job as small as mine. You could call me mean names and I'd still want to do business with you."

Summer stood up tall and let out a laugh. "I'm truly teasing. Women aren't above being assholes, but you don't give off that vibe at all."

Realizing she was dealing with someone who could turn the tables on you in an instant, Kelsey said, "It wouldn't be a good long-term strategy to try to screw around with you. I *really* need this tile."

Summer picked up her phone, looking at Kelsey expectantly. "Let's have that drink. Name the date."

"How about Friday?"

"I'm usually busy on Fridays. Free on Saturday?"

"I can be."

"Then Saturday it is," she said, extending her hand for another shake. "I live in the Strip District. You?"

"Shadyside, but I'm happy to come to you."

"Great." She turned her phone around, and handed it to Kelsey. "Add yourself to my contacts."

"I can do that, but what if you forget my name?"

Summer took the phone back and peered at the screen. "Smile for me." Then she turned the phone around, now showing Kelsey's contact card with her photo attached to it. "When you text me, I'll see your picture along with your info." She tapped at her temple. "I'm a visual person, so I've figured out how to make that work for me." She laughed a little. "But if I had to call *you*, I'd have to go through my photos, which can be a pain in the butt."

"I'll text you when I'm getting ready to leave work on Saturday. Don't plan on happy hour. I'm often stuck there until seven."

She revealed a warm, guileless smile, one that made Kelsey hope the days went by quickly. "If we're lucky, we'll have a very happy hour, no matter what time we meet."

CHAPTER TWO

SUMMER HAD TO RUSH TO spruce herself up a little, but by 6:45 her face was clean, hair brushed, a pressed blouse and clean jeans replaced the gritty, dusty ones she'd tossed into a tote bag, and she'd had time to apply some color to her cheeks and lips. The Friday night gang met at a rotating list of high-end bars around the city, and she was *always* the most casual, not to mention the most gay. But they always had fun, and getting together with old friends put a coda to her week that kicked off her weekend nicely.

Tonight, they were mixing things up a little, meeting at a speakeasy. Summer had never heard of the place, so Leah must have had a hand in the selection. She always valued a well-made drink over being "seen."

By the time Summer arrived, and finally found a place to stow her car, the drinks on the table already had substantial chunks taken out of them. "Well, well, well," she said, standing by the booth with her hands on her hips. "Either you're all very thirsty, or you started early."

"Started early," Leah said. She stood up to kiss Summer, then sank back into the booth and patted the spot she'd occupied. Leah was now nearly on Wendy's lap, but she was always the doting big sister, insuring that Summer could sit next to her.

It wasn't that Summer didn't like her sister's friends, but she probably wouldn't have chosen any of them on her own. They were all roughly the same age, had similar professional rankings, and were all single. When you were forty-seven, as Leah was, your friends' marital status was important. Married women with kids couldn't drop everything to go to Hong Kong for two weeks, as Leah, Patti, and Lori had done in August. Wendy was still wounded that they hadn't waited for her to clear her calendar, but if she hadn't had something valid to complain about she would have definitely made something up.

Summer had seen her sister often since her trip, but this was the first time Leah was wearing a suit that had to have been custom made for her in Hong Kong. "Are you kidding me with this?" Summer said, chuckling as she rubbed her fingers against the material. "This color is absolutely perfect against your skin. And so sexy," she added.

"This old thing?" Leah teased. "I won't tell you what it cost, but we'll probably spend more on drinks tonight."

"Did everyone have something made?" Summer asked.

"Everyone but me," Wendy grumbled. "I'm going to have to go to Hong Kong on my own for that—without Lori to translate for me."

Summer met Lori's gaze, getting a discreet eye-roll in response. "I'd feel sorry for you," Summer said, "but weren't you in Finland at the time? It's not like you were at home twiddling your thumbs."

She felt her sister's hand on her leg and nodded her head slightly. Leah hated to rile Wendy up, so Summer always tried to play nice. That wasn't her instinct, since she thought the other women were all too considerate of her demands, but that really wasn't her business. At forty-seven, her sister had the right to choose her own friends.

"I was in Finland on business," Wendy said, even though Summer could not, for the life of her, figure out what Wendy did for a living. She claimed to be in PR, but she worked from her home most of the time, and also picked up work writing travel reviews. She was one of those people who sailed through life with no visible means of support, but she always had the money to go just about anywhere. *Weird!*

A waiter arrived and Summer pointed at the tea-colored drink her sister was having. "One of those for me, and another round for the table, please."

"Right away," he said, slipping away.

They tended to each pay for a round, but Summer never stayed for the whole evening. She usually paid for the second, then took off before they got to the third. That gave her a little time with her sister, and not too much with the others.

"What's new in the tile business?" Lori asked. They all seemed to find it kind of funny that Summer had a job where she got her hands dirty, but she could tell they were also slightly envious of her not having to spend her day in meetings, or chasing down clients. Her sister had a job that she *thought* she could stand, but even hers was iffy.

"The tile business is just fine. How's the law business?"

"You don't want to know. I mean, you *really* don't want to know," she said dramatically. "We've only been back a few months and I'm ready to take off again. Maybe I'll change my mind and tag along on your Portugal trip."

Summer knew her eyebrows had risen, but she was quite certain she didn't want a fourth on the trip she and her sister had planned. In her experience, three was the right number for a vacation, and given that Patti was the easiest of the bunch to get along with, she was the perfect third. "You'd better make up your mind," she said. "Reservations are tight, since some of the places we're staying only have two guest rooms. You'll have to double-up with Patti."

Lori made a face that would have insulted Wendy, but Patti took most things in stride. "I don't share rooms," Lori said firmly. "Why don't you do a little digging and find bigger places."

"Wish I could, but I've already allocated all of the time I can to planning this trip. But be my guest if you want to take over…" Her sister poked her again, but she wasn't going to give on this. She hated to plan trips, and once she was finished—she was finished.

"How hard could it be?" Lori asked. "Just change things around."

"I doubt it will be hard at all," Summer said. "So…have at it."

Their drinks arrived, and Summer concentrated on taking a sip, not knowing what she'd find. "Ahh…I'm so glad this is whiskey. Every once in a while you order brandy and I can barely choke it down."

"Then ask first," Leah said, giving her a fond smile.

"I like to be surprised," Summer said, which was very true.

"We've all griped about our weeks already," Leah said. "Do you really have nothing to complain about?"

"Not only do I not have anything to complain about, I had something cool happen. A cute woman dropped in, and after I charmed the pants off her, she agreed to go out with me tomorrow night."

"You met someone at work?" Leah asked, her brows rising.

"She came in to talk about tile, and left with my phone number." She blew over her fingers, pretending to polish her nails on her blouse.

"Details," Leah said. "Lots of details."

"Mmm. I don't have a lot. She works at Sedlak Brothers, the home remodeling store. She's super cute. And she doesn't wear a wedding ring." Summer held up her hands. "The bar to entry continues to drop."

"I've got ten years on you," Wendy said, looking sour. "My bar to entry is when a guy shrugs and says 'You'll do.'"

Summer took a quick look around the table, feeling a sharp pang of anger at how unfair life was. These four women were smart, educated, urbane, and attractive. Not only that, they all owned homes or apartments, and appreciated the finer things in life. And not one of them had been able to land a really good date in years—despite each of them longing for a mate. It seemed like every man their age wanted to hook up with the youngest possible woman, which was just dumb. But she couldn't fix society's inequities, much as she'd like to.

"Well, I don't know if this woman will be worth my time, but we spent about forty-five minutes together and I got the impression she's fun. We'll see."

"Who does she look like?" Leah asked. "Anybody famous?"

"No one I can think of. She's tallish, and thinnish, with nice brown hair and good bone structure. Great smile," she added, thinking that was Kelsey's best attribute.

"Who pays when women go out?" Wendy asked.

"I usually offer to split the check, or if it's just drinks I get one round and hope she gets the next. There's no rule."

With envy infusing her voice, Lori said, "God, I'd love to go out with someone who wasn't fixated on showing off how powerful he is. Like I'd be impressed by a guy pulling out a Platinum Card. I've got my own," she said, tossing her thick black hair over her shoulder.

"Kelsey didn't look like she has a Platinum Card, not that I hope she does. I'm looking for a regular woman. Someone who lives within her means would be nice."

"You're really aiming high," Lori said, chuckling. "Wanted: non-bankrupt lesbian."

Summer shrugged. "I'm really not aiming very high. But my arrow hasn't landed on a good target in a year."

"See me in ten," Wendy said. "*Then* I'll feel sorry for you."

Summer was going to toss a comment back, but stopped herself. There was nothing funny about wanting to partner-up and not finding any acceptable candidates. And if she hadn't hooked up in ten years, she might be just as bitter about the whole process as Wendy was.

❀

Kelsey didn't get out of work until close to seven. But she'd made a pretty big sale, and her customer had been pleasant to work with. Not bad for a day's work.

She had time to go home and have dinner, but she decided to head over to Lawrenceville and grab something there. She had a book she was really involved in, and letting someone else make her dinner while she read seemed like a good way to kick off a weekend—even though it wasn't *her* weekend.

A half hour later she was lost in her book, idly slurping down some noodles from a nice little shop that didn't hew to borders very closely. Her noodles seemed Chinese, but there was a bottle of Malaysian hot sauce on the table, along with some Korean hot chili paste. She wasn't a fan of spicy food, so the relatively plain Dan Dan noodles remained unmolested by add-ons.

To waste time, she'd eaten slowly, but eventually her empty bowl was whisked away, and the host gave her a pointed look. As soon as she took out her credit card, her server was at the table, nearly running away with it. One minute later, she was out on the street, glad for the fact that it wasn't very cold out. She checked her phone, and saw that Rob had texted. The spot he wanted to meet at was only about four blocks away, so she left her car where it was and started to walk. By the time she reached the bar, he was standing outside, looking handsome as usual.

Kelsey put her arms around him and gave him a quick hug. "How was your day?"

"Good enough. Have you eaten? If not, I've got to warn you that the food here is terrible, not to mention overpriced."

She smiled. "Then I'm glad to say I have. How about you?"

"I'm trying to cut back," he said as she opened the door. "I'm reserving all of my calories for alcohol."

"Healthy choice," she said, seeing a small table in the back that was free. "I'll grab seats. Order me anything you like."

She was all set up when Rob handed over a beer. "I know you don't like vodka and soda, and I couldn't think of anything more interesting. Is this okay?"

"Sure. I order this lager all the time."

"I know," he said, lifting his chin. "I pay attention, Kels."

They tapped their glasses together and each had a sip. "Good stuff," she said. "So what's going on? I haven't seen you in like ten days. Our schedule's been messed up."

"Nothing good," he said glumly. "I hooked up with a guy last Saturday, and saw him again on Wednesday. Then I had to block him," he said, sighing dramatically. "I thought he had promise, but then he started texting me like six times a day, just to 'check in.' What is there to check?"

"He's barking up the wrong tree if he wants to keep a tight grip on you."

"No, no, he's in the wrong forest," he said, laughing.

She took a look at her old friend when his phone diverted his attention. In many ways, he didn't look very different than he had when they were in school together. Just a little softening under the chin, minor wrinkles around the eyes. But he still had the boyish exuberance he'd shown back then, and she hoped he'd keep that for a very long time.

He slapped his phone down and gave it a malevolent look. "I've got a guy lined up to have a drink with later, but he's jerking me around. If he isn't here by ten, I'm blocking him."

"He's got an hour," she said, checking her watch. "Want me to send him a message telling him what he's missing?"

"That would be an interesting add-on to the apps, wouldn't it? Testimonials." He took another look at his phone. "Ever since I changed my profile to say I was looking for someone to date I'm much less popular. But I'm truly going to give this a try. I'm almost bored of blowing strangers."

"Just shows you can get tired of anything if you do it often enough," she teased.

"That's sadly true. So? What's going on in your world. Since you're out with me on a Friday night, things must be grim."

"They're not grim at all," she sniffed. "I've got a date tomorrow night."

"Really?" He perked up immediately. "Dish, girlfriend."

"Well, she's pretty, she's smart, she owns and runs a business, and she's got a good sense of humor. I'd marry her tomorrow if I could talk her into it."

"Where did you find this gem?" he asked, with his head cocking.

"She fabricates tile, as luck would have it. She's got a nice shop filled with workers, and from what I can see, she treats them like they're human beings." She shrugged. "I'm not kidding about marrying her."

"Name?"

"Summer. Summer Hayes."

"Cute name. Sounds like she made it up."

Kelsey shrugged. "That would only show that she wasn't invested in sticking to things she didn't like. I don't care if her real name is Hildegard Psoriasis."

Chuckling, Rob tapped his glass against Kelsey's. "Many happy returns to you and Hildegard. Let me know when we're going shopping for your wedding dress."

"While I can't see myself in a traditional tux, my dress days are well behind me. We'll have to get creative."

Now he really smiled. Rob loved any reality show that featured weddings—the kookier the better. "I am definitely your man."

CHAPTER THREE

ON SATURDAY NIGHT, SUMMER placed her drink on a table when the door opened to let in a blast of cold air. Kelsey's gaze scanned the small, dark bar, landed on her, then she waved as she walked the few steps. "Hi," she said, looking pretty perky for a woman who'd been at work all day.

"I thought I'd lucked out when I saw this table open, but now I know that was just because everyone else is too smart to sit this close to the door." Summer turned around and looked at the crowd of people who'd stayed well out of the way of the gale that swept through the place every couple of minutes. "If you'd rather be warm, we can stand over there."

Kelsey sat down and took off her gloves. "I'd rather keep my coat on and sit. Is that okay with you?"

"Perfect. I'd rather be a little cold and sit down any day of the week." She held her drink up. "No table service." Standing, she took her wallet from her purse. "I'll treat. What would you like?"

"Um…" Kelsey looked around, possibly seeking a menu or a list of drink specials, but this place had neither. "I'm not too picky. What's good?"

"In the mood for a cocktail? Even though this is a dive bar, the bartender is pretty creative."

"Let's do it," she said, clapping her hands together. "I don't like rum or tequila, but everything else is fine."

"Allergies?"

Kelsey blinked up at her. "Are you going to order something with shellfish or nuts in it?"

"Probably not," she said, trying to look like she was still on the fence about that. "I think it's clear that living with someone who was allergic to soy, chocolate, sesame, and tree nuts made me overly cautious." She smiled when Kelsey's eyes got a little wide. "But I learned how to use an EpiPen, so that was a plus. Be right back with something tequila and rum-free."

Summer tried to slide through the bustling crowd, but a guy spotted her and literally pushed a couple of people out of the way to allow her to get close to the bar—and him. *No way.* She slipped back out of the crowd and went to the far end of the bar, where she could try to catch the bartender's eye while checking her date out.

Kelsey had picked up her phone and started to play with it, giving it her full attention. She *really* was a pretty woman: not in a print model way, but in a symmetrical features, bright eyes, and sensuous lips kind of way. She definitely gave off a gay vibe, but Summer couldn't actually name anything that made her seem so. Maybe the not-so-hidden clue was that her eyes had lit up when she'd spotted Summer. That was plenty. Another piece of good news was that she wasn't sitting there preening, like a lot of people did when they were at a bar. She seemed to have tamped her engaging personality down so that no one gave her a second glance. Was there anything more exhausting than dating a woman who had to try to make everyone in a bar dig her? The answer was decidedly no. Summer had wasted a nice, warm July night with a woman like that, and once was enough.

After returning to the table with Kelsey's drink, Summer raised her glass to tap their rims together. "We're drinking Perfect Manhattans. Just the ticket for a cold, windy night. Cheers."

"Cheers." Kelsey took a tentative sip, then smiled. "Perfect choice. I'm feeling warmer already."

"Our timing was just a little off. Tomorrow's supposed to top out at fifty degrees." She gave the door a scowl. "We wouldn't be shivering if we'd chosen to meet then."

"Everything's about timing, isn't it?" Kelsey leaned over a bit, sliding across the bar-height table with her elbows leading the way. Just being a few inches closer made their chat seem more intimate, allowing her to lower her voice. "I'm glad we chose tonight. When it's cold like this I usually stay home. But I hate to blow a weekend night." Her smile was a little wry when she added, "I guess I'm still holding on to my youth, when every weekend felt like something I couldn't afford to miss."

"I like to go out on the weekend too. I believe I deserve a reward for working hard."

"I do, too, but my real weekend is Wednesday and Thursday. Tonight might be Saturday to you, but it's Tuesday to me."

"That's your schedule every week?"

"Every one. Ten years now."

"You *never* get a weekend off?"

"If holidays align just right we get a whole weekend at Christmas and New Years. Kind of sucks, but I'm used to it." She pointed at the tablet that rested on the table top. "Since this is your weekend, I hope you don't want to spend it talking about tile."

"No need now that I've determined you're not straighter than a stick." She waggled her eyebrows when Kelsey's expression morphed into a wide smile. "I like to be prepared."

"I've never been straight," Kelsey said, looking very happy with that fact. "And I have no intention of changing now. I've been assuming, and hoping, that this was a date."

Summer stuck her hand out and they shook. "I'm in. Let the date begin."

"Okay," she said, rubbing her hands together. "Um, I usually start off with talking about what my date does for a living, but I already know that about you. So let's go a little deeper."

Summer laughed at how sincere she looked. "That's moving quickly, but I like a woman with an agenda."

"Oh, I have one," Kelsey said, her expression still slightly serious. "I'm kind of an optimist, so I think of every first date as the start of something great." She took a sip of her drink, set it down carefully, then said, "I don't like to spend a lot of time dating with no end-goal."

"Tell me more about this goal," Summer said, pretty charmed not only by the thoughtful attention Kelsey was giving to their time together, but the clarity in her blue eyes. If Kelsey was full of BS, Summer would have been astounded.

"I'm in the market for a relationship. If you'd like to make tonight a one-and-done that's fine, but I'd like to know now so I can lower my expectations."

"Mmm." Summer pulled her tablet over and opened it, then spent a moment pulling up her drawing app. She lifted a finger, saying, "Give me a minute or two," then started to sketch with the stylus. "How do you spell your last name?"

"M-a-l-i-a-r."

"Got it." She worked quickly, tamping down her perfectionistic tendencies. Then she turned it around and showed it to Kelsey.

She read it aloud. "Together With Their Families, Kelsey Maliar and Summer Hayes Request The Honor of Your Presence As They Celebrate Their Marriage…" Kelsey looked up, with her gaze a little vacant. "I would have been happy with your being open to a second date…"

"Teasing," Summer said. "Well, not entirely. I'm looking for a relationship, too, and for me, that relationship would be built on monogamy, as well as a public commitment. Are you on my page?"

"I am," she said, with her eyes glimmering in the dim light the candle threw off. "But if we could wait at least a year…"

"Two," Summer said, holding up a pair of fingers. "Once I make a commitment, I'm very tenacious. I don't make them quickly, but I'm very serious about them once they're made." She took another sip of her drink, very pleased with her choice as it continued to warm her. Or maybe Kelsey's sweet smile had done that.

⊛

Kelsey spent a few seconds trying to get a feel for the moment. After she asked about a date's job, she usually tried to clear the decks by learning about past relationships. If her date had fifty of them, all jerks who had fatal flaws, she could chalk the night up as a dead-end, then disappear. But tonight she couldn't work up the motivation to look at the past. Summer made her want to make plans, to think of things they could do together. But Kelsey had to have more info before she could do that.

"How about spending a minute describing your perfect day." She smiled, and admitted, "I got the question from a relationship podcast, but I think it's a good one for getting to know some important things."

A pleased smile settled onto Summer's pretty mouth. "My perfect day? No limits?"

"Well, it has to be reality based. You can't be on another planet, or be prime minister of a very well-run country or anything like that."

"Great. Now I have to start over." Summer scowled briefly, then revealed a playful smile. She tapped at her chin for a few seconds, then said, "I'd get up early and spend some time outside. It's early summer," she said slowly. "A clear, warm day. Maybe a bike ride to a great coffee place. I've got a sweet tooth, and my favorite junk food is donuts, so I'd grab a couple of those. Then…I'd like to stay outside for a while and draw. Any place pretty would be fine. All of that drawing would work up an appetite, so I've got to plan lunch."

She was taking this so seriously that Kelsey was utterly charmed. A woman who jumped right in and tried to play a game was her kind of woman.

"Hmm. Since this is a perfect day, lunch has to be right." She seemed to think for another few seconds. "I'd like something light, and something I don't know how to cook would be best. Ideally, I'd dine with one or two of my favorite people. Then…" She narrowed her eyes, finally nodding. "If my very cool girlfriend wasn't already having lunch with me, she'd come over and we'd do what people do when they're nuts about each other. That would take a while, then we'd nap, with a cool breeze blowing over us." Her smile grew brighter. "If I could manage to have some nice smelling plants right outside my window, I'd appreciate it."

"You've got it. Color?"

"Not picky." She laughed. "That's *such* a lie I should be embarrassed to even say it. I'm extremely picky, but the color would depend on too many factors to pick one without more information. Let's just say they're the perfect color."

"Done. One stand of perfectly-colored, beautifully scented flowers coming right up."

"Then we'd go out to dinner. I like unique food, but it doesn't have to be expensive. Anything with spices or herbs I don't routinely use would be great. But the restaurant has to be on the quiet side. I want to hear every word my fascinating girlfriend has to say."

"That is all very attainable," Kelsey said, so pleased Summer hadn't wanted to spend the day blowing thousands of dollars on silly luxuries. She recalled asking the question once and having the woman say her perfect day revolved around shopping for a designer purse, then showing it off at one of the most expensive restaurants in Pittsburgh. People could reveal a lot about themselves when answering a fairly innocuous question.

"Oh, it is," she said, nodding confidently. "Lastly, I'd like to go for a walk. No place in particular, but window shopping would be nice. And if we happened to run into a good ice cream shop..."

"There are plenty of them in town, and I think I've been to all of them. That's it?" Kelsey asked when Summer gave her a pleased-looking smile.

"Uh-huh. Cuddling in bed while we fall asleep at the end of the day would be nice, of course. Even if my fabulous girlfriend and I didn't live together, the day wouldn't be perfect if we didn't do that."

"Just sleep? No earth-shattering sex to end the night?"

"Done and dusted," she said, clapping her hands together. "Maybe I didn't make it clear how extensive my afternoon lovemaking was. But if I hadn't been able to spend a couple of hours with my divine girlfriend in the afternoon, after dinner would work just fine. I try to be flexible."

"Got it. That's a very good list, and it's not too far from mine."

"How's yours different?" Summer asked, paying rapt attention.

"Well, I don't normally get up very early, since I stay up kind of late. And I don't draw, but I love to sit outdoors on a nice summer day and read. If I could read by a pool, or a lake, I'd be thrilled."

"Ahh. I'd like to draw by a nice lake. Good choice."

"So…I agree on the nice meals, and on spending a long time playing in bed. Actually, window shopping while eating ice cream sounds perfect, too. That's kind of a perfect end to a perfect day."

Nodding soberly, Summer said, "I'll buy that's your perfect summer day, even though you kind of copied off me. How does your perfect fall day differ? What would you do tomorrow?"

Kelsey thought for a minute. "It would be pretty much the same, but skip the pool. If I could truly have what I wanted, and I think I can since I made up the game, I'd be at a lodge with a big, stone fireplace and a comfortable chair to do my reading. That way I'd be close to my room, which I'd use to satisfy my divine girlfriend in every way her dirty little mind could imagine. Not a bad fantasy," she said, almost able to picture it.

"I could get into that, too. I'd like to sit by the window and sketch squirrels gathering nuts, or birds heading south for the winter." Her smile grew brighter. "I love to lounge around in bed when I'm at a nice hotel or a lodge. I'd still want dessert, though."

"Dessert should be a requirement when you're thinking about your perfect day."

"I like the way you think, Kelsey."

"I like the way *you* think." She touched the rim of her glass to Summer's, then drained it. When she stood, she said, "My turn to buy. Would you like a refill?"

"I would indeed."

As Kelsey started for the bar, Summer raised her voice just enough for it to carry. "You're raking up points just by pulling out your wallet!"

⊛

Summer watched Kelsey scope out the crowd, then walk all the way to the end, just as she had done. She wasn't fond of the fact that she watched her date like she was compiling a dossier on her, but that's kind of what your early dates had to be. You needed a lot of information to feel confident about investing your hopes, but you didn't want to be too paranoid, or to look for minor reasons to cross a woman off your list. Still, she was glad to see that Kelsey didn't exploit her attractiveness to sidle up next to a guy and have him come to her aid in getting served faster.

Now her only worry was the speed with which Kelsey had downed that first drink. Summer had arrived fifteen minutes early, so she'd had quite a head-start. But they'd finished at the same time. She was giving that disparity more attention than it deserved when Kelsey returned to set two drinks on the table. Summer took a look at the clear one with a wedge of lime floating in it. "Are you switching up on me? Has your Perfect Manhattan become imperfect?"

"No," she said, smiling. "It was perfect, but I wanted to go lighter."

The drink was close to Summer, and she picked it up to hand it over. "I'm guessing you're a gin person," she said, giving it a delicate sniff. "Hmm…I can't smell any alcohol at all."

A vaguely sheepish expression covered Kelsey's face. "I switched to sparkling water, but I didn't want to make a point of it."

"Because you thought I might feel…funny to want two?"

"I never have more than one on a work night, and I've gotten some not-so-positive feedback on that," she said, her grin sliding into a smirk.

"Then I'll change that up by giving you extra-positive feedback. It was thoughtful of you to buy a round when you didn't really want one, and even more thoughtful to make sure I didn't feel like I was drinking alone." She held up her glass. "Which I don't mind doing, by the way. I don't feel judged when I'm in the mood to drink more than my date does."

Kelsey's smile clearly signaled that she was going to say something playful. "It's fine to feel judged if you routinely call for another drink when everyone else has thrown in the towel. I've got a cousin…"

"Don't we all have someone in the family who insists they just love to have fun when they should probably be scoping out rehab facilities?"

"My cousin isn't at that point, but I'm worried that's where she's heading. She's one of the people who makes fun of me for being a lightweight."

"Is this cousin someone you see often?"

"Just once a year, usually, at our big family and friends vacation. We rent cabins on a lake my parents have been going to since their honeymoon. It's kind of fantastic," she added, with a satisfied smile covering her face.

"Then why wasn't that your perfect summer day?"

"I guess it should have been, but I've never taken a girlfriend with me, so I'm not sure it would be ideal for a dating situation. There are so many people around that I couldn't be sure I could dote on my perfect girlfriend."

"Fantastic answer," Summer said, loving the way this was going. "Tell me more about this big family vacation. I love to date people who either get along well with their families, or are completely alienated."

"Completely alienated? Really?"

"Only because I've known people whose families make their life miserable, but they hang in there hoping everything will miraculously change. That kind of unrealistic hope drives me around the bend."

"You do not need to go around any bends with me," Kelsey said confidently. "I love to spend time with my parents. Actually, I have dinner with them at least once a week. They're a fun hang."

"At least? Like sometimes you see them five times?"

Kelsey laughed, shaking her head. "Never. We usually have dinner on Tuesday night, which is my Friday. But if there's a birthday or something, I'll happily go twice that week."

"Good answer. A woman who likes her family, but isn't tied to them like a leach, knows her limit with alcohol, and is willing to pay for a round." Summer patted her heart like it was racing. "Barely a half-hour has passed, and this is already the best date I've had this year."

"Same goes for me." She smiled a little brighter. "A good first date is awesome, isn't it?"

"Truly," Summer agreed, her mood continuing to climb.

Summer went for the next round, and Kelsey was pleased to see they were both now drinking sparkling water. "I wouldn't normally have needed this," Summer said, "but I'm talking so much my mouth's dry."

"You're not talking too much at all. You're actually painting some nice mental images for me."

"Really? I'm not boring you?"

"I have not had one boring second. In fact, I feel like I can picture the town you lived in when you spent the summer in Italy, and that's a really good thing. I haven't done any traveling to speak of, but if I could have a trip like that…"

"It was fantastic," she admitted. "But I won't be able to do another one like that until I retire. I can't imagine ever being able to be away from work for two months."

"Me either," Kelsey said. "I get thirty days, but I always break it up. Two weeks at the lake, usually a week around Christmas, then three and four day weekends spaced through the year."

"That sounds reasonable. We close for the week between Christmas and New Year's, and for two weeks in July or August, depending on the vote. It's just too damn hot to work all through the summer."

"You vote?"

"About some things. I don't really care when we shut down, so we take a vote. I forget what our schedule is this year. I'm not going anywhere, so I'm not invested in remembering."

"And that's all you get?"

"I can take off a week or ten days without much problem," she admitted. "Actually, I'm going on a trip to Portugal right after Thanksgiving."

"Just for fun?"

"Mostly, but it's also partly for research. I'm always searching for new ideas for my product line, and Portugal's a great place to look."

"Who takes over for you when you're gone? Do you have an assistant?"

"Just Chelsea. But she's more of a receptionist. Different people can step in and cover for me when I'm away, but I try not to take advantage of them. They're busy enough without having to do my stuff."

"You sound like a good boss," Kelsey said, looking thoughtful.

"I try to be." She laughed. "It's not really all that hard if you think of your employees as human beings, and give them a little slack when they need it." She thought for a second, adding, "But I'm not a push-over. If someone can't cut it, I do my best to bring them up to speed. If I can't, I let them go. It's not fair to the others to carry the load for an under-performing employee."

"That makes you an even better boss," Kelsey said. "We've got one woman who does the same job I do, and I swear there's no earthly reason they pay her. She should pay *them* for all of the electricity she uses while goofing off."

"Ooo. Someone sounds bitter," Summer teased. "Tell me what you'd do if you were in charge. One of the ways I try to learn to be a better boss is to talk to people who aren't happy in their jobs."

"Oh, I'm plenty happy," Kelsey said. "I guess it aggravates me that this person's basically stealing from the company by being a goof-off, but it doesn't affect me too much. We get a very modest commission, and I increase it by jumping up and helping anyone who walks in. I guess I benefit from her laziness." She got kind of a dreamy look in her eyes when she said, "But if I was the boss—"

❧

"Favorite teacher," Kelsey said, refusing to even glance at her watch. She knew it was late, but she'd decided to let the chips fall where they may. It had been quite a while since she'd enjoyed a date this much, and she was resigned to gulping down enough coffee to make her brain work in the morning.

They'd already covered where they'd live if they had complete freedom to choose, what kind of house they'd live in, what qualities they required in close friends, what qualities were prohibited in lovers, and what each of them would change about herself if she could only change a single thing. Kelsey still wasn't sure she was happy with her answer, but being more adventurous was something she knew would enhance her life. Summer hadn't had to think for a second before she confidently said she'd be more trusting. That wasn't the most reassuring answer when you were trying to figure out if you were a romantic match, but at least she owned it. Kelsey might circle around and switch her answer to admit she might benefit from being less trusting. She certainly didn't think she was a pushover, but she was always the one hanging on to the tattered threads of a relationship, certain her partner would change if Kelsey waited her out. But…maybe that wasn't the best thing to admit, either. Trying to be more adventurous was a good, safe answer. And at this part of the game, being safe was the smart bet.

When the bartender flashed the lights and yelled out, "Last call!" Kelsey finally took a look at her watch. "Oh, crap," she moaned. "How am I ever going to figure out how much space to allow for Mrs. Reynold's huge collection of Fiestaware?"

"Want me to swing by to help? I don't know anything about space, but I love Fiestaware more than anyone I know. One day I'm going to make a set for myself in a unique color."

Kelsey stared at her for a second as she stood and started to zip her jacket. "You can do that? Seriously?"

Her smug expression was pretty adorable, and it covered her face whenever she talked about her abilities. "If it's made of clay, I can create it."

Kelsey walked over to her side of the table, standing closer than the normal distance relative strangers usually allowed. "On our next date, we're going to talk a whole lot more about your work. I can see how important it is to you."

"It's a deal." Summer stood and started to zip her coat, but Kelsey gently moved her hand away and did it for her.

"I want to make sure you're buttoned up against that cold wind." She tried to make her grin extra playful to make it clear she was intentionally putting it on thick, but she continued to lift Summer's collar and loop her scarf around her neck. "That looks perfect."

Summer looked into her eyes and cocked her head slightly. "I think we should do it here."

"Do what?"

"Have our first kiss," she said, like they'd already decided they were going to have one, and were trying to nail down the location.

"I guess this is as good a place as any," Kelsey said, looking around at the still crowded bar, with all of the die-hards trying to load up on a final drink. "It's not very private…"

"No, it's not." Summer put her hands on Kelsey's shoulders and started to draw her close. "But it's warm. I don't want to be shivering when you kiss me."

"I'm going to kiss you?" Kelsey asked, so close she could see flecks of green and brown in those pretty hazel eyes. "It feels like you're going to kiss me."

With her grin growing as she clearly lied, Summer said, "I can see why you might think that, but you're going to kiss me. I'm *very* passive."

Kelsey tucked her arms around Summer, holding her close against her body. "I am, too," she murmured before dipping her head and pressing their lips together. It was a delightful sensation, with Summer's soft, plump lips so sumptuous Kelsey was amazed she'd waited this long in the night to kiss them. A wave of warmth washed over her, a slight tingling sensation traveling across her scalp, as if someone had lightly tickled the back of her neck.

As they pulled apart, Summer took her phone and held it in front of them. "First kiss selfie," she said, leaning her head against Kelsey's as the flash burst. She didn't bother to look at the result, seemingly happy irrespective of the outcome. Then she tucked her hand around Kelsey's arm and guided her out of the bar and into the cold night that didn't seem nearly so cold now. Either the temperature had warmed up, or a really nice first kiss had made the world feel warm and cosy.

CHAPTER FOUR

THE NEXT MORNING, SUMMER woke at her normal time and convinced her reluctant feet to hit the floor. She would have loved to be able to sleep in on the weekends, while still being bright and bouncy on Monday morning, but that wasn't in her makeup. So she set the alarm for seven every day, even when she'd been out late the night before.

After using the bathroom and brushing her teeth, she went into the kitchen to make coffee. While it brewed, she checked her phone, smiling when she saw a recent text from Kelsey.

"I hope you had as good a first date as I did. If so, you're in a great mood today. I sure am, even though I'm goofy from lack of sleep. Take care!"

Summer was going to leave it at that, but she needed just a little more. *"Why are you up? This is too early for you."*

"True. Fell asleep while reading. Had to get up early to finish the book before I have to leave for work. Being an addict isn't as much fun as it looks. See you!"

A perfect example of a first date follow up. Light and breezy. No pressure. Second date? Wild horses couldn't hold her back.

⊛

Three days later, Summer packed up her things and left the office at five thirty, giving Chelsea a wave when she passed her desk. "I'm heading out to meet with a client. If you need me, feel free to call."

"Got it, boss. See you tomorrow."

When Summer stepped outside, she took in a breath of air, having had no idea the day had warmed up to such a pleasant temperature. Not even needing to zip her jacket, she went to their tiny parking lot and got into her car for what she hoped would be a short trip to Point Breeze.

Using a few shortcuts, she cruised by the big home improvement store about twenty minutes after she'd left her office. Calling Sedlak Brothers a big store was probably not accurate when you compared it to the major chains. But it filled a niche, and she was certain the family continued to enjoy success.

Like the big chain stores, Sedlak Brothers sold building supplies and tools. Lumber, drywall, cement, brick, and stone had been their main products for many years. But when the big chains started to nip away at their profits, they'd added on to the warehouse-style building to create a deluxe showroom for kitchens and baths. Summer had only been inside the addition once, to get the big, fat, "no way" from the owner, but she'd been impressed with the quality of their vendors. If they were stepping up their game even more, they could put themselves into position to compete with the small, but high-end kitchen and bath showrooms that were currently Summer's bread and butter.

She slowed down, seeing that the parking area was packed tight, but she wasn't worried. The neighborhood wasn't often jammed like hers was, and she quickly found a spot on the nearest side street. Hustling to make sure she was on time, she entered through the old warehouse, which had also gotten a facelift since the last time she'd been there. It still wasn't fancy, but everything was arranged nicely, with attractive displays of windows, decking, shingles, and all of the other big-ticket items that made up a home. It wasn't the store for people who wanted one or two choices at the lowest price, but a place like this definitely appealed to people who wanted one step up from builder-grade materials.

There was a slight incline leading to the kitchen and bath displays, and she scoped out the generous work stations tucked away amidst the model kitchens. She had to go all the way to the end, but finally reached Kelsey.

Her work station was kind of huge, and it took Summer a moment to realize the work areas were that big to display different kinds of cabinetry, trim, and drawer styles.

Kelsey's desk was as big as a kitchen island, and neat as well, with colored folders stacked on either side of it and a cup filled with pens and mechanical pencils.

Kelsey was on the phone, and she smiled and held a finger up when Summer got close. Then she pointed to a chair, and pulled down a bowl filled with fun-sized candy bars from her credenza, raising an eyebrow when Summer gave the bowl a long look.

Having a big bite of a Milky Way at the end of the day sounded like a great idea, and she nibbled on it while she waited for Kelsey to hang up.

A folder was open in front of her, and she made notes on a CAD drawing while she spoke. "I agree that you're ahead of schedule on nearly everything, Jake. But it doesn't do me much good to have the fixtures in hand if the valves are back-ordered." She nodded as she set an elbow on the desk and rolled her eyes. "Uh-huh. I'm well aware that you're having trouble with your distribution center. But you promised me the whole order would be here this week. I know it sucks, but seventy-five percent of the total is the same as zero percent."

She stretched across the big desk to reach the candy bowl, so Summer pushed it toward her and got a wry smile in return. A Snickers was in her mouth in a matter of seconds, and she had to chew fast to make her words clear. "The plumber is coming on Friday. The general contractor has put him off three times already, and he's leaving on vacation soon. If I don't have those valves by tomorrow, I'm returning all of the fixtures." She met Summer's eyes and put her hands together like she was strangling the guy. "I *don't* blame you, and I understand you're stuck. But this client would rather have lesser quality fixtures she can pick up from her local home store than wait for High Sierra to get their act together. I hate to dump five thousand bucks worth of fixtures back on you over a pair of three hundred dollar valves, but I have no choice." Jake must have tried to speak, because Kelsey increased her volume and kept going. "When a client starts a job in June, it shouldn't be too much to ask to have it finished by Thanksgiving." She let out a sigh. "Do that. I hope to hear good news by tomorrow afternoon." Then she hung up, not even adding a sign-off. When their eyes met, she said, "My client would go ballistic if I suggested she use cheap fixtures. But if I don't get that order, I'm going to have to listen to her threaten to throw herself off the fortieth street bridge—again. I understand that she wants to show off her house at Thanksgiving, but you'd think I was suggesting she reschedule her wedding at the last minute."

"I feel your pain. I've always found that the people who have the hardest time making up their minds are in the biggest rush once they do."

Kelsey pointed her mechanical pencil at Summer. "That's the god's honest truth. This client dithered around for two months trying to decide which fixtures she wanted. Now she wants me to go to the foundry and hand-forge her brass valves. My great-grandfather had to risk his life as a mill rat, but I'm not up to it."

"Some clients suck," Summer agreed. "But if they weren't picky, we'd be out of a job."

"Also true." She stood up and stretched, allowing Summer a moment to admire the way her navy blue slacks fit. Either they had some stretch to them or Kelsey had them tailored to fit like a glove. That seemed a little extreme, so she must have lucked out and found dressy slacks that really worked for her. "I thought we should meet in the conference room," she said. "I've got a monitor in there, and we can hook your tablet up if you'd like."

"Sounds great. Passing it around is kind of a pain."

Kelsey led the way, pausing at a kitchen display that had an espresso maker built in. "This works if you'd like one," she said, slapping her hand on the machine. "I've gotten to be a good barista."

"I've had enough caffeine, but thanks."

They entered the conference room, and Kelsey got busy, hooking up the device in just a couple of minutes.

"You seem pretty tech-savvy," Summer said.

"Pretty much. I use some complex programs, so I had to get up to speed quickly. Once you understand how some things work, other things don't seem so imposing." Her phone made a noise, and she looked at it for a second. "Roger's here. Ready to rock?"

"Always." When Kelsey looked a little back-on-her-heels, Summer realized her comment was too flirty for work. But it was the truth.

🐝

Kelsey was enjoying the heck out of watching Summer work. She gave off the impression of a very friendly, very laid-back, very competent woman. But there was a well-hidden steel backbone that Roger was actively trying to break. Kelsey didn't know Summer well yet, but she had a feeling he was wasting his time.

Roger Thornhill was one of the top interior designers in Pittsburgh, and she could tell he thought he was slumming to work with Sedlak Brothers. They weren't at the bottom of the barrel by any means, but there were edgier, classier, and higher-end showrooms that had opened up in the last couple of years, and he undoubtedly fit in better with them. But her client's parents and grandparents had been long-term Sedlak Brothers customers, and Kelsey appreciated that the homeowner had even given them a shot. Of course, her client still wanted the best of the best, and Kelsey was determined to give it to her.

Roger drummed his fingers on the conference room table, starting to show his temper, which was an ill-kept secret behind his perfectly-groomed façade. "I understand you need to make a profit, Summer, but you can't be serious about that price."

"I'm pretty serious," she said, still giving him a ghost of a smile. "I know it's a lot of money, but you're asking me to create a six-step tile, and each step adds to the price." She had a sketch pad out, and had been whipping off ideas for the past hour. She tapped the latest sketch with her pencil. "If you'll use one of our existing molds, the price will be a lot closer to what you'd like."

"Isn't the point of a custom tile to get *exactly* the effect I'm looking for?"

"It certainly is. And, as I told you, I can literally do anything you'd like." She paused and locked her gaze on his. "You want to design the tile from scratch, use a non-standard size, a very expensive glaze that's tough to get right, and a detailed, geometric, hand-painted design." She tapped her pencil onto the drawing. "We'll have no trouble doing the work, but the costs add up."

He stood up and tugged at the hem of his expensive-looking jacket. Somehow it hadn't gotten wrinkled even though he'd been fidgeting in his chair for an hour. "Take another look at your numbers. If you can knock off twenty percent, we can do business."

She looked up, with the power shifting just by her remaining in her chair. "I could do that," she said slowly. "But that would mean I was doing the work for no profit. Surprisingly, that's not the best way to keep the lights on at my shop."

"You're not the only tile maker in town," he said, sounding unnecessarily snippy.

"No, I'm not. But most of my competitors are smaller than I am. They won't be able to do this design for less and make any money. And the two that are bigger don't like to go this far from their standard sizes." She batted her eyes at him, making her look not only pretty, but kind of innocent. But her words cut against that impression quickly. "They're even less inclined to work for free than I am."

"Think about it," he said as he put some papers in the leather tote bag that Kelsey would have liked to have stolen when he wasn't looking.

"I will. I'll think about what we'd have to change to lower the price by twenty percent. As is—my price stands."

"I can throw so much business your way you'll have to add staff," he said, slipping on the overcoat that looked like it was made from the softest wool imaginable. "But you have to work with me on price."

"I hear you," she said, still looking as calm as a summer's day. "But adding staff to take on jobs were I don't make a profit seems…" She held up her hands. "Not so smart."

"Call me," he said as he swept out of the room, leaving just a trace of his delightful aftershave.

Summer raised her eyebrows as she waited a few seconds to speak. "I'm not going to work for free so Mister Fancy Pants can buy a thousand dollar briefcase." She started to put her things away. "I'm also not going to call him. If he wants this design, he can make the first move." She stopped and stared at the sketch before she slipped the pad into her bag. "It is a nice design, though. But Jesus," she sighed. "The glaze he wants is really fiddly."

"Fiddly?"

She laughed a little. "One of my studio instructors was British, and I adopted some of his terms. Fiddly bits is one of my favorites, along with 'dropping a spanner in the works.'"

"Cute. I like unique terms."

"Me too." She patted the bag possessively, as if the tiles were in there. "Actually, fiddly is an understatement when we're talking about the glaze he wants. I guarantee that we'll screw up ten to twenty percent of the job, and the way he wants it done gives us just one chance. That's a lot of otherwise perfect tiles to throw away." She seemed to lose a little energy, sliding into her chair and letting out a sigh. "Ignoring the glaze, just making the tiles will take forever. I'm sure it will take my very best fabricator two full days." She drummed her fingers on the desk, clearly thinking. "Fully loaded, he sets me back fifty bucks an hour—"

"Fully loaded?"

"Uh-huh. Salary, overtime, benefits, vacation…"

"You know that number for all of your employees?"

"Of course," she said, like she had the number right on the tip of her tongue. She gave Kelsey a satisfied smile. "I was surprised to find I had a head for business." The smile dimmed when she added, "I'd happily do these tiles at cost to support a charity or a cultural institution, but I'm not going to throw my profit away so Roger looks like a star."

"He'll be back," Kelsey said. "I'm sure he's already gotten the sign-off on the design. I think he's just trying to squeeze you."

"Best of luck," she said, showing a little attitude. "I'm doing just fine, thank you. I don't need to accept jobs where I lose money." She started to put her coat on. "Now, if he'd caught me ten years ago, I would have cut my price by thirty percent. Timing," she added, letting out a short laugh.

"Are you heading home?"

"I'm on my way to Squirrel Hill to see my parents. Unlike you, a family dinner once a month is plenty. Why? Do you want to kiss me again?"

"As a matter of fact, I do." Kelsey stood up and moved over to stand close. "I'd do it now, but even though I'm out at work, I'm not that out."

"How about the weekend? I'm free on Saturday night."

"Then put me on your calendar for our second date. I'd love to have you over to my apartment, but we'd have to get carryouts. I can rarely claw my way out of here before seven on Saturday."

"Then come to my place. I'm busy during the day, but I'll have time to make something."

"It is definitely a date."

"Great. I know you don't have any allergies, but is there anything you don't eat?"

"I'm not the world's most adventurous eater, but I don't dislike much."

Summer reached up and touched Kelsey's chin. It was just a brief brush of her fingers, but it sent a shiver down her back. "I've got your number," she said, adding a coy smile. "I'll text you my address." She took out her phone and moved to stand right next to Kelsey. "First work-date selfie. Smile pretty."

CHAPTER FIVE

THIS WEEK, THE FRIDAY NIGHT gang had decided to meet up at a nice downtown hotel that had a pretty rocking bar scene. Actually, Summer wasn't sure if the actual hotel was nice or not. But the bar up on the top floor provided a great view of an attractive portion of the city, and that made it nice enough for her.

As always, she was the last to arrive, a fact that continually puzzled her. Everyone else had a professional job for a major corporation or large law firm. Shouldn't it be hard for them to get away at five o'clock on a Friday? But she didn't mind bringing up the rear. They'd almost always secured a table by the time she'd arrived, and getting to sit down at the end of the week was sweet indeed.

"Greetings, all," she said when she approached the table on the far end of the crowded room. Given all of the business suits she'd passed, the bar had done a good job of attracting the professionals who were still forced to dress to impress for work.

Leah stood and kissed both of her cheeks, then fondly rested her hand on Summer's shoulder for a moment. "You're looking fantastic, as usual."

"Right back at you, girl. Is that another new dress?"

"Not technically. I bought it last year at the end of the season. This is the first time I've worn it, though. Thank you for noticing," she added, giving her friends a blatant scowl.

"I told you that you looked fantastic!" Lori complained. "I get credit."

"But you didn't specifically mention the dress. Partial credit."

They sat down, and Summer ordered a round when a server approached. She was definitely going to have to pull her credit card out tonight. This place couldn't keep the lights on without charging a lot for drinks. "What did I miss?" she asked after the server departed.

"Nothing, really," Leah said. "Work is slow for everyone but me. We were just trying to decide on our spring or summer trip."

"Why don't we look forward to the one we've got coming up," Summer said, playfully swatting at her sister.

"I am very much looking forward to it," Leah said. "Oh! I haven't gotten to talk to you since last week. How was your date?"

"Make us jealous," Patti said, setting her chin on her linked hands, acting like she was hanging onto every word.

"It was good," Summer said. "Definitely good enough for a second date." She pulled out her phone and showed them the selfie she'd taken. "This was moments after our first kiss."

"Your eyes are half-closed," Wendy said. "And she looks a little hammered."

"She had one drink." Summer looked at the photo again, having to acknowledge she could have done a much better job if she hadn't just stuck the phone into the air and hit the button. "Here's a better photo, taken at her office. This one's minus a kiss good enough to make her look drunk."

"Let me see," Leah said, giving the photo her full attention. "She looks nice. Pretty, too. What's she like?"

"I think she's kind of like me," Summer said, having thought about that a lot. "She seems mature, which goes a long way. And I got a real 'good person' vibe from her. She asked me a lot of questions, which I also appreciated. And she made me laugh."

"That's *huge*," Leah said, going slightly overboard. Summer was sure no one paid her sister to be so supportive, but she acted like it was her full-time job.

"It was definitely nice. She's coming to my house for dinner tomorrow."

"Ooo," Lori said. "That's a big step."

"Not really. She works until seven, and we wouldn't eat until nine if we went out. I'm trying to prevent both of us from starving."

"Will you sleep with her?" Wendy asked. "I mean tomorrow," she clarified. "Do lesbians do that?"

Summer stared at her for a second, often nonplussed by Wendy's boldness. "I'm looking for a relationship, not just a roll in the hay."

"And that means you can't sleep with someone right away?"

"It doesn't mean that at all. It's possible that everything will align perfectly and I'll want to jump into bed with her." She narrowed her eyes, knowing she didn't look very menacing. "But if I do, I'll never admit it."

CHAPTER SIX

KELSEY HAD TO RESIST HER growing desire to push a pair of browsers out of the showroom on Saturday night. She had an image of slapping their backs, yelling, "Save yourselves!" then sneaking out right behind them to hop into her car and hightail it over to Summer's.

When the couple finally dawdled out of the building fifteen minutes after closing, she decided to stop by her own apartment to freshen up first. Having sparkling clean teeth was the minimum when you wanted to kiss a woman, and she definitely wanted to kiss Summer. In her head, she'd kissed her a few dozen times that week, but the real thing was so much better.

As soon as she slipped into her parking spot she ran upstairs, not willing to wait for the elevator, which moved as though it were powered by a couple of mice and a wheel. It would only take about fifteen minutes to drive to the Strip District, and Summer wasn't expecting her until seven, so Kelsey impulsively stripped off her clothes and got into the shower. She wasn't particularly dirty, but it never hurt to smell fresh when you were trying to impress a woman. And while she hadn't gotten any vibes that Summer wanted to hop into bed this quickly, she was going to be ready if she did.

After putting on her newest jeans and a marine blue cashmere sweater, she grabbed her lightweight jacket and made for the door. Just as she crossed the threshold, she remembered she'd bought a bottle of wine, and ran back into the kitchen to fetch it. Now she was good to go, and ran down the stairs and got into her car. But...she hadn't remembered to do the main thing she'd stopped by for. Up the stairs one more time, she stood, panting, as she flossed and brushed while still wearing her coat.

That was a first, but if it resulted in Summer planting a big kiss on her lips, it was worth it.

Back in the car for what she hoped was the last time, she reached Summer's neighborhood in good time for a Saturday night. The place was already starting to hum, but that wasn't odd. Her own neighborhood sometimes seemed noisy, but the Strip District was usually several times as lively. It was close to downtown, had a lot of espresso shops, Italian food markets, and some nice restaurants, but Kelsey wouldn't have lived there if a building paid her to move in. She remembered when the area was just beginning to catch a vibe when she was a young woman, but it had, in her opinion, been too successful. Now, in addition to all of the young professionals who wanted to live close to downtown, swarms of tourists jammed the streets on the weekends, looking for fun. But there wasn't anything special to keep them entertained, from her perspective at least. They just walked slowly up and down Penn, making traffic worse than it had to be.

Kelsey had her phone providing directions, and after leaving Liberty Avenue it kept taking her closer and closer to the river. On the last north-south street still on dry land, her phone told her she'd arrived.

Looking up, she saw one of the new luxe buildings someone had plunked down right on the waterfront. She let her surprise settle, reasoning that she didn't know Summer well enough to even guess where she might live. But she had a regular-girl, artsy vibe that didn't seem to fit in one of these yuppie/preppie/hipster buildings. If Kelsey had to locate Summer somewhere in the neighborhood, she would have chosen the former Armstrong Cork Factory that had been gut-renovated and turned into loft apartments. That building at least had some character.

After finding a parking spot only a couple of blocks away, Kelsey entered the lobby, which was decorated just about as she'd expected it to be—like a designer's concept of a tech start-up. Everything was bright and hard and streamlined, with a guy sitting behind a glass reception desk, giving her a cool appraisal.

"I'm here to see Summer Hayes," she said.

"I'll let her know you're here. Your name?"

"Kelsey Maliar."

He nodded, and dialed, with his wireless headset letting him talk without holding onto anything. "This is Stephen from reception. Kelsey Mally-er is here to see you. Right. I'll send her up." He cut the connection and pointed toward the multi-striped elevator. "Fifth floor. Unit G."

"Thanks, Stephen," she said, then walked quickly to stick her hand in to stop the door after someone got out. By the time she reached the fifth floor, Summer was there to greet her, looking cuter than hell.

She'd pulled her hair back into a messy bun, and had stuck a colored pencil through it to hold it in place. Her face was slightly flushed, probably from the heat of the kitchen, and she'd unfastened three buttons on her navy blue and white striped shirt. She grasped the collar and rapidly fanned herself with the fabric. "I couldn't get my window open. My apartment feels like a terrarium!"

Kelsey put her hand on her back as they started to walk down the bright, colorful hallway, able to feel the heat radiating from her body. "Are you barbecuing? They say that's not a good idea indoors…"

She laughed. "Sure feels like it. I was out all day, and the place was cold when I got home. I made the mistake of cranking up the heat, then promptly conked out on the sofa. I had to run around like crazy to get dinner ready, and…" She stopped and took in a breath. "I'm so glad to see you, Kelsey. I hope you're hungry."

They entered the apartment, and Kelsey's empty tummy really liked what it smelled. "Roast chicken?"

"Right you are. I figured all meat-eaters like a simple chicken."

"Just let me take off my coat." She had it off in a second. "If I knew you better, I'd take off my sweater, too. Did you set the thermostat to the broil position?"

"It's finicky, which is kind of infuriating for a new building. If you can get a window open, I'll be in your debt. I was just mashing some potatoes, although now I want a bowl of ice cream to cool off."

"You go finish what you were doing. I'll handle the window."

Kelsey looked around while she crossed the apartment, seeing that Summer owned some pretty nice furniture. Nothing wildly extravagant, but nicer than most people their age could afford. Given that everything fit together harmoniously, it was clear she hadn't had to accept things her relatives were about to put on the curb.

The window had a tricky catch, one that would have required steel fingernails to pry open. She had a small multi-tool on her keyring, and she used the tiny flathead screwdriver to press the latch while she put her other hand on the frame and gave it a sharp tug. It slid toward her after the metal scraped against the frame, and she smiled when Summer called out, "You've saved us!"

"All in a day's work, ma'am." There were no screens, so she opened the window as far as it would go, then bent to poke her head out to look down at the large deck that surrounded an in-ground pool. She let out a whistle at the sight, but with her head outside Summer probably hadn't heard her. On the way to the front door to fetch the wine she'd brought, she said, "Even if you don't want to date me after tonight, I'm going to try to get invited back during July. Swimming pools are my thing."

"That's what convinced me to move here. I arrived two summers ago, so excited. Then the jerks closed it the weekend I moved in. But I made up for it this past July and August. I sat down there to eat my dinner nearly every night." She looked up from her work and said, "I was amazed at how many people pay for an amenity like that and fail to use it."

"You could give me your entry key to use on Wednesdays and Thursdays and never even have to see me. I'll help you get your money's worth."

Summer pointed at the bottle Kelsey held. "If you bring wine, you're always welcome."

"I made a good guess," she said, proud of her choice as she set the bottle of white burgundy on the counter.

"Ooo. Perfect. Want to put it in the freezer for a minute? I've got my hands full."

Kelsey did as she was asked, then spent a minute watching Summer finish the potatoes and put them into the oven.

"I have to have my potatoes warm," she said, looking up to give Kelsey a smile. "Now for a little gravy, and we're ready to go."

"Can I set the table?"

"Already set. You can put some music on if you want."

"Can do. What do you have…"

"I've got a Bluetooth speaker on that credenza over there. My wi-fi password's on a card on the refrigerator if you want to stream something from your phone."

"I'm on it." After getting her phone on the network, she walked over and noted not only the top-notch speaker, but the quality of the credenza. Well-made cabinetry was never cheap. Making tile must have been about as lucrative as Kelsey had guessed.

Her favorite background music playlist was a big mix of styles. Quiet, slightly sexy, and mostly instrumental. It took just a moment to set it on shuffle and let it go.

"We're ready," Summer said, walking over to the four-seater dining table to place a nicely arranged tray of roast chicken, mashed potatoes, and asparagus on it.

"I'll get the wine."

"Great. Glasses are next to the fridge, and the bottle opener is in the drawer right below."

"Sounds like a good layout. I like having the glasses close to the refrigerator."

By the time she'd opened the wine and carried the bottle and a pair of glasses over to the table, Summer had carved the chicken and was portioning everything out. "Breast or thigh?"

"I like it all. You choose."

Summer met her eyes and nodded. "I peg you as a breast woman."

"I won't argue," Kelsey said, smiling at the banter they'd re-established as she took a seat. "Boy, everything looks good enough to eat."

"I think I nailed it. Hold up your plate." She took her phone and took a quick photo. "I caught you before you tasted anything. Even if it's an awful meal, I'll remember it as a good one when I look at the photo." When she sat, she pulled the pencil from her hair, and shook it out, letting it fall to drape across her shoulder blades. She did that thing from the shampoo commercials, where she tossed her head sharply, then flicked a few reluctant strands back. "So much nicer," she sighed. "I no longer feel like I'm having a hot flash."

"Personal experience?"

"Not yet, thank god. I don't look forward to having to put my head in the freezer, like my mom does, but I think I've got a couple of years before that happens."

"I'm not in a rush, either, but I am looking forward to not having my period any more."

"Silver lining," Summer agreed. "I think we should have some kind of off switch if we decide we don't want to have kids, don't you?"

"I would have hit that switch when I was fourteen," Kelsey said, letting out a soft laugh. "Having kids never seemed like something I wanted to get into."

"It hasn't been a life goal for me, either." She raised her glass and touched the rim against Kelsey's. "To childlessness."

"I'll drink to that." She took a sip. "I don't mean to brag, but this is a nice bottle."

"Two thumbs up. Now…the test." She took a bite of her chicken and smiled as she nodded. "We kind of rock, don't we? A well-cooked chicken and a good wine to match."

"Mmm-mmm," Kelsey said, about to swoon as she took a bite of the juicy meat. "You can cook."

"If I'm going to be immodest, I'll agree with you. One of the first meals I ever cooked was a roast chicken. My mom supervised, but she let me run with it."

"Here's to good moms," Kelsey said, raising her glass again. "My mom's disappointed she won't have grandchildren, but she doesn't give me a hard time about it. How about yours?"

"No hard time for me, either. I have three younger brothers and a younger sister who all have the potential to create the next generation."

"Ooo. Big family." She laughed. "I can't believe we spent like seven hours talking about everything from childhood pets to favorite colors, but I have no idea how many siblings you have."

"Only because I knew we'd get to it. I swear my family means more to me than long-deceased pets. Oops! I forgot napkins." She got up and went back into the kitchen, returning in a minute with cloth napkins that matched the place mats.

"You live like an adult," Kelsey said, smiling so Summer read her comment as a tease.

"I am an adult. But I will admit it's easier to live like one when you have generous parents. My mother loves to shop for...well, anything, really. She hardly seems to mind whom she's buying for. It's the shopping she gets off on."

"That's...as decent a hobby as any."

"I truly don't mean to complain. I definitely benefit from her spending, but sometimes it feels more like control than generosity." She shrugged. "I try to draw a line, but I'm only successful about fifty percent of the time. I'm making progress, but it's slow."

"If I had to pick an annoying trait for my mom to have, spoiling me with gifts would be near the top. But I suppose anything can be annoying if it's done for the wrong reasons."

"I'm not sure if my mom's reasons are bad. I just wish she wouldn't blow all of my dad's money. I assume he'd like to retire someday, but he won't be able to if she keeps up her current pace." She took a sip of her wine. "As you say, there are worse habits for a parent to have."

"I think your family's a rung or two above mine in terms of buying power. My mom would love to be able to shower me with big-ticket items, but she couldn't even consider it. My parents want to retire as soon as they're able to, so they're diligent savers."

"My family's doing well now, but I've been at just about every point on the wealth scale. Well, we've never been crazy rich, and we've never been on the street, but things weren't always so sunny. People say money can't buy happiness, but I can attest that the lack of it can screw things up royally."

⊛

Summer sat on a stool and supervised after Kelsey thoughtfully offered to clean the kitchen.

"Sure you don't want to share the last of the wine?" Summer asked, waggling the bottle in the air. "There's about two ounces left."

"No, you go ahead. To the cook go the spoils."

"Don't mind if I do," she said, pouring it into her glass. "This has been a fantastic day. I went out for breakfast with my mom, then my sister and I spent the afternoon at a museum, and now I'm getting to spend the evening with you. Who could ask for anything more?"

"If you'd gotten to draw for a while, this might have been a perfect day for you," Kelsey said, giving her a very sweet smile.

"Then I'll chalk it up as darned close to perfect. I didn't get to spend the afternoon making love to my awesome girlfriend, either, but good things come to those who wait—so I've been told."

"I've been looking forward to tonight since we said goodbye last Saturday," Kelsey said, looking a little embarrassed to admit that. "I haven't had a second date I've looked forward to as much as this one in a year."

"A year? Really?" Summer took a sip of her wine, feeling the pleasant buzz she got from sharing a bottle along with a good dinner. "I can't imagine anyone as pretty as you are going a whole year."

"I didn't say I haven't had second dates," she said, showing that smile again. "Just that I didn't look forward to them as much as I did this one."

"Then I'm doubly glad you're enjoying yourself."

Kelsey scraped the remnants from a plate into the trash receptacle. "Dating is weird, isn't it? You've got to be open enough so the other person can tell if you might be a fit, but if you're too open you feel a lot worse if they carefully assess your A-game and send you packing."

"Well said. I usually hate dating, since I make up my mind about people in a matter of seconds. The hours really drag when you know you don't want to be there."

"Seconds?" Kelsey said, turning to stare at her. "Are you serious?"

"Uh-huh," she said, realizing she shouldn't have admitted to that. Making snap judgments wasn't the sign of a thoughtful person, and she didn't want Kelsey to think she was flaky. "I've had a lot of therapy, and that's given me a long list of things I'm wary about. You can tell right away if someone is haughty, or overly full of herself, or dismissive, or entitled, or just…wrong for you."

"I suppose that's true. I certainly could have had a better list back when I was just starting out in the dating game. I was like a duckling that imprinted on anyone who showed interest." She held up the platter. "I can't guess where you keep this."

"Bottom pull-out shelf under the silverware drawer."

"Got it." She put the tray away, then started to drain the water from the sink. After putting the dish towel over the handle on the stove, she walked around to where Summer was sitting. "Want to move over to the living room?"

"Definitely." She picked up her phone and put it on silent.

Kelsey stopped right in front of her and smiled. "No selfie?" she asked, taking a glance at the phone.

"Oh, no," Summer said, laughing a little. "I was silencing it. I'm on a big group chat with some friends from college, and the place I worked before I moved back here. Sometimes it can go wild, so I mute it when I don't want to be disturbed. Like now."

"Got it. Just let me know if you want to memorialize anything. I'm ready."

Summer made a quick stop to push the window mostly closed. They'd maintained a polite distance all night, and Kelsey kept that up, taking the far end of the sofa. She crossed her ankle over a knee and leaned back, looking at Summer expectantly.

"I take it you don't imprint on everyone who shows any interest these days?" Summer asked.

"I've gotten pickier, thank god. Actually, much pickier. I'm going on fewer dates, and enjoying most of them more."

"That sounds like a good trend. Do friends introduce you to people?"

"Not often, since I've already met just about anyone a friend wants to introduce me to. I'm working my way through dating apps now." Shrugging, Kelsey added, "I've had decent luck with them."

"That's because you're so cute," Summer teased. "I bet everyone wants to hook up with you."

"Well, not *every*one. Most people, yes, but not everyone. If someone's looking for a Cantonese speaker, I'm rarely the first choice."

"Do you know what you need?" Summer said, standing again and looking down at Kelsey's puzzled expression.

"Cantonese lessons?"

"You need an after dinner drink. Do you like port?"

"I do, but I probably shouldn't. I've got to drive home."

"No pressure, but I've got a credit with Uber. I could send you home in a car, then bring your car back to you before you have to leave for work in the morning."

"Really?" She looked not only surprised, but puzzled. Maybe it was her turn to wonder if her date had a drinking problem.

"Sure. I like to get up early on Sunday and get some things done. Once I return your car, you could give me a ride home on your way to work. Or, if that's not convenient, I could toss my bike in your backseat and ride home."

Kelsey's smile was back. Probably because no one would offer to ride a bike early in the morning if they were planning on getting smashed.

"If you really don't mind, I'd love an after-dinner drink."

Summer went to the little bar cart she kept in the corner. "I've got some choices for you. Port, brandy, or cognac. What's your pick?"

"Let's stick with port. I know I like it."

"Coming right up." She poured the wine into the thin glasses she kept on the cart and carried them back with her. After handing Kelsey one, she sat down again. "I thought your tongue needed loosening before you got into the weeds about your dating habits."

"Not many women tell me that," she said, smiling rakishly as she took a sip. "Nice. That's very nice."

"I don't drink a lot, quantity-wise, but every once in a while I like to get a good buzz on. Tonight felt like that kind of night."

"Mmm. I drink often, but rarely a lot. If I'm at home, I usually have a beer or a glass of wine with dinner, but I never have two if I'm alone."

"You're still hitting my sweet spot," Summer teased. "I like a social drinker who knows when to stop."

"I truly do. I've seen how everyone gives each other the high sign when my cousin's getting sloppy. That's never going to happen with me."

"So…you don't like to date women who embarrass you in public by getting sloppy. What else? Last Saturday you told me you couldn't tolerate cheaters, liars, and users. Anything else on your no-fly list?"

"I honestly don't have a huge number of things on my list. But I'm always more attracted to genuinely nice women. A homely, kind-hearted woman will always win out over a stunner who thinks the rest of the world is there solely to make her life better."

"Personal experience?" Summer asked, cocking her head.

"Uh-huh," she said, smiling. "I was really excited about finally getting a date with a solid ten in the looks department who was about a two in the nice person category. The next person I matched with wasn't nearly as cute, but she was so much more fun to spend the evening with."

"Been there. I'm honestly looking for someone who's easy—" She stopped on a dime. "I don't mean in that way, although it's fine with me if she likes to hop into bed pretty early in the game. I just mean I'm tired of dating women who are easy to offend, or difficult to have a good meal with."

Playfully, Kelsey said, "You date people who don't know how to use utensils?"

"No, but so many people are ridiculously picky about what they'll eat and when they'll eat it. I don't mind if someone's careful about her own choices, but if you lecture me about what *I* order—we're on our last date."

"Oh, my, you've had some bad ones."

"Really bad. Last year, I thought I was getting somewhere with a nice woman who was easy to be with. Then I found out we didn't click—at all —when it came to sex. We'd spent months seeing each other, and I respected her wish to take things very, very slowly. Then I found out she was hiding the fact that she honestly didn't like sex at all." She held up her hands. "That's fine, but that's a big thing to hide while insisting she was just careful."

"Ooo. I would have felt kind of used."

"That's it exactly. I think she knew her lack of interest would ruin the whole deal, so she wanted to make sure I was into her before she told me the truth." She shrugged. "I guess she was right. She would have had to be all-world in every other area for me to give up sex." She laughed. "That's a total lie. Sex is non-negotiable when it comes to girlfriends, but I would have been happy to be her friend. She was a sweetheart."

"I guess you can't create something that isn't there. It's probably best to date people you click with right away."

Grumpily, she said, "It shouldn't take as long to find out if you have a genuine spark as it does to learn to play the guitar."

"I couldn't agree more," Kelsey said, scooting over a little. "Now, I'll grant you that I'm not competent to drive a car right now. But I think I'm sober enough to see if we have any spark."

"I like the way you think," Summer said. "And I like the fact that you have the nerve to try." She put her hand on Kelsey's thigh, pleased when her hand was covered almost immediately.

A surprisingly shy smiled covered Kelsey's mouth. "I haven't even kissed you today, but I feel very sparky."

"Then let's get the ball rolling." She shifted so they were almost facing each other. For quite a few seconds she gazed into Kelsey's eyes. It was the kind of gaze that would normally show you didn't respect a person's personal space—very bold. But Summer was trying to signal that she was willing to lower a barrier. "I think you're special, and I'd be amazed if we couldn't spark a little flame."

"I'm always up for a challenge," she said, slipping her arm around Summer and tucking her into a loose embrace. "Let's see what we've got going on here."

Summer gave her two big thumbs up for being willing to basically put her kissing skills to the test. Most women would have at least been tentative about that, but not her. Kelsey was clearly up to the challenge.

Summer touched her chin, positioning her head for a good angle. Gazing at her mouth, she said, "I don't know about you, but I really like to kiss."

"Then I'm happy to tell you you've come to the right place. When I do it right, kissing feels as intimate to me as anything."

"Let's make sure we do it right." Her hand slid to the back of Kelsey's neck as she leaned in close. Pausing for a few ticks of the clock, she closed her eyes and let herself adjust to her scent, and the warmth of her breath. It was always a heady feeling to let the anticipation build, and she felt it throughout her body, with her heart starting to race.

Kelsey grasped her shoulder to hold her still, then closed the distance between them, with the tiniest sigh leaving her lips when they met. "That's so nice," she murmured when they broke apart.

"I like the way you kiss. Gentle, but not tentative."

"That's me in a nutshell," Kelsey said, just far enough away for Summer to see her smile. "I'm always gentle with delicate things." She put her index finger on the corner of Summer's mouth and traced her lips, sending shivers up her back. "When we were meeting with Roger the other day, I kept getting distracted by your mouth. It's so pretty," she sighed.

"My mouth likes your mouth. Cool, huh?"

"Very." Tightening her hold, Kelsey showed a slightly more aggressive side, kissing Summer until they started to move against one another. "Happy?" she asked when she pulled back for a moment and allowed their foreheads to rest against one another.

"Deliriously," Summer said, chuckling at her own hyperbole. "Seriously. There's nothing I love more than this."

She'd been quite passive up until then, which wasn't odd for her. But when she was turned on bursts of energy came over her in waves, and she really got off on taking the upper hand. She shifted her weight to press Kelsey up against the arm of the sofa and kiss her with more verve, sucking each lip into her mouth in turn, trying to have a piece of her inside her own body. She could feel her shiver, thrilled by the hands that now roamed possessively up and down her back.

"That's so good," Summer murmured. "I love the way your hands feel on me."

Suddenly, she was lying flat on the sofa, with Kelsey hovering above her. Her eyes were shining, and she was shaking a little from the effort of holding herself up. "If you ask me to stop, I will. If you don't…"

Summer was on the verge of putting on the brakes, but then Kelsey lowered herself onto her body, held her face with her hands and claimed her mouth with a drive she hadn't shown even a hint of. It was *fantastic*. Just the way Summer loved a woman to take over and show exactly what she wanted. Even though she had no desire to tell her to stop, Summer didn't want to encourage her further. She was all in favor of making sure there were flames, but definitely not ready to leap into them quite yet.

Kelsey was darned good at reading her signals, even though they'd been non-verbal. She was kissing Summer like she had no control whatsoever, but she didn't go one inch further. And that was a friggin' fantastic attribute in a lover. Having to repeatedly grab a woman's hands to stop her from mauling you was not only exhausting, it was annoying.

Summer hated to bring things to a close, but she wasn't ready to strip off all her clothes and go for it—emotionally. Her body thought she was being an idiot, though, with her clit throbbing painfully to let her know it was displeased.

By shifting her hips, she got a little purchase and was able to press against Kelsey's shoulders. Even though she let out a frustrated sigh, she complied in an instant, allowing Summer to push her away. Playfully, she stuck her lips out and made some loud smacking sounds. "No more?" she asked, nearly slurring.

"If we don't stop now, I'm afraid we won't stop until you've got to leave for work."

Her smile was really cute, so cute she'd probably gotten away with a ton of things as a kid. "It's November, and I haven't taken any of my sick days yet…"

"Can we talk for a minute?"

"Sure." Kelsey reached over and tossed each back cushion to the floor, giving her room to roll over and slip into the space she'd created. Her eyes didn't look hazy any longer, and even though they were pressed up against each other, Summer felt like she could think better now that Kelsey wasn't lying atop her.

She shifted so she lay on her side, facing her. "I'm desperate to keep going, but I don't want to jump into the deep end until I know you better. Is that okay?"

"I'm happy to stop whenever you want." She smiled, looking a little embarrassed. "Well, maybe not happy, but I'd never push further than you wanted to go."

"Then let's just kiss tonight. I feel like I'm getting to know you through your kisses, which are fantastic," she said, tracing Kelsey's warm lips with her index finger.

"If we're going to focus on kisses, we'd better have some more of them," she said, staring at Summer's lips like she was studying them for a test. Kelsey boldly latched onto Summer's mouth as though she owned it, which she did at the moment. She wasn't aggressive, but she was definitely assertive, which was the number one item on Summer's wish list. Very content to let Kelsey kiss her, Summer lay there almost passively, getting more turned on by the moment. But she didn't mind having a thrumming ache between her legs. Deferred pleasure was also one of her things, even though she was tempted to go into the bathroom and peel off a quick orgasm. She was so hot for Kelsey she was sure she could pull the trigger in the time it normally took to pee.

Summer had lost all concept of time, but her watch buzzed quietly, alerting her that it was eleven, the time she tried to hop into bed. Kelsey's head lifted, with a silent question in her eyes.

"My bedtime," she said, feeling like a kid on a school night. "But I'm not a slave to habit. I'm enjoying the hell out of this."

"Me, too," Kelsey sighed. "God knows I love to have sex, but there's something pretty hot about knowing you can't. I think Catholic guilt backfires sometime, making denial super hot."

"I'm not Catholic, and I don't have much guilt. But I am a little cautious." She caressed Kelsey's flushed cheek, now really able to detect the scent of her exertion, which kind of made Summer's mouth water. "I don't normally wrestle on my sofa on a second date." She pulled her close again and kissed her tenderly. "But you're making me go outside my comfort zone. I'm not complaining, by the way."

"I probably rush into sex sooner than I should. But I get turned on and then…" She smiled, once again looking a little embarrassed. "I let my libido make decisions for me, which isn't always the best idea."

"Ooo. Are you saying you're hot for me?"

Kelsey turned her head and blinked a few times. "I'm two minutes from touching myself, and that would embarrass us both."

Laughing, Summer said, "That wouldn't embarrass me at all. If you really want to…I'll watch."

She seemed to really consider the offer, which was also kind of hot. Summer had been lying, though. There was no way they wouldn't both be embarrassed if Kelsey rubbed one out right then.

She playfully put her hand on her zipper, then shook her head. "Can't do it. Want to," she added, "but can't."

Smiling, Summer slid her arm behind Kelsey's head, then leaned over to start to kiss her again. Even though they'd already kissed a lot, the sensation was still fantastic. It had been ages since she'd been so hungry for a woman's mouth, and the way Kelsey returned the kisses showed she felt just the same. "I love this," Summer whispered when they broke apart. "And I know I'll like doing a whole lot more to you in the near future."

"Any chance of a big hug? I get all mushy when I'm turned on. I become an affection junkie."

"All you want," Summer said, wrapping her arms around Kelsey's body as well as she was able, then placing her head on her chest as she held her. "I've had this sofa for at least five years, and I promise you this is the most fun I've ever had on it."

"I have a crush on it," Kelsey said, laughing weakly. "If I could reach my phone, I'd take a selfie." When Summer started to move, she held on tightly. "Kidding," she insisted. "I don't need a photo to remind me of how much fun we've had tonight. Little did I know that delicious meal would be the third best thing about my evening."

"Third?"

"Kissing you for what must have been a half hour is obviously number one, but talking to you is right behind. We did some good work here tonight. I think we've earned a third date."

"Without question." Summer struggled to get to her feet, having to work out a cramp in her knee. "I'm up!" she declared. Looking down at Kelsey, she said, "I really look forward to getting you onto that sofa again very soon."

Kelsey extended a hand, and Summer pulled her to her feet. She was a true mess, and Summer helped her out by tugging her sweater down, then grasping her waistband and centering the zipper, which was off by a few inches. "Much better. You could go out in polite company now."

"I'm going to have to. I've got to get to bed soon."

"Want to sleep here?"

"On the sofa?"

"Mmm." She thought for a second. "I want to say yes to that, but then I'll feel like a prude. I mean, we were pretty intimate just a couple of minutes ago…"

Kelsey put her hands on Summer's hips, holding her in a loose, casual way. "How about this? If either one of us isn't a hundred percent into something—we don't do it."

"Really?" Summer asked, giving her a probing look. "It's that simple?"

"I think so. Especially about intimate stuff. If we're on the right path, we'll get to everything, won't we? Let's not rush."

"Hmm… I don't know what terrible secret you're hiding, but at this point I might be able to overlook it."

"No terrible secrets," Kelsey promised. "I'm just an average Jane who's looking for someone to share her life with." She put her hand on Summer's cheek and stroked it gently. "So far, you're a very good prospect, and I'd like to be the same for you. How about that ride home you promised."

"Let me get my phone." She pulled up the app and handed it to Kelsey. "Just put your address in there."

"All done," Kelsey said, handing the device back. "My ride should be here in three minutes. Just enough time for one last kiss."

"Make it a good one," Summer said, tipping her head back to present her lips.

Kelsey followed through perfectly, putting just enough heat into the kiss to make Summer regret not asking her to stay over. That was great. Wanting more was so much nicer than wishing you'd had less.

CHAPTER SEVEN

KELSEY CHECKED HERSELF OUT IN the mirror the next morning, running her brush through her hair until it looked just right. After grabbing her tote bag, she started down the stairs, getting her coat zipped as she walked. When she reached the lobby, Summer was standing right in front of the door, straddling a sleek-looking bicycle. She looked a little like the people who rode in big groups, with skin-tight black tights and shoes that clipped into the pedals. A bright yellow helmet was atop her head, with her golden pony tail draped over her shoulder. Her jacket was also trim-fitting, and she filled it out to perfection. Kelsey pushed the door open and leaned close to give her a hug. "This car delivery thing would really catch on if you were the person who made the drop-offs. You look fantastic in your bike gear."

"Thanks," she said, wrinkling her nose at the compliment. "This isn't too early, is it?"

"No, not at all," Kelsey said, even though it was a little early. But nine o'clock was a perfectly reasonable hour for a normal person to be up and out. "What's on your agenda for the day?"

"I've already visited my grandmother, and I've had my donut fix, so I think I'll ride until I've worked off the Boston creme I had—in addition to the cinnamon sugar I usually get. Those damn donuts were really calling to me today."

"When did you get up?"

"Seven. Same as always. I was at my grandma's, donuts in hand, at seven thirty. We had coffee and talked about nothing at all until she had to leave for church. That's our habit," she added. "I get to spend a little time with her, and it sets my day off well."

"You visit your grandmother every week?" Kelsey wasn't going to admit how infrequently she'd visited her own now-deceased grandparents, especially since she'd been crazy about them.

"Uh-huh. She's still got a lot of local friends, but three of her closest ones moved to Florida this year. Having me come by cheers her up."

Kelsey wasn't flexible enough to kick herself in the butt, but she should have. Summer had just put things in the perfect context, one she hadn't really spent much time thinking about. And now it was too late to make up for those missed opportunities. Her grandparents had been in failing health in their final years, and slowly began to complain about nearly everything. Kelsey had taken the easy way out and had reduced the frequency of her visits. Yes, it was boring to listen to people complain about their health, but her grandparents were obviously freaked out about having one part of their bodies after another start to break down. She'd been so selfish!

Summer's hand was on her shoulder, giving it a squeeze. "My grandmother's really important to me. An hour of my week isn't much time."

"That's very true. She's your dad's…?"

"Mother's mom. My mom sees her…less often than I do. I can't make everyone do what I want—even though I'd like to have that kind of power."

"I'll do what you want," Kelsey said. "Name it."

"Okay," she said slowly, like she was really giving it some thought. "Go out with me next Saturday night."

"I have plans…" She bent over slightly and placed a gentle kiss to Summer's lips, tasting a hint of the cinnamon from her donut. "That I'm going to cancel. I'll be ready to go anywhere you want at seven o'clock."

"I'll make reservations somewhere. How do you feel about Thai food."

"I don't think I've ever had it, so I'll be ready to start liking it on Saturday night."

"Very good answer," Summer said, wrapping an arm around Kelsey's waist to give her a hug that she was pretty certain would power her through the day.

⊛

Rob usually spent his Sunday evenings at a boisterous gay bar that had a leather scene that popped its head up just one night a week. He certainly didn't give off the impression that he was into leather, usually dressing like your average gay guy in this thirties, wearing tight, knit shirts to show off his pecs, and dark jeans, along with whatever shoes were in fashion. He never spoke about his sexual affinities, and neither did Kelsey, so, even though they were very dear friends, they each had some privacy zones that neither of them seemed eager to breach.

They often met up on Sunday evenings for dinner, since she was always starving when she got off work, and seven was way too early for him to show up at a bar. She had no idea how he implemented major software installations hung over and sleep-deprived most Mondays, but it hadn't seemed to hurt him. He was well-respected at his company, and continued to advance.

Kelsey was waiting for him at an inexpensive Chinese place they both liked, and he slid into a chair after leaning over her shoulder to kiss her cheek. "You look beat," he said, sticking his lower lip out. "Bad day?"

"Not too. It was long, though. No serious customers came in after one, but there were enough browsers to keep me from really getting into any of my paperwork. Just kind of annoying," she admitted. "Not painful."

"I wish you had weekends off," he said, meeting their server's gaze to order a drink. It always gave her pause that a place that specialized in entrees under eight bucks had a full bar, but whatever Rob ordered, they made it quickly and well.

"I do, too," she said. "Especially now—when the woman I'm going to marry is just sitting around on the weekends, waiting for me to sweep her off her feet."

"Ahh!" he squealed, letting out the kind of high-pitched squeak that let every kid at their high school clock him as gay by the end of the first week of their freshman year. "You had a good time last night."

"*Super* good," she emphasized. "I was hooked after our first date, but now that we wrestled around on her sofa for the better part of an hour—I'm even more into her."

He started to laugh. "Lesbians."

She reached over and poked him in his ridiculously muscular arm. "If you don't give me a hard time about not banging a woman on the first date, I won't give you a hard time about not ever having a second date."

Rob gave her a sweet smile and batted his dark eyelashes. "I'm not looking to date. You, however, are looking to have sex, which you seem to have successfully avoided for quite a while."

"You know I've changed my goal. Now that I'm interested in a relationship, having sex with strangers has lost its appeal."

"I'm very glad we're not looking for the same thing," he said, his aging altar-boy appearance likely hiding some pretty racy stuff. "And I'm also very glad you had a good second date. Give me the highlights."

His drink was delivered while she thought. "Mmm. Nothing earth-shattering, but it was all good. Summer's very much what I'm looking for in a woman. She's really easy to be with, she's laid-back, and she seems open-minded. And she takes time out of her week to see her grandmother, so she's nicer than I am."

"You're as nice as they come," he insisted, always on her side. "Anything else?"

"Oh! She can cook, and she's got a big sweet tooth. That's huge."

"Wedding bells are ringing in the distance," he said, cupping a hand around his ear. "You sweet-toothed girls can gobble up your wedding cake all on your own."

On Sunday night, Summer was just starting to clean the kitchen when her phone rang. She almost let it go, but she took a peek after three rings, seeing Kelsey's picture.

"Hi there," she said, after wiping off a soapy finger to hit the button. "I haven't given you a special ring yet, so I didn't realize it was you."

"We're not getting married for two years, so there's no rush to buy me a ring."

"You make me smile, Kelsey, and that's a very important trait. So? What's on your mind?"

"You don't mind my calling, do you? I don't want to be a pest."

"You're nowhere near pest-level. I'm not a big fan of talking on the phone for long periods of time, but I like hearing your voice."

"Just tell me when you've had your fill. I can take no for an answer."

"Got it. Did you just get off work?"

"No, I got out right on time, then met up with my best buddy for dinner. How about you? Was the rest of your day good?"

"Very. After my bike ride, I went to an exhibit at the Glass Center."

"Is that a museum?"

"It's more of a school. But they have an exhibit space, and I wanted to catch a show they have before it closes."

"You know, I've never dated anyone who was artsy."

"Well, given that I'm very artsy, you will have your fill. Luckily, I don't mind going to exhibits alone. But if you want a guide through the art world, I can help."

"I don't know much about art, but I'm certainly not averse to learning more. Maybe we can go to something…" She paused for a moment. "I don't know how we'll go to a single museum with my schedule."

"It's definitely not ideal. But we'll muddle through. Hey. Thanksgiving's Thursday. Are you spending it with your family."

"Oh, yeah. That's set in stone. You?"

"Same for me. But we go all day and into the night. Any chance you could swing by for a late dessert?"

"I probably could. Are we really at the point of meeting each other's family?"

"Why not?"

"I thought your family might like to keep the holiday kind of private."

"Oh, no. This isn't a formal kind of thing. People are in and out all day."

"If you're sure…"

"I am. My family's a big part of my life, and I will always spend a lot of time with them. But…" She paused while thinking of how to describe them. "We're an unusual brood. There are a lot of us, and we're pretty boisterous. If you meet them and decide you don't like them, we might as well call it a day."

"Seriously? You'd stop seeing me if I didn't like your family?"

"Uh-huh. That might sound harsh, but remember what I said on our first date. I'm looking for a relationship, and there's no sense in starting one with someone who isn't into one of the biggest parts of my life. It's better to find out if there are any major stumbling blocks right from the start."

"Mmm. I'm not sure I'd kick you out of bed if you didn't like my parents."

"Well, you should. Girlfriends come and go. Family is forever."

"That's a nice way to think of it. I really want to meet the people you care for so much. I can come around…eight?"

"I'll text you the address. I'm really looking forward to it, Kelsey."

"Me too. Are you working on Friday?"

"I'm not, happily. I like to give my people a four-day weekend whenever I can."

"I'm also getting a very rare Friday off. Maybe we can hang out."

"It's a date. I look forward to having you for dessert on Thursday. In both senses of the word.

CHAPTER EIGHT

ON THE DAY BEFORE THANKSGIVING, Summer was on the production floor, talking to one of her fabricators about a design. She'd climbed up on a work table, a habit so chronic she should have worn light-colored slacks exclusively. The seat of her jeans often looked like she'd been dusted with powdered sugar, which wasn't really the best look for clients.

Running her own company forced her to wear a lot of hats, but the one that fit her best was right here. If she could have made the salary she wanted, she would have remained an artisan. But her dad had convinced her that the lifestyle she'd grown used to needed more income than she could earn via an hourly wage. He'd been right, of course. Not to mention how tough manual labor was on a body. But she still sometimes longed for the days when she'd not give her job another minute's thought once she'd slid her card into the timestamp machine.

They had a big speaker located up in the corner of the ceiling, and Chelsea's voice boomed out of it. "Customer in reception, Summer."

She sighed as she slid off the table. "I'll be back in a second, Fimi. One day I'm going to have to hire a full-time salesperson." She started to walk away, with three people at once advising her to dust off the seat of her jeans. Thank god for observant employees.

When she got to the reception area, she was surprised to see Roger Thornhill standing a few feet away from Chelsea's workstation, gazing at his phone distractedly. That made it pretty clear he was not only unfriendly, he also had to be gay—which wasn't a news flash. Every straight guy from the mailman to the water delivery guy had to be pried away from the always-chatty, usually charming woman.

Summer approached and said, "Hi, there. I wasn't expecting you, was I?"

Dismissively, he said, "I assumed you were always here."

She started to refute that, but it really was true. "Would you like to come into my office?"

"Please."

He had that delicious-looking navy blue coat on again, and as they walked she decided it was cashmere. Who bought a cashmere coat these days? It was beyond silly to have to worry about something that would show salt from the streets, pet hair, and even human hair, when you could have a nice, warm down coat that you could throw into the washer. But Roger probably didn't do his own laundry. She imagined him having a houseboy who did everything, including clip his nails, for what was undoubtedly a meager salary. Roger definitely gave off an "I'll screw you out of every dime I can" vibe.

She let him enter, and he removed his coat and lovingly folded it before draping it across the other chair. "I like your drawings," he said, nodding toward the four companion pieces she had framed and hung behind her desk.

"Oh, thanks. I did those when I was in college."

"Really?" He moved to gaze at them more closely. "They're very nice. I…didn't realize you were a real artist."

"I'm as real as they get," she said, determined not to take offense. "We're allowed to self-identify, since there isn't a board we have to pass."

"Mmm," he said, not even able to laugh at her joke. "Well, I haven't heard from you, so I assume you're not going to work with me on price."

She pulled out a file from her credenza and took out some sketches. "I figured out a way to tweak the design," she said, handing it over. "This one will let me use a standard mold. We'll still do a lot of hand work on it, but going this way will save over twenty percent, while still creating a very individual tile. If your client had both of these lying in front of her, she'd see they were different, but I bet she wouldn't like one significantly more than the other."

He gave the sketch about one percent of his attention, then put the paper back on the desk. "Let's get real, shall we?"

"Sure. I love being real."

He took some papers out of his butter-soft leather briefcase and lay them on the desk. "Take a look at this." He pushed them across the surface and she paged through them.

"My clients paid seven hundred thousand dollars for this house, which was a total wreck. Years of neglect. Water damage. Mold. Asbestos. It should have been a tear-down."

She looked at the black and white photos, finding it looked like it had been abandoned or had been used as a crack house. "I wouldn't have the stomach to renovate this one. It's a money pit."

"Of course it is. But it's also a blank canvas. They're going to spend at least double the sales price renovating it. When they're finished, they want to be in Architectural Digest, and every other home magazine still kicking. Their goal is to impress both themselves and everyone else in Pittsburgh."

"Good for them. What's your point?"

"My point is that they're very wealthy, and very willing to spend whatever they must to have a showplace. Saving a little money on tile means nothing to them."

She reached over and picked up the sketch, replacing it in the folder. "Great. Then we'll get to work on the original design. I'll need a fifty percent—"

"You're missing my point," he said, gazing at her with an unblinking stare. "They don't care about saving money, but I do. I quoted them your original price, and they were fine with it. But I want to increase my margin, and that's where you come in."

"I think that's where I go out," she said, already resigned to having missed out on this piece of business. "I'd love to have you throw jobs my way, but not if I'm going to barely break even on them."

"But you're not looking at the big picture," he said, with his voice gaining some volume. "If I directed even a quarter of my clients here, you'd have to put on staff."

She nodded as she picked up a pencil and twirled it around between her fingers. "So I'd hire more people, spend months training them, and raise my benefits cost. And for that I'd get more business—that you'd keep taking bites out of. Is that the deal?"

"That's a very narrow-minded view," he snapped.

"No, it isn't. That's what's happening to every small business that makes a deal with the devil. No offense," she added, kind of enjoying pissing him off. "Expand the factory, buy specialized equipment, and hire more staff to produce whatever the behemoth demands. Then, once they know you're in deep, they start to squeeze you on price, which they can do with impunity. Eventually, you're doing all of their work at a break-even point, forcing you to make all of your profit from the smaller clients —exactly what you were doing before you landed the huge contract." She tossed the pencil onto the desk, where it rattled noisily before coming to rest. "No, thank you. I'd rather work with people who order ten boxes of tile and pay what I ask—which is a fair price for the skill involved."

He blew out an exasperated breath. "If I hadn't already shown my client this damn sketch, I'd leave here so fast I'd make sparks. But I have, and she loves it." He started to put his papers away, with a very sour look on his face. "There's a new kitchen and bath shop that just opened up in Regent Square. They'll work with me, so I'm going to move this job over there to get a little breathing room."

She stood and glared at him. "You're going to take the business away from Sedlak Brothers? After all of the work Kelsey's done?"

"I'd rather not," he said, raising an eyebrow. "But you're tying my hands."

"I'd like to tie my hands around your throat," she said, surprising the hell out of herself with the uncharacteristic force of her anger. "Feel free to move the business wherever you want." She walked around her desk to stand a few inches from him. "But I'm only making this tile if the order comes from Sedlak Brothers."

"You're not serious," he said, his mouth dropping open. He could obviously see that she was, because he rolled his eyes dramatically. "Aren't you just the perfect little social justice warrior."

"Not really. I just try not to be an asshole. Having Kelsey do all of the plans, only to take the business away from her, is really shitty, Roger. I'm not going to help you screw her over."

He cocked his head, looking at her as though he was just now seeing her. "Which one of us is screwing her? I think that might be you."

"I can't imagine talking about my private life with you. I'm talking about business ethics, which aren't that far removed from regular ethics. Again, trying not to be an asshole is a good place to start."

His eyes were warm and brown and very attractive, as was the rest of him. But he had a dark heart, which made him stunningly ugly in Summer's eyes.

"I wonder if Sedlak Brothers minds if their designers are screwing around with their suppliers? Maybe I'll ask."

She went to the door and stood just outside it. "Get out," she said, making her voice as hard and cold as possible. "I'm not sure I'll make the tile even if Kelsey begs me to, but I definitely will not make it for you alone."

He started to brush past her, and she called out behind him, "Don't even think about bringing me any more business. I'd rather close down than deal with you again."

He didn't say another word, and he was gone by the time she reached Chelsea's desk. She turned to see her receptionist staring at her like she'd grown another head.

"What in the hell was that all about?"

"Pond scum," she said. "You can put a cashmere coat on it, but it's still a slimy, stinking mess."

⊕

She hated to do it, but Summer had to get it off her chest. Calling Kelsey's office number, she connected with her after having spent a minute cooling down. "Hi," she said, realizing she hadn't cooled off enough. "I had a very unpleasant interaction with Roger Thornhill just now, and I thought I'd better give you a head's up."

"Um, can I call you back in a minute? I've got a client here…"

"Oh, shit. I'm sorry I didn't ask if you were free. Call me when you can."

"Give me two minutes," she said, then cut the connection.

The phone rang just a minute later. "What's wrong?" Kelsey said, sounding a little frantic.

"That jerk was here, demanding I cut my price. When I refused, he said he was going to take the project to a different kitchen designer. A new place in Regent Square."

"Oh, fuck," she whispered. "I've spent…god…over thirty hours with my client. She's probably made notes showing how I jumped through hoops to get everything she wants in her oddly-shaped space, and she'll just hand it over to a new designer and say, 'Do this.'"

"I'm really sorry, Kelsey. I probably made it worse by being so obnoxious to him, but here's the bad part. He guessed we were… interested in each other, and he's going to tell your bosses. I'm not sure if he thinks they'll give him a deal, or he just wants to be vindictive, but—"

"Oh, don't worry about that," she said, now sounding almost blasé. "We don't have any rules about who we can date, and everyone here knows I'm gay. It's not an issue at all."

"Oh, thank god. That's a load off my mind."

"Not mine! I want those hours back! Little fucker."

"Me?"

She laughed. "That's not a term I'd use for you. But if I ever see Roger Thornhill on the street, I'll use it on him."

"He might still make the order, since the client really wants it. But I told him I'd only accept it if it came from you, so…we'll see."

"Aww…" she purred, sounding very touched. "You really stood up for me."

"Of course I did. I always will, Kelsey, even if this doesn't work out between us. As I told Roger, I try not to be an asshole."

"You certainly had an interesting day, didn't you? I wish you'd recorded the whole thing. I'd like to hear you losing it at that little shit."

"He'll probably slander me to anyone he has influence over, but I can live with that. I do good work, and my satisfied customers send a lot of referrals my way."

"I'm a very satisfied customer. And whether or not this project comes through, I'll send you every referral I can manage."

"I know you will. By the way, if the order comes through, I'm not going to start on it until your client pays for the cabinets. Roger's the type to swoop in at the last minute and find a way to screw you while making me do a job I don't want to do."

"I really hope this one comes through. I know those tiles will look great, and given what a showoff my client is, she'll invite me over to see them once they're installed."

"I hope it does, too. Without this job, I never would have met you. Roger sucks, but I'll put up with him to get you out of the deal."

CHAPTER NINE

ON THANKSGIVING EVENING, KELSEY drove along the tree-lined streets of Squirrel Hill, noting the neighborhood was ghostly quiet. She'd driven through the entirely residential streets many times, but always during the day, for work. It looked different, more sober at night, when the houses seemed to recede into the darkness.

Having grown up in the near suburbs, it always caught her attention how narrow the lots in Squirrel Hill were. One of the most expensive neighborhoods in town should have sported half-acre lots, in her suburban-centric opinion. But most of these homes were close enough to one another that you could have overheard your neighbors at the dinner table. Maybe that was part of the draw. She'd always gotten the impression that the residents were remarkably close.

Following the directions her phone spit out, she did a double-take when the car started to rumble over cobblestoned streets. Those weren't unheard of in Pittsburgh, but they were more common in the grittier neighborhoods, where remnants of abandoned railroad tracks and tumble-down factories peppered the landscape.

This street was as far as you could get from tumble-down, and she looked up to see a sign that clearly stated "Private Drive." She'd had no idea there were private streets in the middle of the city, but here she was, bouncing along so roughly she'd get carsick if she had to stay on it much longer.

The houses were spaced a good distance from one another, giving them a little room to breathe. Some were quite old, Victorian, at least, while more of them were from the twenties, when heavy manufacturing was going strong, and there was a lot of money thrown around on impressive houses.

There were only a few cars parked on this section of Summer's street, and Kelsey was pleased to see she'd have no trouble parking. But as she got closer to the actual address, the houses got even bigger, and cars filled every spot for a hundred feet on both sides.

The house was as big and impressive as the pristine Queen Anne-style mammoth that stood beside it, but it wasn't nearly as old, or as tall. The brick home was just two stories, and every window glowed with life. The warmth of the light calmed her down a little, for no reason at all. Even snooty jerks could turn the lights on.

Summer had assured Kelsey that she'd be able to slip in unnoticed if she wanted. While she was normally friendly and talkative, even with strangers, she wanted to get the lay of the land before she met everyone. These people were so important to Summer that she didn't want to get off on the wrong foot with anyone.

When she reached the sidewalk of the house she texted Summer, and stayed right where she was until the front door opened. Summer stepped onto the wide, covered porch, cocking her head.

"Is this as far as you're willing to go? I could bring a piece of pie out here, but…"

"I'm nervous," Kelsey admitted. Summer was so forthright that it didn't make sense to hide anything at this point.

"Aww. There's nothing to be nervous about. Almost the whole clan is downstairs in the den now, so we can spend a few minutes talking to my mom. We're the only two upstairs. Promise." She walked down the stairs and grasped Kelsey's hand when she got closer. "The wine's been flowing all afternoon. Everyone's loud, but mellow."

"I didn't have anything to drink. I wanted to be sharp to drive."

"Then I'll pour some down your gullet right now. Good?"

Kelsey smiled at her. "Sounds good. You look very pretty, by the way. Green's your color."

"I would have to say it's my favorite, so I'm glad it's mine."

Kelsey gently touched her shoulder, feeling the crease in her sleeve. "You always look sharp in your nicely tailored blouses."

"Thanks. I send them out," she admitted. "I love a sharp crease, but I'm too lazy to put one in myself."

Kelsey looked up when a woman exited and stood on the porch. Tallish, dark-haired, and stylish, with a pretty smile that brightened when she waved her fingers. "Now I feel like I should cancel," she said.

Summer turned and tugged Kelsey along, and in a second they were all standing on the porch together. "My nearly perfect sister, Leah," Summer said. She squeezed Kelsey's hand, adding, "My 'it's too early to tell how perfect she is' date, Kelsey."

Leah laughed and put her arm around Summer, drawing her close. "One day you're going to date someone who doesn't get your sense of humor. Then where will you be?"

"Single again," Summer said, smiling. "But if someone doesn't get my sense of humor, I've already lost fifty percent of my allure. Might as well cut and run."

"I'm glad to meet you, Leah," Kelsey said, extending her hand for a shake. It was warm enough that Kelsey hadn't worn gloves, but Leah had, and the quality of the leather gave a new, heightened definition to the word "supple."

"Luckily, I not only get, I like Summer's sense of humor. I've decided to assume she's always joking. So far, that's been a safe bet."

"Very safe." Leah checked her watch, a heavy, silver-toned piece that was too weighty to stay flat on her narrow wrist. "I really wish I didn't have to go, but my friends are waiting for me."

"It's fine," Summer said. "I'd rather have you stay, but we've got a lot of people to get through, hoping to make them think Kelsey's 'normal,'" she said, making very dramatic air quotes.

"Let's get together for drinks," Leah said. "By January, I'm going to have some free time."

"No, you're not," Summer said, without any judgment in her voice. "But we'll figure out a way to meet up. Kelsey actually has a predictable schedule, so at least one of us can be counted on to show up."

"I'm predictable," Leah said. "I'm gone at the beginning of nearly every week, back home by the end." Her phone started to jangle, and she slipped it from the slash pocket of her streamlined charcoal gray coat to give it a glance. "Have you ever noticed that some of my friends are pests?" she asked, replacing the device.

"Every time we're together," Summer said. She kissed her sister's cheek, then took Kelsey's hand again. "Have fun, sis."

"Will do. Very nice to meet you, Kelsey. I truly hope we can all get together soon."

"Won't be soon…" Smiling, Summer waved as her sister descended the stairs, on her way to a very nice, very low-slung coupe.

"Your sister makes a nice exit," Kelsey said. "Is she a model or something? How does a woman know how to get into a car that low while wearing a long, dark coat? If that was me, a foot of it would be lying on the street."

"Same here." Summer shrugged. "Leah might look like a model, but she sells glass."

"Glass? Like art glass?"

"Like industrial glass. She travels nearly every week, peddling glass." Summer lowered her voice slightly. "Big secret. You can make a very good living selling something kind of boring if you sell a lot of it."

Kelsey was just going to ask for details when Summer pulled her phone from her pocket, tossed her arm around Kelsey, and snapped a picture. "Meeting the family selfie." She kissed her cheek as she opened the door, then gave Kelsey a gentle push. "Best of luck!"

The moment her feet hit the tiled entry, Kelsey was back on her heels. "Wow," she whispered. "You guys are rich."

Summer pulled her close and said, "Not for long if my dad doesn't set some limits with my mom. She could blow through an unlimited budget." She tugged Kelsey's coat off and hung it on a coat rack. "You get the special spot. The rest of us threw ours on the sofa in the office."

Kelsey had been forced to learn a lot about homes and their styles, and she pegged this one as a 1920s foursquare with grand aspirations. It had been renovated in the not-too-distant past to open it up the way everyone seemed to want their homes now. Open-plan with din, she called the style, knowing people would start closing them up again once they realized how noisy a big house with few sound-dampening walls could be.

The style was as contemporary as the designer could manage, while still fitting the home. Whoever did it was talented, and she sincerely hoped it hadn't been Roger Thornhill. Her gaze traveled over the impressive center staircase, which now partially blocked the view to the back of the home. The office Summer had mentioned was to the left, and looked like a miniature version of a venerable men's club—dark leather and wood in abundance. But the rest of the house was largely neutral, with spots of deeper earth tones here and there. They'd saved the original wood floors, and they glowed from the flattering lights that ringed the coffered ceilings, along with many table lamps to make it seem extra homey and warm.

"Let's go into the living room. You can meet my mom."

"Wish me luck," Kelsey whispered.

"She'll love you. I'm never wrong about things like that." She put her hand on Kelsey's arm and led her into the large room to the left of the stairs. A fifty-something woman stood when they entered and gave them a wide smile. She looked—normal, which was a weird word to use, but it fit. Actually, she would have fit in perfectly well at Kelsey's house, where her female relatives dyed their own hair, painted their own nails, and carefully clipped coupons to save twenty cents on a can of chili.

This woman was, as Kelsey's mom would say, pleasingly plump, and her clothing had probably been bought online. Just a simple green sweater, along with black slacks, and sensible black shoes. The kicker was the large pin she wore—an enameled roast turkey with a slice cut out of it. That was exactly the kind of thing her own mom would have chosen, and that simple detail relaxed Kelsey in seconds.

"Look who I found skulking around in the dark," Summer said, wrapping both hands around Kelsey's upper arm and pushing her around playfully.

"Summer," her mom said in a scolding tone, "you don't know this poor girl well enough to tease her yet. Give her time to get used to your sense of humor."

"She's got to catch up," Summer said. "This is Kelsey. My mom, Beth."

"It's very good to meet you," Kelsey said, shaking her hand enthusiastically. "Summer talks about you all of the time."

"She hasn't stopped talking about you, Kelsey, and I'm very glad she convinced you to stop by."

A middle-aged Latina woman emerged from what must have been the kitchen to speak to Beth. "We're almost finished cleaning up. Should we leave the pies out?"

"Oh, I have no idea. Summer?"

"Sure. Leave them out. I'm sure they won't last the night."

"All right," the woman said. "We'll leave the way we came in."

"Have you been paid?" Beth asked. She gave Summer a searching look. "Will you make sure your dad handled everything?"

"Sure. Be right back," she said, escorting the woman back the way she'd come.

"I hate having meals catered," Beth said, "but with so many people I suppose it is a lot easier." She let out a plaintive sigh. "I just wish the caterers would have brought oyster dressing. Chestnut kind of ruined the whole meal, since Thanksgiving's just a good excuse to gobble up dressing." She shrugged. "I guess you can't please everyone." Pointing at the sofa, she said, "Have a seat, Kelsey. You can sit by the fire while you admire the tiles Summer made."

"Oh, wow," Kelsey said, moving over to the fireplace to trail her fingers over them. "These are gorgeous. This acorn looks so realistic it might have fallen off a tree."

"They're great, aren't they? There are a few other examples of her handiwork around here, but the ones on the hearth are my favorites. She didn't do the acorn personally, but she made the mold for the gourds."

"They're—"

A shriek loud enough to make Kelsey flinch rang out, followed by hearty laughter, probably coming from downstairs. "I don't recognize the voice," Beth said, taking it in stride. "That might be one of the girls my boys brought. I know one's Mallory and one's Taylor, but I'm not sure I can tell which is which."

"Sounds like a big group," Kelsey said. "Do any of your kids still live at home?"

"Oh, god, no," she said, laughing a little. "Thankfully, they're all doing well enough to afford their own apartments. Lucky for them, since I don't have a spare inch."

Kelsey tried not to look as puzzled as she was. There had to be at least four bedrooms upstairs. And if five kids had lived here at one time, why wouldn't there be room for one now? "Um, I had dinner at Summer's the other night. I was impressed by her apartment, especially the decorating." She'd been thinking of how to get that in, since Beth had bought a lot of the furniture.

"I guess it is nice," she said, giving the impression she hadn't ever really thought about it. Obviously, the woman didn't need to be praised from the rooftops for her contributions to Summer's decor.

"Very. Having access to a pool is pretty rare."

"I don't think she cares much for the building, but she got a very good deal on it. Those units weren't renting quickly at first, and she wasn't able to turn down a bargain." She smiled again, clearly fond of her daughter. "Summer's got the soul of an artist, and the savvy of a businesswoman. I'm not sure where she got either trait," she added, "but I'm glad she got both."

Summer entered the room just then and crooked her finger. "Everyone knows you're here, so you've got to run the gauntlet."

Kelsey got up. "Wish me luck."

"They'll go easy on you," Beth promised. "I think the men are still mesmerized by Mallory or Taylor, whichever one has the curves and the blonde hair and the big…" She held her hands out in front of her chest.

"Taylor," Summer supplied immediately. "Not that I noticed."

"Well, that's a couple of things to look forward to," Kelsey said, wishing she could have pulled the words back before they were fully out of her mouth. Luckily, Beth laughed.

"You'll fit in just fine," she predicted. She stood up and reached out to grasp Summer's hand. "Give me a kiss, sweetie. I'm going to bed."

Kelsey did a double take. Who went to bed when she had a house full of guests?

"Really? You're not going to come down to say goodnight?" Summer leaned in and kissed both cheeks.

"I don't think so. That'll take another fifteen minutes, and somebody might tell me who won the game." She smiled at Kelsey. "I recorded the football game, and I want to watch it in bed."

"All right," Summer said. "I won't say anything. We'll see if anyone notices you're gone."

"They won't," she said, walking toward the front of the house. "I know they all love me, even though it might not be obvious."

"Sleep well," Summer said. "I'll call you tomorrow."

Kelsey was still trying to figure out the family dynamic when they passed by a kitchen that even at a glance was super-deluxe. She was tempted to gawp, but Summer was moving quickly. They were partway down the staircase when an older woman started to come up, and they backed up to give her room to pass. "Where do you think you're going?" Summer demanded playfully.

The woman, who was probably in her seventies, gently patted Summer's cheek. "It's too noisy for me down there. I'm going home before I get a headache."

"Want to meet Kelsey?" Summer said, putting her hand on Kelsey's back. "This is the girl I told you about on Sunday." She turned and put her arm around her grandmother. "This is my gramma, Marjorie."

The woman's face lit up, with her eyes looking very much like Summer's. "I was hoping I'd get to meet you. Summer says you're the first normal woman she's been out with in a year."

"That's what I'm going for," Kelsey said. "If I can manage normal, I'm good to go."

"She's cute," Marjorie said, smiling at her granddaughter. "You two look good together."

"Anyone would look better when she was next to Kelsey. Do you want us to drive you home, Gramma? We'd be happy to."

"Kevin's going to take me if he can tear himself away from that game they're playing."

"I'll send him up. Love you," she added, kissing her gently. "See you on Sunday."

"Nice to meet you, Kelsey. Tag along with Summer some Sunday morning. If you like donuts, that is. You won't get anything healthy for breakfast at my house."

"I'd love to," she said, with her spirits rising with each pleasant interaction.

They went downstairs, with Summer quietly saying, "Gramma's still annoyed from my date complaining that there weren't any 'healthy choices' in the house when I took her along one morning. Neither of us likes to have our habits criticized," she added, chuckling.

When they stood at the foot of the stairs, Kelsey took a look around. People filled every seat and much of the carpeted floor, all facing a huge TV, where the group was playing a video game. The TV was on the far wall, with everyone facing away from the stairs, letting her survey them unnoticed.

The generously-sized place was set up like an expensive cocktail lounge, with two leather sofas, and two matching arm chairs able to accommodate six or seven. But there were more people than that, and it looked like everyone under forty was lying on the floor or sitting on a bean bag.

One of the youngish guys turned around and saw Summer, and he got up and walked over. He was obviously Summer's brother, with sandy blonde hair and her same build, except with broader shoulders and enough scruff to show he hadn't shaved all week.

"Gramma's waiting," Summer said. "Are you sure you don't mind taking her?"

"Nah. I've got to work in the morning." He turned toward Kelsey and stuck out his hand. "Kevin. I bet you're Kelsey."

"I bet I am," she said. "Good to meet you."

"Yeah. Me too. Hate to rush, but I've got to go. Gramma's not real patient."

"She's the soul of patience," Summer said. She cuffed him on the jaw. "Get a move on. She's usually in bed by this time."

He laughed, saying, "So are you," then took off, taking the stairs two at a time.

"Hey," Summer said. "I promised you a drink and I haven't delivered. I can make you something now. Cocktail?"

Kelsey took a look at the generous bar, seeing that it was set up with everything she might have wanted. "Do you have any beer?"

"Usually a lot of it." She went behind the bar and pulled out a few bottles from a mini-fridge—all different brands. "Do any of these work for you? Oh-oh," she said quietly. "We've been spotted."

A little girl ran across the room, her pale brown hair bouncing. "Can I have a soda?" she asked, scrambling to climb onto one of the bar-height stools.

"Grab that!" Summer demanded, and Kelsey just got her hand out to steady it. "Poppy," Summer said, very patiently. "You've got to slow down a little. You'd hurt yourself if that chair fell on you."

"I'd jump away," she said, clearly confident in her abilities. She turned to Kelsey. "Who are you?"

"This is my friend, Kelsey," Summer said. "Introduce yourself like we've practiced."

The kid had a cherubic face, along with pale blue eyes and porcelain skin. She looked Kelsey over for a moment, then said, "I'm Poppy Hayes. Pleased to meet you."

"Great job," Summer said, beaming with pride. "Very formal," she added. "Listen to me, kid, and I'll have you sounding like a senior citizen in no time."

The little girl pointed at Summer, but addressed Kelsey. "She's not my mom," she said. "Everybody thinks she is, but she's not."

"Is Summer your…aunt?"

"No!" Poppy said, not having learned to moderate her volume yet.

Summer walked around the bar and wrapped the little girl in her arms, making her try to squirm out of her grip. But she held on tight and kissed her cheeks repeatedly. "This little chimp is my sister."

Kelsey stared at the pair for a moment. "Your sister?"

"Uh-huh," she said, with a playful smile covering her face. "Go get our daddy to come over here," Summer said. "If you bring him really fast, I'll give you a special shot-glass soda."

The kid slid her legs down the stool, then raced over to the group. In a second she was tugging on a man's hand, and he got up and followed along gamely.

"Dad," Summer said, "This is my friend Kelsey. Kelsey, my dad, Matt."

"Oh, the kitchen designer," he said, nodding. He also looked a bit like Summer, his hair sandy like Kevin's. Matt had an easy, engaging smile, and Kelsey wouldn't have been surprised to learn he sold something for a living. Something expensive, given the house. He was probably in his fifties too, not the usual age for the father of a kid who couldn't have been more than four. No wonder Summer's mom had to conk out at nine o'clock. The woman must have been exhausted! Then Kelsey thought of the practicalities, and realized they must have adopted the kid. But who did that when they had five other kids, all adults?

"Did you just get here?" Matt asked.

"No," Kelsey said, "we were outside with Leah for a minute, then upstairs, chatting with your wife."

He cocked his head. "How'd you do that? Lauren's been sitting right next to me." He raised his voice and called over to the group. "Honey? Come over here for a minute."

A woman no older than Kelsey stood and started to walk toward them. She was clearly Poppy's mom, looking like an adult version of the child. Obviously, there had been a divorce Kelsey hadn't heard about.

The woman picked Poppy up when she demanded it, and smiled at Kelsey. "We've been waiting for you," she said. "I'm Lauren."

"My mommy," Poppy said clearly. She held her hands out and her father took her in his arms. "Summer's gonna give me a soda."

"What kind of soda?" Summer asked. "Remember?"

"Shot-glass soda. My favorite."

Summer used a dispenser to pour the tiniest amount of cola into a shot glass, and handed it to Poppy. "Don't spill. Soda's precious."

She listened to the instructions, taking the world's smallest sips.

Her dad gave her a kiss on the cheek. "Finish up, muffin. Time to head home."

Kelsey gazed at him, once again knocked off center. Beth lived here alone? That made it even weirder that she'd gone to bed without saying goodnight.

"No," Poppy whined. "I didn't get to play the game."

"The game's for adults," her mom said. She rolled her eyes as she turned to Kelsey. "We should have never come downstairs. They're playing the goriest game I've ever seen."

"I like it," Poppy said, wriggling to get down from her dad's arms.

"You can like it next time." He switched his hold so he was grasping her around the waist. "The airplane's going to fly low. See how many people you can kiss goodbye when we sweep over them."

The game distracted her, and she stuck her arms out at her sides and straightened out her legs while making a sound not very close to that of a plane. Her dad was laughing along with her as he held her above everyone on the sofas and chairs. She got a few kisses in, and remained in airplane mode as Matt started for the stairs. "Better hurry, Summer. This plane stops for no one."

Summer rushed to kiss Poppy's cheek and scratch her dad's back. Then she hugged and kissed Lauren, turning to Kelsey to say, "Isn't my step-mom smokin' hot?"

"Um..."

"You don't have to play along," Lauren said as she walked over to the stairs. "It was great to meet you, Kelsey. Maybe we'll have time to have a real conversation in a few years." She waved, then scampered up the stairs, where Kelsey could still hear Poppy's loud airplane noise.

"We've made a dent," Summer said, not giving Kelsey a moment to ask who was who. "Let's go meet the rest."

They took the seats Matt and Lauren had vacated, and everyone who wasn't actively playing the video game perked up and looked at them.

"Mom, Dad, this is Kelsey," Summer said, leaving Kelsey significantly more confused than she'd been a minute earlier.

"Robert," a handsome, debonair-looking man said. "And this is my wife, Jackie. We've been looking forward to meeting you, Kelsey. I just wish you'd been able to come for dinner."

"Thanks very much," she said. "I was with my family, but compared to yours, we had a very sedate gathering."

"Oh, we definitely draw a crowd," the woman who'd been identified as Summer's mom said. Kelsey didn't know a whole lot about biology, but she was pretty sure only one of the women so named could actually *be* Summer's mom. Unless Jackie and Beth had been lesbian partners... But that didn't seem likely. Now that she'd had a moment to reflect, Jackie looked a whole lot more like Summer than Beth did.

Jackie was about Beth's age, easily old enough to have given birth to Summer, but she had the pampered look of a woman who lived in a big house in Squirrel Hill. Her hair was a little darker than Summer's, and her eyes a little paler, but her jaw was similar, and she had roughly the same nose. But Jackie had gone under the knife more than once, giving her the plastic, Barbie-doll look a lot of wealthy women adopted. It wasn't Kelsey's preference, but she wasn't invested in telling other people how to look, so she tried not to be too judgmental. People were weird about their faces and bodies, and a lot of them opted for any option to stave off the sands of time—futile though their efforts might be.

Robert, on the other hand, didn't look a thing like Summer. He wasn't quite as tall as she was, and his hair, which was just beginning to gray, was mostly dark and course. His skin was a nice olive tone, and he must have spent time in the sun recently, because he glowed with a tan that made him look robust and vital.

"Does your family live nearby, Kelsey?" Robert caught her attention and held it fast. He had the kind of interested gaze that made you think he was really focused on what you had to say.

"Monroeville," she said. "We moved out there when I was a kid."

"Do you have a big family too?" Jackie asked.

"No, just me. We don't have many local relatives, but my parents got into a social club when we first moved, and those people are like family now. Most of them drop by at some point on the holidays. It's good," she said, smiling.

"If we can distract the boys for a moment, I'll introduce you," Jackie said. "Nick. Andy. Pay attention for half a second."

Two men, who looked like they were somewhere in their twenties, were sprawled atop bean bag chairs, with game controllers on their knees. Two young women leaned against them, not playing, but definitely rooting them on. One of the guys turned around, saying, "Two minutes!" before his attention flew back to the game.

Summer jumped in. "Nick's on the left. He's six years younger than I am. Andy's two years younger than Nick." She lowered her voice. "The women are Mallory and Taylor. They're new."

"They won't last," Jackie said, under her breath. "They never do."

Robert lightly touched Jackie's leg. "I've got to get to bed, honey. Are you ready?"

"I'll stay here and visit for a little while. You go ahead." She kept talking when Robert leaned over to kiss her cheek, reaching up idly to pat his shoulder. "Robert's got an early day tomorrow. Usually his busiest of the year."

He smiled, looking almost pleased when he said, "If I have a big day, I might be able to pay this month's AMEX bill."

Kelsey had no idea what Robert did for a living, mainly since she hadn't known he existed. But she didn't want to ask, especially since everyone seemed to assume she knew.

"I have the day off," Kelsey said. "It's the only Friday of the year we're closed."

"Summer's been telling us about your work," Robert said. "The next time we redo the kitchen..." He gave his wife a fond smile. "And I'm under no delusions that day isn't coming, we'll call. I'd much rather work with someone I know than a stranger."

Kelsey was sure her eyebrows had climbed up her forehead, but she couldn't remain impassive when people kept saying such wacky stuff! Robert didn't know her from Adam, and for all he knew, she was the worst kitchen designer in Pennsylvania. But she rallied, her skills improving with practice, and said, "I'd love to work with you."

"We know a lot of people," he said, flashing a smile that included teeth too nice to have been original. "Next time I hear of someone doing a renovation, I'll definitely send them your way. Sedlak Brothers has been in town since I was a boy. They're trustworthy people."

"I can promise you that's true," Kelsey said, so happy she was able to work for people she knew were honest.

"Goodnight, all," he said, bending over to kiss Summer's cheek.

"G'night, Dad," she said. Kelsey was waiting to see if she called Nick and Andy dad also, but she was leaning toward believing Summer was now out of parents—for the night, at least. There might be another five or six who'd come in with the shift change in the morning. Kelsey still wasn't sure where Beth was. Were she and Jackie Robert's sister-wives? Each in her own bedroom, waiting to see who he chose to sleep with?

"It's kind of peaceful now," Jackie said. "Why don't you hop up and get me some cognac, Summer. You don't mind, do you?"

"Not at all. Kelsey? Anything for you?"

"I never got the beer you pulled out," she said. "We've been so busy meeting people I never picked one."

"I've got other cold ones. What style do you like?" she asked, standing and adjusting her blouse.

"I think I'll have an alcohol-free Thanksgiving," she decided. "I can make up for it tomorrow."

"That a girl," Summer said, tousling her hair. "Planning for a future bender."

As she walked away, Jackie said, "Did you have time to see any of Summer's art work? It's all over the main floor."

"No, I didn't. It's been kind of a whirlwind."

"And you still haven't met her brothers," she said. Jackie stared a hole in the back of Nick and Andy's heads, but they didn't seem to notice. "Those two are more like their father than I wish." She held up her hands. "But they're not my responsibility, so I keep my mouth shut."

Once again, Kelsey wasn't sure who belonged to whom, so she nodded soberly. "Well, from what I can tell, Summer's doing great. I love the work her shop produces."

"She's a very bright girl," Jackie agreed. "In my view, she should have stuck to painting, but Robert talked her into learning a trade. I suppose that was the smart choice, but she has scads of talent." She made a face. "Anyone can learn to make a tile."

Summer sauntered over with an attractive glass filled with cognac. "Is my mother telling you I could have been the next Van Gogh?"

"I have an opinion," Jackie said, not seeming to mind being caught. "I think you could sell that shop to your staff and dedicate yourself to painting."

"I'm not going to do that, Mom. I'm making a good living, and employing a good number of people. I like the security." Summer gave

Kelsey a look, adding, "I have my shop because of Robert, if you've been wondering."

"He offered to be a silent partner, but Summer wouldn't hear of it. Silly," she grumbled.

"It was incredibly generous of him to lend me some seed money, and hook me up with his banker, Mom. That's all I needed."

Jackie gazed up at her for a moment. "The business takes too much out of you. You were so much more lively when you spent your days painting. Your creative urges really got a workout."

"I was twenty-five when I started the company, Mom. I was lively because I was young." She tapped Kelsey on the shoulder. "Come back upstairs and I'll show you the kitchen. You can make suggestions about how to redo it."

"Are you seriously thinking of doing a renovation?" Kelsey asked, turning back to Jackie. "I only glanced at it, but it looked brand new."

"Oh, no, it's dated."

"It was redone about ten years ago," Summer said.

"That sounds right," Jackie said. "Time for a refresh."

"I'd be happy if all of my clients kept to that schedule," Kelsey said, standing and offering her hand. "If I don't see you again tonight, thanks so much for having me." She was pretty certain Jackie lived there, so she felt comfortable in thanking her.

"You should come with Summer the next time she comes for dinner. We'd love to get to know you better."

"That would be great," Kelsey said. "Thanks again."

"After the boys have finished killing all of the cowboys and their horses, and sleeping with all of the loose women in town, I'll give them your regards."

"I'd heard the old west was violent, but I had no idea how violent," Kelsey said, turning her head when a cowboy walked up to another guy and shot him right in the face. "Tough town."

Kelsey followed Summer up the stairs, landing in the kitchen, where the lights had been dimmed to a warm glow.

Summer sidled up her her and slipped her arms around her waist. "Mad at me?"

"Mad? Why would I be mad?"

"Because I knew you'd be thoroughly confused by who was who, and I intentionally didn't warn you."

"That was a little odd," Kelsey agreed. "But I'm starting to learn you like to keep people guessing."

"Kind of," she admitted. She put her hands on the marble counter top on the generous island and boosted herself up. She really liked to sit on counters that were a little high for her. Maybe she just loved dangling her feet. "I wanted to see how you reacted to unexplained relationships. We have a real mish-mash here, and anyone who wants to fit in has to roll with the punches."

"I think I did okay." She chose to lean on the other counter, not having Summer's need to have her feet off the ground. "I was sure Beth was your birth mom, but I couldn't figure out why she was going to bed when the house was full. Then I thought maybe she and Jackie had been lesbian lovers when they decided to have a baby, but I dismissed that idea pretty quickly. My last guess was that they were both Robert's wives, but that didn't really seem to fit, either. Beth doesn't look like she'd be into sharing. I still don't know who Kevin belongs to, but I think I can guess —"

"Got to interrupt. You won't get Kevin's story, since there's a parent missing."

"You've got more? Seriously?"

"Yes. Well, I don't, but Kevin does. Go on with your summary, I just didn't want you to get overconfident."

"Whew." She let that tidbit of info settle, then finished up. "All I was going to add was that Beth was right when she said that Taylor had a nice pair of headlamps. That's my summary."

"You did very well," Summer said, grinning. "The facts are that I'm the only child of the Matt and Jackie pairing. Then my mom married a jerk named Randy, and my dad married Beth. Randy's totally out of the picture, by the way. He and my mom were already divorced when Kevin was born, and he paid neither visits nor child support. Two years after that unpleasant time, Robert swooped in and saved us from living on mac and cheese."

"Your mom married Robert when you were what…eight or nine?"

"Eight. I liked him the minute I met him, and my admiration for him has grown every year since. He's the best," she said, allowing no room for disagreement.

"Of everyone?"

"Mmm…" She sat there swinging her feet for a few moments, then said, "If I'm being honest, yes. Beth comes in second. My mom and dad's stock rises and falls depending on a number of factors. And Lauren's just my pal. She's only a year older, so if we'd gone to the same school we would have been classmates."

"And you're cool with that? The age difference doesn't bother you?"

"Someone has to keep my dad from the poorhouse, and it's not going to be me. I tried to give Lauren some advice before they got married, but she ignored me and went through with it. But…I'm crazy about my sister, so I'm glad Lauren's in the mix."

"So Beth is Nick and Andy's mom?"

"Uh-huh. My dad must have ruined her appetite for men, since as far as I know she hasn't had a date since the day she threw him out."

"Ooo. Bad blood?"

"Not now. But Beth was rock-solid for me when I needed some stability. After she and my dad divorced, I definitely took her side, which must have been hard on him. It was a tough time," she admitted quietly. "But we all get along now to a greater or lesser degree."

"It's going to take me a while to sort this all out."

"Oh! I almost forgot Leah."

"She's…Robert's?" Kelsey asked tentatively.

"Excellent guess. My mom knocked Robert, a widower, off his feet when Leah was getting ready to go to Oberlin. She's been a fantastic older sister, even though she could have justifiably frozen me out."

"I already like her," Kelsey said. "I could see how fond she was of you."

"That's mutual." She grasped Kelsey's sweater and tugged on it so she moved closer. "She and my mom have never been friends, but they're polite to each other."

"Ahh. That would be tough to wind up with a step-mother when you're just about an adult."

"It definitely was, and I admire Leah immensely for never slagging on Jackie, even though she'd be justified if she did."

"Got it. Leah's not only kind, she's got good judgement."

"A hundred percent."

Well, I've got my work cut out for me, but I'll make an effort to keep everyone straight. You could do one thing to help, though."

"Name it."

"Can you refer to all of the parent-figures by their first names? Having two moms and two dads is rough."

"Consider it done. I did that for my ex, so I have practice."

"This has been like walking into class expecting a routine lecture, and having the teacher throw a tough pop quiz at me."

"And you didn't even get a drink." Summer sat up like she'd been shocked. "I didn't even offer you a slice of pie! What a horrible host I am."

"I'm glad on both counts. I ate like I was in a competition today. I shouldn't have another morsel."

"No problem. The pies were only so-so." She slid off the counter and put her hands on Kelsey's hips. "If you'll spend the day with me tomorrow, I'll be a very happy woman."

"Tomorrow? How about now? I could show you my apartment…"

"I would," she said thoughtfully, "but I want to spend some time with my goofy brothers. I don't get to see them very often, and I haven't had a minute alone with either of them. Call me when you get up, and we'll make plans."

"That won't be very early. I sleep in on my days off."

"I'll wait for you," she said, cuddling up against Kelsey's body.

"Okay. I guess I'll take off then."

"Glad you came," Summer said, lifting her head to offer a very pleased smile.

"I am too." She bent her head to kiss her, wishing the kiss could make Summer grab her coat and follow her home. But she just returned Kelsey's hug, then walked her to the door and helped her on with her coat.

"I'm really looking forward to tomorrow," Summer said, leaning against the door, looking mouthwateringly sexy as Kelsey walked out.

"Me too. See you then." The walk to her car wasn't far, but it allowed her a little time to dwell on her disappointment. She was pretty confident her kisses would entertain Summer more than trying to get the attention of the boys, who didn't seem interested in interacting with anything that wasn't flickering on a screen. But Summer was a tough one to pin down. Not surprising for a woman with so many siblings and parents you needed a spreadsheet to keep score.

CHAPTER TEN

IT TOOK KELSEY A WHILE TO get going on Friday, but once she'd had a cup of coffee and a shower she called Summer, reaching her just after nine.

"Good morning," Kelsey said. "I'm finally up and at 'em. Are you still up for getting together?"

"Sure am. When I make firm plans, I follow through." Her short laugh was pretty playful. "But when I'm vague or noncommittal, that's a soft 'no.'"

"Oh, great. Now I've got to gauge whether you're firm or vague."

"You'll be able to tell. I'm not as subtle as I think I am. Want to come over?"

"Absolutely." In the background, she heard a high-pitched voice. "Are you alone?"

"Not at the moment. Lauren's got the day off, and she wanted to go shopping with her mom, so I said I'd watch Poppy for a while."

Kelsey rolled her eyes. While she wasn't anti-child, she was very much pro-Summer, and didn't want to have to compete with a little kid to get her attention. But she would have sounded like a jerk if she pulled out now, so she went with it. "Have you had breakfast? I could bring something."

"Oh, I ate hours ago, and Poppy just had some donut holes. Take your time and have a nice breakfast, Kelsey. It's your day off."

"I guess it is," she said, touched that Summer seemed to understand she wanted to make a rare Friday off a little special.

"Come over whenever you're in the mood. We'll be waiting."

Feeling much better about the day, Kelsey took herself out for a leisurely meal, breaking out a new book for the occasion. Sitting in a cafe, eating a crispy waffle while reading a good book was a hell of a nice way to start the day.

When she arrived at Summer's, she and Poppy were waiting for her when the elevator doors opened, and she couldn't help but smile. The sisters each wore handmade paper crowns, decorated with drawings. Summer's was very professional, but Poppy's was age-appropriate, which meant it was a bit of a mess. But they both looked happy, which perked Kelsey up even further. Hanging out with a bubbly kid could definitely be fun. She just had to adjust her perspective.

"What have you two queens been up to?"

"*I'm* the queen," Poppy said. "Summer's a princess."

Summer shrugged. "I don't really understand the line of succession. It's clearly not based on birth order."

Poppy yanked on the tail of Summer's blouse, and she leaned over to have the kid whisper loudly. "I have to go."

"To the bathroom?"

"Uh-huh. Right now."

"Gotta run," Summer said, swooping the kid up in her arms and racing down the hallway. "I'll leave the door open," she called out.

Kelsey followed along, once again reminding herself that being an only child hadn't turned out to be half-bad. Her sporadic bouts of loneliness when she was young now meant she didn't have to spend her weekends with people she had to carry to the bathroom.

Summer was just shutting the bathroom door when Kelsey started to take off her coat. "Made it," Summer said. "Luckily. Lauren didn't send a change of clothes."

"Do you spend a lot of time with Poppy?"

"Uh-huh. Lauren works, so she has to run all of her errands on the weekend. I try to help out."

"You're a very good sister," Kelsey said. "And Poppy's a lucky one."

"We're both lucky. I'm crazy about her, so it's more fun than a chore. But I'm also trying to give her a good foundation. I can't imagine

Lauren's not going to get tired of my dad's act at some point, and I know how destabilizing divorce can be for a kid."

"What *is* your dad's act?" Kelsey asked, realizing her question wouldn't be answered when Poppy raced down the hall.

"Do you want to keep drawing?" Summer asked the kid. "I've got more of the paper you like."

"Yeah! Yeah!" She ran over to the dining table and climbed onto a chair. By the time Summer went to her desk to pick up some supplies, the kid was slapping her hands on the table noisily.

"Do you want to draw, Kelsey? I've got plenty of paper."

"No, thanks. I'll watch for a while."

"Can we do the zoo?" Poppy asked

"Sure. What animal do you want to start with?"

"Zebra," she said. Turning to Kelsey, she said authoritatively, "It looks like a horse, but it's not."

"Good to know," she said, mimicking the sober expression Poppy wore.

"I have one of your books with animals in it," Summer said, going to a bookcase to search for it. "Got it," she said, thumbing through it as she walked back. Placing the book upright on the table, she said, "You don't have to copy this, but if you want a guide, the picture might help."

"I want it in front," she said, starting to draw the animal head-on. Even though Kelsey wasn't a good artist, she knew that was a tough assignment. But Poppy worked at it for a while, finally roughly adding a tail a few inches above the head and dropping her pencil. "Is that good?" she asked, all but acknowledging it wasn't.

"You've set yourself a tough task," Summer said. "Let's take some pictures, and I'll show you why it's difficult to do it the way you've started out here."

There were some plastic animals in a cubby under one of her windows, probably Poppy's toys. Summer set a cow up on the table and took photos of it dead-on, then she moved around a little, continuing to snap different angles. After downloading the photos onto the big computer at her desk, Poppy sat on her lap while they looked at them. "Here's the one from straight on," Summer said. "See how everything but the face kind of disappears? All you can see is the head."

"I like the head."

"I do too," Summer agreed. "Why do you like it?"

"I just like it. It's pretty."

"Uh-huh," she said, maintaining her patient attitude. "Why do you think that is?" She turned her head to make eye contact with Kelsey, sharing a smile. "I like the head because I can see both of the cow's eyes, and her mouth. That lets you see her personality."

"Yeah. I like her personality."

"I do too. But I also like her spots. And I can't see them if I don't move her a little." She picked a shot where the cow was at a forty-five degree angle. "I like this one. I can see her spots, and her tail, but I still get some of her expression."

"I like her tail too." She jumped off Summer's lap and went back to get her drawing to point. "I got the zebra's tail right here."

"You really did," Summer agreed. "This is a very nice abstract drawing. You emphasized the things you like best. His face and his tail."

"Yeah," she said, clearly pleased with herself. "But I want his stripes too."

"Hmm… Sometimes it's tough to get everything into one picture. Maybe we should do a series."

Poppy clearly didn't understand that one, so Summer added, "More than one."

"Can we do a series now?"

"Sure. Want to do the zebra from an angle so we can see his stripes?"

"Yeah. We'll keep going 'til it's right, okay?"

Kelsey was sure they were going to be at this for hours, but she had to admit she didn't mind much. If someone had taken this kind of time with her when she was young, she might have learned something about drawing. The kid really was lucky.

There was a knock on the door, and Summer said, "I wonder who that could be? Want to find out?"

"Mommy!" Poppy shrieked, then raced to the door to open it.

Lauren was there, and she pulled the little girl into her arms. "Did you miss me as much as I missed you?"

"No," Poppy said, displaying the honesty that only kids could get away with. "We were drawing."

Lauren came in and kissed Summer on the cheek. "Good to see you again, Kelsey. Have you spent the morning wishing for a house full of kids?"

"Not a houseful," Kelsey admitted, "but one like Poppy would be kind of cool."

"Let's hit the road, muffin-top," Lauren said. "I bet your sister and Kelsey have big plans."

Poppy gave Kelsey a long look. It was clear the kid wasn't crazy about her, at least not yet. She cocked her little head and said, "Are you her girlfriend? Do you kiss her?"

Kelsey's eyes shot open, and Summer came to her rescue. She walked over to Kelsey and took her hand. "Remember our rule?" she asked, turning to face Poppy. "We can ask each other any question in the world, but we each decide which ones are about private things that we don't want to share." She got a better grip on Kelsey's arm, tucking it against her body. "Kelsey and I are dating, but we're not girlfriends yet." She narrowed her eyes, still looking playful. "And my kissing habits are *very* private."

"But do you want her to be your girlfriend?" Poppy asked, gazing at her thoughtfully. "Do you like her a whole lot?"

"I do," Summer said. "But you never know how things will work out when you first start dating someone. It's good to take things slow and see what happens."

"Can I have my crown?" she asked, her previous question forgotten.

"Sure," Summer said, going over to pick it up from the floor. "Want me to finish the drawings we did this morning?"

"If you want. But I want my zebra now."

"Good choice." Summer rolled it up and put a rubber band around it. Then she handed it to Poppy and bent over to kiss both of her chubby cheeks. "Love you."

Poppy threw her arms around her and hugged her legs. "Love you, too."

"Thanks so much, Summer. It was a madhouse, but we got everything on our list for C-h-r-i-s-t-m-a-s."

"I know what that is," Poppy said. "It's candy. You always spell candy."

"You're too smart for me," Lauren said, bending to pick her up. "We'll see you two around. Hopefully soon."

"Definitely," Kelsey said. Summer took her hand again, as Poppy and Lauren exited, with Summer making vague plans to drop by on the weekend.

As the door closed, Kelsey said, "I think I just heard you make plans that you're not going to follow through on."

Summer laughed. "I believe you're right. I love the kid, but yesterday and today was enough. I plan on being surrounded by adults for the rest of the weekend." She touched Kelsey's nose, then kissed it. "Mostly you."

"Not during the day," she said, feeling a little glum. "I've got to work tomorrow and Sunday."

"That's why we have to make the most out of today." Still holding her hand, she walked over to the table and gathered up her pencils.

"Is there anything you'd like to do?" Kelsey asked.

"Oh, I thought we'd just hang out. We could go out for a late lunch or an early dinner. Of course, if you twisted my arm, we could go to a museum."

"You know what I'd like?"

Summer smiled at her. "I bet I could guess, but go ahead and tell me."

"I'd love to watch you draw."

Summer looked up, clearly surprised. "You would? Why?"

"Well, we could go to a museum, but I can watch an artist actually create something if we stay right here. I'm fascinated to see the actual process."

"Huh." She had a few pencils in her hand, and she tapped at her cheek with them. "I'd love to draw, but don't feel like you have to make the offer just to be polite. I certainly don't want to bore you to death."

"I wasn't bored when I watched Poppy, so I doubt I'll be bored now. Come on," she urged, putting her hand on Summer's back and rubbing it gently. "Let me see you do something. Anything at all."

"Okay," she said, looking kind of excited. "We have this game called 'fill in the blanks.' Poppy starts by drawing something, then I take a turn and add to it." She moved a pad of drawing paper to pull out a sketch. "I hope it's obvious that she did the throne. I added the ladies, but I didn't have the time to finish them." She laughed. "Rembrandt clearly didn't have child care duties. He wouldn't have finished six paintings in his whole life."

She took a chair and turned it around so she could lean against the back, then put a selection of pencils into a neat row. "You have to let me know if this is boring. I could draw all day, but I certainly don't need to."

"Have at it. I'm really interested." Kelsey sat down next to her to be able to observe her closely. "Can you talk while you work?"

"Usually." She took several shades of gold, yellow, and brown and started to work on the first figure's hair. "If I'm working with oils, I have to concentrate more. But pencils are easy."

"This is so cool," Kelsey said, as Summer started making sure, swift, marks across the paper. "Have you been drawing since you were a kid?"

"Uh-huh. I started early, and never stopped. Once I got some positive feedback, I put even more energy into it." She turned and wrinkled up her nose. "I used to be an approval junkie."

"Used to be?"

"I still love praise, but I don't need outside encouragement any more, and that's been very freeing."

"What kind of encouragement did you get? From school and things like that?"

She revealed a very bright smile. "Well, I hate to brag, but I won the first drawing contest I ever entered. That really gave me a boost."

"You did? What kind of contest?"

"It was a national thing. For Apollo basketball shoes."

"What?" Kelsey gazed at her, puzzled by the cute half-smile on her face. "You won a drawing contest for a national brand? How did that come about?"

"There was an ad they ran on TV when Apollo introduced their kids line," Summer said, her attention back on her drawing. "I had my dad look up the details, and I set about drawing a little girl who jumped so high in her Apollo shoes that she touched a rainbow." A soft laugh bubbled up, with Summer looking absolutely delighted by her tale. "My dad sent it in, and a few weeks later he gave me a letter that said I'd won. I was *so* stoked when I saw two crisp hundred dollar bills in the envelope."

"That's awes—" Kelsey stopped and stared at her. "They sent cash?"

"Seemed perfectly reasonable—when I was nine," Summer added, starting to laugh. "My dad faked the win because he wanted me to feel good about something he knew I loved."

"That's…I guess that's pretty cool," Kelsey said, not at all sure it was a good idea to go into an elaborate lie to boost a kid's confidence.

"It was cool that he wanted me to feel good," Summer said. "Other than that? Kinda whacky."

"Was that a common thing? Oh. You were about to tell me something about your dad when Poppy was out of the room. You were mid-sentence."

"Yeah, I was." She picked up a darker pencil and started to fill in the features of the woman's face. "You asked what my dad's deal was, and I was about to tell you. Professionally, he's a gambler."

"Professionally? That's a thing?"

"Oh, sure. A lot of people make a very good living off playing cards. Sadly, my dad's not one of them."

"Oh. So he's…"

"Usually dodging one creditor to pay another." She smiled when she met Kelsey's gaze. "He's a sweetheart. And he's often got good instincts as a dad. But when you have to move two or three times a year, and you can't reliably keep the lights on, it gets old. He quit a good job to gamble full-time when I was a baby. By the time I was four, my mom was *out*."

"Wow," Kelsey murmured. "That must have been awful for you."

"It was the worst year of my life. And he'd been gone less than a year when my mom started dating Randy. They got married *fast*, and that was way, way too much disruption for a little girl."

"And then they had Kevin, right?"

"Uh-huh. I had a new brother, and a mom whose husband abandoned her. My mom had to fight through her depression to keep her job, since neither my dad nor Randy were able or willing to pay child support. If it wasn't for my gramma, I assume I would have been in charge of Kevin." She looked up and made a face. "Wouldn't that have been interesting?"

"Wow," Kelsey sighed. "That must have been awful for everyone— except Randy."

"It truly was. But then my dad married Beth and things got better pretty quickly." Her smile grew as she continued to make decisive marks with her pencil, creating an angelically beautiful woman right before Kelsey's eyes. "Beth was a godsend for both my dad and me. She always welcomed Kevin along on the weekends, giving my mom a break. She's just the best."

Kelsey put a hand on her back and scratched it. "I'm really glad you have her."

"I am too. My mom…I mean Jackie, didn't like it when I started calling Beth 'mom,' but she got over her hurt feelings eventually. Beth did a ton of mothering, so she deserved the title. Still does," she said, firmly.

"And then your mom met Robert, right?"

"That took another year or two. We had some rough times trying to keep the lights on, and finally couldn't make rent. My grandparents took us in, but that wasn't ideal since they only had a two-bedroom house. But we learned to get along in a small space, and we all had enough to eat. I can't complain."

"How did your mom hook up with Robert? Having two small kids would make her toxic to most guys, right?"

"Mmm." She nodded while moving down to work on the woman's luxurious purple dress. "Long story. My dad, Matt, that is, had some cash burning a hole in his pocket when he and my mom got engaged. He did his usual and bought a ring much nicer than he could afford. My mom was somehow able to hold onto it for quite a while, but when things were really bad she went to Robert's flagship jewelry store to try to sell it. I guess someone called him out of his office to see if he was interested, and to hear him tell the tale, he fell for her on the spot."

"Love at first sight," Kelsey said.

"I guess it was—for him," she said, with her voice darkening a little. "I'm still not sure she loves him even half as much as he does her. But..." She paused for a few seconds, seeming to think before she spoke again. "She makes him happy, so even if she can't stand him, he's unaware."

"But...they've been together for a long time, right?"

"Uh-huh. They had a big twenty-fifth anniversary party two years ago. Quite the blowout."

"Well, that kind of sucks. He seems like an awfully nice guy."

"The nicest. If he'd married Beth, they'd be the world's best parents. But something about my mom really does it for him, and that's all that matters."

"When did you start thinking of him as a dad?"

"Really quickly. He was reliable, stable, kind, patient, encouraging. Everything a dad should be. Leah was just about an adult, so he seemed to look at me and Kevin as second chances to help raise a pair of kids. We were desperate for stability, so we really lucked out."

"After some tough years," Kelsey reminded her.

"Everyone has tough years," she said dismissively. "I got some of my worst ones out of the way when I was young. If you get to choose, I think that's best."

"Ooo. Are those pearls you've got on the dress?"

"Uh-huh. I thought a couple of long strings of pearls worn like bandoliers would look cool. I'm going to give her a hammered gold belt to dress it up even further."

"This reminds me of sketches I've seen in fashion magazines. But more finished."

"I can see that. I could do a better job with paint or watercolor, but this will be nice. I like to frame the good ones and give them to Poppy. It's a thing we do a lot."

"Best sister ever," Kelsey said, giving her back another scratch.

"Mmm. Can you rub my shoulders a little? I let my head drop when I'm concentrating, and always get an ache in my neck."

Kelsey got up and stood behind her, then started to massage the tight muscles. "You're awfully tense here," she said. "Let me know if this hurts."

"It does, but it will feel better soon." She turned and smiled up at Kelsey. "I have confidence in you."

She kept rubbing, starting to dig into the muscles. "Did you go to school for art?"

"Yep. I got an MFA from a school in Southwestern New York that has a great ceramics program."

"Really? You majored in ceramics?"

"Uh-huh. I might have stuck with painting, but I had a good teacher in high school who tactfully praised me as an excellent copyist."

"Is that…an insult?"

"Oh, yeah," she said, laughing softly. "She was right, but it still stung." She pointed at one of the pieces that hung on her bone-white walls. "That one is a sinful rip-off of Chuck Close. The still life over on that wall looks like a rough copy of a John Currin painting, and the last big one there is a very good copy of Hope Gangloff's style. If I put that in her studio, she might worry she was suffering from memory loss, but I bet she'd claim it."

"Be right back," Kelsey said, walking over to the closest painting. It was large, probably five feet wide and seven feet long, and extra compelling because Summer was the model. From a distance it had looked like a regular photograph taken when she was quite young. Larger than life, it showed her simply standing, legs spread, hands at her sides. She was wearing a colorful blouse and faded jeans with rips in the knees, exposing some skin. She was shoeless, and looked really carefree. But as Kelsey got close, she saw that it wasn't a single photo at all. It was composed of a huge number of tiny photos, each of Summer, somehow working to show light and dark and depth and shadow.

"How in the world…?"

Summer was by her side, and she tucked an arm around Kelsey's waist. "To make this time-suck, I had to take over seven hundred and fifty photos of myself, then work for months to get them placed properly. I could tell you how I did it, but the end result is much more interesting than the boring details."

"I'm stunned," Kelsey said. "This is so far out of my imagination I can't…"

"You know what I said earlier about not needing a lot of validation?"

"I remember."

"I don't believe I realized that praise made me hot." She grasped Kelsey's hand and tugged her over to the sofa. "Let's go make-out like teenagers."

"I could be convinced."

"I love the feeling of wrestling around on the sofa. It reminds me of being in high school, playing around in the basement, hoping my mom didn't come downstairs."

"And that turns you on? No judgement," she said, laughing at how silly this all seemed.

"It appears that it does."

Kelsey grasped her by the hips and pulled her onto her lap. "I didn't do this in high school, so I don't have the same memories, but if I'm going to have to grapple on the sofa, you're the one I'd choose to do it with."

&

They grappled until the throbbing between Kelsey's legs was beginning to be more annoying than pleasurable. Today she hadn't even tried to go further, having gotten the clear message that Summer just wanted to kiss. But once Kelsey really got into kissing, her body wanted to keep going until it got some satisfaction, and she was quickly getting to the point where there was going to be a fight between her conscience and her libido. Tenderly, she slipped her arm under Summer's head and tumbled her onto her side. "Remember that breakfast I told you about?"

"Uh-huh." She patted Kelsey's belly. "Is it all gone?"

"Totally. How about your donut holes?"

Smiling, she said, "They were gone by ten. I could cook, but I'd have to go to the store first. Should I? Or would you rather go out?" Her smile grew a little impish. "Or we could go chow down on leftovers at my parents' house. They'd like that."

Before Kelsey wasted a moment thinking over her idea, it was out of her mouth. "If we're going to raid our parents' fridge, shouldn't we take turns?"

"Seriously?" Summer said, looking delighted. "You're ready to introduce me to your parents?"

"Why not? I've met yours. All of them," she stressed. "I've only got the usual number, so you won't need a diagram."

"I'm in," Summer said, bubbling with enthusiasm. "Call and make sure they're into it."

"Oh, they will be. My mom has already threatened to drive up and drop in one night if I don't introduce you soon."

"Sounds like my kind of mom. Can't wait."

CHAPTER ELEVEN

KELSEY SEEMED SLIGHTLY TENSE ON the drive, but that only made sense. While Summer hadn't been nervous on Thanksgiving, she'd given everyone strict orders to be welcoming, and had tried to keep Kelsey in sight at all times. It was human nature to worry a little bit when your new girlfriend met your parents. And as much as Summer tried to act like they were just casually dating, they were hurtling toward girlfriend status. But even though they were moving faster than she'd wanted to, she couldn't help herself. When you met someone who had no glaring faults, who also turned you on like crazy, it was nuts to keep her at arm's length.

They were flying down Parkway East, with traffic much lighter than usual for late on a Friday afternoon. There was a billboard well off the highway, and it caught Summer's attention. "Have you ever been to Kennywood?"

Kelsey gave her a glance. "Have I ever been? I've never missed a year, and I plan on keeping that record going until the end. You?"

"Oh, yeah." She nodded, lost in thought for a few moments. "I'm not sure that I remember this perfectly, but I have a very clear image of holding my dad's hand just before we went in." She tried to open her mind to all of the sensations. "It was super hot, and we were in the blistering parking lot. I remember him squatting down and giving me a very stern lecture about how I had to hold onto his hand no matter how hot it was." She laughed a little. "I can still see beads of sweat running down his face, and I remember being frightened, since he made it seem like some unnamed force might pull us apart." She put her hand on Kelsey's leg, something she found herself doing often. "I think that was the first time I went. If my memory's right, that might have been the first time he had to take me somewhere by himself. He was probably petrified he'd lose me."

"Ooo." Kelsey shot her a sympathetic look. "You were so young when your parents split."

"I was. And Robert was four long years in the future. Those gap years were pretty rough." She took a breath, trying to clear out some unpleasant thoughts. "But my dad was trying to stay close and keep me entertained. I'm sure he didn't really want to go to a theme park when it was a thousand degrees out, but this was before Beth arrived on the scene, so he had to figure things out for himself."

"Mmm. My dad knows the place backwards and forwards, since he worked there when he was growing up. We went a couple times a year, but I remember going with just my mom—" She stopped on a dime, then cleared her throat. "I must be thinking of something else. We always went as a family."

"I haven't been since I was nineteen or twenty. A bunch of my friends and I would get high and stumble around the place until we spent all of our money on deep fried cheese on a stick, and those fantastic fries they made." She laughed. "Someone would invariably wind up vomiting in a trash can, and they'd ask us to leave." She gave Kelsey another pat. "Your dad worked there, huh?"

"Sure did. He grew up in Munhall, and he makes it sound like working at the park was a rite of passage."

"I love it," Summer said, already thinking about wandering around the park with Kelsey. "The old wooden roller coasters are the best. They look like they could fall apart at any minute."

"That's what you like about them?"

Even from the side, she could see Kelsey's eyebrow rise. "Of course. What's the point of a roller coaster if you're a hundred percent sure you'll survive? It's the threat of danger that makes them fun."

"Hmm… I think I'll pick the rides when we go. My family always goes on Slovak Day, so mark your calendar."

Summer leaned over and slipped her arm around Kelsey's, careful not to impede her driving. "I'm getting excited about the thought of going to Slovak Day with you."

"You are?" Kelsey turned her head just an inch or two to meet Summer's gaze.

"Sure. You wouldn't take me if we weren't serious about each other. If we're solid enough for Slovak Day, I'm going to start looking around for wedding venues."

"I wish you weren't kidding," Kelsey said, with some definite longing in her voice. "I wouldn't marry you this week, but…" She laughed. "You could convince me that Valentine's Day wasn't too soon."

"Slow your roll," Summer said, making sure she sounded like she was teasing. "After a year, we can start thinking about the future. For now, we're plenty busy with the present."

⊛

Kelsey was more distracted than she should have been, but hitting a spot of traffic made her concentrate again. They went from slow to stopped, and Summer took out her phone and determined that there was an accident up ahead. The delay was only supposed to last fifteen minutes, so Kelsey put the car in park and decided not to care. There were worse things than being stuck in traffic with Summer.

"Hey," Summer said, with a strange intensity to her voice. "How do you want me to be around your parents?"

"Uhm…" Kelsey took a look, seeing a perfectly sober expression on her face. "How about being the same person you've led me to believe you are. Whoever that is seems great."

"I'm not joking," she said, and Kelsey could see that was the truth. "What if your parents ask about my…I don't know. What if they want to know about my past relationships? How frank should I be?"

Kelsey sat up a little taller in her seat. "Are you saying there's something you want to hide? And if so, maybe you'd better tell me what it is."

"No, no," she said immediately. "I have nothing to hide. But I don't like to get ahead of things. You and I haven't talked about hundreds of topics, so I want to stay away from them until we do. But sometimes parents are *very* inquisitive..."

Kelsey nodded, feeling some of the tension that had started to build die down quickly. "My dad might ask about your business, or where you grew up. My mom won't be even that nosy. She's very hands-off when it comes to girlfriends. She'll grill *me* like a well-done steak," she added, laughing a little at that. "But she'd never do that to you."

"Great." Summer eased her seat back, a contented smile covering her face.

"Uhm, now that you've brought it up, want to tell me about these past relationships? It didn't dawn on me that we haven't done that."

"We will," she said, now seeming very casual. "I've just had one, so it won't take long."

"One?" Kelsey was sure she was teasing, but Summer didn't immediately follow up with the real number.

"Yup. Natalie Hartley. I worked in New York for a couple of years after I graduated from college, then I moved back to Pittsburgh to start my business. About a year after that, I met Natalie, and we were together until a little over two years ago."

"Got any more details?" Kelsey asked, seeing that Summer was being oddly circumspect.

"Sure," she said, smiling warmly. "But it's hard to summarize a long-term relationship while stuck in traffic."

"You can summarize a little," Kelsey urged. "Then we can talk more when we have time. I...uhm...who broke it off?"

"I did," Summer said, with a flash of pain crossing her features. "I wish I hadn't had to, but I did."

"We're stuck here for a few more minutes. Give me your top five reasons for calling it quits."

"How about one? We're not together now because of a single issue, but it was a big one." She took a breath and paused for a few moments.

"Natalie couldn't stand to be alone." Shaking her head, she said, "That sounds like the dumbest reason in the world to break up with someone you love, but I was starting to resent her, and you can't be consistently loving to someone you resent."

Kelsey's heart rate had picked up quickly. That sounded like a spectacularly bad reason to break up with someone!

"I don't need a whole lot of alone time, but I need some. Natalie, on the other hand, needed none. When I wanted to do something she didn't want to do, she'd tag along, which should have been fine. But it wasn't," she emphasized. "Having a woman follow you around a museum, spending more time checking her watch than the art..." She shrugged, looking kind of helpless.

"You broke off a long relationship because she didn't enjoy museums?" Even hearing that sounded awful!

"Of course not," she said, giving Kelsey a brief scowl. "It's just that she kind of hated them. Eventually, I stopped going, since it was easier to do what she liked." Her eyes had taken on a dull quality, and her voice was filled with sadness. "She was kind, and thoughtful, and very sweet to me. Loyal as a hound. But she was too needy for me to handle, and she wouldn't consider going to therapy. I truly had to end it." She sounded like she was going to cry when she added, "It broke my heart, but I had to."

"You couldn't just do what you wanted and tell her to stay home?"

Summer shrugged. "I tried all sorts of things, but none of them worked. She got hurt easily, then I'd have to spend the rest of the day reassuring her that I loved her. It got to be exhausting, and that's not how I wanted to spend the rest of my life." She put her hand on Kelsey's leg and patted it. "I could go into much more detail, but that's a good summary. So what's your number? Committed relationships only."

"Two," she said. "One early on when I was more like Natalie than I care to admit, and another that lasted about two years."

"When did it end?"

"It's been two Christmases."

"Tell me about that one, since it's more recent."

"There's not a lot to tell. We got along well, and I thought we had a lot of potential. But then Ashley got an offer to move to California for a job. I didn't want to go, and she didn't love me enough to stay."

"Ouch!"

"Yeah," she said, nodding. "It hurt. But finding out your girlfriend values her career more than you is a good thing to learn pretty early on."

"Do you ever regret your decision?"

"Not really." She waited a second to deliver the punchline. "She didn't fit in out there for some reason. Didn't even last for her whole probationary period. So three months later, she was back. I'm still kind of amazed that she assumed we'd get back together."

"No chance, huh?"

"Zero," Kelsey said firmly. "I can overlook a lot, but once you abandon me—we're done."

✺

As soon as they were dumped onto Penn Highway, Kelsey exited and headed for a nearby residential neighborhood. They were soon surrounded by car dealerships, strip malls and every kind of chain store under the sun, which quickly segued into an almost bucolic neighborhood, with modest ranch homes set well back from the curving street.

"I bet we're close," Summer said. "You act like you're on auto-pilot."

"Yeah," Kelsey said, clearly more nervous now that they were almost there.

"I'm sure I'll like your parents," Summer said quietly. "And if I don't, I'm a very good liar. I swear you'll never know if I hate their guts."

That made her laugh, and she spared a bit of her attention to give Summer a smile. "I know you'll like them. I'm just nervous."

"Does that mean you think they won't like me? They'd have to be crazy not to," she said, trying to make Kelsey laugh again.

She didn't. Instead, she pulled over to the side of the road, put the car in park, and took Summer's hand. "I know they'll like you," she said, very sober. "I'm just a little worried that… I know you wouldn't consciously judge us because we're on a lower economic rung than you are, but…"

"Kelsey," she said, stroking her tense face. "We were on food stamps until my mom married Robert. My dad declares bankruptcy every eight years like clockwork. When my family was in dire straits, it was because we spent money we knew we didn't have and weren't likely to get." She leaned close to kiss her pale cheeks. "Your family might live in a less expensive neighborhood, but I bet they're not mortgaged up to their eyebrows."

She smiled thinly. "My dad has a credit card so he can move through the world, but he only uses it when it's absolutely required. They carry cash, and if they don't have enough on them, they don't buy it."

"Wouldn't you rather be related to people who play by the rules? Come on now," she said, giving her a tap on the chin. "Quick story. My dad bought a massive TV when I was a kid. The biggest one I'd ever seen. Then a couple of guys came in during *Caroline In The City* to take it off the wall and carry it away." She let out a growl, adding, "That was my favorite show of my entire life. A woman who got to draw all day? I was *in*."

"The guys just took it?"

Laughing softly, Summer said, "You're obviously a woman who isn't used to having stuff repossessed. Yes, they just took it. Of course, my dad had thrown the old TV away, since it wasn't up to snuff. Took a month to get a replacement that wasn't even as big as the one we'd started with, and by the time the cable was back on the show had been canceled. Bastards."

"Wow," Kelsey whispered. "I can't imagine living like that. We were all about safety and security. My mom always teases that they're going to be very wealthy, as soon as they're dead. They're so heavily insured it's almost funny."

"My dad's insurance is having someone who seems lucky blow on his dice. Now let's go meet the prudent people who raised such a lovely woman. I can't wait."

Within ten minutes, they were all down in the den, watching the big screen TV that was definitely not going to be repossessed. Summer had never voluntarily watched a hockey game, but there they were, watching *Philadelphia's* team, which was more than strange.

George, Kelsey's dad, was an avid Penguins fan, and since his team wasn't playing, it was imperative that he watch a rival. Summer was glad she hadn't told Kelsey that a major ongoing argument between her and Natalie was how much time they spent watching sports together. Summer voted for none, while Natalie could get invested in watching a sport she'd never seen before and would never see again. Summer still recalled being stuck in front of the TV while they watched people toe wrestle, still a little annoyed that she'd never get that hour of her life back.

The ridiculous part of that ongoing argument was that she had no judgment about Natalie's obsession. She simply didn't share it. But having Summer sit close and comment on the action was a big part of the fun for Natalie.

Looking over at Kelsey, Summer detected a little of the locked-in attention that Natalie used to show. But Kelsey had never mentioned being into sports to any degree, which was a good sign. Natalie never would have spent consecutive Saturday nights away from an arena or her television.

Luckily, Kitty, Kelsey's mom, didn't seem to mind watching men skate after a puck, even though she clearly wasn't invested. In that way, she was definitely a better partner than Summer had been.

"Your turkey's delicious," Summer said, taking a bite of dark meat that was surprisingly moist. "Ours was decent, but it was cooked off-site. That can't compare in my book."

"Your dinner was…brought in?" Kitty asked.

Summer liked the timid way she got that out. Kitty was kind of a doll. Not very tall, and quite slight, with fiery red hair, worn short, and eyes that seemed unnaturally green. She looked nothing at all like Kelsey, with her pale skin looking like it might burn from having the lights on too bright. It was hard to tell in November, but Summer bet Kelsey would tan well, if she chose to. But even though they didn't look alike, you would have pegged them as mother and daughter from a block away. They just seemed remarkably fond of one another, with Kitty touching Kelsey gently every time she made a point.

"Yes," Summer said. "I don't know if you've spoken to Kelsey since last night, but she learned I have a pretty big family. My mother doesn't enjoy cooking, so they have most of their parties catered." She shrugged her shoulders. "They have a very nice kitchen, but my mother doesn't really know her way around it, and hasn't given any indication that she wants to learn."

"Well," Kitty said, clearly puzzled. "I guess there's no sense in making a big meal if you don't get any enjoyment out of it."

"I'm glad you get enjoyment out of cooking," George said, pulling his attention from the TV to give Kitty a smile. "'Cause I sure do enjoy the way you make Thanksgiving. Best dressing anywhere."

"Oh, George, dressing is the easiest thing in the world to make. I'm sure mine's no better than anyone else's. You're just used to it."

Summer watched them banter back and forth, pleased to see they seemed so well matched. Kelsey was a lucky woman to have parents who dug each other.

George didn't look much like Kelsey, either, but he might have resembled her more if it was clear what color his hair had once been. He only had a little of it left, covering only the back of his head from ear to ear, clipped very short. He made up for the lack of hair by maintaining a neat goatee, but that was almost all gray, not giving any hints as to its former color.

George had dark brown eyes, and they showed just as much emotion as Kelsey's pale ones did. Actually, after observing him for a few minutes, his personality seemed a bit like Kelsey's—friendly and even-tempered. Summer was pretty sure Kitty could have ruled the roost if she'd wanted to, but she didn't seem like that was her thing at all.

Summer wasn't sure how she'd gone several weeks without asking Kelsey about her family, but she hadn't, and it would have been odd to ask what kinds of jobs each of them had at this point. So she stuck to idle chit-chat, determined to grill Kelsey all the way home.

Kitty turned to her and said, "I didn't get a chance to talk to Kelsey earlier, so I didn't hear about your family, Summer. Did you say how many sisters and brothers you have?"

"Three brothers and two sisters," Kelsey cut in, eyes twinkling. "Summer's older sister is forty-seven, and her younger sister's just turned four."

"Four?" Kitty's eyes flew open wide. "Did you say four?"

"Yes," Summer said, elbowing Kelsey playfully. "She's trying to be funny. My parents have been divorced forever, and each of them had second marriages with kids. Then my dad went for a third, which I'm glad to report he's still in, and he and his wife had a little girl."

"Summer's step-mom's only a year older than she is," Kelsey said, drawing a glare.

"She thinks she's going to tell all of my family secrets, but believe me, I've only told her ten percent of them. We're a colorful bunch."

"So are we," Kitty said. "Why..." She furrowed her brow as she thought. "We haven't put our Christmas lights up yet, and that's wild for us."

"I'll do them on Sunday," George said. "I've never waited longer than the Monday after Thanksgiving, and I'm not going to start now. I just wish I could bring a cherry picker home from work. I'd have that roof outlined in ten minutes." His eyes twinkled when he added, "Yinz are comin' to help, right?"

Ahh. The beauty of Pittsburghese. George didn't rely on it heavily, but Summer bet his parents had. She regretted that she met few people now who filled their conversations with it, since so many people were teased out of it when they went to college, or worked with people who didn't use it. That was class shaming, pure and simple. Regional accents rocked.

"I don't know much about heavy equipment," she said, "so I don't know for sure what a cherry picker is, but I'm going to guess it's one of those things where you sit in a basket-like cage and move around in the air."

"Correct," he said, after waiting to swallow another big bite of dressing. George wasn't exactly fat, but he had a belly that Summer fervently hoped wasn't in Kelsey's future.

"Do you operate that from the basket, or the ground?"

"Basket." He laughed a little, making his eyes turn into slits, another feature Kelsey didn't share. "When I'm out there repairing a high-power line in a storm, the last thing I want is some jag down the ground moving me around."

Summer smiled to herself, loving the way he dropped prepositions and said "down" as "dahn." She gave herself points for figuring out what he did for a living just by letting him talk. "You're a brave man," she said. "I'd be afraid to be up in that basket on a calm spring day."

"I'm not brave," he said, scoffing at the compliment. "My dad knew a guy who worked for an electrical contractor that snared a big job rigging high-power lines for the city. I didn't know nothin' about electricity, so I hightailed it over to a trade school and took to it pretty well. It was late summer when I finally got hired, and I was happy to be working on my tan while I learned to fly around in the sky. Then we got our first sleet-storm, and I wanted to cry." He laughed, compelling Summer to laugh along with him. He'd probably told that tale a hundred times, but both his wife and daughter laughed too. That was a great sign of a happy family. No one was sick of the joke inventory.

※

Summer needed to use the rest room, and Kelsey went with her to show her which way to turn. On the way to the hall, Summer paused at an occasional table to pick up a framed photo. Little Kelsey was in a blue plaid uniform, holding her mom's hand. Kitty was also wearing a uniform —well, part of a uniform. Her bright red hair looked even brighter with a school crossing guard's white hat neatly settled on her head. "Look at you two!" Summer exclaimed. "Was this first grade?"

"Second," Kelsey said. She took the photo and gazed at it for a moment. "I can't even tell you how much I loved having my mom walk me to school. I had to get up like forty-five minutes early to go with her, but I looked forward to it every day." She placed the photo back on the table. "I knew she was there to watch out for every kid, but it felt like they were all incidental. My mom was there to make sure *I* was safe."

"That's so sweet." Summer took Kelsey in her arms and gave her a gentle kiss. "Does she still work?"

"Uh-huh. I think she'll stay on until my dad retires. It's just two and a half hours a day, but she kind of loves it."

"You know what I love?"

"Tell me," she said, like she already knew the punchline.

"I truly love dating women who appreciate their parents. That knocks about fifty percent of the problems out of a relationship." She put her hands on Kelsey's shoulders and looked into her eyes. "Promise you don't have a gambling problem, and we're set."

She laughed in the way a person hiding a gambling problem would have difficulty doing. "Not only do I not have a gambling problem," she said, bending over slightly to place gentle, playful kisses all across Summer's face, "I am debt free, I've got a 401-k that I contribute the max to, and I have enough savings to cover all of my bills for at least six months." She wrapped her arms around Summer's waist and delivered a very hot kiss. "Oddest flirting I've ever done, but whatever works for you works for me."

Kitty wouldn't accept any help in cleaning up, so Summer and Kelsey got ready to take off, since tomorrow was a work day for Kelsey. Near the front door, a partial wall was filled with framed photos. As Summer had expected, there were a lot of them. An intact family with only one kid would understandably focus intently on her.

The first one, of Kelsey in a gold cap and gown, looking really happy to be getting out of high school, made Summer chuckle. "Look how young you were! So innocent."

"That lasted a while," Kelsey said. "My heart didn't turn to stone until I was in my twenties."

"Ha! You're still as pure as a little lamb." They moved along the wall, with her commenting, "You keep getting smaller. I'd think the pictures would start with you as a baby and work up. You've got them arranged funny."

"Then you should have started at the other end of the hall."

When they neared that end, the photos abruptly jumped from chronicling every school grade to just a few of an adorable baby with a mop of dark hair and deep blue eyes. "My god," Summer murmured. "Why aren't there hundreds of these? You should have had an agent, Kelsey."

Kelsey's shoulders moved up and down in a "Why are you asking me?" kind of gesture. "This was years before we got a digital camera. I guess having to pay to develop the film made them satisfied with a few." She smiled at the photo of her as about a six-month-old. "I was a cute baby," she admitted. "But I got gawky pretty fast." Kelsey tugged her back to when she was a young teen. "My legs almost go to my armpits here."

Kitty walked into the hallway and put her arm around Kelsey's waist. "Wasn't she the prettiest little girl you've ever seen? Sweetest, too."

"I bet she was even a good baby," Summer said. "She probably never cried."

"Oh, I'm sure she... I mean, I think she was a perfectly normal baby, crying, and fussing, and sleeping a lot. It's when she started to grow up and develop her personality that she stood out. She was the most loving, grateful child I've ever met. So polite."

"She still is. Kelsey has very good manners."

"Oh, I know," Kitty said. She stood on her tip-toes to kiss Kelsey's cheek. "I'm so lucky to have her."

"That's enough of the mushy stuff," Kelsey said, acting a little gruff. "You're embarrassing me."

"I'll call you and we can dish about her," Summer said. "Kelsey can't complain if she doesn't know we're doing it."

Kitty looked a little nonplussed, but Summer was used to that. A lot of people didn't get her sense of humor right away, thinking many of the comments that she clearly intended as jokes were totally serious. But she was confident she'd win the Maliars over. They were crazy about Kelsey, and when they figured out that Summer was crazy about her too, they'd all be fast friends.

🌀

"Yinz be careful out there," George called from the doorway. "Them steps can be slippy."

"Why don't you say 'slippy?'" Summer whispered as they approached the car. "That's one of my favorite bits of Pittsburghese."

"I don't know if I started speaking like my dad and was warned off in school, or if I never picked it up. My mom doesn't use it like my dad does, but she has a few words that tag her as a Pittsburgher."

Kelsey was laden down with enough turkey to keep her in lunches for a few days, and she struggled to jam the containers on the floor behind her seat. When she had everything where she wanted it, she started the car and gave Summer a smile that seemed slightly shy. "Did you like my parents?"

Summer wiped at her forehead. "Whew. I'm so glad I don't have to lie." Unsnapping her seatbelt, she leaned all the way over and gave Kelsey a long, tender kiss. Staying right where she was, with their lips an inch apart, she whispered, "I think I could come to love them. They seem like very good people, and it's clear they're mad about you. That's two big thumbs up."

"I was pretty sure you'd like them," Kelsey said as Summer slid back into place. "I just wasn't sure what I'd do if you didn't."

As Kelsey put her hand on the shifter to put the car in reverse, Summer stopped her. "I know this sounds like I'm repeating myself, but that's because I am. If you go out with someone who doesn't like your perfectly lovely parents—break up with her. Seriously. You can't have a long term relationship with someone who can't at least act like she likes the people you love." Tapping her temple, she added, "Get your head on straight, girl. Your family is your center. Everything else has to revolve around that."

"Oh, sure," she said, giving the car some gas. "Easy for you to say. You're not going out with someone objectively awesome."

"We're both *sub*jectively awesome, but I'm kind of stoked that you think no rational person would find me lacking in any way."

"Is that what objectively awesome means?" she asked, shooting Summer a quick look. "I guess I should have studied vocabulary better." She laughed to herself as she guided the car around like she didn't have to think at all.

About ten minutes after they'd left the house, they approached a surprisingly big campus. "I thought I'd show you my school," Kelsey said.

"This is your high school? How many kids? Ten thousand?"

"Community College of Allegheny County—Boyce Campus. I only earned an associate's degree, but I was proud of it."

"You graduated? Why didn't I see a photo of your graduation on the Kelsey Maliar Walk of Fame?"

She smiled at that. "I didn't want to pay for the cap and gown. An associate's degree didn't seem like that big a deal, especially when my friends were all at Pitt or Penn or CMU. It felt odd to make a big deal about my graduating from Harvard on the Mon when my friends thought they'd just finished their sophomore years."

"The what?"

Kelsey let out a laugh. "You probably didn't have one friend who went to community college, did you."

"Um, no I don't think I did."

"Well, community college isn't exactly the toughest place to get into, but you've got to admit CCAC's the best school on the Monongahela, right?"

"I can't think of another who'd beat it," Summer said, finding Kelsey's self-effacing humor pretty charming. Summer took a look at her, watching her pale eyes scan the campus. "Are you...unhappy you didn't continue on? You did well enough to transfer, right?"

"Easily," she said, turning to smile. "I took all of the honors classes they offered, and did well in them. Pitt would have been happy to have me."

"But...?"

She continued to look across a wide athletic field to the campus buildings beyond. "I studied English because I didn't have any idea of what I wanted to do with my life. I enjoyed it, but it seemed kind of dumb to go into debt just to earn a degree I wouldn't use."

"But why wouldn't you—"

"Who do you know who actually uses an English degree? I didn't want to teach, and I didn't want to continue on to grad school. I felt ready to get a job and strike off on my own, so I did."

"You found a job right away?"

"Oh, I already had the job. I started working for Sedlak Brothers as soon as I got my driver's license and could get there from here. I worked twenty hours a week from the time I was sixteen until I graduated from CCAC."

"Are the Sedlaks family friends or something?"

"Not too far from that. They're Slovak, and people we knew told John Junior they knew a girl who was willing to work hard."

"And that was you."

"Sure was. They offered to send me for CAD training if I wanted to take over for a woman who was retiring. Those jobs don't come up often, so it was too good of an opportunity to pass up. That pushed me into giving up on getting a bachelor's degree, and I don't regret that decision."

"And you don't have any student debt."

"Precisely zero," she said, smiling. "Part of the reason I took honors classes is that they refunded your tuition if you got a 'B'. Let me at 'em," she said, growling. "Free classes? I would have worked my ass off to get an 'A plus' if I'd had to."

"I can see you as an English major. Do you still like books?"

"Yeah," she said, turning quickly to give Summer a smile. "I probably don't read with the same attention I did when I had to analyze a book, but I've never lost my love for novels."

"I never gained a love for novels. If we eventually live together, you can fill all of the bookcases."

"I am up to that challenge. I've already got a running start."

CHAPTER TWELVE

THE NEXT EVENING, KELSEY SURVEYED the small dishes that dotted the table at the Thai restaurant that Summer had picked. While not normally needing a huge meal, this was kind of ridiculous. Poking at one of the two salads with her fork, Kelsey said, "This is the papaya?"

"Uh-huh. I think you'll like it."

She met Summer's eyes. "Is more coming?"

She shook her head, offering a funny smile; one that Kelsey couldn't read. "We can order more if you'd like to. I just thought it would be a good idea to eat light."

"Mission accomplished."

Summer had shown a fairly hearty appetite during their other meals together, so this tiny amount of food was truly puzzling. They were sitting next to, rather than across from one another at the table, and Kelsey looked up sharply when Summer's hand landed on her leg, then slowly and teasingly climbed until it was nearly at her crotch.

"Don't you hate having a full stomach when you're lying down?" She met Kelsey's eyes and gave her a smile that turned racy very quickly. "I'd like to end our date in the horizontal position. Naked."

"Check!" Kelsey's hand was in the air in less than a second.

"We don't have to rush," Summer said, pulling her hand down and waving their server away. "It's only seven fifteen. We've got all night."

"What if you change your mind?" She was totally serious about that, but tried to make it sound like she was joking.

"Not a chance. I would have invited you up last night, but it was getting late and I didn't want to be in a rush."

"I don't want that either," Kelsey said. She laughed, having to admit she was lying. "Well, I do want to rush, but I know that's not a good instinct. Slowing down and savoring things is a much better way to go." She took a bite of the papaya salad, pleased to find that it was kind of perfect. Light, flavorful, and not overly spicy. "That's really good."

"One of my favorites," Summer said. She took a bite of the cucumber salad that had some suspicious looking red flakes on it. "This one's good, too, but maybe a little hot for you. Sorry about that. Want a noodle salad? I'm sure we could get one in a couple of minutes."

"I'm fine sticking with the papaya. Actually, I'm not really thinking of the food any more."

Summer took her hand and held it for a few seconds. "I'd like to put our cards on the table—while there's still a table to put them on."

"Okay. Which of my cards do you want to see?"

"I just want to make it clear what I'm looking for, and make sure I know the same about you."

"Good idea. What's on your wish list."

"I don't think this is a news flash, but I like to be crystal clear." She took a breath as her gaze grew serious. "I'm looking for a loving, supportive, monogamous, sexually satisfying relationship. Does that sync with your list?"

"Perfectly," Kelsey sighed. "I want a committed relationship with a woman who's willing to work through our problems—which I'm not idealistic enough to think we won't have."

"Same page," Summer said. "I hope talking about this now doesn't seem too…analytic. But I like to talk things out before my libido gets involved."

"You're acting like an adult, and that's not a slur in my book."

Summer took another bite of the cucumber, obviously satisfied with just that tiny amount of food. "Getting excited," she said, her eyes sparkling. "We have similar goals, and I'm pretty sure you're not a sociopath. I'm ready to hit the gas."

"I'm not a sociopath," Kelsey said, "but if I were, I'd lie about it…"

"Right!" Summer laughed. "It's really hard to spot one, but I'm feeling very confident about you. Seeing how you interacted with your family helped a lot, so I'm very glad you suggested we head down there last night. Good instinct."

"If that's not enough, I can produce another character witness. My friend Rob has known me since high school. You can grill him about my well-hidden faults."

"I bet you don't have a single one. And I'd love to meet Rob soon, but don't forget that I leave for Portugal on Friday night."

"I forgot about your trip!"

"I didn't. That's why I thought tonight was the perfect time to get to know each other much better." She leaned over and spoke softly, with Kelsey watching her sexy lips move. "I've been dreaming about having sex with you, and my patience is at an end." Her sweet smile changed just a little, quickly adding some spice. "If I rock your world, you won't even be tempted to look for a new girlfriend while I'm gone. What do you say."

Once again, Kelsey held up her hand. "Check!"

⊛

Since they were closer to her side of town, Kelsey suggested they go to her apartment. During the short drive, she worried about whether she'd neatened up before leaving for work that morning. She usually did, always feeling more settled to come home to a clean place, but she was still concerned—about everything. There was no better time to obsess about every facet of your hygiene than when you were about to go to bed with someone for the first time. Had she flossed her teeth that morning? Had she used a washcloth to scrub behind her ears? Exactly when was she due to get her period? It was either two or three days, which wouldn't be a problem at all. But what if she'd miscounted…

Her checklists were still running through her head when she pulled into the building's lot. Of the two guest spaces, one was still open. She quickly texted Summer, telling her to take number 14.

Kelsey got out of her car and walked over to take Summer's hand when she exited.

"This cute little thing is yours?" Summer asked, tilting her chin to assess the three story building.

"Uh-huh. I've been here since I started to work full time—literally the day after my last exam at CCAC."

"It's cute. Kind of petite."

"Kind of," Kelsey admitted. "Four units per floor. All one bedrooms."

It had gotten pretty nippy out, and they rushed to enter the lobby, which wasn't much of a lobby at all. Just a little blip of an entryway, with all of the mailboxes tucked away on one of the walls. Kelsey pointed to the elevator. "We can ride up if you want, but it's the slowest elevator in all of Pittsburgh. Noisy, too."

"I'm happy to walk."

Kelsey led the way, pushing open the fire door that led to the industrial-looking stairs, painted a dull, dark red. Sometimes she wished she lived in a fancier place, but her rent was kind of a steal, and she was simply never going to be a person who valued a little flash more than savings. She'd only taken a few steps when Summer patted her ass. "Does walking up these stairs every day give you that muscular butt?"

"Maybe." She turned slightly to smile back at her. "I wouldn't ever complain about the stairs if you were behind me doing that."

"I like to distract myself when I'm exercising. I usually think of how I'd draw something, but tonight I'm thinking about getting your slacks off." She plucked at the fabric, giving Kelsey's butt a pinch in the process. "I don't know where you bought those, but they look fabulous on you."

"Aren't they nice? Lots of stretch, and no wrinkling. I bought two pair in blue and two in black when they went on sale."

"We're doing great at flirting," Summer chuckled. "I've had more intimate conversations with my gramma."

"Give me a minute. I can't flirt while I'm trudging up my steps." They finally reached the third floor, and Kelsey held the door open. "Right this way," she said. "I'm the last one on the left." She got her keys out and opened the door, relieved to see that she'd cleaned up after making coffee. "My humble abode."

Summer entered and did a very quick scan. "It's cute." She took Kelsey's hand as they walked toward the windows. "I can see from a glance that you like to watch TV and read books. Oh! You listen to music while you're reading books. Those are serious speakers."

"Pretty serious," Kelsey admitted. "They also provide sound for the TV. Good ones let you crank up the volume a bit without driving your neighbors nuts. More treble and mid-range, and less booming bass."

"Okay," Summer said, pasting on a very big smile. "Now that we've got that settled, I guess it's time to take off our coats and jump into bed." She slapped herself in the forehead with her gloved hand. "I will never, ever, again announce my intentions before I'm actually carrying them out. This is the least romantic lead-up to sex that I've *ever* been responsible for." She put her hands on Kelsey's waist and looked into her eyes. "I'm sorry I didn't handle this well. I wanted tonight to be special."

"It will be," Kelsey said, gentling her voice. She took off her gloves, then quickly shrugged out of her coat before tossing it onto a stool that sat underneath the breakfast bar. Then she carefully slid Summer's coat from her shoulders and pulled her gloves off. "Let's just act like we normally do. We'll wind up where we wind up, okay?"

"I'd love a do-over," she said, looking relieved. "Can we sit down and listen to some music?"

"Sure can. How about a glass of Port?"

"You have some?"

"I bought some," Kelsey revealed. "I wanted to have some for when I lured you into my lair."

Summer smiled at her for a long time, holding the look. "One of the things I like best about you is how thoughtful you are. That's *huge*, Kelsey. Really huge."

"Thanks," she said, almost sure she was blushing. "My mom always says that it costs nothing to be thoughtful."

"I've love a splash of Port. I'd offer to turn on your sound system, but it looks complex."

"Not too." She walked over and picked up the remote, clicking it on. "I think tonight is a good night for...standards."

"Standards?"

"Yeah. Ella, Lena Horne, Dinah Washington… American standards."

"Why not?" Summer sat on the sofa and kicked her shoes off. "I don't know why you listen to music that's older than my gramma, but…"

"I listen to everything. But I got into the genre a while ago, and I find it soothing. Kind of sexy, too." She bent over to kiss Summer's head. "Be right back with your Port. I don't have the right kind of glasses, but you're too polite to complain about that."

"Oh, glasses don't affect the taste. I wouldn't have bought the ones I have for myself. Gift from mom."

Kelsey quickly splashed some Port into two glasses, then sat next to Summer on the sofa. Gently, she tapped their glasses together. "To us," she said. "Whatever we do tonight will be fun. And that's what's important."

"You're right," Summer said, giving her glass another "tink" against Kelsey's. She took a sip, then smacked her lips for a moment. "That's a nice Port you have there."

"Thanks. I go to a wine shop in the neighborhood, and the guy who runs it usually makes good recommendations."

Summer took another small taste, then set her glass on the coffee table. "Remember when I told you that I found I have a head for business?"

"Sure. You found you're more analytical than you would have guessed."

"All true. But I've been mulling that over, and I feel like I've been letting the analytical predominate to a certain extent. That's not great. When I plan less and go with my instincts more it feels more natural." She took Kelsey's hand and kissed it gently. "I've been trying to analyze whether we'll make a good couple. Which can be a fun exercise," she added, "but I can't use checklists or spreadsheets to know if we'll be a match. That has to come from here." She took Kelsey's hand and pressed it to her breast, smiling at her with a very open expression. "I've got to trust you and let you inside to find out if a relationship's in our future."

"Yeah," Kelsey murmured. "That's exactly what you have to do. But I know it's scary." She laughed a little. "I've jumped right into bed with women I knew I wouldn't want to spend a lot of time with, but I don't do that any more. Now that I'm looking for a relationship, I'm much more careful."

"It's an awful system, to be honest. You're supposed to open yourself up physically and emotionally to someone you don't know well at all, hoping, with little evidence, that you'll want to be with them for a very long time." Her eyes widened. "Actually, you're hoping you'll wind up knowing them better than anyone on earth. It's so front-loaded!"

"It's definitely too front-loaded. But if you didn't have the drive..." She scooted a little closer, now able to sniff Summer's spring-like scent. "If your body didn't go on full-alert when you were around someone you were really attracted to... You'd never have the nerve to show so much of yourself. It's...a lot!" she admitted, laughing at how odd it really was to have sex with someone for the first time. "Remember when you were a kid and you finally understood what sex entailed? It took me forever to believe it."

"It sounded like the most disgusting thing in the world," Summer agreed. "I thought you'd have to be stark-raving mad to let a guy put his penis inside you. Well, I still think that," she said, chuckling. "I've always been one hundred percent gay."

"I'm so glad you decided to play for my team." She tucked her arm around Summer and felt a wave of pleasure pass through her when she molded herself to Kelsey's body. "Let's act like lesbians."

"I love acting like a lesbian," Summer sighed, tilting her head back to present her lips to Kelsey. "My favorite role."

Kelsey held off for a couple of seconds, loving the feeling she got right before she kissed someone she was really into. That extra moment or two of anticipation always gave her chills. She placed her hand on Summer's cheek, and stroked it gently before dipping her head and kissing her firmly. Almost at once, Summer's hand went to the back of

Kelsey's neck, and she pulled her in, no longer playing around. She was ready to be kissed seriously.

"Perfect," Kelsey whispered when she paused for a second to take in a breath. They were both ready to get down to business now, and Kelsey led the way, pressing Summer up against the sofa to probe her sweet mouth with her tongue. She tasted so fresh, so clean. The tiny bit of alcohol they'd had wasn't enough to overtake the bright flavors of their salads, with Kelsey able to detect hints of cucumber and lime still on her breath.

Summer clung to her tightly, really getting into it. There was nothing that Kelsey loved more than kissing a woman who made it clear how much she was enjoying herself, and Summer was definitely doing that. Her hands were in Kelsey's hair now, and they occasionally slid across her scalp, making chills pass over her in waves. *Delightful!*

Kelsey had no idea how long they explored, but they were both running out of air. Summer's chest continued to press against Kelsey's as she panted softly, their desire growing with every moment that passed.

"Come to bed with me," Kelsey murmured, drunk with desire.

Summer was on her feet in a second, tugging at Kelsey's hand. "I never thought you'd ask," she said, with a cute smirk covering her face.

Kelsey stood next to her, trying to take a moment to calm her nerves. She let her gaze travel over her bookcases, photos of family and friends, all of her furnishings, purchased with care. This was her place, curated and organized her way. But she was ready to let Summer all the way in. Into her life, into her home, into her body, and into her heart.

Summer was no rookie when it came to having sex with someone she didn't yet know very well. Going to an arts and crafts-focused university, and being immersed in the art world during her twenties had exposed her to a lot of expressive, emotional, lusty people; and she'd definitely been eager to join in the fun. But once she'd settled down with Natalie, she'd gotten out of practice. In the last two years, she'd had some very quick romances that she'd tried to convince herself might lead to relationships, but, in retrospect, she'd slept with those women mostly because she was horny. To her surprise, those quick dalliances hadn't been very satisfying. While she didn't regret giving casual sex another try, she wasn't really built for it. She wanted to know a woman thoroughly, and she wanted to reveal the deepest, most hidden parts of herself to someone she could trust. You could only do that with someone you were confident wouldn't stomp on your heart.

Her previous attempts to create sexual chemistry when none existed made her sure that opening herself up physically was the best way to know Kelsey even better. And even though she wasn't naive enough to think she knew her deeply, she already trusted her, which gave her the confidence to take the next step.

But all of that didn't completely relieve her anxiety. She *so* wanted this to work out. But she had enough experience to know that you could match in fifty difference ways, yet be a total mismatch because of a single item. At this point, Summer was almost certain there was nothing that would throw Kelsey out of the game. She had all of the critical attributes: she was mature, financially prudent, self-sufficient, independent, honest, thoughtful, and kind. If they had a decent sexual connection—all systems were go. And from the fire in those sea-blue eyes as they walked into the bedroom together, Summer's confidence that their connection would be more than decent shot up.

"You look tired," Kelsey teased when Summer nearly collapsed onto the bed, so ready to get going she felt a little weak.

"Not tired," she said, holding up her hands and twitching her fingers to indicate Kelsey should join her.

"I kind of hate trying to get undressed while lying down," she said, grasping the top button of her shirt to pop it open. "Mind if I do it… now?"

Holy god! Kelsey was offering to put on a show. Nothing worked on Summer's libido like a woman who had enough confidence in her body to own her sexual desire. An awesome body wasn't required to give her a boost, but from what she'd seen… "Please," Summer said, sitting up a little by propping herself up on her elbows, not wanting to miss a thing.

Kelsey got a little cockier as her buttons popped open, revealing a hint of her white bra. "Your eyes are about to burn a hole through me," she said, locking her gaze on Summer. "I'm getting the feeling you like watching me undress."

"Love," she said, rendered unable to emit more than single words.

"Love, huh?" She'd finished unbuttoning her blouse, but she didn't take it off. Leaving it open so that Summer could catch glimpses of her was perfect. Just *perfect*. Kelsey unfastened and unzipped her slacks, then let them fall to the floor. Her underwear wasn't fancy, or colorful, but the white undies with the high-cut leg made her look tall and lean, with just a little muscle showing on the side of her leg.

"Hot," Summer managed, frustrated with herself for being unable to express herself more eloquently.

"I can't wait to get into bed with you," Kelsey said, standing up tall to shake her shoulders and let her blouse slide down her arms. Before Summer could say a word, they were lying next to one another, with Kelsey's warm, soft skin pressed against her.

"So nice," she murmured, finally able to shake off her languor to let her hands trail up and down Kelsey's back, finally settling on her ass. "Happy," she said, still largely inarticulate.

"Me too." Kelsey sat up slightly and set about undressing Summer in a quick, forthright manner. When Summer started to sit up, Kelsey held her in place with just a finger pressed into her sternum. "I've got it," she purred, looking thrilled to handle this all on her own.

Summer lay there, carefully watching Kelsey transform before her very eyes. No matter how much you thought you knew a person, being surprised once you hit the sheets was, in Summer's experience, common. Kelsey didn't give off much of an "I'm in charge" vibe in her daily life. Well, maybe about work. But when they were hanging out together, she was always concerned with Summer's wishes and plans, nearly always deferring. That pointed toward a woman who'd be either tentative, or, at most, egalitarian in bed. But she was ultra-confident, a little forceful, and clearly in charge. How perfect was that? It was such a relief to not have to run the show.

Once Kelsey had unfastened or unzipped all of Summer's clothing, she leaned over to ramp up her kissing game, which was already excellent. Gently, she wrapped her arms around Summer and pulled her into a sitting position, then tossed her blouse and bra aside. Kelsey tightened her hold, rubbing her chest against Summer's, making her nipples harden when they brushed against the little bit of lace on Kelsey's bra.

Summer crossed her wrists behind Kelsey's neck, holding on as well as she could as kisses rained down on her in an unceasing stream. It felt like an hour had passed, but that wasn't possible. That was just the sensation of being thoroughly loved by a woman who knew exactly what she wanted. Every moment was distinct.

With a great deal of tenderness, Kelsey lay her down again, then rolled her onto her side, while tugging her jeans and undies down. It took just a minute, then Summer felt the cool November air kiss her bare skin. With a burst of activity, Kelsey removed the last bits of her own clothing, then pulled Summer into her warm embrace once again.

"Can I just hold you for a while?" she asked softly. "I really do get all mushy when I'm turned on."

"I love to be held," Summer murmured. "Especially by you."

"This is fantastic. I can finally touch you like I've been dreaming of. I just want to relish this...closeness."

"You could make me cry without much effort," Summer admitted. "I feel so tender toward you."

"Yeah, that's it. I feel tender."

They held each other for a few minutes, with Summer feeling very emotionally open, so trusting of the woman cuddling up against her. She'd been certain she was ready to test their sexual compatibility, but she was learning so much more than that. And everything she learned was making her crazier about Kelsey than she already had been. What a delicious night this was turning out to be!

Kelsey tilted her head, gently pressing their lips together. Then they started to kiss again, with the heat slowly building. In just a few seconds they were moving against one another, rubbing their bodies together forcefully, clearly each trying to experience every bit of pleasure there was to sample.

"I love this," Summer murmured, feeling like all of her nerves were involved now, each of them firing a little bit of joy straight to her brain.

"Every minute's better than the last." Kelsey lifted her head slightly, then started to move down Summer's body, grinning. "I think I'm on a roll." In just a second or two she was settled down between her legs, gently moving Summer around until she was satisfied. "Perfect," she murmured, almost to herself. Then she went for what she clearly craved, tasting Summer without the slightest hesitancy. "So happy," Kelsey murmured when she paused for just a second.

"Me," Summer said, with the most fantastic sensations zipping all over her body, starting at her center and radiating out. "I'm happier."

Kelsey lifted her head, speaking clearly. "If there's anything I can do to make this better—tell me or point me in the right direction. My goal is to please you. Anything you want is exactly what I want."

"That's a wonderful goal," Summer sighed. "So far, you're doing just great without any help."

Their eyes were fixed on one another, with a very tender connection holding them in place. "Do you like this?" Kelsey asked, entering her gently.

"Like's not a strong enough word," Summer said, unable to hold her head up another moment. When a woman was making love to her so well she liked to lie back and relinquish all control. Nearly any sensation was welcome.

Kelsey wasn't content to simply keep doing the same things. She varied the pace, the pressure, whatever she could try—clearly getting off on hearing Summer moan her satisfaction. As much as she tried to hold back a little, Kelsey kept pressing her, silently urging her to let go. Finally unable to resist her for another moment, Summer took the brakes off and just let her body revel in all of the sensations that buffeted her. A few seconds later, a climax she hadn't even seen coming hit her hard, making her gasp in surprise. "Whoa!" she called out, completely taken aback. "No warning whatsoever!"

"Sorry?" Kelsey said, grinning impishly when she tilted her head to meet Summer's eyes.

"You're sorry you had me so turned on I couldn't focus?"

"Well," she said, slowly crawling up to lie next to Summer. "That would be a weird apology. But if you like knowing one's coming…"

"Feel free to surprise me. Any time," Summer said. "How about one of those mushy hugs? I need some cuddling, too."

"With pleasure." Kelsey got an arm under Summer's neck, then pulled her onto her side so they were pressed against one another firmly. "That was more fun than I've had in a long, long time. I think we've got some spark."

"Tons," Summer agreed. "I usually like giving as much as receiving, but that experience is going to be a tough one to beat. You figured me out *fast*."

"Oh, I bet there's a whole lot I don't know about you," Kelsey murmured softly. "But I can't wait to learn."

Kelsey knew it was too soon to declare her love for the woman who was touching her so gently that all she could do was purr like a kitten. But she sure wanted to. Summer *got* her. Not just sexually, but that was part of it. The bigger part was how she just took Kelsey at face value, seemingly perfectly accepting of all of her little quirks. Summer was easy, in the most positive sense of the word.

Kelsey nuzzled against her, seeking her mouth again. When their lips met, she got that flash of deep connection, that urge to merge with this beautiful, gentle woman. They'd get there. She was nearly one hundred percent certain of that. And that was a very nice way to feel about a woman you'd only known for a few weeks. It was actually kind of remarkable, leaving her to imagine how close they'd be after two months…two years. The possibilities were endless.

※

Sometime in the night, Kelsey woke, feeling the need to use the bathroom. Starting to sit up, she flinched when Summer stretched her body out and tossed a hand over her head. The night came back to her, and she sat there grinning, amazed that she hadn't remembered everything the moment she woke. But she remembered now, and she gazed at her, amazed by how pretty she was. She hadn't put her hair up, and it now splayed across her pillow case, a golden halo that framed her face beautifully. Kelsey slid out of bed and tiptoed over to pick up Summer's phone. She knew her passcode was T-I-L-E, and she entered it to reveal the home screen. Normally, she wouldn't have taken a photo of a sleeping woman, but using Summer's device gave her control over the image. If she hated it, she could delete it.

The lamp had a dimmer switch, and Kelsey turned it on slowly, stopping when she was able to get the camera to focus. She took a few shots of Summer, still touched by how innocent, yet sexy she looked. Then she got on her knees right next to the bed. Holding up a thumb while she smiled like a fool, she took a selfie, knowing Summer would appreciate it. Their first time making love selfie would always make her laugh, and that was a great way to start what Kelsey hoped was a very long-lasting relationship.

※

Summer woke with a sigh, then closed her eyes almost immediately to snuggle into Kelsey's warm embrace. Was there anything better than making love for an hour or two, then falling asleep like you'd been drugged? Summer was pretty sure there wasn't. Although waking up with someone you were really into was a close second.

She was almost asleep again when she realized there was some muscular tension coming from Kelsey's side of the bed. "Awake?" she asked softly.

"Uh-huh. I know you're going to visit your gramma this morning, but do you have anything planned for the rest of the day?"

Summer opened her eyes, seeing Kelsey gazing at her. "Nothing planned. Why? Don't you have to go to work?"

"Well, I should…" She smiled. "But I've covered for one of my co-workers a few times. If she's available, would you like to spend the day together?"

"Yes!"

"Oh, what a nice way to answer," Kelsey said, smiling happily. "Let me see if she's up for it."

"Do we have time to snuggle more if you do have to work? On a cold morning, there's nothing I like better."

"It's just eight. Worst case, we've got over an hour."

"Come here," Summer said, opening her arms. "I want you close."

"Nowhere I'd rather be," Kelsey said. She fired off a text, then dropped her phone and snuggled in. It was going to be a *great* day.

⊕

At nine forty-five, Kelsey opened the passenger door for Summer, then raced around to her own side of the car. "It was nice of your grandmother to go to a later mass so we had more time to talk."

Summer put her hand on her leg and gave it a squeeze. "It was nice of you to go with me. She likes you," she said, giving that leg a firm shake. "So do I."

Kelsey patted her belly. "We're full of donuts and coffee, and we've got a couple of hours to kill before lunch. Let's stop by your apartment and get some art supplies. Then we can hit up a museum."

"What?" Summer asked, with a delighted smile covering her face. "I assumed you'd want to spend the day in bed. Not that I'd argue with that idea…"

"We'll have plenty of time for that. Museum first. Nice, leisurely lunch next. A spirited bout of sex, followed by a nap should hold us until dinner. How does that sound?" She turned to see that delight now entirely suffused Summer's expression.

"You're trying to recreate my ideal day, you romantic devil!"

"Doing my best," Kelsey admitted. "As soon as places start to open I'm going to make lunch and dinner reservations. I don't want any unexpected glitches."

Summer leaned over and kissed her cheek, staying close to nuzzle against her for a moment. "You are a very unexpected surprise, Kelsey. A truly delightful one."

It was nearly eleven when Summer dashed back to Kelsey's car that night. The icy breeze that blew through town had obviously kept all of the sane people at home. Kelsey got in and rubbed her upper arms briskly, with her breath visible in the car. "Well, now we know how to make sure we have a good ice cream place all to ourselves."

"Thanks for not trying to convince me to window shop while we ate our cones. We'll have to save that element of my perfect day for this spring." She grasped the fabric of Kelsey's coat and pulled her over for a kiss. Her lips were chilly, and her cheeks even colder, but Summer was able to warm them up pretty quickly. "If my sister wasn't going on this trip to Portugal, I'd cancel. But I just can't flake out on her."

"You should go," Kelsey said, gently stroking Summer's cheek with her gloved hand. "I'll be waiting for you."

"Can I text you? Call you?"

"I hope you do. I don't leave for work until nine forty, so you could call me in the morning if that works out."

"If I don't freeze to death before I get out of Pittsburgh," she said, pointedly looking at the heater.

"Forgot!" Kelsey started the car and turned the heater on high. "Do you think you'll have time to see me this week? I'm going down to see my parents on Tuesday night, but I'm otherwise free."

"Do I *want* to see you this week? One hundred percent. Do I think I'll have time to focus on you?" She saw Kelsey's smile dim, but she had to be honest. "I'm going to be swamped. I've got to finish a million things at work, and I'm locked into going to a winter concert at Poppy's preschool on Thursday." She took Kelsey's hand and held it to her chest. "Why don't we just relish this perfect day until I get back?"

"All right," Kelsey said, clearly disappointed.

Summer cupped her cheek and added, "The last part of my perfect day was snuggling with my awesome lover. Back to your apartment?"

That high-wattage grin was back in an instant. "I normally stay up until one, but I'm very eager to hop into bed this instant—with you."

Summer hadn't set an alarm, mostly because she rarely needed one. She stretched a little, getting a few kinks out, then turned onto her side, gazing at a soundly sleeping Kelsey. She was a very pretty woman, made even prettier by the unguarded, innocent expression that covered her face when she slept.

They'd only cuddled the night before, which was oddly reassuring. When she'd told Kelsey about her perfect day, she'd made it clear that sex in the afternoon, done right, was plenty for her. But that didn't necessarily mean it was enough for Kelsey. The fact that she didn't even attempt to get anything started last night showed that she not only listened, she honored Summer's wishes.

Kelsey might not have known how important that simple thing was, but it was vital. And her instinct to place a gentle kiss on Summer's lips and hold her in a tender embrace might have been the sexiest move she'd made all day. Trying to satisfy your lover's physical and emotional needs was the hottest thing around, and Kelsey had shown she was pretty expert at both. Summer had no idea why she was single, but she was determined to change that status—hopefully permanently. *Now* they were girlfriends.

Chapter Thirteen

ON THE FOLLOWING SUNDAY NIGHT, Kelsey sat with Rob at one of their regular haunts, having dinner. She'd been a little distracted, but he hadn't seemed to notice. He was usually very attentive, not to mention perceptive, but he was planning on hooking up with a guy he'd met the week before, and he couldn't contain his enthusiasm.

"He was honestly the perfect man," he said, with a dreamy look in his eyes. "We got along like gangbusters, and when we finished he switched over from his…" He stopped, honoring their unstated agreement to keep sexual details to a bare minimum. "He turned into a perfectly normal guy. Honestly, Kels, it was like a regular date." He said that with such puzzlement that she wasn't sure how to respond.

"Is there…some kind of rule that you can't have a regular date with a guy you like having sex with? I know a lot of guys who do."

"There's no rule," he scoffed. "I just don't meet many…okay, any guys I want to see for more than sex. Eric's the first in a long time."

"I'm happy for you—" Her phone buzzed, and she smiled as she picked it up. "But I'm happier for me. I've got to take this."

"Go. Go," he said, shooing her away.

Kelsey grabbed the phone, and her coat, and raced out of the restaurant. She'd lucked out by having a mild night to take a call outdoors. "Hi," she said, giddy with excitement. Having a new girlfriend was like being on a roller coaster, and at this point, the car was going up and up and up.

"Hi there. It's one o'clock in the morning here, and I'm so stuffed I will never be able to sleep. So I thought I'd call you and moan about how good the food is, while complaining about how little control I have over my appetite."

"Are you trying to make me feel bad about my mediocre order of loaded nachos? 'Cause you are."

"Ooo. Am I interrupting your dinner?"

"Well, I'm having dinner with Rob, but you're not interrupting us. I told him you might call."

"Call me when you get home, Kelsey. I'm sure I'll be up for another hour—at least."

"Sure? I don't want to miss the chance to talk to you."

"I'm positive. I'll stay up even if I get tired. I miss you," she said, sighing softly.

"We'll eat fast. I love Rob, but he's no you."

✿

Kelsey almost felt bad to rush through dinner, but Rob didn't seem to mind at all. He really loved the Sunday night leather scene, and assured Kelsey that getting there early might be a good tactic. As soon as she kissed him goodbye, she got into her car and dialed Summer, while fussing with her earphones. "Hey," she said, fumbling to put the correct one in. "Sorry if I sounded weird. I put the wrong earphone in."

"You're in your car?"

"Uh-huh. Couldn't wait," she said, surprised at how excited she was just to have a few minutes of Summer's time.

"Ooo. You're revealing how much of a sweetheart you are. I really like that, Kelsey. I never feel like you're playing with me, or hiding your feelings."

"I definitely like to play with you," she teased. "But hiding my feelings would only hurt me in the end. Eventually you'd find out about everything, so why not put it out there right now."

"I really look forward to finding out all of your secrets. Your quirks. Your fears. And your turn-ons, of course."

"Some of those sound more fun than others. Ask Ashley about my quirks. One or two of them grossed her out." She'd gotten too cold, so Kelsey started up the car and pulled out of her parking space.

"Hey now, you can't drop that and not follow up!"

158

Kelsey laughed. "It's nothing bad. She was…kind of rigid. Not in an awful way, but if she ordered a BLT, she didn't want the restaurant to, as she said, play tricks with her. I remember one time she ordered one and it had cheese. Even though she took it off, I could tell that kind of ruined it for her."

"Oh, damn. That couldn't be less like me. I'm one of those people who hunts down the unexpected. Actually, I had a fried chicken BLT not long ago that I was crazy about."

"Mmm. I think I'd like that, too. I certainly don't mind traditional things done in a traditional way, but improvisation's good if it's done well. Except at Thanksgiving," she added. "Don't try to substitute goose or duck for turkey. That's not going to fly."

"Next year, we're going to spend the day with your parents. We'll swing by mine for the evening."

"Really?" Kelsey said, delighted that Summer was already making plans that far ahead.

"Yeah, I think so. I need to see my family, of course, but our gathering is so loosey-goosey that it wouldn't hurt a thing to have us drop by late in the day. Your family has a more traditional meal, so being there for it would mean more to them."

"That's exactly true," Kelsey said, feeling her eyes fill with tears. "I'm so grateful that you recognize that. Being an only child puts some pressure on me that makes it tough to ignore family traditions."

"I get that. My mom—Jackie—will be upset, but Robert will understand. If I can keep him happy, I'm good."

"Well, damn," Kelsey said, sitting at a light. "We've already got Thanksgiving sorted out. Which part of Christmas is most important to you?"

"Christmas Eve," Summer said. "If I'm around then, I can watch Poppy open her presents, then pick my gramma up and take her to midnight mass. Everything else is optional."

"I think we're good to go. My parents go to midnight mass, too, but it wouldn't break their hearts if I didn't join them. Being home in the morning on Christmas day is the only mandatory thing."

"Your parents have a guest room. After we go to mass with gramma, we'll drive to Monroeville and wait for Santa to wake us."

"I can't even tell you how happy that would make my mom—and me," Kelsey said, determined to spend some time when she got home buying matching Christmas pajamas for the two of them. If you were going to jump into the Christmas spirit, you might as well jump high.

🙠

Two nights later, Kelsey sat on one of the molded benches at the bowling alley not far from her parents' home. She'd been bowling with the group for years, ever since she was forced to pick a sport for a PE requirement during her first year at CCAC. Once the class was over, a group of them kept meeting up, eventually joining a league. All of these years later, they were still at it.

While they were putting on their shoes, Courtney pulled out her daughter Ava's recent art project to pass around. Kelsey found herself staring at it with more than polite interest. "How did she know how to do this?" she asked, amazed that a little kid could create such a complex, three-dimensional piece.

"School," Courtney said. "I'll agree that Ava's is good, but some of the other kids' projects were amazing." She gave Kelsey a tap on the back of her head. "She *should* be able to do something like this at twelve."

"Oh. Right," she said, nodding robotically. "She's twelve." The fact was that they rarely saw each other outside of the league. A few of the others got together socially, but Kelsey was sure that was because a couple of them had kids at the same time, and sometimes babysat for each other. Looking around at her friends, she was amazed that one of them had a kid who could play the piano, perform gymnastics, and make art good enough to actually get pleasure from it. She passed the tablet computer to Stephanie, still thinking about how quickly the time had passed.

"When are you going to bring this new girlfriend down so we can take a look?" Brittney asked. "We missed the last one completely."

"Yeah," she said, scratching her head. "It was a rare day I could talk Ashley into coming down here. My parents were always nice to her, but she just wasn't into going out of her way to get to know my friends and family." She smiled. "That won't be a problem with Summer. If she was in town, I bet she would have come with me tonight. She's bound and determined to win my parents over—not that she'll have a hard time. She's very likable."

"You said she *makes* tile?" Brittany asked. "Like…herself?"

"You weren't here last week when I made everyone sick by droning on about how artistic she was, so you're going to have to catch up later, Brit. But, yes, she owns a small company that makes tile."

"Discounts?" she asked, cocking her head.

Kelsey laughed. "I'm sure she'd give my friends a break. But even twenty percent off would still make them super expensive. If you need tile, I can get you some that has a handmade look, but isn't. Save your money for the unique stuff for after you've put your kids through college."

"I'm just praying they want to follow in my footsteps. CCAC worked great for me, so I'm trying to sell the kids on it."

"I'm with you," Kelsey said. "If a kid does well in community college, then I'd pay for them to go on. If not—get a job, junior."

⯃

The next night, Kelsey walked in the door at six thirty, carrying enough vegetables to make herself a hearty salad. She put the canvas bag on the counter, then started to take off her coat. Before she could take it into her bedroom to put it in the closet, her phone chirped. Taking a peek, she saw a text from Summer. *I'm in bed. Alone. Want to join me?*

FaceTime, Kelsey texted back. *Give me five minutes.*

Rushing to change into her pajamas, she went back into the kitchen to twist a big carrot away from its top, then quickly peel it. Grabbing her tablet, she sat down on the sofa to wait for the device to chirp. The moment it did, she accepted the call. "Ehh... What's up Doc?" she asked, sticking the carrot into her mouth.

"Not what I expected," Summer said, chuckling. "Did I catch you in the middle of doing something...interesting?"

"Just trying to get something into my stomach. I've been home for about six minutes, and I'm starving."

"Ooo. You're getting a carrot, when I'm unable to sleep because of the prawns with garlic and ginger, and the grilled octopus..."

"Adjust the camera angle," Kelsey said. "I want to see if your tummy's sticking out. It sounds like you do nothing but eat!"

Summer smiled at her, and did exactly as she'd asked—but sexily. After Summer had tossed off the sheet, she held her phone so it was aimed at her belly. Then she slowly pulled up her shirt, keeping going until a hint of the undersides of her breasts were exposed. Her hand went to her stomach, and she trailed her fingers over it teasingly. "What do you think?"

"I think I'd like to be in Lisbon right now," Kelsey sighed. "Could you have picked a worse time to travel? I'm filled with NRE, and I've got no way to express it."

"NRE?"

"New relationship energy. That's what Rob calls it." She laughed. "I don't know how he knows about it, since he hasn't been in a relationship since we were twenty-two."

"Ahh... Yeah. I'm filled with NRE myself. Glad I got my own room," she added, grinning slyly. "I woke up thinking about you this morning, and had to touch myself before I even got up to use the bathroom."

"I'm more of an evening person," Kelsey said. "I like to think about you all day, then touch myself to relax enough to sleep."

"You know, I don't know what your ideal is. Sexually."

"You mean frequency?"

"Sure."

"Hmm. What would I choose if I could have exactly what I wanted... That's kind of hard to say. When I'm not dating anyone, I touch myself a couple of times a week, more right before my period, less during it. But when I'm with a new partner, every day isn't out of the question."

"Good answer," Summer said. "Very good answer."

"I guess I'd like to get into a two or three times a week groove. But I'm flexible."

"I know," Summer said, her voice having turned a little sultry. "I think my schedule would be close to yours. But it's almost impossible to have too much sex at first."

"Right with you on that," Kelsey said. "I'm up for twice a day when I really vibe with someone new. There have been weeks when ten times is just right."

"Ten times?" Summer laughed. "You might be the first woman I've been with who has a more robust sex drive than I do. I'm not complaining, by the way. I can ramp it up."

"I think we'll just fall into a rhythm that's right for us. I'm not worried about that," Kelsey said. "I just wish I could be in your arms right now. It's kind of great, but kind of awful to be able to see you lying there, looking good enough to eat, but be unable to touch you."

"It's sweet torture that's going to end in three days. Get ready to rumble, good looking. I'm so hungry for you I'm ready to come home early."

Kelsey held up the carrot, grinning. "Grab a bite before you get on a plane. You'd be disappointed if you came all that way and just got this for dinner."

❦

Two days before Summer was set to return, Kelsey got up at the crack of dawn—for her. It was only seven, but nine was her preferred waking time. It was noon in Lisbon, though, and she and Summer had found that was the best time of day to insure they could have a long chat. She picked up her phone and dialed while walking into the bathroom to pee, not wanting to waste a minute.

"Hi there," she said when Summer answered. "What have you gotten up to today?"

"Smooch," she said, always starting off their talks with a kiss. "Just the usual. I got up pretty early and went to a little place near the apartment we've rented and had coffee and a pastry." She laughed. "I'm not even going to tell you how good the pastries are here. But the one I love is called God's bread, and the name's not deceiving."

"Hungry," Kelsey interrupted. "Don't taunt the hungry people."

"You're up so early you'll have plenty of time to get a donut as soon as we hang up."

"This is true…"

"Then I sat and sketched until Leah finally showed up. We waited around for Lori to arrive, but then it was time for me to eat again. The Portuguese like to have a cup of coffee and a pastry at eleven, so once we did that we were all finally ready to start the day."

"At eleven," Kelsey said, amazed that Summer would waste the whole morning just sitting.

"Closer to noon. This was ten minutes ago, Kelsey. Leah and Lori went to do a little shopping, and I'm walking around a park near our apartment. It's a nice one," she added. "Only having you here could make it nicer."

"I've never been to Europe, but you're making me want to go."

"Never?"

"Not even once. None of my friends have been, either. We're homebodies."

"You don't have to travel for me," Summer said. "I've got plenty of travel buddies. But if you want to…I'd love to have you with me any time I go."

"That's so nice," Kelsey sighed. She stood and left the bathroom, deferring the flush for after she hung up.

"The thought of traveling together?"

"No," Kelsey admitted, chuckling. "The fact that you'd go on your own if I didn't want to join you. That takes a lot of the pressure off. Know what I mean?"

"I think so. It makes things tough when you start to fall for a woman and feel like you have to take up her hobbies and like her travel plans and…all of the stuff."

"Yeah. All of the stuff. I don't feel that pressure with you. I was talking to my friends when we were bowling on Tuesday, and I got the impression they felt sorry for me. Like you going on your trip meant I wasn't worth sticking around for. But that's bullshit, and I made it clear that's not the kind of relationship I wanted."

"Know what I want?"

"No, but I'll try to give it to you if I can."

"I want to come home on Saturday and spend the night in your arms."

Kelsey sighed. "I want that, too. I tried to find someone to take over for me at work on Sunday, but no dice. People are already booked up with holiday parties. But I'm all yours on Saturday night."

"We land at five, so I'll be home just about when you're off work. Want me to have the car service drop me at your apartment?"

"Yes," Kelsey said immediately. "That's exactly what I want. On Sunday we can get up early and go visit your gramma. Then I can drop you off and head to work."

"My gramma will be around after Mass," Summer said, cranking up her sexy voice. "If I only have you for a couple of hours on Sunday morning, we're going to spend it making sparks fly."

CHAPTER FOURTEEN

ON SATURDAY EVENING, KELSEY WAS nearly home when her phone buzzed. She instructed it to read her the text, smiling when the robotic woman's voice said, "Whoever's in charge of customs should have his head on a pike. I've got about forty-five minutes to flush the last hour from my brain so I can focus on you alone. Can't wait!"

She and Summer had been texting all day, so Kelsey knew she'd gotten upgraded due to Leah's exalted status and points. That meant she would have had dinner. But Kelsey was starving, and with a forty-five minute cushion she was able to race across town to pick up a couple of things. She might be cutting it close, but sometimes the risk was worth the reward.

⊛

An hour later, Kelsey had set out the treats she'd bought, and had opened the bottle of Douro Branco she had chilling in a plastic bucket. It wasn't the silver ice bucket she assumed Summer had, but Summer had easily convinced her that things didn't hold a huge place in her life. She was kind of agnostic about stuff, as a matter of fact, which was yet another great quality.

Kelsey had been able to squeeze in a shower, and was just zipping up her jeans when the buzzer sounded. "I'm coming down," she said as she hit the entry key, then raced for the stairway, with the cool air making her still wet head cold. But that was probably a good thing. Anticipating Summer's return had made her temperature rise, and running down the stairs was adding a degree or two.

When she flung the door open, Summer was sitting on her suitcase, looking like she was waiting for a bus. "I was going to try to carry this thing up the stairs, but that seemed less than—"

Kelsey grasped her gloved hands and pulled her to her feet, planting a kiss to her lips before Summer was all the way vertical. They held each other in a very snug embrace, with Summer rubbing her face against Kelsey's neck when the kiss finally ended. "Missed you so much," she murmured. "Next trip, I'd love to have you with me."

"Just tell me how much to save, and I'll get right on it."

"Poland. You've got fifteen months. Leah's in charge of planning. I'll call her tomorrow and tell her I need my own room." She looked up and gazed into Kelsey's eyes, looking tired, and a little pale, but very, very happy. "We'll have dinner with the girls. Other than that, it'll just be you and me."

"Can we swing by Slovakia?"

"Consider it done. We'll peel off from Poland early and hire a guide. Leave it to me."

Kelsey pressed the elevator button, and the door creaked open. "I haven't taken this since I bought my TV. Hope it works."

Summer pulled her suitcase along, then put her arms around Kelsey as the doors reluctantly shut. "Want to make the trip seem shorter?"

Nodding, Kelsey faced her and wrapped her in her arms again. "I don't care if this is the longest elevator trip in history." Their lips met again, with Kelsey thrilled at how quickly they'd reconnected. It seemed like they'd just seen each other the day before, which was kind of awesome.

This time the elevator felt like it had sped to the top, even though she was sure it had sauntered along, same as usual. But when you were kissing such a delightful woman, time really flew. The doors rumbled when they opened, then Kelsey pulled the suitcase, with Summer holding onto her free arm tightly. "I'm so happy to be home," she sighed.

Kelsey opened the door, and helped Summer off with her coat. "I'll just hang this in the coat closet," she said, draping it neatly across the back of her reading chair.

"What's this?" Summer asked, standing by the wine bucket.

"I assumed you would have eaten, but I wanted to make your return as gentle as possible. I stopped by a Portuguese restaurant in Shadyside and bought pastel de nata. They looked so good I bought three."

"There's only two..."

Patting her stomach, Kelsey said, "I had to make sure they were up to snuff. Which they were," she said. "My wine guy said this white would go well with them, so we've got a whole meal. Wine and pastry."

"Such a thoughtful woman," Summer murmured, holding Kelsey again, then tilting her head slowly until their eyes met. "Such a beautiful woman." She traced her lips with her fingers. "I've thought about kissing you more times than I can count. It's so nice to actually be able to put those dreams into action."

Kelsey dipped her head and really gave her a hot one, releasing just a little of her pent-up desire. After a few seconds, Summer started to get into it, holding on tighter and eventually pressing Kelsey up against the wall. "That pastel is not going to get eaten if we keep this up," Summer murmured, still gazing intently at Kelsey's lips.

"I'm happy to jump into bed right now. But I thought you might like to shower and change. I pulled out some pajamas for you..."

Stepping back, Summer gazed at her for a few seconds. "So many decisions." She nodded. "A glass of wine, a little dessert, then a shower. Look at how decisive I am," she added, chuckling.

"Have a seat. I'll serve you."

"Every sentence sounds better than the last," she said, with her laugh sounding a little faint.

"Tired?" Kelsey asked as she put the pastry on a plate.

"Not horribly. I was able to get a long nap on the plane." She laughed. "Even if my sister was a horrible traveling companion, I might go with her just for the upgrades. Business class is so much nicer it's not even funny."

"So I've heard. My grandmother used to tell me about her flights back to Ireland. She made it sound like she was treated like royalty, but

I'm sure she didn't have the money to go business class. Have things changed that much?"

"Deregulation," Summer said. "Airlines used to compete on amenities. Now it's bare-bones so they can be the cheapest. Then they add on all of the things that used to be free. No matter what, the consumer will be screwed." She took the glass Kelsey handed her and they tapped them together. "I'd toast to the American dream, but that's too depressing." She leaned over and placed a soft kiss on Kelsey's lips. "To us. That's something I can pledge allegiance to."

"To us," Kelsey agreed. "I'm so glad we're on the same continent again." She took a sip, smiling at Summer. "My wine guy comes through again."

Summer nodded, then took a bite of the pastel de nata. "Just like Lisbon," she sighed. "What a nice, soft landing you've provided. Portuguese wine, pastry, and all-American kisses."

Kelsey put her arm around Summer's shoulders, with a sense of peace filling her when they each moved closer. "Tired?" she asked. "It's midnight in your brain."

"I'm tired from traveling, but I've been staying up late so this isn't even past my bedtime. But Monday morning's going to be a beast." She rubbed her shoulders against Kelsey. "I'm not going to think about that. I'm just going to enjoy tonight." She reached for her plate and brought it close. "Take a bite," she said. Kelsey did, then Summer nibbled at it. "This is better than the last one I had in Portugal. You did well."

"Thanks. I had to wade through all of the review sites to finally decide this place in Shadyside must be legit. It was top-rated everywhere. We'll have to go have a real dinner some night."

"Whatever you want," Summer said, so amenable when she was tired that Kelsey was pretty sure she'd agree to just about anything.

"Let me know if you want that shower. I'll fetch your pajamas."

"I would like one," Summer said. "And I'd like you to go with me."

"Really?"

"Uh-huh." She stood up and pulled Kelsey along with her. "Bring the pastry and a glass of wine."

Up for anything, Kelsey tagged along, pleased when Summer started to undress on the way to the bathroom. It was so nice to be with someone who didn't mind being naked. Her blouse and jeans were on the floor by the time they entered the bathroom, then Summer stood in front of Kelsey and gazed at her expectantly. "Want to finish?"

"I was just going to ask if I could."

Summer stuck her hands up in the air, and Kelsey smiled at her as she reached around and unfastened her bra.

"Ahhh," she sighed. "Freedom."

Kelsey whisked her undies off, then couldn't resist holding her close and kissing her, finding it hot to hold a completely naked woman when she was fully dressed. "This is fun," she murmured when Summer pulled away to turn on the water.

"I'd drag you in there with me, but I can see you got a jump on me. Your hair's still damp." She leaned close and sniffed all around Kelsey's neck. "The scent of a freshly showered woman is one of my favorite things."

"Some people don't like to smell soap or perfume, but I'm not one of them. Of course, with a few well-placed kisses I can get into sex just about any time. But if I had my choice, recently brushed teeth and clean skin is my preference."

"Mine too." She picked up the pastry, took a big bite, then washed it down with some wine. "I will deliver a sparkling clean body in just a few minutes."

"I'll be waiting. And watching." She laughed. "You don't mind if I watch, do you?"

"That's why I dragged you in here. Foreplay," she said, waggling her eyebrows.

"I'm not sure I need any," Kelsey said, chuckling softly. "I could have gotten busy in the lobby."

Summer left the bath for a second, returning with her toiletries. Pulling out some clips, she bent over and gathered her hair, then affixed it to the top of her head, sticking clips here and there to keep it from tumbling down. "I don't want to waste time drying my hair." She stood up and gave Kelsey a noisy kiss. "I've got better ways to spend the evening."

When she stepped into the shower, she adjusted the head to hit her on the chest. "Ahh," she sighed. "The second I step into warm water, I start to relax."

"I've never watched you shower," Kelsey said. "I might start getting up every morning to start my day off right."

Summer put her face close to the door, giving Kelsey a pointed look. "At seven thirty?"

"Why don't you start showering at night? Doesn't seven thirty p.m. sound like a better time?"

"I thought that would make you rethink. Such a night owl." She turned and gazed at Kelsey for a moment. "But the thought of having you watch me shower, then pulling you into bed for a raucous roll in the hay isn't a bad idea at all, is it. Bite?" Summer asked, opening the door a crack to stick her head out.

Kelsey almost leaned in and bit her neck, then it dawned on her that she wanted some of the pastry. "Open wide," she said, placing it right at the door to protect it from spray.

"I love this," Summer sighed, securing the door again. "While you watch me shower at night, will you always bring along a snack?"

"Absolutely. I just wish my shower was a little larger. I'd love to get in there with you, but we'd be bumping into one another."

"Not a bad idea… I've been thinking about bumping against your body kind of a lot." She turned to let the water cascade from her shoulders all the way down. Her nipples got hard in a second, with Kelsey unable to take her eyes off them. When Summer picked up the soap and worked up a lather in her hands, Kelsey was finally able to switch her focus, now expanding it to gaze at her entire breast when

Summer lifted her arm to wash herself. What great entertainment this was! She might be able to stop paying for cable if Summer's skin didn't get too dry from an hour long shower every night.

Summer had been acting like she was all alone, which was kind of cool. Then she turned and moved her face very close to the door. "Do you like watching?"

"A lot," Kelsey admitted. "After not seeing you for over two weeks…" She gazed at Summer for a few seconds. "There isn't a part of you I don't want to just stare at."

"As soon as I've washed all of the good parts, you can do a lot more than stare." Continuing to hold Kelsey's gaze, she put a little soap on her hand and propped her leg on the lip of the tub. Leaning forward, her hand slipped between her legs. A remarkably sexy smile curled her lips as she washed, then cupped water in her hand to rinse. "I know you're going to get me dirty again in no time at all, but I want to start off nice and clean."

Kelsey wanted to just watch for a day or two, but found herself on her feet. "You're clean enough." She grabbed two towels and tossed one over the door for Summer to take. When the water stopped, she slid the door open and started to efficiently dry Summer's body, wishing it was warm enough for her to lick the water off with her tongue. But December in Pittsburgh didn't really allow for that kind of play. They'd have to wait until summer for that. Luckily, she wasn't in a hurry.

"Let me help you slip into this," Kelsey said, holding up the blue and red flannel pajama top.

"Perfect. You can put the bottoms away. No need," she said, smirking.

Kelsey helped her out of the tub, then wrapped her snugly in her arms. "Could I be happier? A sweet-smelling woman, still warm from the shower, wearing just a top." Her hands went to her ass to grasp and squeeze her flesh. "And I get to touch her just about any way I want." She tilted her head down and placed a long, soft kiss on Summer's lips. "I think I'm as happy as I get."

"Not even close. Do you want to go into the living room and have me sit on your lap and make you wish we were in bed? Or should we cut to the chase?"

"Chase," Kelsey said. "Definitely chase." She turned and ran for the bed, launching herself onto it. "Ready!"

Summer walked up to her and put her hands on Kelsey's belly. "I missed touching you," she said, looking kind of wistful. "Even though I love traveling, and I love spending time with my sister, there was something missing." She pushed Kelsey's sweater up a little, then bent and kissed her skin, making her squirm. "You."

"I'm glad that you went," Kelsey said. "Honestly. If each of us can do the things that make us happy—even if that isn't something the other wants to do—we've got a much better chance at making this work. I'm truly looking forward to being in a fully adult relationship."

"That's one of the things I like best about you," Summer admitted, climbing onto the bed to sit astride Kelsey's hips. "You're not a fragile little thing, ready to shatter at the slightest bit of pressure. That's such a relief. I can't even tell you how reassuring that is." She leaned over, holding herself just a few inches from Kelsey's face. "That doesn't mean I won't support you when you're feeling fragile, because I definitely will. I simply don't feel like I have to worry about you all the time."

"You just have to worry about seeing me often enough. Our schedules might be a problem…"

"I don't think so. We get off work around the same time. Spending a few hours a day together is great. Really."

"I don't know," she said, certain Summer knew she was teasing. "I think you're going to have to convince me."

"I really, really want to be your girlfriend," Summer murmured, with a totally serious look covering her face. "If you'll just give me a tryout, I'll do my very best to impress you." She removed the clips from her hair, then ran her fingers through it. Once she had it straightened out, she tossed it over her shoulder and gazed into Kelsey's eyes. "Why don't we get started on giving me a serious case of bed head?

"That's not a bad idea…"

In a flash, Summer was off the bed. Quickly, she unzipped Kelsey's slacks and pulled them from her. In another second, she'd grasped her by the elbows and was pulling her into a sitting position. Before Kelsey could speak, her sweater was off. Then Summer kissed her with a stunning amount of passion, really going for it. Kelsey's libido had just been waiting for the invitation, and she felt a wave of desire hit her. Her hands slid under the roomy pajama top, delighted by the feel of Summer's smooth, cool skin.

Without realizing Summer had unfastened her bra, Kelsey blinked in surprise when she was lowered to the bed again, with the straps tickling her arms as it slipped away. "When—"

Pressing into her, Summer took over completely, with her hands roaming up and down Kelsey's sensitized body as her mouth was nearly devoured. "I thought about doing this to you nearly every day I was gone," Summer murmured, stopping for just a second to catch her breath.

"Welcome home," Kelsey sighed, thrilled to be gazing up into the prettiest hazel eyes on earth.

❀

It was after ten, but Summer had gotten a rush of energy from her last orgasm, and she couldn't even think of closing her eyes. They were under the blanket, but she was going to have to toss it off. Kelsey's body was pouring off so much heat they might not even need a sheet.

"You know what's funny?" Summer asked.

"I know a few funny things. But I'm interested in your perspective."

"I was just thinking of how I love to start off lovemaking with a squeaky clean body. But once I'm in a sex haze, I love all of the scents. I mean, they actually make me hot." She sniffed all around Kelsey's body, very easy to do since she was lying between her legs, with her head on her thigh. "You've got a very compelling scent."

Kelsey laughed a little. "This might sound odd, but I just got an image of a restaurant."

"A restaurant? How…?"

"When you walk in, you want a clean tablecloth, with spotless glasses and shining silverware. But after you've eaten, it's kind of pleasurable to look at the mess you've made. I hate it when you go someplace really nice and they're cleaning up all of the time. I like for my table to remind me of what a great meal I had."

"Something else we agree on," Summer said, not yet having found any major differences. "I certainly don't mind if my plate's whisked away the second I finish, but I prefer to be left alone. Especially when I'm with someone I care for. When we go out, I don't want anyone to come near. I want to concentrate on you."

"You do a really great job of that," Kelsey said, slipping her fingers into Summer's hair and gently scratching her scalp. "Even though we've only slept together a few times, I have no doubt that you're into me when we're making love. You commit," she said, laughing a little. "I never worry that I'm taking too long, or that your jaw's getting sore. I can relax."

"I'm known for my stamina," she said, letting out a soft laugh. Shifting to be able to climb up and lie next to Kelsey, she added, "A stray thought never enters my mind. I find you so fascinating that there's no room for one."

Kelsey put her arm around her and pulled her very close. "If I haven't made this clear, you were missed."

"I feel like I was missed. Coming home has been the highlight of my trip." She met Kelsey's eyes, seeing they were getting a little droopy. "I can't guarantee I'll be up with the dawn, but if you get up before I do, and you want to continue to welcome me home, you have my explicit permission."

"That might be in twenty minutes," Kelsey said, ineffectively hiding a yawn.

"I look forward to being woken any old time. I've got two weeks worth of kisses stored up, just waiting to deliver them right to your sweet mouth."

The next morning, Kelsey stood next to Summer at the bathroom sink, both brushing their teeth. After they'd rinsed, Summer leaned against the sink and held Kelsey in her arms, cuddling her like a kitten. She loved the way she smelled in the morning, and the warmth of her body perked Summer right up. It was like having a drink of sunshine, even when it was drizzly and gray outside.

They started to kiss, neither one of them wanting to waste one of their precious minutes. Summer was disappointed she hadn't set an alarm, but she'd decided to go easy on herself. Adjusting to the time change was going to take her a while. When she reached down to fill both of her hands with Kelsey's flesh, a loud, unpleasant buzz sounded. "What in the heck is that?"

"Someone calling from the lobby. Probably kids." She was obviously able to ignore the insistent noise, but Summer didn't have that ability.

"Mind if I go tell them to buzz off? Literally?"

"I'll do it." She kissed Summer one more time. "Don't go away."

"There aren't any windows in here," she called after her. "I'd have to sneak right past you to escape."

She heard Kelsey speaking, and expected her to return in seconds. But then she spoke again. Summer couldn't hear the words, but there was a quality to her voice that wasn't right. Puzzled, she walked into the living room to see what was up. Kelsey was right in front of her intercom—a metal square by the front door with a speaker and two buttons. She was clearly trying to be quiet, but Summer heard every word.

"Absolutely not. You may *not* come up."

A woman's voice crackled and cut out, but Summer heard her as well. "I only want to talk to you for five minutes, Kelsey. You owe me that much."

Kelsey had clearly forgotten her goal to speak quietly. "I owe you nothing! I'm not going to buzz you in, today or any day, so just leave. Please," she said, sounding like she was about to cry.

Summer was beyond puzzled, not thinking that any of Kelsey's exes would be desperate to have her back at this point. But she didn't want to eavesdrop. If something weird was going on, Kelsey would tell her.

She started for the bedroom, hoping she could close the door and shut out the voices. If that didn't work, she'd get in the shower. It was bad enough to fight with an ex. The last thing you wanted was a witness. She'd just gotten to the bedroom when the woman's tear-filled voice rang out, echoing through the living room.

"How can you be so cruel? You honestly won't spare five minutes for your own mother?"

"You gave up the right to call yourself that when you took off. My *real* mother would never show up at my house, uninvited, and try to force her way in."

Summer froze, then turned to see Kelsey leaning against the wall, pale and shaking. Rushing to her before she slid to the floor, Summer got an arm around her waist. The back of Kelsey's T-shirt was already damp, and she truly looked like she might faint.

The woman spoke again. "Please, Kelsey. Don't shut me out like this. Please."

Summer looked at her for a second, then quietly and calmly said, "Do you want me to go downstairs and handle this?"

She pulled her lips into her mouth, biting them until the flesh around them was an eerie white. Then she managed to say, "Buzz her in."

Summer reached up and left her hand on the buzzer for a moment. "Are you sure?"

She just nodded, not very convincingly, but Summer hit the button, letting it ring out harshly for several seconds. "I'll put my pants on and go meet her at the elevator. Come on," she urged. "Take a moment to get yourself together." She led Kelsey into the bedroom and guided her over to the bed. Then she bent over and looked into her eyes, seeing they were close to glassy. "Take some deep breaths. You don't have to rush." Cupping her cheek, she added, "It'll be okay, Kelsey. Promise."

Only many years of having to be fast on her feet with bill collectors, repo men, and various branches of law enforcement had given Summer the chops to handle situations like these. Of course, she had no idea what circumstances had led to this person showing up, but Kelsey clearly had two mothers—and only wanted one.

※

It seemed to take forever, but the elevator door eventually opened. Summer had walked down the short hallway to wait, and when the door slid open she let out a gasp. While the woman wasn't a dead-ringer for Kelsey, she might have been a warning sent from the future.

The woman looked like she was in her sixties, and had spent a good portion of her time on earth being beaten down by someone, or something, or maybe even struggling with a chronic illness.

Her hair was mostly very close to Kelsey's color, but it was beginning to gray at the temples. It was long enough to be pulled back in a ponytail, revealing features that would have made her quite attractive if she hadn't looked so haggard.

If Summer had seen this woman on the street, she wouldn't have paid her any attention at all, even though she was taller than average, and had those pretty, yet worn features. She was one of those people who blended in with the woodwork.

Summer put her hand out and forced herself to offer a welcoming smile. "Summer Hayes, Kelsey's…" She didn't know how to finish that sentence, given she didn't know what Kelsey wanted her to reveal, so she added, "Friend."

The woman looked dazed, as well as tentative as she exited the elevator and blinked at Summer a few times. "I'm Marianne Fencik," she said, still standing right in front of the elevator door.

Summer wasn't sure what to say, so she went with her usual—tell the truth and deal with the fallout. "Obviously, Kelsey's not happy that you stopped by. She's getting herself together now. Um…I didn't know you existed, so I'm a little out of my depth here."

The woman tilted her head, giving Summer a curious look. "Are you Kelsey's girlfriend?"

"Yes. We're just starting out, but yes," Summer said, revealing more than she normally would to a perfect stranger. But it seemed vital to be forthcoming. While she had no idea what had gone on, Marianne and Kelsey were both shook. Badly. And when emotions ran high, Summer liked being as honest as possible. "Even though we haven't known each other long, I'm very fond of her."

Marianne nodded, then she stood up straight and stuck her chin out, looking a little more sure of herself. "It's taken me years to get up the nerve to do this, and now that I've come this far I feel like I *can't* leave without seeing her."

"I think she's willing," Summer said, starting to lead her down the hall. "Well, not willing, but… I think she'll come out of her room if we give her a few minutes."

As they walked, Marianne seemed to loosen up slightly. "I'm so sorry for coming at this time of day, but I've tried every other hour, and she's never home. I'm leaving town tomorrow, so I had to be more aggressive. I thought by coming early I might catch her before she could get away again."

"Um, she hasn't answered when you've been here before?"

"I haven't bothered to ring. Kitty told me what kind of car she drives, so I could see she hasn't been home."

"Kitty?" Summer knew her mouth was gaping open, but this story was getting weirder by the minute.

"Do you know Kitty?"

"I do. Not well, of course. But I've been there for dinner." They were at the door, and she pushed it open, relieved to see that Kelsey was still hiding in her room. Actually, that might have been a bad sign, but it was helpful since Summer needed a minute to get settled.

Marianne stood in the doorway, looking around like she was investigating an animal's den, worried the beast might emerge at any second and maul her. Her mouth slid into a smile as her gaze landed on the bookshelves that filled the window wall. "She still loves to read," she said softly, tearing up.

"She does," Summer said. "Reading sometimes makes her stay up too late at night, but once she gets started on a book she likes, she can't stop. Um, we haven't made coffee yet, but I could use some. Can I interest you?"

"I think I'm jittery enough, but I'd love a glass of water."

Summer walked over to Kelsey's coffee maker and started to busy herself with setting it up. Then she flipped it on, slightly calmed by the reassuring noises of the heating element. After filling a glass with water, she walked over by the bookcases and handed it to Marianne. "Looks like we've got a few minutes. Are you willing to tell me what the deal is? Are either of the people Kelsey claims as her parents biologically related to her?"

"George is. Kitty's her step-mom."

"Ahh. And you...don't live around here?"

"I moved to California when Kelsey was very young," she said, with her gaze dropping to the floor. "I haven't seen her since she was about to enter second grade." She bit at her lips, mirroring the gesture Kelsey had made just a few minutes earlier. "I tried to reach out to her, of course, hundreds of times, but she took Kitty on as her mother, and wanted nothing to do with me."

"As a second-grader?" Summer asked, stunned.

"I called, I wrote, sent presents..." She sighed heavily, looking absolutely bereft. "There was nothing I could do to reach her. If it hadn't been for Kitty letting me know Kelsey was doing well, I might have lost my mind."

"She's in touch...regularly? Does Kelsey know that?"

"Not regularly," Marianne said clearly. "It's been years since she's told me anything to speak of. But I wrote and called so many times after I got to Pittsburgh that I must have worn her down." She met Summer's gaze and said, "I've just lost my brother, the last of my immediate family. I think that made her feel sorry for me."

"I'm sorry to hear that," Summer said. She might have gone on, but it was odd offering condolences to a total stranger. When you didn't know the deceased or the survivor, you were just saying sympathetic words that you couldn't have connected to emotionally.

Summer walked back over to the coffee maker and poured a cup, adding a splash of milk. Warming her hands on the cup, she went to sit on the sofa, reassured to be seated on a piece of furniture she was somewhat familiar with. In times of stress, she loved to have a few recognizable signposts nearby. "My mind's reeling," she admitted, "but I'm clear-headed enough to know you two had better get busy if you're going to have any time to talk. Kelsey's got to be at work soon."

Marianne's face fell. "On a Sunday?"

"She works every weekend." She put her cup down and stood. "Be right back."

She opened the bedroom door tentatively, but Kelsey wasn't in the room. "Kelsey?"

"I'm in here."

The bathroom door was mostly open, revealing a sober-looking woman standing in front of the mirror, hands on the counter, leaning over to stare at herself. She'd taken a very quick shower, and was fully dressed in a dark sweater and jeans. She looked a bit like she was about to enter a church for a funeral, and knew she had to gather her composure to get through the service.

Summer put a hand on her shoulder, then stood close and leaned against her. "I don't know about you, but I'd rather be kissing."

Her mouth twitched slightly, hinting at a smile. "Ditto. Instead, I'm trying to decide if I could survive the jump from the third floor. You know, I could have saved fifty bucks a month if I'd taken the first floor unit, which would have come in handy today. Serves me right for being such a spendthrift."

"What do you want to do?" Summer scratched her back through her sweater, smiling when Kelsey closed her eyes and pushed back against her hand.

"I want to call in sick, go back to bed, and pull the covers over my head. I don't want to think, I don't want to talk, and I don't want anyone to talk to me."

"Okay," Summer said, patting her briskly. "I'll see your guest to the door, then go home and wait for your call." Adding another pat, she said, "It's all right if it takes you a few days to get back to me."

She'd no sooner turned than Kelsey grasped her from the back and hugged her. "I can't do any of that, but thanks for letting me have the fantasy. Do you mind if I go talk to her for a minute—alone?"

"Not a bit. Oh. She asked if I was your girlfriend, and I confirmed that I was. Just an FYI."

"Mmm," she murmured. "That's fine."

"Why don't I just sneak out. You need some privacy."

"No!" She actually looked a little panicked. "If you can wait, I'd appreciate it. I might need a push to get me out the door. I've got appointments scheduled back-to-back, so I've got to go in."

Summer picked up her phone and went to her purse to pull out her earphones. "I'll listen to music." When it was clear Kelsey wasn't able to open the door, Summer went to her and wrapped her in a hug. "You're not a little girl anymore. You and your…mother are both adults. You've got this," she insisted.

"Thanks. Um, I guess I've got some explaining to do," she said, again not meeting Summer's eyes.

"We've got plenty of time for that. Go on now," she urged. "Adult to adult."

She stood up tall and squared her shoulders. "Thanks," she said, striding for the door.

⊛

There was an old woman standing by the window. Graying hair, lined face, posture a couple degrees off vertical. In Kelsey's head, her mother was a young, dark-haired beauty, with gorgeous skin, and pale, curious eyes. But this woman looked like all of the joy as well as the color had been sucked right out of her. How had her eyes gone from robin's egg blue to gray?

"Hi," Kelsey said, startling the woman, who turned toward her now, with her jaw starting to tremble. Slowly, a tentative smile formed, and she spoke, with her voice hurling Kelsey into the past.

"What a beautiful woman you've become."

"Thank you," Kelsey said, shaking so hard she knew her voice was trembling too. "Um, you obviously know I'm not interested in seeing you, so…" She paused, too polite to finish the sentence, even though she wanted to.

"Your uncle died last week, Kelsey, and I'm having a memorial service for him this afternoon. All of the Fencik cousins I'm still in contact with will be there and I thought…" She took a breath. "It's been *so* long. I thought there was a chance you'd come."

Now that she was talking, or stating her case, she looked a little more vital. Her color got better, making her skin less chalky. But it was still hard to look at her and remember the woman who'd walked out of the house that spring day, carrying a single suitcase while crying like she'd lost everything.

"I can't," Kelsey said "Even if I didn't have to work, it's just been too long. I've moved on, and I assume you have too. I think it's better to go on like we have been."

Her mother came closer, approaching her like she would a snake. "But you're my child. I'll never move on from you. Never."

Looking at her was too weird, so Kelsey went into the kitchen to pour a cup of coffee. "Um, I understand we come at this from different perspectives," she said, fumbling with a cup and nearly dropping it. "So let's say that *I've* moved on. Kitty's my mom." She turned her head to see the stricken look on her birth mother's face. Thankfully, that wounded expression didn't give her even a hint of pleasure. Those early teenaged fantasies where she went to California and beat this woman to a bloody pulp had stopped long ago. Now she just wanted her to go away. "Um,

I'm sorry about your brother. I don't remember him very well, but you were close, right?"

"Of course we were," she said, starting to cry. "You were crazy about him, Kelsey. You don't remember when he'd take you down to the fire station and let you sit in the truck?"

A memory hit her and she nodded. "I'd packed that away," she said softly. "But, yes, I remember. I guess not seeing him for so long…" She was compelled to add something hurtful, but got hold of herself. It was silly to make a big deal of her uncle having dropped her like a hot rock so long ago.

"That wasn't his choice."

"Doesn't matter," Kelsey said crisply. She wasn't about to get into an argument over who did what and why they did it.

"Are you…" Marianne sucked in an audible breath. "Are you happy, sweetheart?" Tears were coursing down her cheeks now, but Kelsey's heartstrings were only mildly tugged. Complete abandonment did a pretty good job of severing even the strongest bond.

"I *am*," she said, putting some extra emphasis into her words. "My parents have been awesome."

"And you have a girlfriend who seems very kind."

"She is. So…I'm fine. I've got a good job that I like, and my life is going well."

"What do you do? I've spent an awful lot of time trying to find out anything about you, but your Facebook page is locked down and you don't seem to have anything else. I thought everyone used LinkedIn."

"Not me. I'm pretty private," she said, not adding that she'd been very careful with her online presence, never even using a photo of herself in her profile expressly so she couldn't be found. The last thing she was going to do was make it obvious where she worked. She would *not* be stalked.

She took a big gulp of coffee, then set the cup down. "I…It's hard for me to be this cruel, but I don't want to have a relationship with you. I think it would be better if you'd try to do what I've done. Stop thinking of the past any more than you have to."

"You're my child," she said again, jerking backward as if Kelsey had slugged her. "I think of you every single day, and I always will."

"I'm sorry," Kelsey said, her stomach burning from the tension. "I wish you could forget about me, but I guess that's asking a lot." She walked over to stand in front of her birth mother, somewhat cheered to see that they were eye-to-eye. In her now infrequent nightmares, her mother towered over her when she violently pushed Kelsey away and slammed the door in her face.

Kelsey extended her hand, nearly touching the tan ski jacket her mother wore, just to make sure she was real. But she pulled back and stood there with her hand hovering in the air for a few seconds. "Again, I hate to be rude, but I've got to get to work."

It had been a while since Kelsey had to occupy her mind while stuck in a church, but at that moment her mother looked exactly like an image she'd seen of Our Lady of Sorrows. The portrait showed the Virgin Mary with a face lined with pain, looking like an old, beaten-down woman, so strikingly different from the paintings of the vibrant woman-child who'd agreed to bear Jesus.

Kelsey wished with all of her might that she could pull some sort of positive, nurturing connection to this woman from her memory bank, but she'd intentionally deadened herself to whatever lingering love...or heartache she'd retained. There were simply not enough embers to even consider stoking a flame of connection.

"I'm sorry I can't give you what you want," Kelsey said, struggling to keep her voice firm. "But I can't. I'd prefer you didn't contact me again, but...that's probably not realistic either." She stopped when she considered that her careful and intentional plans to remain off the grid hadn't worked. "How did you find me?"

"Don't be angry with her," she said quickly. "Kitty mostly ignores my calls and letters, but I badgered her enough this time that she finally answered."

"That's…disappointing," Kelsey said, with her stomach turning at the concept of her mom betraying her so cruelly.

"She's a mom too, honey. I think she put herself in my place."

Kelsey raised her eyebrows, tempted to unload about how her real mom would have died before abandoning her. But she didn't want to go down that road. If she let even a portion of her anger out, it might knock the whole damn building down.

"All Kitty gave me is your address. No phone. After I leave tomorrow, I won't be able to call you."

Kelsey looked into her eyes, with the vaguely creepy sensation of looking into a mirror to the future. If she could manage it, she was going to avoid having her heart broken. Her mother was only around fifty-five, but looked much older. "As I said, I think that's best."

Clearly defeated, the woman started for the door, almost idly commenting, "I was surprised to learn you were lesbian."

"There's a lot you don't know," she said, with a suddenly unquenchable desire to hurt her. A desire she hadn't had even a flicker of for over ten years burned so bright it made her blood boil. "When you abandon your child, you miss a few highlights when you drop in a quarter of a century later." She opened the door, having to stop herself from grasping her by the shoulder and throwing her into the hallway. "Don't come back," she said, turning her back as she shut the door hard. She knew she should have felt bad for being so abrupt, but she couldn't afford to see her mother's face when the door slammed. The last thing she needed was another image to burn itself into her memory. The ones she had from her childhood were bad enough. That worst one, the one she'd worked so hard to block, came back again. Her mommy rushing to the car, head down, crying piteously, while Kelsey tried to understand why a short trip to visit a relative in California was making her so terrifyingly sad.

❧

When Summer was tense, or irritable, or bored, or preoccupied… Whenever Summer had the *opportunity*, she drew. She didn't have any supplies with her, but Kelsey had a computer and a printer on a small desk, and a mechanical pencil and a felt-tipped marker lying next to some paperwork. That wasn't much, but the mechanical pencil and a sheet of paper from the printer tray worked well enough.

She was listening to some Liszt, and started thinking of the tiles she'd done for the Pittsburgh Symphony. She wasn't a huge classical music fan, but there was a frantic piano piece she liked and often played when her nerves needed calming. She had no idea if playing wild music calmed other people down, but it seemed to work for her.

Drawing a clarinet from memory wasn't the easiest thing in the world, mainly because she didn't think she'd ever held one in her hands, but she thought she was doing a decent job. She must have been concentrating pretty well, because she levitated when Kelsey touched her shoulder.

"Jesus!" she gasped, clutching the placket of her shirt. "My startle response must be off the charts."

"Sorry," Kelsey said, looking very hangdog.

Summer tugged her earbuds out and stood up. "How are you?" she asked, gripping her upper arms and looking at her carefully.

"Not great. But I've got to get to work." She looked around, seeming puzzled. "Can you push the button on the door when you leave? It'll lock when you close it."

"I can go now."

"I don't want to rush you…"

"Are you sure you're all right? I can drive you to work if you want. You look pretty out of it."

"I'm all right," she said, nodding. "I'm…" She nodded again, with a little more confidence. "I can pull it together."

"Are you sure?" Summer slid her hand up and cupped her cheek. "Promise you're all right to drive."

"I promise," she said, with her focus sharpening.

"All right. I was going to have dinner with my parents…Robert and Jackie, but I'm going to cancel. Come by my apartment when you're through for the day. We can talk if you want, but if you don't want to I can at least feed you."

"I'm all right," she said, putting her hands in her hair and smoothing it out. "I really am. I appreciate your offer, but I think I'd rather come home and go to bed. I'm not going to be good company."

"I'm not looking for entertainment," Summer said, searching her eyes. "I want to take care of you if you're shaky."

She let a slight smile show. "Talking about under-cabinet lighting, knife drawers, and gap fillers all day should snap me back into my routine."

Summer continued to look at her eyes. "Hiding out when you're upset isn't the best idea…"

"I know that," she said, her voice now gentle. "I just need to let things settle. Give me a little time."

"Okay," Summer said, pulling away. "You can have as much as you need." She picked up her coat and her purse, then gripped the handle of her suitcase. "Are you ready?"

"Yeah, yeah," she said, clearly distracted. "I've got to drop you off."

"I can call for a car. Seriously."

Kelsey put her arms around her and hugged her tightly for just a few seconds. "I wish this morning had been a hell of a lot less tense." She checked her watch. "I can drop you off, but I'll be cutting it close."

"Go. I'll call a car and lock up when it gets here." She tilted her head to kiss Kelsey's cheek. "Call me," she said, as Kelsey walked toward the door. Summer was tempted to call Sedlak Brothers and tell them Kelsey was sick, then pin her down to find out what in the holy fuck was going on. But that wasn't her style. She could wait to hear what she hoped would be a perfectly logical reason for withholding the fact that Kelsey had turned her back on her birth mother. That was going to have to be one fuck of a fantastic reason, but the woman she was falling for wouldn't have hidden it without cause. But what on earth could that cause possibly be?

Chapter Fifteen

Kelsey had four appointments to slog through, with one drop-in waiting over an hour for her to finish with the previous client. Now it was six o'clock, and she was grimly driving to her parents' home.

She had a key, but never used it. They weren't formal people in any way, but she liked to respect their privacy. Until now, she'd always been sure they respected hers, too. Now even that foundational belief was shaken.

Her mom answered the door, and the moment she saw Kelsey's face she started to apologize. "I talked to her the day her brother died," she said, with the words tumbling out while Kelsey was still in the doorway. "She sounded so heartbroken, honey. I thought about how supportive you were when my sister was going through her chemotherapy, and I thought you might be able to help her like you did..." She pressed her lips together and started to cry, something Kelsey had seen her do very rarely. "I know I shouldn't have spoken to her, but I just...couldn't turn my back."

It was impossible to simply stand there like an oaf, watching her mom cry, so she walked inside and closed the door behind herself. After shrugging out of her coat, she bent over to wrap her in a hug. "It's all right," she soothed. "I know she appealed to your good nature."

"She's missed so much. It breaks my heart."

"Uh-huh." Kelsey patted her, then stood up. "Is Dad downstairs?"

"Sunday night football comes on in two hours," she said, blotting her eyes with a tissue she'd pulled from a handy box. "You don't expect him to miss a minute of the pre-game, do you?"

"He's going to wonder who you're talking to, but I'd like to have a minute alone. Is that okay?"

"I don't think he heard you come in. If he had, he'd be yelling up the stairs, right?"

"I guess you're right. The Maliar intercom," she said, making a familiar joke about her father's ability to make himself heard through layers of plasterboard and insulation. She sat down on one of the seldom-used floral wingback chairs in the tiny living room, watching her mom take the other, using just a third of the cushion to perch on the edge, expectantly.

"I can understand how she appealed to your good nature, Mom, but why didn't you tell me you'd given her my address. Feeling trapped like I did was an awful way to wake up."

"I'm so sorry," she murmured, looking totally humiliated. "I thought there was a chance you wouldn't connect, and then you wouldn't even have to know about it…" She trailed off, then meekly added, "I was afraid to admit what I'd done."

Kelsey's anger started to evaporate. Her mom had been put in an awful position, and being angry with her just wasn't right.

"Let's put today aside. How often have you talked to…Marianne," she said, deciding she liked the distance it created to call her birth mother by her first name.

Her mom closed her eyes for a moment. "Not that often. Definitely less than she wanted."

"And this started…when?" she asked, realizing this was going to be like pulling teeth.

Her mom sighed and let her head drop slightly. "I knew about the whole situation before we married, of course. But your dad didn't warn me that she might call."

"And she did?"

"Right away," her mom said, nodding soberly. "She had a million questions about you, and I couldn't tell her it was none of her business." She blinked slowly. "She's your mother, honey."

"You're my mom," Kelsey said, not willing to give an inch on this one. "You're more of a mom than she ever was."

"Okay," she said softly. "Marianne gave birth to you. I can't imagine that's something you can just walk away from. Not if you're any kind of decent human being."

"A decent human being doesn't walk out on her little girl," Kelsey said, feeling her anger start to burn again.

"You know it wasn't like that. She didn't want to leave you, honey. Things were very, very tough for her, and she did what she thought she had to do."

Kelsey gazed at her for a long minute. "What would make you leave me behind to move across the country? I'm serious, Mom. What would it have taken?"

"I wouldn't have ever left you," she said quietly. "But I've never been in Marianne's situation. You never know what you'll do until you walk a mile in someone's shoes."

"But you just said you wouldn't have done the same thing."

"I…I'm mentally healthy, Kelsey. Your mom wasn't. At the time, that is. She seems okay now, but she was in a bad place then. And while I know it feels like she cut off ties with you, you know that's not true."

"It *is* true," she said coldly. "Phone calls and presents aren't substitutes for reading to your child and tucking her into bed. Who was there when I was sick? You were. Who cuddled me when I had nightmares? You did. You're my mom, and even though I had to go through hell to get you, I'm very, very happy with how things turned out." She got up and knelt next to her mom's chair, leaning in to hold her in a tender embrace. "You're the mom I chose, and that's the best decision I ever made." She kissed her cheek, then patted it noisily. "Now stop talking to Marianne. She has my address, and if she wants to contact me, she can. Okay?"

Her mom looked at her for a long time, seeming to really study her. "Did you let her explain herself? Did you even let her into your apartment?"

"I let her in," she said, getting to her feet. "Actually, I only did that because of the pleading look Summer was giving me. That wasn't a surprise, since she's nicer than I am."

"No, she's not," her mom said, gazing up at her with moist eyes. "She just hasn't been hurt like you have."

"I think she's been hurt a lot, Mom. I can pretty much guarantee she's more resilient than I am."

"So? Did you let Marianne talk?"

"Not really. I didn't want to have to go to work with swollen eyes, so we were only together for a couple of minutes."

Her mom blinked up at her. "You just let her leave?"

"Um, it's more accurate to say I told her to leave, and pretty much slammed the door before she was all the way out." She winced at the astounded expression that covered her mom's face. "I'm not exactly proud of that, but she wouldn't take no for an answer."

"She has a story to tell you, Kelsey. An important one. I honestly think you should hear her out. It's the Christian thing to do."

"Uh-huh." She reached down and took her mom's hand, easily pulling her to her feet. "Let's use the Maliar intercom to see if Dad wants to share some popcorn while he watches the game."

"How do you know we've already had dinner?"

"It's after six. That's the sweet spot for the dessert window. I'd bet my paycheck you finished your meal at least a half hour ago."

Her mom gazed at her for a minute, clearly wanting to continue the Marianne conversation, but respecting Kelsey's boundaries. "You win this time. But one of these days we're going to surprise you and eat late. I might get your dad to wait until…six thirty." She let out a laugh. "I'd have to move the clocks forward, but it could happen."

After struggling through the worst mood she'd been in during her adult life, Kelsey finally texted Summer on Tuesday afternoon. They didn't have a break room at Sedlak Brothers, but most people swung by the espresso maker in the Italian country kitchen at some point in the afternoon just to get away from lookie-loos and the phone.

She set her phone down on the counter and busied herself making a cappuccino, impatiently waiting for Summer to reply. It took her ten minutes, but the ellipse eventually flickered to life.

Good to hear from you. Want to come over tonight?

Kelsey picked up the phone and replied. *I will skip my bowling league to meet up. What time?*

I'll be home by six. I'll make dinner.

Let me pick up carryouts. Do you like Italian?

Love it, she typed, adding an emoji of pasta and another of red wine. *See you soon.*

Kelsey put the phone in her back pocket and swallowed her short drink in one gulp. She had a lot of work to finish before she could leave, but she was going to take off on time, even if she had to come in early on Friday to finish up. She'd kept Summer waiting long enough. They had to talk.

CHAPTER SIXTEEN

THEY'D NEVER SHARED ITALIAN FOOD, so Kelsey was flying a little blind when she ordered their dinner. She picked pasta, chicken, and a couple of vegetables, assuming Summer would like at least one of them. The guy at reception announced her at six thirty, and she smiled as the elevator door opened and Summer stood there.

"I love the fact that you come down to the elevator. It's very welcoming," Kelsey said, sliding an arm around Summer to pull her close for a kiss. "I hope my animal-like reclusiveness hasn't driven you mad. When I'm upset, I tend to hide under the porch until I'm sure it's safe to come out."

"Mmm," Summer said, looking up at her. "I'm just the opposite. I want a load of attention when something's bothering me. I need too much, if you ask Natalie."

"I have no plans on asking Natalie anything," Kelsey said as they started to walk back down the hall. "You know how a novel can have an unreliable narrator?"

"I think so. I'm not much of a reader, as you know, but I assume it's someone you're supposed to believe, but can't."

"Right. Natalie's an unreliable narrator. If she let you go, her opinion is worthless."

Summer touched her back as she guided her in and locked the door. "Well, I'm the one who pulled the plug. But she had a lot of opportunities to make me not want to, so I guess her opinion is a bit suspect." She took the bag from Kelsey's hand. "This smells fantastic."

"It usually is. This is my go-to spot when I need to carbo load before a big race."

Summer raised an eyebrow as she pulled plates out of a cabinet. "You're a runner?"

"Not yet," she said, maintaining a straight face. "I want to make sure I like everything about running before I commit to it. I started with carbo loading, which I'm really fond of. I just haven't graduated to the next step yet."

Summer walked around the counter and put her arms around Kelsey's waist. Then she rested her head on her shoulder while letting out a heavy sigh. "Even though we've only known each other for a month, you've become a habit. It's only been two days, but I was having withdrawal symptoms all morning."

Kelsey tilted her head so her chin rested upon Summer's. "I'm really sorry I went to ground. I don't know how to break the habit, but I'm willing to try."

Pulling away, Summer said, "It's not a problem now, but it might be if we eventually live together. It would be weird living in silence for a day or two, especially if I was desperate to talk."

"Then I'll figure out a way to change before we move in together. I can be very determined when I have a goal."

"Wow," Summer said as she started to open the containers. "My goal is to not keel over after eating all of this."

"We don't have to gorge ourselves. I bought things that will warm up well for lunch tomorrow."

"I thought you said you worked hard when you had a goal. We have to make a huge dent in this. Mmm. Mmm," she sighed. "I love eggplant parm. We might have to arm wrestle over it if it's your favorite too."

"I'm crazy for the spaghetti ai limone. Lemony goodness in a light cream sauce and shrimp in every bite."

"Now I want that. We still might have to wrestle."

"Maybe after dinner," Kelsey said. "Wrestling with you is better than all of this food put together."

Summer passed by her, with the pasta on a plate. She held it under Kelsey's nose for a second, saying, "I bet you don't think that when you're really hungry."

"I'm *really* hungry. Let me wash my hands real quick then we can dive in."

"Mine are already washed, and I can't guarantee I'll wait for you."

"Kind of harsh, but fair." Kelsey stood at the sink and scrubbed her hands, watching Summer arrange the food carefully, clearly trying to make it look as good as it smelled. She approached everything like it could be made better with a little composition, a very appealing trait.

"Okay. I'm clean and hungry. Let's get at it."

Summer stuck to her favorite, whipping through a hearty portion of the eggplant while Kelsey forced herself to eat slowly so she didn't get too full too fast. They barely spoke, but things felt easy between them, which was a massive relief. Some women would be prickly for weeks when they'd learned you'd kept something big from them.

Slamming her fork to the table, Summer pushed her chair back. "That evil eggplant's going to entice me to eat the whole order. Really good stuff," she said, smiling at Kelsey. "Thanks for taking care of dinner. I certainly don't mind cooking, but I love to have dinner simply appear once in a while."

"You've got to have a bite of this spaghetti. The chicken marsala will be good tomorrow, but this loses something when it's warmed up."

Summer took the offered bite, then pushed Kelsey's hand down to the plate so she twirled her fork again. "More," she demanded. "That's sinfully good."

"I'm sure I'll finish this if you let me, so I'd appreciate some assistance." She held up another forkful. "Open wide."

Summer grinned at her as she took the bite, moaning with satisfaction. "So light. So lemony." She kissed her fingers, then cast a glance at the broccoli raab, which had been ignored. "I should have started there, but I never do. Sorry no one loves you, healthy green vegetable."

"It's not perfect on the second day, but I'll eat it tomorrow," Kelsey said.

Summer stood and started to move the plates into the kitchen. Kelsey followed behind and put a hand on her shoulder. "Let me clean up."

"Later." Summer took her hand and led her over to the living room. Kelsey took the sofa and Summer turned to the left, settling onto one of her comfortable upholstered chairs. "As you might guess, I've got some questions about what happened on Sunday morning. Should I start?"

"I could probably save you the trouble and just put out the facts, but feel free."

"All right." Summer tucked a foot under herself, perching like a bird as she leaned against the arm of her chair, shifting forward to be closer to Kelsey. "My big question is why didn't you tell me Kitty was your stepmom. That's a big detail to omit."

"Um…" She leaned back and thought for a minute. "To be honest, I try really hard to forget we're not related by blood. Sometimes I do such a good job of it that it doesn't occur to me to mention it."

Summer stared at her, looking pretty unhappy. "You're not serious, are you?"

"I am. Totally."

"Kelsey," she said, with her voice low and soft. "It's not possible to forget your mother abandoned you."

"I think it's close to possible. Really. I'm getting the impression that you think I was intentionally keeping Marianne's existence a secret, but I wasn't. I raced you down to Monroeville because I wanted you to meet the important people in my life. My birth mother isn't in that category." She heard her voice rising and gaining a little volume. "She just isn't."

"Okay," Summer said, nodding slowly. "I can understand wanting that to be true. And maybe you've spent hundreds of hours in therapy working through all of your feelings. But even if you've had the best therapy in the world, being abandoned by your mother leaves a mark, Kelsey. Come on now. Let's face facts."

"I am! It's a fact that I rarely think of her. It's a fact that she's not important to me. And it's a fact that I don't want her in my life."

"But—"

"I don't have a lot of memories from when she lived with us, but I recall a woman who, I now realize, was dreadfully unhappy. Anxious. Depressed. Emotionally unavailable. Then Kitty arrived, and I found out how fantastic it was to have a mom who wanted to be there. I got an upgrade," she insisted. "I started out with a fairly shitty mom, and eventually got the one I should have had from the beginning. My mom's the best," she said firmly.

"But you had to have been—"

"I will admit that having Marianne leave screwed me up for a few years," she interrupted. "But I got over it." She leaned over to rest her forearms on her knees, getting a little closer to Summer. "I know you've had some traumatic things happen to you."

"Of course I have. Quite a few."

"Have you told me about every single one of them?"

"I haven't. No," she said softly. "We've just scratched the surface, Kelsey. Some stuff has to come up organically."

"Why?" she asked, certain she was winning the point.

"Because it shows really bad judgment to start off a relationship by giving a woman a typed list of all of the shitty things that have happened to you. I like to reveal things when they come up…" She wagged her finger at Kelsey. "I see what you're doing, and I don't like it. This isn't a minor thing. It's got to be the biggest trauma of your life."

"It has been," she admitted. "And I would have told you about Marianne if I'd thought about her when we were together. But she honestly hadn't crossed my mind for a while. I have a nice, secure vault in my head where I store my memories of her. When some event made the vault open up, I would have talked about her."

"That…works for you?"

"Uh-huh. Really well."

"What about when we were at your parents' house? Are you seriously telling me you didn't think of Marianne when I asked why you had so few baby pictures on your wall?"

"I thought of her briefly," she admitted. "But then my mom walked over and Marianne disappeared again. I swear that's true. My mom is the fresh air that blows the bad stuff out."

She tilted her head, clearly puzzled. "You couldn't possibly recall much about Marianne's leaving. Yet you still have no interest in hearing her out?"

"None. She's like the old beater I got when I learned to drive."

"The woman who gave birth to you is like an old car?"

"In a way. That car served its purpose, then I traded it in. The car I chose for myself, the one I'm still driving, is exactly what I wanted. I never, ever wish I could drive the old one again. It doesn't cross my mind."

"Um, I'm really not trying to hurt your feelings," Summer said, sounding a little tentative, "but that's a pretty awful way to think of your birth mother. She sure acted like she cared for you deeply."

"Not deep enough to stick around. She chose her own happiness over mine, and that's not something a good mom would do. Sorry," she said, truly ready to put this to bed.

"Do you know why she left?"

"Yep." She could feel her features harden. "She was cheating on my dad, and when she was caught, she moved to California to start over." She slapped her hands together as if she were dusting them off. "No fuss. No muss."

"Oh, Kelsey," Summer said, with so much empathy infusing her face it made Kelsey ache for her young self. "I'm so sorry." She took a breath. "That sounds a little like Kevin's situation. He hasn't invested a moment trying to track his dad down. Randy's history—justifiably." She reached across and took Kelsey's hand, holding it tightly.

"That sounds about right. Marianne wanted out, and I let her go. She might want to act like a mother now, but I've got one who fulfills all of my mothering needs."

"But Kevin's situation is a little different." Her voice got even softer when she said, "He only knows Robert as his dad. But it's not like that for you. You had a real relationship with your mom, even if she was… distracted, or depressed, or whatever."

"I know that," she said, drumming her fingers on the arm of the sofa for a minute or two, anxious to make this stop. "Okay," she said, leaning over again. "Try this analogy on. I was a little acorn, just beginning to sprout in the shade of an unhealthy oak. The oak fell, leaving me more light and air and room to grow. I could spend my time longing for that oak, but I chose to be thankful for the sun, and the fresh air, and the space I have. All of that is because of Kitty's love and attention. She's given me the tools I needed to grow. She's my sun."

"All right," she said, still speaking quietly. "I'll try to think of Kitty and you the same way I think of Kevin and Robert. I acknowledge Randy as Kevin's birth father, but that's only genetics. Robert is his dad."

"That's absolutely the same for me. Marianne was a sick oak tree who fell and got covered up by the forest floor. I acknowledge her—reluctantly—and that's all. She hindered my growth much more than she helped." She stood up, hoping it didn't seem rude to take off so soon after dinner. But she didn't have the stomach to talk about Marianne for another minute. "I'm getting groggy. Probably from carb-loading. Mind if I head home before I conk out?"

"It's only seven forty-five." She stood up as well. "Let's get a little air, then I'll walk you to your car. It's not too cold for you, is it?"

"You're asking if it's too cold in December to go for a pleasant after dinner stroll?" she asked, cocking her head. "That can't be a serious question."

"Come on," Summer said. "We don't have to be out for hours, but I ate so much I'm uncomfortable. I need to walk off two or three calories."

"All right," Kelsey said, even though she wanted to just go home and sleep for twelve hours. "I don't want to go too far afield. Do you have a favorite route?"

"Not really. We can do a little window-shopping. I like seeing the holiday touches stores put up."

"Need help with your coat?"

Summer stopped in the middle of putting it on. "Do you like to help?"

"I've never realized this was a habit," she said, grasping Summer's hair into a ponytail and holding it up to kiss the soft skin. "But your neck smells so good I look forward to doing this."

"Surprising, but charming."

They walked down the hallway together and went down on the elevator. Once they'd passed through the large lobby, Kelsey pulled on her gloves, and raised the collar of her coat. "Brr…"

"It's nice out," Summer said, giving her an elbow. "You were playing fast and loose with the truth, Ms. Maliar."

"Well, it's cold compared to August…"

Summer took her hand and they walked to Smallman, which was largely deserted. "Not much to look at here," Kelsey said.

"No, but it's quiet. I decided I'd rather talk than shop."

Internally rolling her eyes, Kelsey knew what the topic was going to be. But she wasn't going to start. If Summer wanted to belabor the issue, she was going to have to be in charge.

"Uhm…do you think your certainty that you don't want kids has something to do with Marianne?"

That was a surprise question Kelsey hadn't seen coming. She spent a moment thinking about it, with the answer creeping up on her. "I guess I'd be surprised if it didn't. How about you? You seem just as certain as I am."

She nodded slowly. "I've got some worries that I'd be more like Jackie than Beth. But the bigger issue is that I'd want to be a full-time mom, and that can't happen."

"So if you partnered with someone with a ton of money, you'd…?"

"Probably not at this point, since I'm quite happy with the status quo. But it wouldn't be off the table if my partner *really* wanted to be a parent. How about you? Is there any flexibility on your side?"

"I don't think so. But I'm open to getting a pet," she said, trying to make the conversation lighter. "Preferably one that didn't have to be walked on cold mornings."

Summer put her arm around Kelsey's waist and pulled her in. "I realize you don't want to talk about her, but I have so many questions about Marianne and all of the repercussions of her leaving. I need some answers, Kelsey. I honestly do."

"Why?" She stopped, with Summer turning to face her. "I told you everything that matters. She didn't like the life she'd signed up for, so she found one she liked better. I found a mother I liked better, and I've moved on. What else do you need to know?"

"So much," Summer sighed. "I've got a list a mile long."

With her temper starting to flare, Kelsey said, "I'm never going to want to talk about her. That's just a fact."

Summer gazed at her for a minute, with her gaze scanning all across Kelsey's face. "Being abandoned by your mother has repercussions. If we're going to be in an exclusive relationship, we can't just shut off big parts of our lives."

Kelsey closed her eyes, trying to make this whole topic disappear. But it was clear Summer wasn't going to allow that to happen. "I'm not ready to talk about her. Give me a few days. Or a week. Let me calm down about this."

Placing her hands on Kelsey's shoulders, Summer said, "I can see that I'm badgering you, and I wish I didn't feel the need to. But I have to know how this has affected you. I can't just let it slide."

"I wish you could just believe me. Marianne's in the vault."

Summer stared at her for a few moments. "If that's true, you wouldn't need a week to calm down enough to answer some questions."

Was anything more annoying than having your girlfriend make a point you were desperate to refute, but finding yourself unable to? *No!* "I'll think about it," she grumbled. "Then we can talk. Can we head back to my car now? I'll give you a ride home so you don't have to be out alone."

"That's fine," she said, softly, giving every impression that it wasn't fine at all. But Kelsey couldn't be railroaded into talking about something she had very purposefully stored away. She'd talk about it when, and if, she was ready.

CHAPTER SEVENTEEN

SUMMER HAD FIRMLY RESOLVED TO let Kelsey bring the topic of her birth mother up. While she didn't like having to be passive about it, when someone had locked something away so purposefully, it had to be tough to voluntarily bring it up again. But even though she hadn't broached the subject on their infrequent texts, Kelsey was still distant. She didn't seem to have any real excuse for being unavailable the rest of the week, only proposing vague plans for Saturday night.

When Saturday rolled around, Summer decided to give her until noon. If they didn't have anything set by then, she was going to tag along with Leah and her pals. Dinner at an expensive Italian steakhouse didn't appeal to her at all, but she wasn't going to sit home and pout.

Finally, just before Summer was going to text her sister, Kelsey proposed that she make dinner, and they agreed to meet at a market by her apartment so they could pick something they both liked. But that slowed them down pretty significantly. It was seven thirty by the time they arrived at the apartment, where they paused while Kelsey got her mail.

They each carried a bag of groceries up to the third floor, the weight slowing them down. Once they got inside, Summer set her bag on the counter and tried to catch her breath. "I thought I was in decent shape, but that bag felt like it weighed fifty pounds by the time we hit the third floor."

"The cheap woman's version of the gym." Not even winded, Kelsey looked at her mail with a small portion of her attention, tossing each piece onto a pile clearly meant for the recycling bin.

Summer shrugged out of her coat, then picked up the stack of junk. "Want me to throw this out? I have to pass by the recycling center on my way to the coat closet."

Kelsey's apartment was so stripped down that they'd given several spots pet names. Besides the upholstered chair being the coat closet, the sofa was the dining room when the TV was off, and when they lowered the lights and turned it on, the living room became the media room. The eighteen inches of counter space in the kitchen was the prep island, so even having mail lying there made it too crowded to work. For a woman who sold kitchens, Kelsey's could only serve as a "before" picture in Sedlak Brothers' advertisements.

Summer picked up the pile, noting one of the envelopes was hand-addressed. "I think you missed something real," she said, pulling it out.

"No, I didn't. Toss it, please."

Summer looked at it carefully, seeing it was sent from Santa Barbara, from an "M. Fencik." "Oh, Kelsey, do you really want to do that?"

"Sure do," she said, taking off her coat and grasping Summer's from her hand to carry them both to the chair. When she turned, Summer hadn't moved.

"I'm not interested. Pitch it, please."

"What if she's saying something important?"

"Like what? I assume my grandparents are both dead now, and no one informed me about that. I only had one uncle, so who's left?"

"No cousins?" She walked over and put her hands on her waist, always feeling emotionally closer when Kelsey was in her arms.

"I have no idea if my uncle married, or had kids, so your guess is as good as mine. But if I have any, I've never met them." She moved her finger in a circle, indicating that each thought led to the next. "I have plenty of relatives. My real mom's sister and her family live in Maryland. I see them a couple of times every year. While my cousin can be a pain, my aunt is just as sweet as my mom. I'm perfectly satisfied with my current crop of relatives."

"What in the fuck is wrong with your mother's family?" Summer snapped. "You had grandparents? Local ones?"

"Munhall. Is that local enough? I could ride a bike there if I had to."

"And you honestly think they didn't even try to contact you after your mother left?"

"If they did, I never heard about it."

"Were you close?"

"I guess not. At least not compared to kids I knew." She was quiet for a few seconds, then said, "I remember a girl in kindergarten talking about her grandparents taking her to Disney World over the summer, and I thought about how weird that would be. Really," she stressed. "I couldn't imagine going on a trip with my grandparents. Actually, I don't recall ever being alone with them. So even when I was little I knew we didn't have the same kind of connection some other kids had. But I remember them, and their little chihuahua, and I definitely noticed their absence."

"God!" She took the envelope and tried to tear it in half, furious on Kelsey's behalf. The paper tore easily, but there was something inside too thick to yield. As the envelope ripped, some photos fluttered to the floor. The top one had to be the first photo ever taken of Kelsey. Summer quickly picked them all up, holding them to her chest. "I think these are the baby pictures that should be on your mom's wall. Are you sure she doesn't want them? I can't imagine she wouldn't be thrilled to see what you looked like as a newborn."

Kelsey walked over and took them, scowling at the first image. "I look like a hairless cat. All wrinkly and pink, with slits for eyes." She handed them back to Summer, seemingly completely uninterested. "I know you can't resist," she said, moving away to arrange the groceries they'd just bought.

She was damned right about that. When getting information from your girlfriend was as tough as mining for diamonds, you had to exploit whatever sources you had. "You're a sweet little toddler here, and you must have been about Poppy's age in this one." She held the photo up, but Kelsey turned away to wash her hands at the sink. "So cute," Summer murmured. "This was probably your first day of school."

"I've got a great photo of my first day of second grade. That's just as good as first."

For the first time since the day they'd met, Summer had the stomach-flipping feeling that this might be something they couldn't get past. If Kelsey was this inflexible, this unwilling to even discuss something that had affected her so deeply, she was making a pretty clear statement about how she'd be about any upsetting topic. And if there was one thing Summer knew, it was that she could not be with someone who not only shut down at first, but refused to revisit the topic at all—even after having a week to open up.

"There's a letter," she said, holding it up. "I'll put it aside for you to read later."

"You can put it aside if you want, but I'm not going to read it." Kelsey walked over to slide an arm around Summer's waist, while taking the letter from her hand. "I know you don't understand this, but I don't want to hear anything she has to say. Honestly, if she was writing to tell me she was a billionaire and wanted to give me all of her money, I wouldn't take it. She is dead to me," she said clearly.

Summer gazed into her stormy eyes for a minute, unsure of what to do or say. She was about to pick up her stuff and go home when Kelsey's features softened. "That's how I feel, and I'm not interested in changing. But you clearly need to learn more. So feel free to read her letter, talk to my dad, my mom... Hell, contact Marianne if you want to. Just leave me out of it."

Calmly, Summer composed her thoughts. "Here's the deal," she said as Kelsey moved back to the counter to finally start making the salad they'd agreed on. "I'm not interested because of idle curiosity. I'm interested in what went on because that kind of abandonment has to leave scars. Major childhood traumas reverberate through a person's lifetime. Especially something like abandonment."

"I know that," she said. "But I've dealt with it. My life is good, Summer. You've seen that for yourself."

"I have. But just having Marianne in this apartment for five minutes has put a barrier up between us. I know it's partly because I want you to talk, but I think it's more than that. Having your mother leave the house one day, never to hear from her again…" She stopped, feeling a little sick to her stomach when a memory hit her. "That happened to me with a woman I dated for about a month, and I can still ruminate about it when I'm feeling vulnerable."

"Read the letter," Kelsey said. "And I'm serious when I said you should talk to my mom and dad. I'd just like to be left out of the loop." She stopped cutting up a red pepper to add, "For now, at least. I'm open to trying to get comfortable taking about her." A wan smile made her look a little more like herself. "I think I need to re-set the combination on the vault."

Unsure of whether it was a good idea to proceed, Summer gazed at the handwriting for a few moments. Marianne had clearly gone to school when teachers focused on penmanship. Her words were on a sharp, but invisible horizontal line, each taking up the right amount of space. The woman should have been an architect. Of course, maybe she was. For all Summer knew it was equally likely that she was a spy or a stone mason. The letter was short, and she found herself reading the words before she could put another moment of thought into whether she should.

Dear Kelsey,

When I moved to California, your father allowed me to take the majority of the photos we had of you. They're precious to me, but I thought you might want to see some of them. I had copies made, which I enclose.

It might be a foolish dream, but I hope in looking at these you'll see how much you were wanted, and how much both your father and I loved you.

I don't think Kitty has seen these, so please share them with her if you'd like. She won't be surprised to learn what an adorable baby you were, but I think she'd still like to see the evidence.

When you stayed with me in Santa Barbara, I tried to send a few of these home with you. But you weren't interested in looking at them, much less carrying them back to Pennsylvania. I hope you've changed your mind, and can get a little pleasure out of seeing what an innocent, beautiful little girl your father and I were blessed with.

With all my love,

Your mom, Marianne

Summer's hand dropped, with the letter falling to the floor. She stooped to pick it up, feeling a little wobbly when she stood. "When did you stay with Marianne in California?"

Kelsey stopped as though she'd been flash-frozen. Gripping the counter with her hands, she began to speak, sounding more like a computer-generated voice than herself. "I have to think. Can you finish…" Then she turned and went into her bedroom, with Summer able to hear her close the bathroom door.

Furious with herself for pushing it, she started to work on the salad. It only took a minute or two for her to realize that reading the damn thing had been the right choice. If Kelsey wouldn't deal with this, Summer was going to have to call it quits. While she thought she could handle most issues, she couldn't deal with even minor ones alone. Learning the scope of the aftereffects from Marianne's abandonment now, when they were still in the early days, might save a much bigger heartache down the line. Still, even though she knew this was the right time to talk, the prospect of having the conversation was still stomach-churning.

A few more minutes passed, then Kelsey came back into the room, pale and anxious-looking. She stood right in front of Summer and spoke softly. "Marianne left the day after I finished kindergarten. She was gone all summer, returning right before the school year started. I think she moved into an apartment or a house." She stopped, put her hand on the counter, and took a few breaths. Her skin had grown even paler, and Summer thought she might be shaking. "Actually, I'm not sure if she came back to our house and then left, or if she went directly to her own place. That's very blurry."

"That makes sense," Summer said. "Trauma fucks with your memories."

"Right. So...they told me next to nothing, but I'm sure she didn't stay in Pittsburgh for long. It was still warm out when she left for good, so that couldn't have been more than a month or two." She took another breath. "When I finished first grade, she came back to drag me to Santa Barbara for the summer."

"Um, I truly don't want to be a jerk about this, but you've been telling me she abandoned you. But that doesn't sound accurate..."

She finally looked into Summer's eyes to wearily say, "Why couldn't you throw the fucking envelope away when I asked you to?"

"I'm sorry," Summer said, standing next to her and tentatively putting a hand on her back. "But this changes the history, Kelsey. It does."

"No, it doesn't." She took Summer's hand and walked over to the sofa, where they both sat. "I only have one vivid memory of the first time she left, but they clearly made up a lie."

"A lie?"

"Yeah. They told me she had to go visit her aunt. They made it seem like it was some kind of emergency, which I bought, since she was so freakin' upset. So for that whole summer, I thought she was coming back. Like any day." She shifted around to face Summer. "How would you deal with your mom leaving you for a couple of months when you were five fucking years old? No real explanation. Not even a fucking phone call." Her features screwed up tightly and her voice rose. "I'm dead certain about that. I did not speak to her for at least two months, and I spent a fuck-ton of time sitting in the living room, desperate to leap into her arms the minute she came back up that sidewalk."

Summer grasped her hand and held it tenderly, with tears rolling down her cheeks before she even knew she was crying. "That breaks my heart. It truly does."

"It broke mine too," she said quietly.

Her voice was softer when she continued. "I have very few memories of what happened when she came back, but, like I said, she left for good not long after I started first grade. I spent the whole year dealing with the loss, then she shows up—unannounced—to drag me to California. I mean that literally. I'm surprised the police didn't investigate why there was a child being forcibly dragged onto a plane."

"You honestly didn't know you were going?" Summer asked, stunned.

"No idea. I'm certain no one asked my opinion. I was just taken, like I was a fucking possession. I missed my dad, I missed my friends. And the whole time I was there, I was worried I was going to be forced to stay. As the days went by, I convinced myself my dad, the only person in the world I could rely on, was trying to get rid of me."

"I would not have handled that well," Summer admitted. "I don't think anyone would. That's why you need to talk about this. To get some of your feelings out."

"I don't want them out!" She jumped to her feet and walked to the other side of the room, not a very great distance. "If you'd let this go, I could leave her and her memories where I want them. In the fucking vault!"

Summer took a few deep breaths, giving Kelsey a moment to calm down. "Have you ever worked through your feelings with a therapist?"

"No," she spat. "That would be like opening a vein, which I'm not going to do. It was horrible, okay? I was a terrified child because my mother left me, but I healed with Kitty's help. So stop trying to rip the god damn scar open!"

Summer jumped to her feet and clutched Kelsey in a snug embrace. She was radiating heat, with the back of her blouse damp. "I'm so sorry," Summer whispered. "I know you want to lock this away, but you can't. It's like a bad seal on a pressure cooker. If you don't release the steam, it will blow when you least expect it." She pulled back and gazed into her turbulent eyes. "I just want you to have a safe space to get some of your anger out."

"Getting my anger out will never be safe," she growled. "I could knock down half of Pittsburgh with the anger I have for that woman. And if she doesn't leave me alone, I'm going to move and not give the post office a forwarding address." She grasped Summer tightly and enunciated clearly. "I've lived here for thirteen years, and my rent is a steal, but I'll leave tomorrow if I have to."

Summer touched her face, holding it gently. "I'm going to write to her and tell her to leave you alone. I don't want to start a relationship with her, Kelsey. I promise that. But I want to make it clear that she's torturing you. If she truly loves you, she'll stop."

"She didn't love me," Kelsey said, with her teeth clicking together softly as she spat the words out. "If she had, she'd be in Monroeville this evening, making my dad dinner."

⊛

After they had their salad, a tense affair, Summer went home when it became clear that Kelsey was too keyed-up to interact. The moment she got home, she pulled out her phone and dialed the Maliar home. She'd gotten the number when she'd wanted to call to thank Kitty and George for their hospitality after Thanksgiving, and this was only the second time she'd used it.

Kitty answered on the second ring. "Hello?"

"Hi, Kitty. This is Summer Hayes, Kelsey's…girlfriend?" she said, annoyed with herself for making it sound like a question.

"What's wrong, Summer? Is Kelsey all right?"

"She's upset, but otherwise fine. Her…birth mother sent her some baby photos. That part went down all right, but Marianne mentioned the time Kelsey went to California to visit. When I pressed her to tell me about it, she really went off on me. She got more and more upset, and eventually said she'd move if Marianne didn't leave her alone."

"Oh, goodness. She loves that apartment."

Kitty sounded as distraught as Kelsey did, and Summer felt like she'd made another forced error. "I'm sorry if I'm upsetting you—"

"No, no, I'm glad you told me. I doubt Kelsey would have."

"Kelsey told me she didn't mind if I talked to you, or even Marianne, about the whole thing, but… I don't know if that's smart. Do you think I should write to tell her to leave Kelsey alone? I'm kind of at a loss here, Kitty. I want to help, but I'm so unsure of what happened and why…"

"Good lord," she sighed. "This is all my fault. Why was I so weak? Marianne's not exactly a stalker, but she will *not* give up."

"So this has been going on for a long time?"

"Oh, it was awful at first," she murmured. "After George and I married, we arranged for a weekly call. Marianne called religiously, but Kelsey steadfastly refused to talk to her. Marianne was in tears, Kelsey was in tears, I was in tears. George was so angry it was impossible to even talk to him about it. Everything was just awful."

"It certainly sounds it. I can't imagine having to leave, and I can't imagine being left."

"That's it exactly. My sympathy has its limits, since I think Marianne made some very unwise choices. Still, I've been after Kelsey for years to establish some sort of relationship. Shouldn't you have some sympathy for someone who's tried so hard to apologize?" She made a soft noise, kind of like a hen. "This is Kelsey's only blind spot, but it's a big one. She has no sympathy whatsoever for Marianne, and I think that's…well, it's cruel. I hate to feel that way, but I do."

"I can see that," Summer said. "I probably shouldn't say this, but I'm worried about getting closer to Kelsey. Not being able to forgive is…big."

"Oh, Summer, don't say that. Kelsey's one of the best people I know. She's just been so hurt that she can't get past this. Everyone has a few blind spots, don't they?"

"Sure. God knows I do. But I still worry about this."

"Let me handle Marianne. The last thing she needs is another way of getting to Kelsey. She'd pull you in for sure."

"All right. I was hoping you'd do that."

"Stick with my girl," Kitty said firmly. "The luckiest day of my life was the day I met George. I love him to death, but even he knows Kelsey was my real prize. I guarantee you'll realize how special she is if you can get past this little rough spot."

"Thanks, Kitty. Make sure you tell Marianne that Kelsey's not kidding. She'll move if she has to."

There was a significant pause, then Kitty said, "Kelsey's never kidding when it comes to Marianne."

Chapter Eighteen

A WEEK HAD PASSED, WITH Summer finding herself increasingly troubled that they weren't keeping in touch like they had before Marianne had burst onto the scene. She reassured herself that Kelsey was simply having a hard time putting everything back into the vault, but she found herself obsessing over the distance when she tried to sleep. Her own guilt over stirring up the hornet's nest just made her feel worse, so she tried to give Kelsey the space she needed to feel safe again. But a work opportunity had come up that afternoon, and she texted Kelsey with a proposal.

I need to go to NYC for a day. Since I can pick when I go, I thought I'd go on Tuesday evening, and come back on Thursday. Want to go with me? I'm planning on driving, and I'd love the company.

It took just a minute for her to reply.

I'd love to go. I haven't been to NY for a couple of years. Next week?

That would work out great. I'll make the reservations.

If I have to pay for my own room, go cheap <s>

I'll get one big room. The client's paying, so you'll just have to cover your own meals.

I'll bring cans of tuna and a loaf of bread. New York's expensive!

Would you mind if I could arrange to have dinner with some of my college buddies?

Love to. Maybe they'll pay!

They made arrangements for Summer to pick Kelsey up from work on Tuesday evening, and she got a little thrill when Kelsey loped out of the door right at six.

She'd changed into jeans and a parka, and when she got into the car Summer tugged at the pom-pom on the top of her knit hat. "You look so cute in that."

"My mom made it for me. I got to pick the color."

"Bright pink matches your cheeks when you're in the throes of passion," Summer said, hoping it wasn't a mistake to tease about sex.

She pulled the hat off and took a long look at it. "I turn this color? That must be kind of weird. I'll have to do it in front of a mirror to see if you're screwing with me."

Summer almost said she was looking forward to screwing with her again in the near future, but there hadn't been a glimmer of sexual interest on either side since the morning Marianne had appeared. "Hungry? I haven't eaten dinner yet."

"Starving. Busy, busy day. People must be off for Christmas, and they're wasting their holidays looking at cabinets. What would you like?"

"I like junk when I'm on a car trip. Do you like fast food?"

"The faster the better," she said, already showing that she was going to be a good travel companion.

※

They'd driven about a hundred miles, and were now getting into a groove. The car had the pleasant funk of discarded fast food containers, and Kelsey was rooting around for a bag she'd placed in the backseat. "Ahh, got it," she said. Sticking her hand inside, she started to pull things out. "M&Ms, Oreos, Kit-Kat, and Junior Mints. What's your pleasure."

"You brought snacks? Excellent."

"They always jack the price up on the Interstate." She laughed. "I probably saved thirty cents by buying everything near home."

"I admire your planning. I think I'll wait until my attention starts to flag to snack."

"You still need to pick. I like them all, so I'll take the leftovers."

"Let's see," Summer said, tapping her fingers against the steering wheel. "What would wake me up? Mints, I think. Put those aside for me."

Kelsey handed them over. "You'd better keep them. I unconsciously eat when I'm bored, so they might disappear." She ripped open the Kit-Kat, since it was her least favorite. "I'm happy to drive if you want a break."

"I'm happy to let you. Let's stop in an hour and get out to stretch our legs."

"Works for me." She reclined her seat a few inches, always finding a position change allowed her to sit comfortably for longer. "You haven't told me about this job. What's going on?"

"Oh, it's a pretty big one, but they're jerking me around. It's for a new condo building downtown. They want something unique for the bathrooms, and the entryways, but they're being a little cheap." She turned and gave Kelsey a wry smile. "I'm working with the developer's interior designer. I get the feeling he thought he could get custom tile for fifty percent less than he'd have to pay in New York. He seems to think everything in Pittsburgh costs like a nickel."

"I wish," Kelsey said.

"I've been looking to buy a house soon, and I've been both surprised and dismayed at how consistently prices keep climbing. The 'Burgh is happening."

"Buying a house? Like a single family?"

"Uh-huh. That's the main reason I rented my current apartment. I didn't care for it, but it was cheaper than the ones I liked better, and I knew I wasn't going to be there long."

"Ahh. You've been planning."

"That's a common theme with me. I want a bigger kitchen, a guest room, and a dedicated space for my art. I hate having to work at the dining room table."

"I've never looked for a house." She thought for a second. "Ever. Can I help?"

"Sounds like you don't know how to," Summer teased. "But I'd love to learn together."

"Oh, this is going to be cool. Where are you looking?"

"Mmm. If I could live wherever I wanted, I'd pick Mt. Washington. A view of the city would be sweet."

"What's stopping you?"

Summer gave her a quick look. "Have you ever tried to drive to Lawrenceville from Mt. Washington at eight in the morning? As much as I'd like a view, spending time sitting in traffic is never going to work for me."

"Okay. So you're looking for a place close to work. Anything else?"

"Ideally, I'd buy something old, but totally fixed up." She smiled. "As you might guess, I have very definite ideas about what I want, and no one has renovated a place the way I'd like. I've been checking out places on the internet for months, but all of the ones that have been done well are way out of my price range. I've been on the verge of giving up."

"No, no. There's a house for you. We'll just have to look harder. I'm good at picturing the potential of a run-down place. A few thousand bucks spent on tile and paint can heal a lot of scars."

Summer turned again and shook her head slowly. "You're wrong about the price tag on tile. The roof might be falling off, and the heating system might be shot, but my tile has to be stunning."

❧

As soon as Kelsey finished her Kit-Kat, she pulled out her phone, saying, "Can I be the DJ?"

"Absolutely. I love music, but I forget to put it on. I get into my own thoughts..."

"I have something going all the time. I usually joke that the thoughts in my head scare me too much and I have to drown them out, but you'd believe that."

Summer shot her a look, seeing she was smiling as she thumbed through her tunes, with the brightness of the screen giving her a ghostly pale look. "I don't think you're tormented on a daily basis, but even if you were that wouldn't send me running for cover. Everyone has issues. Working through things is both the best and the worst part of being in a committed relationship."

"I'll admit I'm occasionally tormented, but as long as people stop poking me with sticks…" She turned and gave Summer a warm smile. "I'm talking about you, in case you hadn't guessed."

"I had a feeling. So? What's my personal DJ going to play? What's your jam?"

"My jam," she said, sounding formal, "is pretty wide-ranging. I use streaming services to get recommendations, and they've figured out I only want to listen to women. I must be in the 'pop/rock/new country/folk' category, with a note that I'll pass on things with even a hint of testosterone."

"That's a good category. Mine would include punk and hip-hop and alt rock for when I'm working on something that gets my blood pumping, and a little classical for when I'm working on something calming. And I don't mind testosterone a bit—in my music." She laughed. "But I don't use any of those sites, and I'm too lazy to search for new stuff. Most of the music on my phone is from college."

"Then you definitely need a personal DJ. You're in luck to be stuck in the car with a good one."

Summer took the last turn driving, and as they passed a sign signaling the road ahead was winding she said, "See that sign?"

"Sure."

"When I was young, my dad told me that meant you were in an area where snakes chased your car."

"What?" Kelsey asked, starting to laugh.

"He was always making stuff up for no reason at all." She turned briefly and met Kelsey's gaze. "I think that's how he kept his lying muscles in shape."

"Damn it, I was just thinking it was cute that he was fanciful, but you had to ruin it with reality."

Summer laughed at the pouty face she was making. "He also told me that the dead animals we'd see on the side of the road were napping."

"Ooo. Those were some long naps."

"Right? When I told him I was worried about them getting that close to the road, he said it was the sound of cars that soothed them to sleep."

"Not bad. If you're going to lie, be able to back it up." The rhythmic sound of the car going over the bumps in the road was actually soothing, and Summer spent a moment thinking that her dad's tales had mostly been benign.

"Hey, I just thought of a goofy thing my dad told me," Kelsey said.

"Hit me."

"When I was little, I wasn't very interested in sitting down and watching a football game, which he really wanted me to do. He figured out that I'd jump through hoops to get one of my favorite cookies, the oatmeal ones with the chocolate drizzle? Know what I mean?"

"I think so."

"Well, he told me they were special NFL cookies, and the league had a rule that you could only eat one per quarter."

"Seriously?" Summer said, laughing at the amount of time George had to spend to come up with that one.

"Seriously. I had to be there for the whole quarter to get one of those babies. I'd be watching that clock tick off the time more than the game, but it made him happy to have me running around the room acting like I liked football."

"And you grew to love it."

"I did. But only the Steelers. When they get knocked out of the playoffs, I lose interest."

"Got it." She thought for a moment. "Aren't parents kind of weird? We rely on them for everything, yet they screw with our trust just for fun."

"Only my dad," Kelsey said. "I think it's a guy thing."

"Maybe. I guess my moms didn't do things like that. Huh," she said thoughtfully. "I'm sure someone has written a scientific study on why fathers taunt their kids, but I'll go along with your theory. It's just a guy thing."

They didn't reach the hotel until after one, but it had been nice to enter Manhattan in the wee hours. Summer had chosen a moderately-priced chain hotel near Wall Street, and she was pleased to see there was a public lot nearby. For a mere forty-five dollars, she'd be able to leave her car outside for twenty-four hours. It wasn't highway robbery, since no one had used force, but it was close.

Summer didn't travel often, so she didn't have any loyalty status, but someone more important than her must not have showed up that night. While the room they were assigned wasn't large, it had a wonderful view, with tall towers nearly filling the window.

"Even with all of that light, I bet I'll fall right to sleep," Kelsey said.

"I think there are blackout curtains. I assume they're mandatory." She pulled the thick vinyl halfway closed. "I'll button it all up before we try to sleep."

"I'm going to try as soon as I use the bathroom. Dibs!" Kelsey took her backpack and ran into the little room, leaving Summer to change into her pajamas while she waited.

Kelsey emerged, wearing a long-sleeved T-shirt and her underwear. "All yours," she said. "If you take longer than three minutes, I'll be asleep."

"I'm pretty fast," she admitted. "I'm a professional lesbian."

She did her usual nighttime tasks, then slid the pocket-door open. Kelsey was in bed, lying on her side while she held a fluffy pillow in her arms. She looked so pretty with the dim light shining on her face that Summer felt a pull she would have gladly given up sleep for. But Kelsey was still not giving off any sexual vibes, so she crawled in behind her and put a hand on her waist. "Goodnight," she whispered.

Kelsey turned her head as far as she could, and placed a soft kiss to Summer's lips. "Cuddle?"

"Love to." That was the truth. She wished they were still connecting on a sexual level, but cuddling was a close second on her list of favorite things to do.

225

Summer tried to shut out the annoying sounds that pulled her from a deep sleep, but they kept tugging at her. She felt like she'd been fished from a deep pool, and when she broke the surface she realized she'd been dreaming. She fluffed up her pillow and turned over, and in moments was almost out again. Then a frightened whimper made her fly up into a sitting position. Still groggy, but with her pulse racing, she realized where she was. Kelsey was clearly having a bad dream, making little noises that Summer simply couldn't ignore.

Stealthily, she cradled Kelsey in her arms, doing her best not to wake her. At first, she went rigid, then she sighed and let her body conform to Summer's. She lay as still as she could, hoping Kelsey would settle down. But that wasn't to be.

"What...?"

"I'm sorry," Summer said. "You were having a nightmare and I tried to soothe you back to sleep."

"Thanks. That was nice of you." She sat up and brushed her hair back with her fingers, then blinked a few times to clear her eyes. "I haven't had one of those in a very long time. Scary," she added.

"Want to talk about it?"

Kelsey pulled the covers up over her shoulders, looking like a kid who didn't want to face something that frightened her. "Um...I had the nightmare because we keep talking about it. I told you I do just fine when I pack everything away, but I'm always worried you're going to make me dig it all up again."

Summer sat up and gently stroked her leg through the cover. "We didn't talk about it tonight, Kelsey. Actually, we haven't talked about it since I read the letter. Have you been struggling ever since?"

"Not a lot," she said, possibly fibbing. "I just get the feeling you're going to bring it up when we're together."

Still patting her, Summer said, "You've been distant. Is that why?"

"Yeah. I guess," she said, not looking up.

"Listen to me," Summer said soberly. Kelsey looked into her eyes in the darkened room. "To help you feel safe again, I'm happy to act like you were born when you were in second grade. You had Kitty then, and were on a good trajectory." She leaned close and kissed her cheek, which had become chilled. "I'm on your side."

She gazed into Summer's eyes, holding the look for a long time. "You'd really just skip over that part of my life?"

"If doing that would make you feel safe, definitely."

"But you made it clear you were worried about how this would affect me. Like long-term."

"I am concerned about getting into a committed relationship with someone who's tormented about something and won't discuss it." Kelsey started to speak, but Summer pressed a finger to her lips. "I'm concerned," she stressed. "But learning more about you might show me my concern is overblown. If you want to lock this away like you have been, I'm willing to not bring it up again. No pressure." She shifted so she could reach her lips. "You're not just this one thing, you know. You're interesting, and funny, and kind, and smart, and really, really sexy. I think we get along great, which is the most important thing, right?"

"We get along great," she agreed, with a slight smile showing.

"I care for you, Kelsey, and I want you to do what works for you. If those nightmares will go away by locking this down, we'll do that."

"I think they will. I swear I hadn't had one since a woman I was into started texting another woman when she was at my friggin apartment. The jerk left her computer open in my living room, and I saw a screen full of flirting."

"That made you have nightmares? I...I need to know these triggers, Kelsey. I sure don't plan on sneaking around, but I wouldn't have guessed that would bring you back to your trauma..." She took a breath. "Is it because your mom was screwing around with some guy?"

Kelsey gave her a look that brought her up short. A deep stare that seemed to go right through her. "You're making assumptions. I'm sure I never said Marianne was screwing around with some guy."

"What? I'm sure you said she cheated on your dad…" Kelsey continued to stare, her gaze burning hot. "Oh, shit," Summer said. "Your mom was with a woman?"

"Yes," she said quietly. "She left my dad for a woman."

"Jesus," Summer sighed. "Was she a lesbian before she married your dad? Or did she…" She sucked in a breath when Kelsey continued to give her a dark glare. "I'm sorry. We're not going to talk about her. I'm sorry I asked a follow-up. It just caught me by surprise."

"It's all right," she said, scooting down so the covers went up to her nose. "I volunteered info that time. My fault."

"No, you were right to correct me. When I found out, I would have felt like you were lying to me, and that's one of *my* triggers." She leaned in to wrap Kelsey in a hug. "Everybody has things that create hurdles to being close. But we can get over them if we're willing to put the effort in. Promise."

They were nose-to-nose, and Kelsey finally revealed a genuine smile. "I like you," she said. "I like you a lot."

"Same here." They kissed, tenderly, then Summer found herself yawning. "I've got to get to sleep. My alarm's going off in two hours."

Kelsey's arm popped out of the covers and she stroked Summer's cheek. "Don't be shy about letting me sleep in."

"I won't be shy at all. I'll be finished by noon, then we can do whatever you want until dinner. We're meeting April and Samantha in the East Village at seven."

"Let's go see that Neapolitan Christmas tree at the Met. That sounded great."

"I think that's what *I* want to do, but I'll let you be generous." She kissed her again, very gently. "Sleep until noon if you want."

"I normally don't, but I might try. I hope your meeting goes well."

"Thanks. Now close those pretty eyes and get some rest."

Kelsey woke when a shaft of sunlight painted a stripe down her body. She was hot, and still a little groggy, but she checked her watch to see it was after nine. Summer had snuck out of the room soundlessly, which was an awesome trait in a girlfriend.

Getting up, she noticed the pod-style coffee maker resting in a nook by the door. She wasn't wild about the coffee they produced, but it was quick and didn't require that she put on pants to be able to drink a cup. Kelsey reached for a small pad of paper that was leaning against the coffee maker. Summer had probably used felt-tip pens or markers, since the lines were thin and sharp, saturated with color. The drawing depicted a steaming mug of coffee looking quite appetizing, but next to it was a container of the noxious chemical known as non-dairy creamer. The top of the container was torn off, and a red plastic straw lay next to it. In the corner of the thick paper Summer had outlined a rectangle upon which she'd titled the piece. "Despair. Markers on Card Stock. Summer Hayes."

Kelsey opened the mini-fridge, seeing every kind of soda, and a few brands of beer, but no real milk. Having Summer go to the trouble of making a sweet little drawing just to cheer her up at the thought of no real milk was beyond thoughtful. Even if Summer hadn't had a load of other qualities Kelsey found irresistible, her drawing skills alone made her a ten out of ten.

Chapter Nineteen

On the Sunday after their trip, Summer went down to the lobby of her building that evening, waiting for Kelsey to text her. As usual, she was right on time, and Summer went out to jump into her warm car.

"Chilly out there," she said, rubbing her arms. She leaned over and kissed Kelsey's cheek before she started to put her seatbelt on.

"The car didn't warm up until I was on your street. I hope my mom's making something that will stick to our ribs."

"Whatever she makes will be nice," Summer decided. "And if it's awful, I can fake enjoyment."

"Nice to know," Kelsey said, giving her a weak slap on the leg. "I'll have to look for clues you can't fake next time we..." She waggled one eyebrow, never getting it to do what she wanted, a gesture Summer found consistently cute.

"That I don't fake. I'd only be hurting myself by lying about an orgasm." She patted her gently. "I wouldn't have any reason to fake one with you, by the way." She didn't add that they hadn't acted like lovers since Marianne had come on the scene. Summer was willing to be patient, but they were going to have to talk about that—soon.

Her dad opened the door, welcoming them both with hugs and kisses. That made Kelsey smile. Her dad was always friendly to the women she brought home, but he didn't usually start with the cheek-kisses until he'd known a woman for quite a while. He was jumping ahead with Summer.

"I'm running behind," her mom called out from the kitchen. "You'll have to forgive me for being rude."

They walked into the kitchen together, with Kelsey nodding in satisfaction when she saw her mom's phone lying on the window sill, cranking out her disco playlist through the speaker Kelsey had bought her last Christmas.

"I can't listen to The Hustle and not dance," Kelsey said, earning a very fond look from her mom.

"Wait until I wash my hands—"

Playfully, Kelsey put her hands on her mom's hips and turned her around. "Stick your hands in the air, girl. No one cares if they're dirty."

It took just a second for her mom to get into the groove, with them mirroring each other perfectly. "Best dance partner I've ever had," Kelsey said, beaming at Summer.

"You're teaching me that, post haste," Summer said, her smile bright.

"Oh, no. Kitty O'Hara Maliar's the dance teacher around here." Kelsey busted out her best disco move, showing off a bit as she shot her arm in the air and swung her hips.

"Woo hoo!" Summer said, clapping her hands. "You two should take this act on the road."

They hadn't gotten started right at the beginning of the song, and it ended before they'd finished their whole routine. But as soon as the next song started, her mom clapped her hands and said, "Time for the bump."

Kelsey followed orders, having to bend her knees to get her butt at the same height as her mom's. *Disco Inferno* thumped in the background, and they danced while they both giggled. Dancing wasn't a rare occurrence at her house, but she'd never done it in front of a girlfriend.

"Let's just order a pizza," her mom said, unable to stop laughing.

"Pizza?" Her dad looked like he'd been slapped. "I've got my mouth all ready for stuffed pork chops."

"Party pooper," her mom said, kissing Kelsey's cheek when she presented it. "I'm so glad you girls came tonight." She hurriedly washed her hands, then gave them both proper kisses and hugs. "You both look so nice."

"Summer does, for sure," Kelsey said. "Isn't that a cute blouse?"

"Oh, Summer could wear a paper bag and look pretty. It's not the clothes, it's the girl."

"I'm coming over here for dinner all the time," Summer said, clearly pleased by the friendly greeting. "No one at my house ever tells me I'm cute."

"You're not cute," Kelsey's dad said, as if he'd already given the matter some thought. "You're pretty." He must have heard himself and decided he'd been too forward, because he shut his mouth quickly and turned for the stairs. "Hockey's calling," he said, walking fast.

Kelsey put her arms around Summer and hugged her from behind, quietly saying, "I think my dad's got a little crush on you."

"A big one," her mom said. "I've never met a man who didn't act a little stupid when a pretty girl was around. They must not realize they're being so darned obvious."

"You can't blame him, Mom. Summer's the prettiest girl I've ever brought home. God knows I wasn't able to stop myself from flirting with her, and I was working!"

"Oh, you," her mom said, patting her cheek. "Go put your coats away. I made some deviled eggs you can nibble on while the chops bake."

"My favorite," Kelsey said.

"That's why I made them, honey. I know what you like."

Kelsey led the way down the hall. "We can put our stuff on the bed." She'd intentionally chosen her parents' room, and after Summer had put her coat down Kelsey handed her a framed photo. "My mom keeps this on her dresser," she said, waiting for Summer to look at it and smile.

But tears appeared in those hazel eyes in mere seconds. Her finger hovered over Kelsey's face, then she looked up at her. "You look so happy," she whispered.

Kelsey stood by her and gazed at the photo. Her parents were standing in front of the altar of the parish she'd been born into, while she stood in front of them, wearing a very fancy dress, the nicest she'd ever owned. In her hand was a simple bouquet, and she flashed the happiest grin imaginable.

"Doesn't my mom look beautiful?" she said, still confident she was the prettiest bride in history.

"Very," Summer said, perfectly serious. She looked up and grinned. "Your mom's cooking caught up to your dad somewhere along the way. He was kind of skinny when they married."

"I don't think he was ever skinny, but he's certainly filled out." She took the photo and replaced it. "I just wanted to show you how quickly I got on board about their marriage. I think that was the happiest day of my life."

Summer turned to gaze at the photo for another minute. "You really do look like a happy little girl. Is that your church? It's pretty."

"No, that's in Munhall. The wedding was in May, and we moved here in June or July. I just remember it being hot."

"You didn't mind moving? I had to do it a lot, and I can't even tell you how much I hated it."

Kelsey waited until Summer was looking at her, then said, "I'm the one who wanted to move." She didn't add anything, but she hoped her expression made it clear she didn't want to talk about it any further.

"Got it," Summer said. She put her arm around Kelsey's waist. "What are we waiting for? We've got some deviled eggs to chow down on, and if we have time, I'm going to get a dance lesson."

Her mom and Summer had gone upstairs to talk about knitting projects while the game was tied. That seemed crazy to Kelsey, but she knew Summer didn't like any part of hockey, and her mom obviously didn't mind having an excuse to sneak away.

The Penguins squeaked in a goal while the Flyers were a man short, and after celebrating for a moment, Kelsey got up and went over to the bar her dad had installed. It wasn't as fancy as the one at Summer's house, but it got the job done. She pulled a beer out of the mini-fridge and waggled it when her dad turned her way.

"Well, I'd say no, but I hate to have you waste the trip. You having another?"

"I think I'll hold at one. I drove." She twisted off the cap and delivered the beer.

"Thanks, honey. Think we should have the girls make us some popcorn?"

"I don't need any, but I'll run up and make some if you want me to."

"Nah," he said. He patted the seat next to him. "We've got a minute alone. Tell me what's going on."

"With…?"

"You and Summer," he said, like that was obvious. "Your mom told me you had some choppy waters after Marianne got your address." He shook his head. "First time I've known your mom to get into something like that. Surprised the holy hell out of me."

"Me too." She and her dad didn't usually get into very deep discussions, keeping their conversational topics to sports, local politics, and their jobs. Oddly, they also talked about Marianne once in a great while. She felt a little more comfortable talking to him than her mom, since it felt like they'd both been wronged. Plus, her mom was too soft-hearted to see the situation the same way they did. She took that Christian forgiveness thing to its absolute limit. "I didn't give Mom a hard time about spilling the beans, but I wanted to."

He put his hand on her shoulder and gazed at her soberly. "She didn't mean any harm. You know that."

"Oh, I know. And after Marianne forced her way into my house, I saw how determined she can be. She'd roll over Mom with no problem at all."

"I don't remember Marianne as being very pushy," he said, with his gaze shifting up to land on the wall behind her. "Actually, I try not to think about her at all, but sometimes…"

"Me too," Kelsey said. "I've been pretty successful at shutting her out of my memory, but ever since she showed up on my doorstep, my sleep's been screwed up."

"Not the nightmares again," he said, staring at her in alarm.

"Some," she admitted. "Summer really tries to get me to talk about the whole thing, but I don't want to. She's promised she won't bring it up again, but there's…something between us now that wasn't there before. A little distance."

His look grew even more worried. "Unless she's hiding something, she's the best girl you've ever brought home. Might be worth going out of your way to figure out what the problem is."

"She's definitely worth going out of my way for. But…" She shrugged. "I'm not sure what to do."

He gave Kelsey a gentle tap on the shoulder. "You know, sometimes you have to do things you don't want to do to keep a woman happy. Maybe you *should* talk about it."

"Really? Do *you* talk about it?"

"Hell, no," he said, shaking his head briskly. "But I'm not having nightmares about it, and your mom isn't poking me to get me to talk."

"What if she did?"

"Now? What would I do if she wanted me to talk about it now? After all this time?"

She nodded, and he made a funny face as he thought about the question. Then he shrugged. "If it meant a lot to her, I'd do it. I sure as hell wouldn't want to, but I would. Jesus," he grumbled. "I took dance lessons for her, so talking couldn't be much worse than that." He gave her another poke. "Don't screw this up, Kels. Summer would fit right in with us. I can see her out in the backyard at one of our barbecues, can't you?"

"I can," she said, allowing herself the pleasure of daydreaming about Summer flitting around, chatting up all of their family friends, something none of her previous girlfriends had even tried to do. "I really can."

They'd just been in the car for moments, but Kelsey decided to get it out of the way right then. She cleared her throat, and said, "Do you want me to talk about Marianne just for me? Or do you think taking it off the table will hurt our relationship."

Although Kelsey was watching the road, Summer flinched so hard she caught it out of the corner of her eye. "Where did that come from?"

"Mmm, I was talking to my dad, and he told me to not be hard-headed about the whole thing." She gave Summer a quick glance. "I can dig my heels in pretty quickly, but I know that's not a great trait."

"No, it's not a great trait, but it's not the worst one either. If I had to pick an annoying trait for you to have, I might actually choose it."

"You don't have to pick just one. I've got plenty. So? What do you think?"

"Um, I think you'd be happier if you got some of your anger out. That's my main wish for you. But not being able to ask questions and learn things about your early years is kind of tough." She paused for a moment, clearly turning this over in her head. "There's a good chance it'll get in the way. I'm willing to date someone with all sorts of issues she'd rather not talk about, but I can't see myself going deeper if the early years have to be top-secret."

"Why? You've told me a little about your early life, but not much. I think I'd be fine not knowing the details."

Summer gazed at the side of her face. "I told you about the big stuff so you'd have some perspective. Stuff will come up because of some of my early traumas. That's guaranteed. Knowing I earned my right to overreact might make you more understanding." She gripped her leg firmly. "Isn't that important?"

"I guess," she said, almost able to see the situation from Summer's perspective.

"The same thing is true for you. You'll overreact because of things I have no knowledge of. Over time, that will hurt us."

Kelsey thought that over for just a minute, knowing she didn't have a defense. "What if I take off the top-secret classification. Would you feel better if you can ask questions?"

"That might do it." She rubbed her hand over Kelsey's leg again. "But I really don't want to upset you when you're already feeling shaky. If you need another few weeks…"

"Let's give it a try. If I hate it a whole lot, we'll reassess."

"That sounds more than fair. But I don't want you to be worried about this. Why don't we just open things up once in a while? Like I'll ask you a question or two every Sunday. Would that work?"

"I can't know unless we try," she said, already feeling sick to her stomach at the prospect. "Since it's Sunday, I assume you want to start. I bet you've got a list."

"Not a list…" She put her hand on Kelsey's leg and rubbed it briskly. "Well, maybe I have something close to a list." She took an audible breath. "I've got one that I've been thinking about since we were in New York."

"Shoot."

"Did knowing your mom was a lesbian make it hard for you to come out?"

"Yes," she said, giving Summer a brief glance. "Are we done?"

"We are if you need to stop."

Kelsey rolled her eyes. It would be easier if Summer just held her down and went down the entire list. One day of torture would probably be better than getting poked repeatedly. But she'd agreed to the plan, so she had to pony up. "I can give you a little background. It didn't really hit me that I was gay until I was out of high school."

"But you said you didn't date guys. I know you couldn't get through high school with no one chasing you like mad."

"Thanks," Kelsey said, sparing her a grin. "You're right. Some guys were interested in me, but I wasn't interested in them. I'd convinced myself it was each particular guy I didn't like, rather than the whole group. I got away with that since I hung out with a bunch of girls, all of them super involved in school. Not one of us dated anyone seriously all through high school."

"Really? None of you?"

"If someone got interested in a guy, she'd kind of split off from the bigger group. And that only happened a couple of times. I think all of us were focused on the next step. We wanted to get out of high school and reassess once we were in college."

"Ahh… You hung out with the National Merit Scholar girls. The ones who took all the AP classes they were allowed."

"Pretty much," Kelsey agreed. "Even though I wasn't trying to get into Penn, or Princeton, like most of them were, I loved that they didn't spend their days mooning over some dorky guy."

"I can see that would have felt like a safe haven for you." She patted her gently. "And I bet you could have gone to Penn with no trouble if you'd really wanted to. You're one smart cookie."

"Ehh," she said, shrugging. "I did all right. But I didn't have any clear career goals, and I didn't want to saddle myself with a ton of debt, so I went to CCAC to see if I liked college enough to pay big money for it. Right away, I started to meet women who openly identified as gay, something that hadn't happened at my high school."

"And these lesbians…interested you?"

"Yeah. Too much," she said, grimacing. "I tried to convince myself I was just fascinated by them because they were unique, but I couldn't keep that up forever. I still didn't dive in, though. I just stewed about it the whole time I was at CCAC." She chuckled softly. "I think I secretly thought that having lesbian friends was kind of like being gay myself."

"You never poked your head into the LGBT club offices?"

She shook her head. "My campus didn't have one. But even if we had, I wouldn't have gone. I was living on my own before I got up the nerve to put myself out there."

"Poor girl," Summer soothed. "You probably had some Catholic stuff going on, plus you were freaked out to be following in your mom's footsteps…" She gripped Kelsey's leg. "Were you worried about upsetting your parents?"

"My dad," Kelsey said, her voice growing hoarse as the emotion hit her. "I didn't know what he thought about Marianne being gay, so I couldn't guess how he'd feel about me. I was pretty sure he wasn't going to be happy, though."

"How did he take it?"

"Better than I could have hoped. I talked to my mom first, since she'd help me bury a body with no questions asked, and she dropped some very big hints. By the time I was sure, he'd been waiting for me to bring it up, and he acted like it was no big deal at all." Her stomach was in knots, and she added, "Just one more phase of my life that Marianne made tougher."

Summer's voice was very soft when she said, "I bet your dad wasn't as understanding when Marianne was in the same position."

Kelsey turned and looked at her for longer than she should have, then turned the wheel to center herself in her lane. "Marianne and I have never been in the same position. I could have married some poor guy and popped out a baby or two in hopes of fitting in, but I didn't even consider it." She took in a breath, determined to keep her voice level. "When other people's lives are involved, you figure out your shit before you pull anyone else in."

CHAPTER TWENTY

SUMMER WAS SWAMPED AT WORK on Wednesday, spending most of the day on the production floor working with one of her designers.

The day had been so busy that she'd ignored her phone. It was after seven when she went back to her office and checked to see a text from Kelsey that was four hours old.

She dropped into her chair and put her feet up on the corner of the desk, relief flooding her when she leaned back to stretch her muscles out. "Hi," she said when Kelsey picked up the call. "Sorry I didn't see your text until now. Too late for dinner?"

"I haven't eaten yet, so I'll still follow-through on my offer to cook, but it'll take a while if I start now."

"Let's go out. Do you mind coming over to my neighborhood? There's an Indian place I like on Penn that's usually not hard to get into."

"Send me a link. I'll meet you there."

"Great. I'll be the woman with two drinks in front of me. I'll order one for you when you arrive."

"Sounds like someone had a bad day. I'll try to cheer you up."

"I'm already cheery. Just tired. But I'll get a second wind when I see your pretty face."

"Same here. I can't wait to see you, even though I don't like Indian food. Bye!" she added, hanging up before Summer could reply. She almost called back to change restaurants, but she loved Indian food, and was certain she could find something on the menu that Kelsey would like, or at least tolerate.

⊛

Kelsey seemed pretty pleased with her dinner, sticking to appetizers to avoid the curries, which she claimed destroyed her entire intestinal track. If they wound up together, Summer would have to tame down Kelsey's portion of half of the things she liked to cook.

While Kelsey said she was happy with her vegetable samosas, and she ate nearly all of the spinach and artichoke raita, she seemed very tamped down. "What's on your cute little mind?" Summer asked, tapping her hand with a papadum. "You don't seem very bubbly tonight."

"I'm not." She picked up a samosa and nibbled on it, not even attempting to dip it in any of the delicious sauces. She must have *really* hated spice. Kelsey kept her attention on the unused sauce containers, clearly avoiding eye contact. "The friggin' Genie's out of the bottle, and I have no idea how to get her back inside."

"I'm going to need a little more detail," Summer said. "You lost me at Genie."

"Marianne. Now that I've been face-to-face with her, I can't act like she doesn't exist."

"Ahh. I can see that would be just about impossible. Seeing her had to be…" Summer paused, not knowing how to finish her thought. "I can't guess how it would feel."

"Awful. Really awful. It's screwing with every part of my life." She sighed heavily. "My sleep, my concentration. My sex drive."

"Mine hasn't been great either. I think we feed off each other."

"Makes sense. I'm desperate to get back to normal, but I'm kind of at a loss…"

"Do you have anyone to talk to?" Summer asked gently. "How about Rob?"

"He doesn't know," Kelsey said, flinching slightly.

Stunned, Summer said, "You haven't told your best friend?"

"No. And I'm worried he'll be hurt, so I haven't had the nerve. I thought I might get through this rough patch and wouldn't have to bring it up." She finally met Summer's gaze. "But I don't think that's going to happen, and I don't want to develop a drinking problem, which is the only thing I can think of to help me get to sleep. It's time to bring the big guns in." She pursed her lips for a minute, then said, "Will you help me find a therapist?"

"I will," Summer said, her heart starting to race. While she knew therapy would be tough for Kelsey, she'd never said anything that made it clearer she was willing to work to have a good life. And if she was willing to work for herself, she'd put that same effort into them, which nearly made Summer click her heels with joy.

The whole week before Christmas Kelsey was moody and quiet. She was never short-tempered, though, which made her mood less of a burden than it would have been if she was outwardly cranky. This was clearly a year Kelsey needed extra family time, so they spent most of the holiday with their respective families. By the time she got home on Christmas day, Summer texted Kelsey, and she agreed to drop by her apartment when she left Monroeville.

When Summer went down to the elevator to welcome her, Kelsey looked not only tired, but drained. Like she'd had some of her life-force pulled right out of her body.

"Hi," Summer said, wrapping her in a hug. "Merry Christmas."

"Thanks." She seemed to want to hang on for a while, and Summer kept trailing her hand over her back. "I had a good day," she said, finally standing up. "Got to pay my annual visit to my parish church last night."

"My gramma almost guilt-tripped me into going with her, but I convinced Kevin to take over for me," Summer admitted. "So you're holier than I am."

They started to walk down the hallway. "Are you Catholic? Like baptized and confirmed and stuff?"

"Nope. My mom wasn't into it, and my dad didn't care either way. Gramma's into it big, though, so I try to tag along when I can manage. I just wasn't up to it this year."

They went inside, and Summer went to the counter to pick up the present she'd wrapped. "I have a little Christmas spirit just for you though," she said, presenting it as Kelsey was still taking off her coat. "I'm not good at waiting, if you hadn't noticed."

Kelsey reached into her coat pocket and pulled out a small box, carefully wrapped. "Merry Christmas," she said, finally showing a broad smile. "I hope you like it, since I can't take it back. No pressure," she added, smirking.

"Open yours first. Hurry," Summer said. She really did hate to wait.

Kelsey took the paper off with care, then lifted the top of the box. "Holy shit!" she gasped. "How did you do this?"

Summer stood next to her, admiring her handiwork. "I took the selfie from our first date and...made it more attractive," she said. "I was going to use Photoshop, but I decided I could do a better job with watercolors. Do you really like it?"

"We look gorgeous!" She took another look at Summer. "I mean, you really are gorgeous, so it's totally accurate where you're concerned, but... damn. I'm a good looking woman if I look like this."

"It's very realistic," she said, putting her arms around Kelsey and holding her tightly. "You're beautiful inside and out."

"I haven't been feeling very beautiful. Or sexual." She pulled back and looked at Summer carefully. "Are you losing patience with me?"

"Of course not. Once you get some of your feelings out, you'll start feeling more like yourself. It might not be fast, but it will happen, Kelsey. I'm sure of that."

"I keep thinking of what you told me on our first date. Having a sexually satisfying connection was pretty high on your list."

"It was definitely on my list," Summer agreed, "but it wasn't at the top. I can be very patient when I know there's something good waiting for me. And you showed me clearly that we get along very, very well when we're both into it. I know our connection will be great when you're feeling better. No pressure."

Chapter Twenty-One

WITH RECOMMENDATIONS FROM HER former therapist, as well as a few friends, Summer had come up with a list of five therapists for Kelsey to contact. She'd settled on one very quickly, and at Summer's urging she'd made her first appointment for a Wednesday afternoon, her Saturday. Summer wasn't positive Kelsey would feel like she'd been dragged over hot coals, but she was certain it wasn't going to be easy for her. At least she'd have her Sunday to recover if opening this up was as tough as Summer assumed it would be.

On the day in question, Summer told Chelsea she had to run out for a while, then raced to her car in the bitter wind that had all of Pittsburgh in its icy spell. Traffic wasn't bad, but it still took her longer than it should have to get over to Walnut Street in Shadyside. That meant she might have missed Kelsey, especially if the therapist conducted forty-five minute sessions, which were becoming the norm. The office was in a two story building that held a national eyeglass chain on the first floor. Because it was a bustling commercial street, there was no building-owned parking lot. So Summer drove along slowly, knowing she could find Kelsey's very practical steel grey car if it was still parked. It took some careful surveying, but she finally found it on a side street.

Summer slowed down, able to see that Kelsey was sitting in the car. Her seat must have been reclined, since her head barely showed through the driver's side window. Summer pulled up alongside and gave her horn a honk. When Kelsey didn't flinch, she did it again, and again, finally getting a response. Her head lifted and she gazed at Summer with a befuddled expression. Then the window lowered and she said, "Have I been here for hours? It's still light out."

It took a second to have that make sense, then she realized Kelsey was asking if Summer's work day had ended.

Ignoring the question, she said, "Why don't you hop in and let me give you a ride home." She tried not to make it clear that it was a big deal that Kelsey was nearly lying down in what had to be a freezing cold car, but quickly decided fooling her was going to be super easy.

"I'm fine," she said wanly.

"Please? I'm worried about you. It's too cold for you to be sitting here, Kelsey."

"Is it?" She looked like she wasn't sure what day it was, much less how cold it had gotten.

"It really is. Come on. Hop in."

She nodded, then made her seat more upright. When she started to get out, Summer called out, "Roll up your window."

After another blank stare that lasted a lot longer than Summer was comfortable with, Kelsey nodded, put her key back in the ignition, and rolled it up. When she got in Summer's car, she met her gaze.

"You didn't have to come find me. I could have gotten home on my own." She took in a breath. "It was just taking me a little while to get my thoughts in order."

"You can do that once you're home." She reached over and grasped her gloved hand. "Starting therapy is rough, and I wanted you to know that I've got your back."

"Thanks," she said, lowering her head as she spoke softly. "I'm not surprised by that, but I'm glad."

"I've got to get back to work, but I'm going to come by when I'm finished. Think of what you'd like for dinner, and it's yours."

"Um, sleep?" She let her head recline to settle upon the headrest. "I'm so tired."

"Well, I'm coming over anyway, even if it's just for a quick check-in. I'll bring something you can eat for lunch tomorrow if you aren't hungry tonight. Okay?"

Kelsey gave her a long look, then nodded. "I'd like to go to bed and sleep until Friday when I have to go to work, but Jean suggested I'd feel better if I interacted with people."

"First name? Pretty informal," Summer said, giving her a smile.

"Yeah. She's one of the clinical social workers on the list, not a psychologist. I liked her."

"I'm really glad. One of my friends from college recommended her."

"She seems nice. But I'm so tired," she repeated, barely able to get the words out.

"I'll get you home now, but I'll be back by seven at the latest. Should I take a key?"

Kelsey blindly stuck her hand out and dropped her key ring into Summer's hand. "Take mine. I won't need it."

"Um, don't you have to unlock your door?"

"Oh. I guess I do need it."

"I'll buzz you when I get back," Summer said. "But you'd better answer. I'm pretty tenacious when I have to be, and I'm determined to check in on you."

"I will," she said, leaning her seat back to stare out the window on the short drive to her apartment, remaining utterly silent.

❦

Summer was swamped for the rest of the afternoon, but thoughts of Kelsey kept interrupting her concentration. She felt more than a little guilty, acknowledging she'd helped push her into therapy. But she was willing to live with the guilt, knowing that over the long run Kelsey would find some relief. Therapy certainly didn't make your problems go away. Not by a long shot. But a good therapist could help you face difficult issues and figure out how to live with them. That might not have sounded like a great deal, but Summer knew just how freeing it was to work your way through anger.

Finally able to wrap things up by seven, she swung by a Vietnamese place not too far from her office. She would have stopped at a good Jewish deli, but she didn't know of one on the way to Kelsey's, so she picked up the Vietnamese equivalent of chicken soup and continued on her way.

Kelsey's car was within walking distance of her apartment, but Summer didn't want her to have to go out of her way to fetch it. So she spent a couple of minutes trading places, leaving her own car in the spot Kelsey's had been in.

Once she arrived, Summer had to buzz several times to get Kelsey to answer, but she finally did. Summer walked up, and when she opened the door to the hallway Kelsey was standing in front of the elevator doors, staring blankly. If she'd been even vaguely on her game, she would have recalled Summer always took the stairs. Besides, the elevator noise was tooth-rattling, not something you could ignore if it was moving.

"Hey there," Summer said, walking up from behind her to scratch her back.

Kelsey turned slowly, looking as bewildered as she would have if Summer had scaled the side of the building. "Did you walk up?"

"Uh-huh."

Kelsey was wearing a pair of light blue flannel pajamas and a blue and white robe that looked like it had been made from a blanket. Very cozy-looking. Summer put her arm around her and led her down the hall. "I like your robe."

She took a look to see what she was wearing. "Oh. Thanks."

They reached the apartment, and Summer pushed the partially-open door wide, then followed Kelsey in. Her purse was lying on the sofa, but that was the only sign of life in the living room. Taking a glance into the bedroom, Summer could see that she'd done as she'd said she was going to do and had been in bed.

"I brought you some pho. Want a little bit?"

"Not hungry." She looked longingly toward her messy bed. "I appreciate that you came, but I think I'm just going to get back in bed..."

Summer took her and pointed her in the proper direction. "You go ahead. I'm going to eat my pho, then I'll package up the rest for you to eat tomorrow. I'll come in and say goodnight before I leave, okay?" She looked so vacant. So…disconnected. But she nodded and walked toward her room, removing her robe and letting it fall to the floor as she crossed the threshold.

Summer fussed with the packaging and finally got the dish out. She normally would have ladled some into a nice bowl, set the table, and eaten like it was an event. One thing she'd learned about living alone was that treating yourself as well as you treated a guest was a key to happiness. But she didn't want to go digging around in Kelsey's things, so she just used the plastic utensils that came with the order. After slurping down less than half of the large container, she put the top back on and stored it in the refrigerator.

Quietly, she went into the bedroom. The bedside lamp was on, but it looked like Kelsey was already asleep. After turning it off, Summer leaned over to kiss her cheek, but Kelsey reached out blindly to grasp her wrist, holding it tightly. With her voice trembling, she said, "Will it always be this hard?"

Summer's heart broke, and she could see, even in the faint light, that Kelsey looked haunted. "Scoot over a little." When she did, Summer sat with her back against the headboard, legs straight out in front of herself. "Put your head right here," she said, patting her lap.

It took her a minute to get in the right position, but Kelsey finally lay back down with her head on Summer's thigh. The sigh she let out would have been funny if Kelsey hadn't looked so damn bereft. But she did, and all Summer wanted to do was comfort her to let her know she'd support her in any way possible.

"Do you like to have your head rubbed?"

A one-shouldered shrug wasn't a very positive response.

"How about this?" With a gentle touch, she started to run a finger across Kelsey's features.

"Nice," she said, closing her eyes.

"Just relax and clear your mind. Concentrate on my fingers as they move across your face."

"Okay," she whispered. "I like this."

"Then I'll keep doing it. I'll do anything to help you feel better. You know that, right? You trust me to try to help?"

"Yeah," she said. After a pause, she added, "But you're the one who pushed me to go to therapy, so you're on pretty thin ice."

With a quick laugh, Summer said, "I'm guilty as charged. But I swear I only pushed you because I'm sure you'll feel better—eventually. Choosing therapy's kind of like the situation you'd find yourself in if your leg was broken. You *could* ignore it and have a bad limp for the rest of your life, but if you have it taken care of properly, eventually you'll walk without pain."

"I haven't ever broken a leg, but it definitely feels like something's fractured." She touched her forehead. "In here."

"No, it's not," Summer soothed, continuing her slow, tender face massage. "You've been trying to stuff some serious pain down for an awful long time, Kelsey. Starting to open that vault is going to be hard, but it'll be worth it. Trust me on this, okay?"

"I feel like I'm at the top of a really steep slide and I've already let go. It's too late to turn back now."

On Super Bowl Sunday, Summer sat on the floor of the den of her parents' home, watching a pre-game show she could not possibly have cared less about. She would have skipped the entire event, but this was a good time to see her brothers, who always showed up when there was a big screen, lots of food, and cold beer.

She was certain Beth, Nick and Andy would've been written off the guest list long ago if both Summer and Robert hadn't urged her mom to be more expansive. To the boys, Jackie was just their dad's first wife. They'd spent very little time with her while they were growing up, and they had next to nothing in common. And no one could accuse Jackie of being overly solicitous of people she didn't want something from. But Robert was a firm believer in having everyone connect a few times a year, and since he didn't mind paying a caterer, Jackie didn't have a good excuse for paring down the attendees.

Andy was sprawled across a bean bag, looking kind of boneless. He'd always been a little like an invertebrate, but Summer had assumed he'd straighten up and sit in a chair like other adults when he was one. But so far he'd maintained his childlike posture, which his girlfriend seemed to think was cute.

Andy grasped Summer's boot and tugged on it. "Do you love me enough to make some more nachos? We destroyed the ones Mom brought in ten minutes."

"Of course I do." She pulled her foot away and poked him here and there with the toe of her boot. "How much do you love me? I'm not into unrequited love."

"What do you want?" His head was below level, and when he looked at her he was practically upside down.

"Go with me to look at houses next weekend. My lease is up in September, so I've got to get moving on this. Literally."

Andy had gone through a couple of job changes already, but he seemed to like his new gig as a real estate agent. He gave Summer a long look. "I've got to spend a whole day looking at houses for some nachos?"

"Looks like," she said. She wanted some, too, but she made it a habit not to give in to her brothers' requests without getting a little something back. Both of the boys had some of their father's bad instincts, assuming good things would fall into their laps without much work on their parts.

"Deal. But the nachos better be good."

She gave him another gentle poke. "My nachos rock, and you know it. Be back in a few."

When she got up, Leah did too. Her arm settled around Summer's shoulders as they walked toward the stairs. "Do you think Kelsey's going to make it?"

"I hope so." She walked in front and waited for Leah when they hit the landing. "It's impossible to predict what mood she'll be in, so I certainly won't be surprised if she bails."

They went into the kitchen, pulling out another giant bag of tortilla chips, along with the Texas-style chili Beth had brought. Then containers of cheddar cheese, jalapeños, and sour cream were placed on the counter. They each took a sheet pan and started to construct.

"At least she's still going to therapy," Leah said. "Having your mother abandon you isn't the kind of thing you can get over without a lot of work."

"She's actually going twice a week now," Summer said. Leah was the only person in the family she'd told about Kelsey's background. Beth would have been interested, but Leah was a fellow therapy fan, so she knew what it could deliver—and what it couldn't. And while Summer trusted Robert with her life, she hadn't mentioned it to him, mostly because she didn't want him to let it slip to her mom. Jackie made up her mind about people quickly and permanently, and she didn't want her to put Kelsey into the "damaged" category.

"Ooo. That must be costing her an arm and a leg."

"She doesn't have much choice." She stopped and gazed at her sister for a moment. "When I learned about Marianne, I will admit to being pissed about being kept in the dark. Now? I'm glad I didn't know earlier, since I would have taken a pass."

Leah let out a wry laugh. "Given I've refused second dates because a guy lives on the wrong side of town…"

"I'm not as bad as you are," Summer said, able to call her sister on her ridiculously high standards. "Except for this one thing, Kelsey's kind of perfect. But this is a very big thing, and I'm not at all sure she'll be able to get through it."

"Does anyone ever change?" Leah asked gently. She wasn't totally cynical, but she was in the neighborhood. Not having anything close to a relationship since she was in her twenties had made her a little negative about the possibility of love.

"I'm not expecting her to make massive amounts of quick progress. But she's shut down almost totally, so I have no idea how she's doing."

"You mean she won't talk about it?"

"Much worse," Summer said, starting to carefully spoon chili onto the tortilla chips. "She's withdrawn in every way. I make it a point to go over to her apartment after her appointments to make sure she gets dinner. But once we've eaten, all she wants to do is turn on the TV and stare at it. I don't think she'd know if we were watching a basketball game or 'Antiques Roadshow.' She stares at the TV with no expression at all."

"Oh, that's bad. Really bad."

"Agreed." Summer got out a grater and started to work on the cheese. "Our romantic relationship has fallen off a cliff, too. I usually take her to bed and rub her back or something, but that's the extent of our physical contact."

"So you're more of a nurse than a partner."

"That about sums it up. Which is fine," she rushed to say. "That's what she needs now, and I'm happy to offer any help I can. But…" She trailed off. "I'm not sure the spark's going to come back."

Leah gave her a loving smile. "She's lucky she's got you. Of anyone I know, you're the one who'll hang in there."

"Hanging in has never been my problem," she admitted. "But I've got to acknowledge that having this pop up after I was certain I'd found someone with no significant emotional baggage sucks."

"I hate to see you hitching your wagon to a woman who shuts down when she's in pain. You've worked hard to get out of caretaker mode, Summer. Don't get into another situation like you had with Natalie."

She let out a sigh as she tried to make sure the cheese adorned the field of chips in an even layer. Meeting her sister's gaze, she felt herself begin to smile. "Everyone's entitled to one big flaw, right?"

Leah raised an eyebrow. "You've spent thousands of dollars in therapy to get over trying to fix people. Why even be tempted to get into that again?"

"Because Kelsey's really trying to work through this." She started to whip up another batch of guacamole by thwacking a knife into a halved avocado. As she wrenched the pit out, she found herself laughing. "Once she makes some progress, I'm hoping she'll want to kiss me with a little more heat than she uses with her mom."

"Seriously? It's…"

"Her sex drive has flown the coop. But it was robust before this all happened, so I hope that's just a glitch."

"Well," her sister said, stressing the word hard. "That would be a deal-breaker for me, but my list of deal-breakers has always been longer than yours." She laughed a little. "The only guys who show any interest in me lately look like they carry around a DNR order."

Summer wiped her hands and gave her a long hug. "I wish the guys you liked had the brains to see what a jewel you are."

"Well, they don't, but at least I'm not sitting around waiting for them. My life is pretty stress-free, and that's partly because I'm not trying to please a guy all of the time."

"Probably true. This has been stressful for me, but I'd still rather be with Kelsey than any other woman I've met. I was truly hoping to wind up with a lover who didn't need to spend most of her net worth on therapy, but that wish has not been granted."

"Well, when you add that caveat, you cut down the dating pool by well over half. God knows I've never had a mentally healthy lover, and I've been looking for one since I was sixteen."

CHAPTER TWENTY-TWO

SINCE SHE'D STARTED THERAPY, Kelsey needed significantly more contact with her parents. At first, Summer assumed she was working through some things with them, but it eventually became clear that simply being in their presence calmed her. So they started going to Monroeville for Sunday dinner. In a normal world, that would have been too frequent a visiting schedule for Summer. But Kelsey clearly needed it, so Summer tried to focus not on what she lost—Kelsey's undivided attention, and what she gained—a nice meal with people she enjoyed.

After a few weeks of mostly listening to Kitty and George try to draw Kelsey out, Summer realized she had a resource she'd been overlooking. She needed to throw some light on this process, so when they arrived she urged Kelsey to go downstairs to have a beer with her dad. She didn't argue about much these days, pretty much doing what she was told without complaint. After sneaking over to the stairs to make sure Kelsey wasn't within earshot, Summer quietly closed the door. Kitty had just put some potatoes on to boil, so she wasn't actively busy.

"You've got to help me out," Summer said quietly. "Kelsey and I are spending a lot of time together, but I can't tell if this is the new normal, or if you think she'll emerge from this…zombie-like state she's in."

Kitty looked stricken for a few seconds, then she took Summer by the hand and led her through the house to step outside. "If anyone asks, we're admiring my spring flowers," she said, taking a quick look at the front door.

"If I'm putting you in a bad position…"

"Of course you're not. You care about Kelsey." With another brief glance at the door, Kitty said, "I didn't know Marianne well, but I knew her well enough to speak to her when she and Kelsey arrived at school."

"Arrived at school…? Are you talking about her childhood?" She touched Kitty's arm, making sure her voice was warm and understanding. "I'm very interested in Kelsey's early years, but I'm asking about something specific, Kitty. I can't hang on here if Kelsey's never going to —"

"Background," she said. "Let me give you some. I think it will help."

"Okay, but we don't have much time…"

"I don't need much." She took a breath and said, "When Kelsey started kindergarten, I'd see her and Marianne every morning. You know she was a teacher at our parish school in Munhall, right?"

"I know next to nothing, Kitty."

"Well, she was. I didn't know the Maliars, other than by name. But when Marianne started bringing Kelsey to school we spoke every morning. Kelsey was a little shy, but game," she said, with a tender smile covering her face. "You know how it's clear some kids really want to interact, but they don't demand attention?"

"Sure."

"That's how Kelsey was. She and I joked around, but Marianne didn't join in." She seemed thoughtful for a moment. "She wasn't standoffish. She just wasn't good at smalltalk. Anyway, the rumor raced around the whole parish that Marianne had flown the coop shortly after that school year ended. No one knew why she'd left town, but people assumed something was seriously wrong—with her or her marriage." She looked very disapproving when she added, "People gossiped so much. It was the talk of the town."

"I'm sure it was," Summer acknowledged. "Having the mother of a small kid take off must have been major news."

"Prior to this, the hottest gossip I ever heard was when someone's daughter converted to Judaism to marry a boy she fell in love with. This was a *much* bigger story," she stressed. "I always went to the earliest mass, and I started seeing Kelsey sitting in the back with George. They left early every week, just so they didn't have to talk to anyone, I suppose."

"Got it," Summer said, knowing they didn't have much time, and wanting to get as much info as Kitty could share.

"So…when the school year began, I was thrilled to see that Marianne had returned. But Kelsey was different. Startlingly different. That formerly playful little girl held onto her mom's hand like an eel. They'd pass by me every morning, but Kelsey didn't even look up. She was a different kid."

"I'm sure she was," Summer said, aching for the little girl who had to have been so confused.

"It didn't take long for some busybody to snoop around, and when the school confirmed that Marianne and Kim, another teacher, were living together, and sharing a bedroom…they were both fired. Then everyone knew. I mean *every*one."

"Brutal," Summer murmured.

"Of course it got worse. Marianne and Kim moved to California, and Kelsey started to approach the building like she was terrified of it. George did everything he could to drop her off quickly and get to work, but she made a scene almost every day. Nothing loud, of course. Just a small child, crying her eyes out while she held onto her daddy. It broke my heart," she stressed, looking like she could cry even now. "I didn't live too far from them, so I approached George, who I don't think I'd ever been introduced to, and offered to pick Kelsey up on my way to work."

"You did?" Summer stared at her. "Just like that?"

"I thought I could help," she said simply. "Gossiping about the child wasn't doing her any good. She needed *help*."

"And Kelsey bought into this?"

"In seconds. I convinced her that I needed an assistant," she said, smiling with a little hint of pride. "When she thought she was helping, she got right into it."

"Amazing," Summer murmured. "That was such a generous thing for you to do."

"Nonsense. She was a little girl in trouble. Every person in that school should have helped out." She shook her head, looking like she could go on if she had time. "So I had my helper, and that let Kelsey have her little cry while still at home. That made things better for her, too."

"I can't imagine…"

"So…here's my point. For months—at least three or four—Kelsey mostly nodded or shook her head when we were together. I kept her right by my side until the bell rang, so we were together for close to an hour and a half every weekday morning, and an hour at the end of the day. But I don't think she volunteered a single word. Sometimes I thought she'd lost her ability to speak," Kitty added, seemingly on the verge of tears. "But then George and I started to talk every evening, just so I could tell him how she'd been…"

"And he fell for you like a lead weight," Summer teased. "As any sane guy would have."

"Oh, stop," she said, giggling like a kid. "We hit it off, there's no doubt about that. And I was so fond of Kelsey that I might have married George if only to be there for her."

"She was a lucky kid. You saved her, Kitty. There's no doubt."

"She might have come out of it fine," she said, very unconvincingly. "But I'm glad I was there. By the end of that year, George and I were very close. Things nearly went off the rails when Kelsey was forced to spend the summer in California, but we got her back on track fairly quickly." She smiled again, with Summer easily able to see the love she had for her daughter. "As soon as we told Kelsey we were going to marry, she started acting like the little girl I'd first met." She put her arm around Summer's shoulders and gave her a hug. "I'm telling you this only to let you know that she's resilient. It's just that she starts off in a…I don't know what you'd call it, but she goes silent when she's hurt or confused. It takes her a while to get past that, but she does, Summer. I've seen it happen several times, and she *does* get past it."

"I truly want to support her. I'd do anything I can to help. But she doesn't seem to want a thing, Kitty. I go over there twice a week to make her dinner, but I'm not sure she'd notice if I stopped. I've never been close to anyone who shuts down like this. I'm patient, but…"

"Stay close," Kitty said, grasping Summer's hand and holding on tightly. "I know she'll be more like herself once she has a little time."

"I hope so," Summer said, now sneaking glances at the door the same way Kitty was. "I was very attracted to the woman I first met, but I'm not even getting a glimpse of her now."

"She'll be back," Kitty said, full of certainty. "I'm just so sorry George and I didn't send her to therapy when she was a child. That was... unforgivable. We just didn't know," she said. "In Munhall, you only sent a kid to see a psychiatrist if they were in real trouble." She looked very grim when she added, "The only child I knew who went was caught torturing and killing animals."

Summer had often wondered why George had left Kelsey to figure this out for herself, but if no one else was sending their kids for counseling, it must not have been an option in your parenting toolkit. It was odd for Summer to reconcile, having grown up just an hour's drive from Kelsey. In her friend group, not going to therapy during high school made you the odd woman out.

Kitty started for the door quickly, saying, "I forgot all about my potatoes!"

⊛

The potatoes had been saved, and fifteen minutes later they sat in the dining room, with the window cracked open to let in the scent of the hyacinths Kitty had placed in the window boxes.

Kelsey had been picking at her food, even though Kitty had made meatloaf, one of her favorites. She'd lost weight, but not because Kitty and Summer hadn't done their best to get her to eat on the days she was feeling particularly bad.

She put a bite of mashed potatoes into her mouth, but seemed to have a difficult time swallowing it, even with Kitty's delicious mushroom gravy on top. Dropping her fork noisily to the table, she looked up as each of them stared at her.

"Well," she said, being very dramatic—for her. "It looks like you're all going to get what you want."

"What do we want?" George asked, looking like a bear caught in a trap.

"Jean agrees with you. She thinks I'm only going to make progress if I talk to…her."

Summer and Kitty exchanged furtive looks, but Kelsey caught them. "Are you happy now?" she demanded.

The looks on Kitty and George's faces made it clear that being loud and dramatic was a rare occurrence. They looked so stunned that Summer guessed they wouldn't reply at all, so she jumped in.

"I can't speak for your mom and dad," she said, locking her gaze onto Kelsey's, "but having you miserable doesn't make me happy in any way." She reached over and took Kelsey's hand, displaying more affection than they normally did in the house. "We all want you to find some peace. And if you could get that by wiping Marianne out of your memory bank, we'd all support that."

"I sure would," George said, his cheeks flushed. "I'd pay good money to wipe her out of mine. And don't put me in the camp of people who want you to see her. I wouldn't look outside if she was standing on my front lawn."

"Don't ever say that again," Kitty snapped, the first time Summer had ever heard her come within a mile of a sharp word. "If your therapist thinks you should talk to Marianne, we'll support you."

"Me too," George said, possibly having been kicked in the shin. "Just 'cause I wouldn't do it doesn't mean you shouldn't." Kitty held Kelsey's free hand tenderly. "We all love you, sweetheart," she said, pulling Summer right into the bosom of the family by using a simple pronoun. "Are you going to write, or call—"

"Jean thinks I should visit," Kelsey said, looking ill. "She wants me to spend some time with her and get the whole story. Since Marianne came here last time, Jean thinks it's my turn to go there."

"And you're willing to?" Summer asked.

"No," she said, snapping the word off crisply. "But I've got to get out of this funk. Jean's been telling me to do this for a month, but I've been fighting tooth and nail."

"That's my girl," Kitty said. "You never give in without a fight."

"Jean says I'm fighting myself," she admitted. "And I'm just about punched out." She met her mom's gaze. "I'm terrified of going."

"Santa Barbara in March? I'm ready," Summer said. "When do we leave?"

"You'd go with me?" she asked, her voice trembling slightly.

"So would I," Kitty chimed in.

George cleared his throat. "I've never been to California. How bad could it be?"

⊛

By the time they'd left the dinner table, Kelsey was much calmer, but not much more talkative. It actually took her an hour, but she finally offered up the fact that Jean had suggested she go alone. Kelsey didn't seem clear on what her reasoning was, but it made a certain amount of sense to Summer. If she or Kitty were there, Kelsey would have to spend some amount of time interacting with them. The visit was going to be much harder for her than therapy, so being alone to stare at the TV was probably all she could manage.

After they said their goodbyes to Kitty and George, Kelsey started up the car, then backed out of the drive. When she turned for the highway, she said, "I bet you're glad Jean wants me to go alone. Nobody wants to go to Santa Barbara for more of the same. My wanting to cry but not allowing myself to. Not speaking for the most part. Etcetera. Etcetera."

"I'd *much* rather go with you. Honestly. But I think Jean might be right. Having me or your parents there might put more pressure on you." She patted her gently. "And the last thing you need is more pressure."

CHAPTER TWENTY-THREE

KELSEY HADN'T EXACTLY BEEN ignoring Rob, but she was close enough to doing that to feel bad about it. They usually got together on Sunday nights, but she'd been so needy for family time that she hadn't reached out to him recently. And, despite all of his excellent qualities as a friend, he was utterly passive when it came to making plans. If she didn't make the overtures, they didn't get made.

On Monday afternoon, she sent him a text. *I've been a huge slacker. Got time this week to hang out?*

He texted back in less than a minute. *How about tonight? Miss you!*

I can do it. 7:30? Your choice of restaurant.

Let's go upscale. Andrea and Betty's. 7:30 unless you hear different. XO

Satisfied that she'd taken the first step, she was now able to worry about the content of their conversation. How did you tell your supposed best friend that you'd blatantly lied to him for half of your life?

Andrea and Betty, whose real names were neither Andrea, nor Betty, ran a small, intimate, farm-to-table restaurant not too far from Summer's apartment. It was a little expensive for Kelsey's tastes, but the food was always excellent, as well as unique. She'd really enjoyed her pasta with a wide variety of mushrooms, and was still munching on the focaccia their sadist server kept replenishing. Even though she'd lost weight, she didn't really think it was wise to put back every pound in one night—but she had no control when it came to any form of freshly baked, bread-like food.

Rob had clearly noticed, because when the server came to see if they wanted dessert, he handed over the empty bread plate. "I'll have an espresso. And my friend will *not* have any more focaccia."

Kelsey smirked at him as the server walked away. "Who said I don't want dessert?"

"You'll explode if you jam any more carbs down your throat. And you never like coffee after dinner. I'm just saving you the trouble of thinking."

"You're good at that," she said, getting more nervous by the second. "You know what else you're good at?"

"Yes," he said drolly, "but the things I'm best at are of no use at all to you."

Ignoring his sexually-driven banter, she continued, "You're good at taking me as I am. That's huge to me, Rob. Knowing I have a friend I can ignore for a couple of months, then jump right back in with is very comforting."

"I love you," he said, tossing that sentiment off easily. "Whether I see you every week or twice a year, I still love you." He had a spoon in his hand, and he tapped her on the wrist with the bowl. "Have you been spending your Sunday nights with Summer?"

"Yes, but also my parents. I've…" She swallowed, finding the words almost stuck. "I've needed more support than usual recently." His eyes widened, but he didn't speak. He was good at letting her get to things when she was ready. "When I was a kid, something really traumatic happened to me. So traumatic that I've never talked about it to anyone outside of my immediate family."

"Jesus, Kels," he whispered.

"It's bad," she admitted. Letting out a breath, she steeled herself. "My birth mother fell in love with another woman, and moved with her to California. I hadn't seen her since the summer after I finished first grade, but she came to town a couple of months ago—determined to pick up right where we left off."

"Jesus fucking Christ!" His words had a lot of emotion behind them, but he'd whispered them. "You can't be serious."

"Oh, I'm serious. Her name's Marianne, and I've spent most of my life trying to forget she exists."

"Who's Kitty?"

"Stepmom, technically. But I don't think of her that way. I think of Marianne as…I'm not even sure how I think of her. But I truly wish I didn't have to think about her at all."

"What kind of…narcissist would abandon her child and then come back decades later—uninvited." He stopped and quietly said, "She was uninvited, right?"

"Right. Her brother died—locally—and she manipulated my mom into giving her my address. She showed up at my apartment when I was getting ready for work one morning." She closed her eyes briefly. "I spent much of the next couple of days either in bed with the covers over my head, or explaining to Summer why I'd kept such a massive secret." Bitterly, she added, "She still doesn't understand that part. She doesn't specifically say that, but I can tell."

"Hey," he said quietly, leaning back in his chair when a server delivered his espresso. "You're not hurting Summer, or anyone else by keeping this to yourself. Your secrets are yours to keep." He gulped down his espresso, then moved the cup and saucer away to slide his hand across the table and grasp hers. "They wouldn't be called secrets if they were things you wanted to talk about."

She gazed at him for a moment, kind of knocked off her feet by how understanding he was being. "You're not angry with me for never telling you?"

"Did you keep it a secret because you thought I'd be an ass about it?"

"No!"

He gripped her hand tighter. "Then why would I be angry with you? We've all got secrets, Kels. But now that this one's out I've got a few questions. Do you mind?"

"Let's settle up and walk around the neighborhood. Then I can tell you about my friggin' trip. That's not a secret, but…" She reached for her wallet. "It's been a tough couple of months, buddy, and I'm afraid it's not going to get better for quite a while—if ever."

⊛

They'd walked and talked for nearly an hour, with Kelsey feeling a little more grounded, and much more relieved than she'd been at the beginning of the meal. Having a friend who acted like you expected him to was very soothing.

They were near their cars, and he put his hands in his back pockets and rocked a little. "You know I'd go with you if you needed me to," he said, his expression surprisingly sober. Rob didn't usually act very serious, no matter the topic.

"I do," she said, grasping him for a quick hug. "I know I can rely on you. I'm just sorry I've been ignoring you. I know it's not a good excuse, but I didn't want to talk about Marianne, and I knew I'd have to if we saw each other."

"Don't worry about it. If I'd been desperate to see you I could have called." He gave her a funny look, then quietly said, "I've been wondering if you've been keeping your distance because you didn't want me to meet Summer."

"Well, I kind of don't," she said, "but that's definitely not the reason I've been absent. That's one hundred percent avoidance."

He blinked at her for a moment, clearly puzzled. "You honestly don't want me to meet your girlfriend?"

"No, no," she said quickly. "I *do* want you to meet her. Just not right now."

"Am I going to be more socially acceptable later…?"

"No!" She replayed her last words, then realized how they must have sounded. "It's just that the time you and I have together is precious. Summer would fit in just fine if we wanted her to, but I'm not sure I do." She shook her head, after having thought it over for only a second. "I'm pretty sure I don't want her to. You and I talk about us stuff, and I don't want to have to get her up to speed. It just never works," she decided. "She sees her sister almost every week, but she's never invited me. I think we both prefer having separate friends."

"God knows I do," he said, smirking. "I never enjoyed having to share you with Ashley. She was nice enough, but conversation didn't flow. We couldn't use shortcuts."

"Exactly. There's nothing wrong with having separate friends—for a while at least. Once we move in together all bets are off, but for now let's be just a twosome."

Summer had tried to back off, letting Kelsey handle all of her travel plans on her own. It only took her a week to arrange everything, which included switching around her therapy schedule so she could see Jean the night before she left. On that night, she stumbled out of the office, nearly falling on her face. Good thing she had the ability to right herself, or she would have spent the evening in the ER getting her nose reset.

It was just getting dark, and Summer flashed her headlamps from the side street, managing to light Kelsey up. She peered down the street, nodded, then walked toward the car. Summer lowered the window when Kelsey didn't reach for the handle on the passenger door.

"You really don't have to spend your evenings watching over me," she said, sounding, and looking, tired.

"Does that mean you don't want to have dinner? I have a real hankering for that lemon pasta you introduced me to."

"I doubt that I'll be good company." There was still no expression on her face. Summer couldn't tell if she was getting the brush-off, or if Kelsey simply didn't want her to go out of her way.

"I'm very good company," she said, trying to keep it light. "So you can just eat something good while I entertain you. Come on, Kelsey. Even your stretchy slacks are starting to look big on you. You need some carbs."

She sighed, sounding like she so often did now—like the weight of the world rested on her shoulders. "Okay. Let's each drive to make getting home easier."

"Uhm...the plan was for me to take you to the airport in the morning. I thought I'd stay over."

"That's too much trouble," she said quickly. "I'm only going to be gone for two nights. The parking fee won't kill me."

"Whatever you want," Summer said. "I'll meet you at the restaurant?"

Kelsey stood up, then leaned over again a second later. "Do you really want to take me tomorrow?"

"I've already arranged to go in late. So…yes. But I don't want to crowd you if you'd rather go on your own."

Kelsey opened the passenger door and slid in, turning to give Summer a hesitant smile. "I just despise being so needy," she murmured. "I feel like I'm a child again, and I hate it."

"That won't last. At first, it's common to feel like you're the age you were when you were traumatized, but I promise that passes."

Kelsey clicked her seatbelt and reclined her chair slightly. "Why doesn't your therapist tell you stuff like that? A roadmap would be nice."

"I can give you the benefit of my many, many years of therapy. If you've got a question—just ask."

Nodding, Kelsey said, "That would require talking, and I've made it clear that's not what I'm best at right now." She frowned. "Is that common, too?"

"Not for me. But I'm sure it's not uncommon. Up for some pasta?"

"Sure." She finally showed a smile. "And I'm definitely up for spending the evening with you. You won't mind if I grab onto you like I did my teddy bear, will you?'

"I'd be honored," Summer said, meaning that very sincerely.

While Kelsey was getting ready for bed, Summer stayed in the living room, torn between going home and staying. Ever since Marianne had appeared, Kelsey had begun to remind her of Poppy. The kid was mature for her age, and had an independent streak a mile wide. But she truly needed help—often—to get anywhere. But the more she needed assistance, the less she wanted it. Summer had no doubt that Poppy would walk into traffic if something caught her eye, but she hated having you hold her hand, and would sometimes dissolve into a puddle of tears when you insisted. Not every time, of course, but often enough to make you wish she'd hurry up and mature just a little bit more.

Kelsey wasn't exactly like that, but she was close. She needed comforting, and hundreds of hugs. And she definitely needed to talk about what was on her mind. But she had a very, very hard time accepting the things she most needed. So Summer had been holding off on even offering some of the support that used to keep them connected.

The last time Summer and Kitty had a little confab, she admitted she was worried about whether she could hold on for much longer. Clearly, if Kelsey didn't get through at least some of this, Summer couldn't stick by her. Being with a woman who wouldn't talk and wouldn't be physically intimate was a nonstarter. But it wasn't fair to Kelsey to be looking for an escape route. Summer had to make a commitment to stick with her, or get out now. Being on the fence wasn't the way to treat someone you cared for as deeply as she did Kelsey.

She closed her eyes as she repeated what was going to be her new mantra. They were in this together, for as long as it took. So long as Kelsey was trying, and Summer believed with all of her heart that she was, they would remain a team.

CHAPTER TWENTY-FOUR

THE NEXT MORNING, KELSEY switched off her alarm before it rang. She'd been up since four, certain she hadn't slept much even before then. She was going to be a mess this evening—when she was going to be expected to be open, trusting, and talkative—after ten minutes of sleep.

Summer was lying on her side, facing away from Kelsey. It might be hard to get the physical contact she needed without waking her, but Summer was so eager to help Kelsey knew she wouldn't mind being woken. But that seemed risky. There was every chance she'd pull away if Summer got too close. Actually, being with her while she was asleep was kind of perfect. Kelsey turned onto her side and shuffled closer, resting her head on Summer's pillow. Then she took in a deep breath, desperate to smell her hair, or any other calming scent she could pull in. Closing her eyes, she buried her face in the golden strands, while tucking her hand around her waist to pull her close.

If only they could get back to where they'd been just a couple of months ago. A time so close and yet so very, very far away. How had the days gone by so fast? Or was it so slow? Kelsey wasn't sure which it was, but she was dead certain she wished it was still November, and that her birth mother had never, ever found her.

⊛

Late that night, Summer leapt for her phone when it rang at one o'clock in the morning. The second she picked it up, Kelsey started to talk so quickly that Summer had to jump in almost immediately. "Kelsey! Slow down. I missed the first part of what you said."

"I said," she repeated, sounding past furious, "that I'm coming home tomorrow morning. I haven't changed my reservations yet, so I can't give you the details. I'll do that after we hang up."

"Hold on a minute," Summer said, having never heard her sound so...frazzled. "Tell me what happened."

"There's nothing to tell. Marianne is a jerk, and her leaving was the best thing that ever happened to me."

"Kelsey," she soothed. "Tell me what happened. Come on now. Slow down and tell me what she did to hurt you."

She blew out a breath that must have made her lips flutter, given the odd sound. "You mean after she spent the first fifteen minutes of our tender mother-daughter chat giving me a hard time about coming in the middle of the week when she was still teaching?"

"Ooo. Did she really?"

"Yes," she said, quieter now. "She...I guess she wasn't trying to give me a hard time. But she honestly expected me to come and stay for like a week or two. And she definitely wanted me to wait until she was on vacation. I blew a lot on last minute tickets to friggin' Santa Barbara, and she couldn't be thankful for that?"

"That would have hurt my feelings," Summer said. "A lot."

Kelsey was quiet for a moment, then said, "I don't think she had any idea she was being rude. I don't know if she's always this clumsy in social situations, but I'm damn glad I take after my dad. I'd lose my job if I was as blunt as she is." After less than a second, she added, "She insulted my job!"

"What? Why on earth—"

"She's upset that I didn't finish college. In her mind, I'm some kind of genius who should be teaching at the university level—even though I never, ever wanted to do something like that. She's got this whole life made up for me—but it's not the life I *chose*."

"I'm so sorry," Summer soothed. "Did you get anything out of the evening? Anything at all?"

"Not much," she grumbled. "She spent the entire night telling me about what happened the year she left. But how does that fix anything? That's water under the god damned bridge. I understand that her life was unmanageable, but what am I supposed to do about that?"

"Do you want to tell me…"

"No," she said briskly. Then she proceeded to do just that. "Long story short: She figured out she was gay when she fell for Kim. My dad wasn't sympathetic. He wanted her to shut it down and never bring it up again. Her parents had a homophobic fit. She was on the verge of a nervous breakdown, and her aunt in California let her come out here for a while so she could figure out what to do. She… She blames me!" Kelsey shouted. Details of her evening must have kept popping up, since each of these exclamations seemed to surprise her.

"What? She blames you for what?"

"After Marianne returned to Pittsburgh, when I was about to start first grade, she and Kim moved in together. I don't remember telling anybody anything, but I don't think she's lying…"

"Why would she lie—"

Kelsey was talking to clear her head. That much was obvious. They weren't truly conversing.

"Marianne says that I told my teacher that she and Kim lived together, and that they slept in the same bed. A day later, they were both fired after they admitted they were a couple. She honestly implied that I did that to hurt her! But how could I hurt her by talking about something I was totally perplexed by? My mother left our home to move in with one of the third grade teachers, and I was supposed to just go over there on the weekends and sleep on their sofa? No explanations?"

"Oh, Kelsey this sounds so fucked up. I'm so sorry you went all that way just to have her treat you so badly."

"She's not trying to," she sighed. "Her wife kept butting in to apologize for her. She was like an interpreter for the rude."

"That's…"

"It was weird. Marianne must be a good math teacher, because she was more like a computer than a person. No warmth at all. She just wanted to throw facts at me and have me forgive her."

"I…I can't imagine how you must feel."

"Drained. Exhausted. Furious."

"Do me a favor, will you?"

"If I can."

"Sleep on it tonight. See how you feel in the morning. If you're sure you want to leave, you know I'll be at the airport to pick you up tomorrow night. But if you can possibly get anything out of staying another day…"

"If I wasn't too tired to get on my laptop and change things around, I'd argue with you. But I am, so I won't."

"It sounds awful," Summer soothed. "But you're there. Just remind yourself that tomorrow can be the last time you see her if you choose. Get what you need from her, Kelsey. Whatever that is, try to get it."

"Little late for that," she said, with a bitter edge to her voice. "I needed a lot when I was a little girl, and I sure as hell didn't get it then. Why would things be different now?"

⊛

The next night, Kelsey was far too tired to be coherent, but she knew Summer was waiting for her to call. It was late, after one at home, but she'd promised, so she dialed the phone and managed to smile when Summer answered. "I woke you up," Kelsey said, able to envision her; sleepy-eyed and groggy.

"Just resting my eyes. How are you?"

"A little better," Kelsey admitted. "Not good, mind you, but a little better. When I made Marianne run into her house, crying, Kim came out and explained a few things. That kind of helped."

"Kelsey! What happened?"

"Not sure," she said. "I think that was when she insulted my dad. Hard to tell. There were quite a few times I wanted to tell her to go fuck herself."

"Want to get into any details? God knows I'm interested."

"Mmm. The only thing Kim said that stuck with me was that my grandparents threatened to go to court to get custody of me if Marianne stayed in Pittsburgh. Her dad was friends with our parish priest, the one who ran my grade school, and he's the one who fired her and Kim. Kim believes he did it because my grandparents told him to, which might be true."

"What horrible people. I'm glad you didn't stay in contact with them."

"Yeah, that seems like a blessing. Kim's pretty laid-back, and she talked about them like they were vipers."

"That sounds like a compliment."

"Right? So Kim and Marianne believed the state might pull their teaching licenses if they stayed, but that seems a little extreme to me. We're talking the nineties, not the fifties."

"They must have been terrified!"

"Yeah, they must have been. Having your parents threaten to take your kid away from you just because you're a lesbian sucks."

"So...you have a little more sympathy for her?"

"Not much," Kelsey admitted. "But I understand her situation better. We'll see."

"Where did you leave things?"

"Marianne is going to take the morning off so we can have breakfast together. Then she's going to take me to the airport. Hey... Do you mind if my dad comes to pick me up tomorrow night? He really wants to."

"Oh, no, that's fine," Summer said. "Do you think you'll be up for a visit on Friday?"

"How about Saturday? I've got Jean scheduled for Friday, and I'm sure I'll be wrung out after catching up at work."

"Saturday it is," Summer said. "Just remember. You have some control. If you change your mind and don't want to meet for breakfast, you can just take a cab to the airport. Marianne has no control over you now."

"You're sounding more like Jean every day," she said fondly.

"All of those years of therapy have to have some payoff. I'll see you on Saturday, okay? I'll cook."

"Looking forward to it. Thanks. For everything," she said, misting up a little as she hung up. What a fucking day it had been!

Kelsey hadn't been able to sleep a wink on the flight, even though she was dog-tired. At least they were on time, which was some cause for celebration. She'd taken only her usual tote bag, not wanting to have to fight for space, so she was able to dash out of the terminal quickly.

Her dad was usually kind of a genius at being able to pause at the curb, and his good luck continued today. The moment she exited, his lights flashed and she jogged down the sidewalk to his truck. She was feeling more emotional than usual, and just seeing the sturdy, beefy vehicle made her feel safer.

She opened the door and climbed in, seeing her dad's anxious expression even in the relatively dim light. "Hi," she said, nearly losing her breath when he reached over and wrapped her in a very fierce hug.

"I thought about you every damn minute you were gone." As he let go, he said, "They never tell you when you bring a baby home from the hospital that you'll still be worrying about her over thirty years later."

"There's a lot they don't tell you," she agreed. "Lots of people seem to know the secrets, but they don't share much."

He was watching her as if he expected her to do something weird. Like he wasn't quite sure who was going to return from California. Then a traffic enforcement guy slapped the rear of the truck, and her dad put it in gear. "Was it hard?" he asked, his voice having dropped down to its lowest register.

"Sure was. Very hard. But I'm glad I went." She gazed at the side of his face, seeing how tense he looked. "I feel like a massive weight's been lifted off my shoulders."

His concerned expression morphed into a grin. "Then I'm really glad you got yourself over there. I didn't know how it'd work out. Your mother's..." He shrugged. "She's not the easiest person in the world to talk to."

Kelsey regarded him for a minute. "Personal question?"

"Sure. Why not?"

"What made you marry her?"

"Oh, gosh," he said, letting out a stream of air, like the hissing of a deflating balloon. "That's a good one. Tough question, Kels."

"Really? You married the woman, and you can't say why?"

He shrugged, looking helpless. "I dunno. She was pretty," he said, sounding like he'd forgotten that detail until that minute. "Prettiest girl I ever went out with."

"Uh-huh. Is that all?"

"No, I guess not." He fixed his attention on the road for a minute, but she could tell he was distracted. "Um, she was smart, and that was nice. Most of the girls I'd dated were big dummies." He looked thoughtful for a few seconds, adding, "She wanted to work, and I knew she'd have a good, reliable income coming in once she got her degree. She'd qualify for a pension, too, and that was a big seller."

Kelsey raised her left hand and ticked off her index and middle fingers. "So...pretty and willing to work. That's it?"

"You make me sound like an idiot," he grumbled. "Who knows why you do things? I was barely twenty. A good-looking girl who didn't need a lot of hand-holding wanted to marry me." He pointed his thumb at himself. "I didn't think I was going to do any better, so why not?"

"Wow," she muttered. "I hope you've got a better answer than that if Mom ever asks why you proposed."

"Oh, yeah," he said, very confident. "I was thirty by then. I knew what was important."

She didn't have the nerve to ask what that might be, worried he'd say beauty and heterosexuality.

"If I'd had any sense, I would have figured out she just wanted to get away from those parents of hers. But I let her convince me we should get married pronto."

"Huh. I can see that," Kelsey said. "She's pretty determined when she wants something. Um, was she always so...what's the word? Blunt?"

"Oh, yeah," he said, nodding. "But that's not such a bad thing. I always knew where I stood with her. She'd tell you if your tie looked stupid with your suit without tip-toeing around. And she didn't need all of that Valentine's Day stuff, or any of that." He laughed. "She wanted a new vacuum cleaner for her birthday one year, and she went to pick it out herself. I kind of miss that," he said, looking a little wistful.

"Again, I wouldn't share that with Mom. She wouldn't appreciate knowing you hated giving her presents. Most women wouldn't," she added. "Marianne's not the norm, or at least she struck me as a little off the mean."

"Yeah," he said, nodding. "I never dated anyone quite like her. That's why it surprised the hell out of me when she came back from California to tell me she was in love with someone else."

Kelsey stared at him, mouth agape. When she finally got her mouth to work, she said, "What? You didn't know until she came back?"

"First time I heard anything about it. She was depressed...or whatever's worse than depression. I tried to find her a place, like a hospital, but our insurance wasn't good enough to get her into anywhere decent. The public hospital that had room for her was a real nightmare, so when her aunt offered to take her, that seemed like the only choice."

"So..." She took a breath, forcing her voice to remain level. "You're saying she didn't want to leave?"

"I don't know, Kels," he said slowly. "She went without much argument, but that was after I took her with me to check out that mental hospital. That place would have made just about anyone agree to just about anything."

This new tidbit of information was enough to make her sick, but Kelsey pressed on. "You're saying that when she came back—a month or two after you were going to commit her to a mental institution—you kicked her out of the house? I...I assumed she was exaggerating."

Soberly, he shook his head. "If Marianne tells you something, you can pretty much believe it." Pursing his lips, he stared at the highway for what seemed like a long time. "What was I supposed to do? Your wife's depressed because she's been mooning over some girl from work—for years. Did she tell you this crush she had lasted for three or four years?"

"No, she—"

"She started to work at the school when you were just a year old. Near as I can tell, she and that woman started something up right away."

"I…didn't know that," she admitted.

"Well, she did. So what was I supposed to do? Tell her it's just fine to be in love with somebody else?" His voice grew louder, more pointed. "How many guys would put up with that? I don't know one!"

"She didn't know she was gay when she married you, Dad. She didn't figure that out until she met Kim."

"So?" He seemed to forget he was driving, turning to stare at her for a few seconds. "How does that change anything? She made a damn vow, Kelsey. Before our friends, before our families, and before God. I understand she figured something out later, but…" He made a dismissive gesture with his hand. "So what? Do you think I never met someone I liked better than Marianne? Hell, yes, I did. The girl who dispatched the trucks was a real sizzler, and I could see she liked me, too." He paused a second, sticking his chin out. "Know what I did about that?"

"I have no idea, but you'd better say you did nothing."

"Better than that. I stopped going inside the building to get my route. I stayed outside and had someone from my crew go get our marching orders. I stood out there during thunder storms, snow, icy rain. I knew I couldn't be tempted by something I couldn't see." His eyes were flashing when he added, "That's what you do when you make a promise. You keep it!"

"I don't disagree, Dad, but I think this might be different. Finding out you're gay makes you see the world in a whole new way. It sure did for me."

"Great," he said, snapping the word off sharply. "So you see the world in a new way. Go right ahead and do what you've gotta do—later. After you raise your little girl." Quietly, he added, "You really do see the world in a whole new way once you have a baby. And where I come from, you stuff your own wishes in a sack until that baby grows up."

"That would have been nice," Kelsey agreed. "But Marianne thinks everything worked out for the best because we got Mom in the deal."

"It worked out great for me. Kitty's the best wife a guy could ask for. But for you?" He shook his head slowly. "You would have been better off with Marianne, even though Kitty's a better mother in every way that counts. Marianne was your mom, and that's not a job you quit, Kelsey. It's just not. Maybe she got the life she wanted, but she put you through hell to get it. And for that, I'll never forgive her." He met her eyes again. "There'd be a special place in hell for her if I was in charge."

"Damn," Kelsey said, barely letting any air out to speak the word. "You really hate her."

"She hurt you so she could have what she wanted. Damned right I hate her, and I'd hate anyone else who did the same. No one screws over my little girl and gets a medal for bravery."

CHAPTER TWENTY-FIVE

ON SATURDAY EVENING, SUMMER fumbled for her phone, finally convincing her fingers to work well enough to slide across the screen. "Hello?"

"Were you asleep?" Kelsey asked.

"Must have been. Busy, busy day. Are you on your way?"

"Uh-huh. Want a rain-check?"

"No!" she said, sitting up and making herself sound more awake than she was. "I've already made dinner. I was just sitting down…"

"Lying down sounds more accurate."

"Well, I certainly didn't start out that way. But I must have been at least half asleep at some point. My jeans are off."

"What?"

"I was fully dressed, and now my jeans are on the floor. God knows what goes on when I nap."

"I'll be over in about fifteen minutes. I can't wait to see you. Pants-less."

"I can straighten up," Summer said. "I'll be ready for company."

"Leave 'em off," Kelsey said, with a hint of sex in her voice. "I haven't seen your cute little butt in months."

"Will do." Summer got a zing of excitement racing through her body. That had been the last thing she'd expected to feel, but you never knew what was going to happen when Kelsey was around. That wasn't always a good thing, but if she was feeling even a little of her usual playfulness, things were definitely looking up.

⁂

Summer went into her bathroom to brush her teeth and take her hair out of its ponytail. She almost put her jeans back on, but her knit boxers were cute, and she thought Kelsey might get a kick out of them. Now that someone was making boxers specifically for women, they finally fit properly, with no baggy butt.

She answered the call from the doorman, telling him to let Kelsey in, then went down the hall to fetch her. In just a minute or two the elevator doors slid open and she reached in to grasp her hand and pull her out.

"Don't you look cute," Kelsey said, smiling warmly. "Are those octopus on your undies?"

"Uh-huh. Cute, aren't they?"

"Very. I like the combo of the royal blue top and orange undies. I didn't know octopuses came in blue, but they match nicely."

They reached the apartment door, and Summer nudged it open. As soon as they got inside, she tucked her arms around Kelsey and held her close. "I saw you Tuesday morning, but that hardly counted since we were both half asleep. So it's been…forever," she sighed. She looked up, seeing Kelsey nod slightly. "I missed you."

"Me too." She pulled away, with Summer feeling a little pang of longing at how readily she'd broken their connection. But Kelsey was just taking a minute to set her tote bag down and remove her coat. Then she reached for Summer's hand, and led her over to the sofa. Summer sat down, pleased when Kelsey dropped to the cushion next to hers. Then a lean arm settled around her shoulders, and she couldn't stop herself from snuggling up close. "I've missed this so much."

"Me too. Next time I go to California I'm not only staying long enough to get a better feel for the place, I'm taking you with me. Jean was wrong. It would have helped to have you there. Marianne had her cornerman, and I needed mine." She touched Summer's cheek. "How would you feel about watching Marianne and me in the ring, ready to knock each other's blocks off."

"I'm glad you want to go back," Summer murmured. "And I'd love to go along to support you." She sighed when she snuggled a little closer. "How are you feeling?"

"Not great." She shifted around a little. "I'm still tired. And I've obviously got lots to unpack, as Jean says."

"I don't doubt that. You had a very rushed trip." They were sitting so close Summer had a hard time focusing. She pulled back slightly to meet Kelsey's gaze. "I hope you're giving yourself some props for how brave you were. You impressed me this week. A lot."

"I did?" Her eyebrows rose in unison. "What impressed you? My sniveling?"

"I know you're teasing, but I'm being entirely serious. You were very brave. I don't think I'd have the guts to face someone I'd spent many, many years making into a ten-foot-tall ogre. Working on childhood trauma's tough stuff." She put her hand on Kelsey's jaw and looked into her eyes. "So are you."

"It was easier after that first night," she said, with her voice now soft and reflective. "Once I got past my anxiety, it wasn't easy by any means, but it wasn't so frightening." She smiled. "I guess I'm proud of myself, too. I'm feeling more normal in some ways. Like everything's on the verge of snapping into place." She leaned over and whispered into Summer's ear. "On the way over, I was fantasizing about you not wearing pants. It's been weeks since I've had even a hint of a racy thought." She leaned over further, pressing her weight into Summer. "I like racy thoughts."

"I do too." She kissed Kelsey's cheek. "I knew they'd come back soon." Tickling under her chin, she smiled when Kelsey started to giggle. "You're so cute I don't even have words to describe you."

"You are," Kelsey said, her smile disappearing as a look Summer hadn't seen since Marianne's visit had snatched it away. This was her "I'm into you" look, and having it appear made Summer tingle from head to toe. "Kiss me," Kelsey whispered. Her voice was soft, yet close to forceful. Summer loved the timbre, along with the implication.

Kelsey didn't always take the lead, but she was never shy about expressing what she wanted. For a change, it was fun to have her sit back and toss Summer the ball. She felt a burst of energy, coupled with the heat of her desire, and it made her whole body hum.

"I'm going to enjoy this," she purred, getting right down to it by wrapping her arms around Kelsey and pressing her up against the back of the sofa. "I've missed your lips," she murmured when she came up for a breath after their first long connection.

"I've kissed you every time I've seen you," Kelsey said, with her gentle smile making her eyes crinkle up slightly. "You can't deny that."

"Then I'll edit my statement. I've missed your tongue." She leaned into her and held her face tenderly, letting her tongue dart into Kelsey's mouth, thrilling to the warmth, and the sexy sensation that made the hairs on the back of her neck stand up. "Mmm. You taste so good."

"You do too. Minty," Kelsey said, smiling. "You brushed your teeth just for me, didn't you."

"I did. I combed my hair, too. I wanted to look nice for you."

"You always do." She picked up her hand and delicately traced around Summer's features. "Every time we kiss like this I think of how lucky I am to have you in my life." She froze for a second. "I mean, I'm lucky just to have you to talk to. But to add this…"

"I know," Summer said, sighing. "I've missed this too. It adds a little something. Something that makes me feel so…" She thought for a minute. "I was going to say close, but that's not it. I've been feeling super close to you, and we've been kissing like sisters."

"Pretty close sisters," Kelsey added. "I'd be a little freaked out if my sister kissed me like you do. No matter how chaste, there's always a little bit of heat there."

"I certainly hope so," Summer said, giving her a gentle bop on the shoulder. "You really do make me think of the next kiss. It's hard to stay focused since I'm always wondering if I'll get another. I'm a glutton when it comes to you." She was hit by a surge of desire, and she gave into it, shifting her body so she could straddle Kelsey's lap.

"Well, that was a surprise," Kelsey said, with her eyes having gone wide.

"A good surprise?" No wonder she'd never been drawn to take the lead. The rules weren't obvious!

"Uhm...not a bad surprise," she said, clearly hedging.

Summer slid off her lap, trying to tamp down the shame of not having been able to recognize Kelsey's signals. "I didn't mean to push you. I thought I was getting some vibes..."

"They're there," she said firmly. "They're just not fully there. But I'm thrilled I had even a glimmer of desire today. I haven't been this... whatever I am...since I was pre-pubescent. I've been afraid it was never going to come back."

Summer had been thinking exactly the same thing, but Kelsey didn't need to know that. "It will," she insisted, with her belief growing. "Good things come to those who wait." She kissed her cheek and stood. "Ready for dinner? It's been waiting, and I'm pretty sure it's good."

"Let's do it," she said, looking just a little uncomfortable at the double entendre she definitely hadn't intended to make. They still had quite a way to go, but at least Summer knew the sexual pulse still beat in Kelsey's heart.

⊛

After dinner, they sat on the sofa, with a little more distance than they'd had when Kelsey had first arrived. She wished she felt like grappling like they had after their first dinner together, but she simply wasn't there yet, and rushing it seemed very unwise.

"We didn't have much time to talk when you were in California," Summer said. "Got anything else you'd like to tell me?"

"Mmm. Not really. I mean, I could tell you all sorts of stuff, but I have more...impressions than specific memories."

"What about that? Your general impression, that is."

Kelsey nodded, having been thinking about this nearly non-stop. "I think Marianne is stuck. You know those pictures she sent? Of me?"

"Sure."

"Well, the originals are all over her damn house. It was kind of creepy, to be honest. A couple of dozen photos of a baby, then a toddler, then a little girl. But they stopped abruptly and there aren't any more. It's like the kid died," she said, still getting the creeps when she thought about it.

"Ooo. I didn't think of it that way."

"Yeah. In her head, I'm still like five or six. She's got this crazy idea that we can just pick up where we left off, but that can't happen. At best, we'll be able to have some kind of interaction, but I'm never going to think of her as my mother again. You get one bite of that apple."

"I think it's admirable that you're willing to work on having some kind of relationship. That shows you've got a tremendous capacity to forgive."

"Yeah...maybe," she said, not at all sure she agreed she did. "We'll have to see how it plays out."

"Anytime you want to talk..."

"I know," she said, smiling at Summer's hopeful look. "If you're not rabidly curious, I'd rather talk about her in therapy. That kind of keeps a lid on it."

"I'm definitely curious, but I'm not rabid," she said, revealing a wry smile. "Over time, you'll talk more when you're comfortable. That's just how therapy works."

"I'll trust that's true, since you're a pro. Oh! I think I caught Jean doing a therapy trick last night."

"A trick?"

"Uh-huh. I wanted to check with you to make sure I wasn't just being paranoid."

"I can't wait to hear this one."

"Well," Kelsey said, stretching out a little to get more comfortable. "Marianne told me some stuff that kind of threw me for a loop. I started to talk about it last night, and Jean kind of redirected me. It was about stuff that my dad did or didn't do, and Jean definitely acted like it was a non-issue. I'm thinking she doesn't want me to delve into my dad's behavior at this point."

"Mmm." Summer looked a little concerned, then nodded. "That might be a therapy trick. I've been redirected quite a few times." She put her hand on Kelsey's leg and rubbed it gently. "It might be a good idea to work through your feelings about Marianne first. Then you can think about your dad." She held onto her leg for a moment, increasing the pressure. "Given how you two interact, I don't think you've got some massive, unresolved issues hidden deep in your psyche."

"God, I hope not," she said, worried about exactly that. "I...couldn't." She stopped herself abruptly, unwilling to even think of what would happen if she found some horrible trauma lurking around.

"A lot of bad stuff happened—to both of you," Summer said, her gaze filled with empathy. "I'm sure it would help to talk about some of the mistakes your dad made. But there's no rush, Kelsey. He's a solid guy."

She nodded again, feeling a little relief. "I know he is. But..." She closed her eyes briefly. "Marianne told me he's the one who cut my grandparents and my uncle off. Once my grandparents threatened to try to get custody of me, he told them he'd call the police if any of them ever stepped onto our property."

"I can't say I blame him on that..."

"No, it made sense to keep an eye on my grandparents, who sound like horrible people, but he cut my uncle off just because he was afraid he was in cahoots with them." She shrugged. "That wasn't really necessary. Letting me think I was so unlovable that my mother, my grandparents, and my uncle had all dropped me like a hot rock was unnecessarily cruel. My dad never explained any of that. He just let me...worry."

Summer wrapped her in a tender hug, murmuring into her ear. "He probably didn't know what to do. He was flying blind, Kelsey. That doesn't mean you don't have a very valid complaint. But I'm pretty confident he was floundering."

"Yeah, you're right." She sat up a little and let out a breath. "How can I be so tired when it's not even nine o'clock?"

"Stress," Summer said immediately. "Why don't you lie down on the sofa and let me rub your back. We definitely don't need to be feeling sexual to be loving toward each other, right?"

A wave of panic hit Kelsey so strong she felt like she might be sick. "You say that like you think that part of our relationship is...over. You don't think that, do you?"

"No, no, not at all." She put her hand on Kelsey's shoulder and looked at her for a few seconds. "Have you ever had periods where your sex drive has gone missing?"

"None that I can think of..."

"So this isn't something that's come up for you throughout your life?"

"No," she said, so glad she was certain of that. "I meant it when I said I haven't been like this since I hit puberty."

"It's stress," Summer said, seeming so sure of herself. "Trust me on this. If your sex drive has always been reliable, having it go on the fritz when you've had this kind of turmoil isn't surprising. Really."

"God, I hope so," she said, still kind of shook.

"A lot is going on in your head," Summer soothed. "When you sort things out, and have a good plan for how you want to go forward, you'll start feeling normal again."

"I guess I have to believe that." She let out a breath, not as confident about the future as Summer seemed to be. "Could you do that thing with my face? Where you just touch it for a while?"

"Love to. Get comfortable and we'll see if we can work a little of that stress out."

Kelsey lowered herself so her head was resting on Summer's leg, then shifted around until it was supported at the right angle. "Nice," she said, hearing how heavy her sigh was.

"Are you awake enough to talk about something?" Summer started to let her fingers drift lightly over Kelsey's face.

"Uhm...don't make it anything complex. I couldn't do quadratic equations right now."

"Easier than that. My lease is up in September, and I'm ready to start looking for a house."

"Jealous," Kelsey said, starting to really relax. "I'm a couple of years away from that. I've got a down payment saved up, but I figure I'll need at least fifty thousand for renovations—if I'm lucky."

Summer tickled the tip of her nose. "Why not get a jump on things? I'm pretty sure I've got the money together..."

Kelsey's eyes popped open. "Are you asking me to move in with you?"

"More than that. I'm asking you to help me buy the house we'll live in. I want to make sure we agree on what and where and...everything."

"Seriously? You think we're at that point?"

"Well, no, I'm not sure," she said, her brow furrowing a little. "But I think we're close. That's why I'd like to go ahead and buy it in my name. That's...easier," she said. "If we're at the living together point in September, we could have both of our names put on the title. And if we're not, I'd be set with a house that an expert put her stamp of approval on."

"Ahh," Kelsey said, seeing the logic now. "I guess it would be kind of weird to have you buy a house I hated, then decide to move in together in six months or so."

"Right. If we do it together, we could make sure it was something both of us really liked. What do you say?"

"I say that sounds like the best idea I've ever heard. But my downpayment is locked into a five year CD that won't come due until—"

"Not a worry. If we move in together, we can equalize over time. Or we can just throw all of our money into a pot and not worry about who puts in what."

"That might take a little time for me to get used to," Kelsey said. "I'm kind of protective with my savings."

Summer gave her a pinch on the cheek. "As someone whose father spent us into the red a few times a year, I've clearly got my own stuff. But those are issues we can work on. I'm just trying to see if you'd like to be part of this decision."

"Nothing I'd like better," Kelsey said, pushing her shoulder against Summer's leg as she felt even sleepier. Or maybe being close to Summer simply made her feel safe and secure enough to fully relax.

CHAPTER TWENTY-SIX

KELSEY WALKED OUT OF HER therapist's office on an April evening, pleased only by the weather, which was kind of perfect. Just cool enough to need a light jacket or a sweater, with the scent of all sorts of blooming plants wafting through the still, night air.

Just before she reached her car, a pair of headlights flashed. Recognizing Summer's little sedan, she walked over to it and bent over when the window slid down. "Stalking me?"

"Uh-huh. Want to go for a ride?"

"Do you have a destination in mind?"

"I do," she admitted, smiling so sweetly that Kelsey felt her mood improve slightly. "My brother saw a house during the brokers' caravan today. He's sure I'll like it, and he's arranged for a showing at seven thirty. Are you ready to start our search?"

"I haven't eaten…"

"I'll buy you ice cream," Summer said, using a sing-song voice.

"First? Or do I have to tromp around a house for hours on an empty stomach."

"Hop in. I think we can get to the ice cream shop and still be on time." Kelsey walked around to get in, then leaned over and kissed Summer's cheek.

"Where are we getting my dinner?"

"Have you been to that place on Butler that uses a hand-rolling technique?"

"Do you think this is California?" Kelsey asked. "What's wrong with a scoop of chocolate ice cream with a ladle full of hot fudge?"

"Therapy didn't go well, huh?" Summer asked, her voice full of empathy.

Kelsey gazed at the side of her face as she started to drive. "Not very. Not that it ever goes great."

"Remember my broken leg analogy. No one likes wearing a cast," Summer said, reaching over to scratch Kelsey's leg. "They're uncomfortable, they make your skin itch, and they smell awful when you've had one on for a while. You had a bad break, Kelsey and therapy's your cast. You'll get there, but you can't rush the healing process."

"That's true, I guess. When did you break your leg, anyway?"

"I've never broken a thing," she said, letting out an impish laugh. "But Kevin did. I learned from his misfortune."

Summer parked in front of the house, reclaiming her ice cream from Kelsey, who'd been trying to spoon bits of it into her mouth at the stop lights. Andy had texted to say he was running late, giving her time to eat slowly, but the ice cream was really good, and she had a hard time taking it easy.

"Nice looking house," Kelsey said. "Sturdy. Solid. I bet it was built in…1920."

"That old? Really?"

"Sure. The homes in this whole part of Lawrenceville are around a hundred years old. This one's got all the markings of a bungalow from that time. I like that it's brick," she added. "We won't have to worry about the wooden footings being rotten."

"Mmm. Brick means I wouldn't have to paint it, either, but it's a little…staid, isn't it?"

Kelsey smiled at her. "It wouldn't be after we played around with it. It could be like a mullet. Business in the front, party in the back."

"My mom's brother had a mullet. Loooong after they'd gone out of fashion, by the way. When I was a kid, I thought it was way cool."

"Here comes Andy. You know, he walks a little like you do. Very smooth."

"Hmm. I don't see it." She put her hand on the door. "Ready?"

"One last bite," Kelsey said. "I'm not going to ruin my record of never leaving a bite of anything sweet."

Summer got out and waved at Andy. "Hey there," she said. "I didn't mention this earlier, but Kelsey and I are going to shop together."

He walked over and opened Kelsey's door, putting on a little charm. "Hi," he said, giving her a hand to help her exit. "You two are ready to buy a house together, huh?"

"Maybe," Kelsey said. "We're going to agree on the house, then see if we want to live together. We like to do things out of order."

"Sounds like a new way to buy a house, but I'm used to Summer never following the rules." They started to walk toward the front door. "This place was remodeled just once," Andy said, "probably in the seventies. They didn't do the bathrooms, so they're still original, which might be good if you like the vintage look."

"Sometimes I do," Summer said. "So long as they're not pink."

They walked up the few stairs to the front door, and Andy used the lock-box code to let them in. "An older couple lives here, and they've let a lot of things pile up. You're going to have to imagine how it will look empty."

Entering, Kelsey stopped in the doorway, staring at six overstuffed, corduroy-covered recliners jammed into the front room. "Nice," she said, with a playful smile. "Just enough chairs for all of your siblings."

Summer put her arm around Kelsey. "You can snuggle up next to me. We'd fit in that one for sure," she said, pointing to one that was wide enough to be a loveseat.

"Those are some massive chairs. At least nothing clashes, huh?"

"I'm so glad we're doing this together. It's great to have a partner who can find something nice to say about almost anything."

❦

They'd been poking around the house for a half hour, with Kelsey looking carefully for signs of trouble. While she worked primarily with kitchens, she also did baths, an occasional entryway, and a few fireplaces. That had exposed her to all kinds of building products, and listening to the problems that cropped up for her customers during their home renovations had clued her into an awful lot of things to avoid.

When they'd finally looked at every nook and cranny, they said goodbye to Andy and got into the car. Summer gazed at Kelsey for a moment, then said, "I'm tempted. What do you think?"

"It's got great bones. I'm sure there are all sorts of deferred maintenance issues, because there almost always are, but the roof's only five years old, the furnace is about the same age, and the water heater's brand new. That's fifty thousand dollars they've invested." She nodded as details floated through her head. "I like that they left out a file filled with all of their receipts for the big-ticket items they've paid for. Organized people tend to do the little things that keep a house in good repair."

"Mmm. Yeah, that was nice. But the street is a little busy."

"That will be mostly during the day. It's definitely quiet now."

"I guess it has been. I'd actually love being twenty feet from Arsenal Park. We'd be able to walk to fireworks."

"It's a sedate house," Kelsey said. "More of a place I'd see for myself, rather than you." She gave Summer a smile. "It's pretty working-class. A good Slovak house."

"I'm not a working-class girl, but I'm not the fancy type you seem to think I am. I want a house that's just big enough for the two of us, with a large enough yard to easily accommodate parties."

"This definitely fits the bill."

"So…it's minimally acceptable?" Summer asked with a concerned look. "You've been pretty hands-off. I can't tell what you think of it."

"I like it a lot," Kelsey said. "Having the original woodwork largely unpainted is huge. Plus, the hardwood floors just need sanding and a new finish. Two working fireplaces is a big deal. You don't see that every day."

"Don't forget the original stained glass over the fireplaces. That was super cool."

"Honestly? I don't think we're going to do much better in a home this age, at this price. Of course, we'll have to rip out the nasty carpeting and paint the whole place, but we wouldn't have to do a lot of remodeling right away."

"Oh, yes we would," Summer said, obviously certain of that. "I'd tear that mess of a kitchen right out of there. To the studs," she said, making a face.

"Then let's talk kitchens," Kelsey said, getting a little thrill at being able to use her hard-earned knowledge. "There's room for a 36-inch cooktop, double wall ovens, a standard-sized dishwasher, a 24-inch sink, and a slim refrigerator. And if you wanted to have a narrower sink, you could buy a wider fridge."

"You can really tell all of that?" Summer asked, raising an eyebrow in question.

"Sure can," she said, beaming a smile. "Didn't you wonder what I was doing walking around with my tape measure?"

"Why did you have one? You didn't know we were going to see a house."

She patted her tote bag, the one she carried most of the time. "I've always got it. You never know when you're going to have to measure a kitchen."

"Kind of cool," Summer said, giving her a wink.

"We'll sit down and talk about how you cook and what your storage needs are, and I can come up with a cabinet plan. It won't be a huge kitchen, but you'll be able to fit everything we need in there."

"I'll redo the entryway tile…"

"And the bathrooms."

"Only if we have to," she said, surprising the heck out of Kelsey.

"Really? Everyone wants a fresh start in the bathroom."

"I thought they were kind of cool. I loved the old claw-footed tub, and the sage-colored tile in the master bath was really sweet. I'm not going to buy a hundred-year-old home and try to make it look like it was built last week."

"Sounds like you could be on the edge of making an offer."

"Only if I have your buy-in. What do you think?"

Kelsey had been thinking about it since Summer had picked her up. "I think Lawrenceville is the perfect spot. Not too far from my job, and even closer to yours than you are now. It's bustling, but not as jammed as your neighborhood."

"I've been shopping online for months, and this is the best I've seen for the money. If I make an offer with an inspection contingency, I can get out of the deal if we change our minds."

"Well, well, someone's been doing her homework."

"I'm not as thrifty as someone else I know," she said, patting Kelsey gently. "But I don't throw my money away. I've been reading up on the pitfalls of home buying for over a year."

"I'm excited! I didn't think you could perk me up after therapy, but you've managed to."

"I've got some skills," Summer said. "Now I'm going to go home and talk to Andy about making an offer. I thought this would take months, but we might actually buy a house!"

"I'm..." Kelsey closed her eyes and let herself feel the anxiety that was starting to grow. "I'm not comfortable putting an offer on the first house we see." She took in a few deep breaths, consciously calming herself. "But it's a very good house, and someone will snap it up by the weekend. I'm going to work through my discomfort." She stuck her hand out, and Summer shook it. "Let's buy ourselves a house."

On Sunday, after spending the first half of the day at the shop mentoring a couple of high school kids who were considering going to college for ceramics, Summer swung by her dad and Lauren's house to pick up Poppy for a trip to the Botanic Garden.

When she pulled into the drive, she noticed her dad's usual car had grown. A big, black SUV filled the space, with a temporary plate fluttering in the breeze. Poppy raced out of the house and flung herself at Summer's legs. "Daddy bought a car!"

"I see that," Summer said.

The front door opened again, and her dad and Lauren emerged. "Want to ride in style? We're not going anywhere..."

Summer gave her dad's cheek a kiss, then did the same for Lauren. "I think I'll stick with my own. I like being able to put it into a tiny space."

"You can't beat German engineering," her dad said, gazing at the huge car like it was a gorgeous woman.

"I'm glad you like it," she said. Poppy tried to open the door, but she didn't have the key.

"The sound system's better than the one I have in the house. Want a test ride?" He loved having new toys more than Poppy did.

"Maybe when we get back." She bent to pick Poppy up. "Ready to go look at some flowers?"

"I want to take the big car. Daddy said we can."

"Happy to," Summer said. "But daddy needs to go with us. I don't know how to drive it." She gave her father a pointed look, and he easily went along with the lie.

"We'll teach Summer how to drive it soon," he said. "Today you can go in a car that you're almost big enough to drive."

"Not too far from the truth," Summer said. "Ready to go?"

Poppy raced over to the passenger side of the car. "When can I drive? When I'm in first grade?"

"A little later than that," Summer said, waving goodbye as she made sure Poppy was buckled into her car seat properly. "You've got to wait until your feet touch the pedals."

"I could use a stick," she said, clearly thinking this through.

Summer turned on the car and started to guide it down the street, slightly troubled by her dad's insistence on German engineering. Last time she checked, they had pretty good engineers in America, as well as Japan, and Korea. But she was sure he'd never considered going for practicality. He had to have the biggest and the best, even if the repo man would be hooking it up to a tow truck within a year. Thank god his profligate ways weren't genetic.

As Summer had expected, Poppy was largely unimpressed by the flowers, but she was very taken with the Lotus Garden, as well as the pond. Summer wanted to paint the scene, charmed by the tranquility of the space, but Poppy was determined to destroy the very tranquility Summer loved by trying to throw pebbles from the bridge. The kid had a good arm, nearly able to hit the ducks floating around. Poppy would need close supervision for a couple more years, but no ducks were going to be murdered on Summer's watch.

Around four, Summer dropped her off, laughing to herself when her dad and Lauren emerged from the house. They were holding hands and Lauren leaned her head on his shoulder as they all chatted for a few minutes. Both had the look of a couple who'd enjoyed a rare afternoon of sex. Lucky devils.

"Any news on the house?" Lauren asked.

"I didn't pull you into the text chain? I obviously had a misfire, since I meant to." She smiled. "After a little back-and-forth, the seller accepted our offer. Closing's in 60 days, but we're not planning on moving in until my lease is up. We've got lots of work to do."

"So you're honestly going to buy a house with Kelsey?" her dad asked. "Don't let Natalie hear that. She bugged you for *years* to convince you to buy."

"Natalie's definitely not in my text chain," Summer said. "And, yes, I'm ready to move in with Kelsey. We're not a hundred percent, but we're close enough to make plans together."

"How are you going to do the financial stuff?"

Summer had already decided to reveal the minimum. No matter how many years passed, she didn't think she'd ever trust her dad when the subject of money came up. "That's still a little up in the air. We don't want to get ahead of ourselves. I'm going to handle the downpayment, which is going to tap me out." That wasn't exactly true, but it was true enough.

"I'm gonna help make the tiles," Poppy said.

"I just bet you are," Lauren said. "You'll be good at it, too."

"I'm good at everything," the kid said, clearly not beset by much self-doubt.

Summer bent over to kiss her and offer a hug. "You're very good at giving hugs, Pops. I can always rely on you for a great one."

✦

Then it was off to Sedlak Brothers. Kelsey might have had too much wine the night before when she'd made the vow, but she'd sworn she wanted to end her Sunday talking about the kitchen remodel.

The store itself was kind of dead late in the afternoon, with the design center even quieter. As Summer walked along the various displays, she considered how it had been set up, something she hadn't bothered doing the last time she'd visited.

Each designer had a work station fitted out with kitchen cabinets, repurposed to hold files rather than boxes of pasta and cans of soup. One was country French, another Tuscan, another kind of modern. There were seven fully fitted-out kitchens, each one lavish, probably to show how you could blow your entire budget without even thinking about it.

Summer meandered through them, taking a slight turn to find herself in the cabinet hardware display, then another where samples of ceramic tile lived. She spent an extra minute there, checking out the competition. Some of the stuff was top-quality, mostly hand-made stuff from Spain, Portugal, and Italy. There was only one other American manufacturer of custom tile, an outfit from Chicago that specialized in Prairie-style designs. Her tile would fit into the store pretty seamlessly, and might fill a niche that no one else had. Kelsey had already made some overtures about carrying Pittsburgh's Finest, but she had to get approval from the head honcho. But Summer wasn't in a hurry. She was barely able to keep up with their commercial work, a situation she was pretty darned happy with.

Finally she reached Kelsey's desk, finding her on the phone. Seeing her face light up at the end of a long day made the journey well worth it. Summer sat down and removed her lightweight jacket, then spent a few minutes really looking at Kelsey's area.

299

Hers was a little bigger than the others, maybe because it was up against the back wall. Not having to fit into an angled path gave her a couple of extra feet. Her desk was dark, with a mahogany stain, and the desktop was marble; cream-colored, with a lot of seams of pale grey. Hanging cabinets on the wall would have held a whole lot of files, and given how clean her desk was, those files got put away the moment they weren't needed.

She didn't have a lot of knick-knacks displayed, but Summer smiled at a photo of Kitty and George, obviously taken at their twentieth wedding anniversary. They were both beaming, with a big cake in front of them, their joined hands on a knife, ready to cut.

"I'll put your picture up as soon as we're officially engaged," Kelsey said, her voice filled with mischief.

Summer met her gaze, seeing that her eyes were a little droopy. "Are you sure you want to do this? I can see you're tired."

"Never too tired for you. I told my parents we'd be there by seven, so we've got almost two hours."

"That should be plenty."

"To start," Kelsey said, seemingly seriously.

"Two hours is only a start?"

"Unless you truly don't care and you're willing to let me fit everything together in the way I think is best."

"Um…" She stared at her for a second. "Isn't that the point? You're the expert."

"No way! This is going to be ours, not mine. You have your own way of using a space. You don't want my vote to be the only one that counts."

"Are you sure about that?"

"Pretty sure. You're easy going about a lot of things, but not design." She picked up a mechanical pencil and started to sketch. She didn't have the hand of an artist, but the drawing of five boxes quickly made her point. "I've got 182 inches to work with on the north wall. I could put in five 36 inch bottom cabinets and four 36 inch top cabinets. That would give us a load of storage. But do you have that many pots and pans and dishes to fill them? I certainly don't."

She made another drawing with a big box, then a narrow one, then a sink, then two more big boxes, each with an accompanying narrow one. "Same space with a farmhouse sink, which I think would be nice under the window, a spice rack, a nook for cutting boards and sheet pans, and another one for plastic bags and aluminum foil." She looked up. "You're a particular person. You're going to have a lot of opinions."

"But I'm not sure what my options are. I didn't get involved when Robert and Jackie did their remodel."

"I've done a few," Kelsey said, twirling her pencil in her hand, trying to look cool, and succeeding. "I'll walk you through it. Today I just want to get a feel for how you like to use your kitchen. Then I'll work out some plans for how we can get what we want in the space we have available."

"Is there enough space? You mentioned taking out the wall between the living and dining room, but that means we'll lose the wall for placing cabinets."

Kelsey smiled. "You have no idea how few people think of that when they're itching to remove every damn wall in the house." She sketched the raw space, and put the dimensions on top. "We're at roughly fifteen by eight. That's about 120 square feet if we don't include the south wall. That's plenty for one or two people's kitchen storage needs." She looked up, with a sweet smile on her face. "Hopefully two."

"I'm more than hopeful," Summer said. "I'm confident."

"Right. Back to the present. If you take out this whole wall, you'll lose about 12 feet of space for hanging cabinets. But then we could put in an island, which everyone wants."

"I'm not sure. There's a part of me that would like to keep the place looking as close to original as I can. But I don't want to be too precious about that."

"Let's do it both ways." Her smile was playful when she added, "I don't normally encourage people to blue-sky their plans. But I'm willing to do a dozen iterations if that'll make you happy. You're special."

"I feel special," Summer said, barely able to recall feeling so down about Kelsey just a couple of weeks earlier. Falling in love was like being on a roller coaster. Sometimes your stomach felt like it was in your throat. Other times, like right now, your girlfriend gave you such a sweet, love-filled smile that you truly felt like you were right at the peak, with not even gravity having the power to pull you down.

CHAPTER TWENTY-SEVEN

THE NEXT AFTERNOON, SUMMER WAS at work, pondering some ideas for their kitchen. She wanted something that was very personal, but it was important to keep the period feel of the house. Early twentieth century was her focus, but it had to have a little Summer flair, which was proving to be tougher than she thought it would be. She'd talked to a helpful research librarian, and was looking forward to digging into some of the catalogues the big retailers put out in the teens and twenties. It had never occurred to her to see what Sears and Montgomery Ward had been pedaling to homeowners during the time her house had been built, but, as usual, a good librarian was worth her weight in gold.

When her office line rang, she picked it up and answered absently, using her work response. "Pittsburgh's Finest. Summer Hayes."

"Summer? This is Kim Albright." She hesitated for a moment. "Marianne Fencik's wife."

"Wha... Who?" Summer stumbled. Then her thoughts got clear. "How did you get my number?" she asked, forgetting her manners completely.

"I'm sorry for tracking you down, but we didn't know how else to get any information..."

"About what?"

"Well, Kelsey told us about you and your tile business, and it wasn't hard to find you..."

"Great. You went around Kelsey to find me. Do you really think I'm going to talk about her without her permission? If so—"

"Please!" she interrupted. "Just hear me out. Marianne's a nervous wreck, and even though I know we should be more patient, it's very, very tough to be on pins and needles."

"Patient about what?"

"It's been two weeks since Kelsey left. We thought… We'd *hoped*," she stressed, "that her visit would have at least opened up the lines of communication. But—"

"You're telling me that Kelsey hasn't called, right? And you think I can make her?"

Kim let out a breath, audible over the line. "I don't know what I thought you could do. But Marianne's so anxious I'm afraid she's going to start having panic attacks again, like she did when we first moved. If you love Kelsey, you have to understand how hard it is to watch the woman you care for suffer."

"Of course I do," she said, gentling her voice. "And I wish I had some way to help, but I don't. I can't get involved, Kim. This is Kelsey's issue. One hundred percent."

"I understand," she said quietly. "I honestly thought that seeing Kelsey would take away some of the pain Marianne's been stuck in, but it's done the opposite. She got close to her goal, after being almost certain she'd never reach it. But now that she's had that little bit of success, she wants everything. It's awful," she added quietly. "My heart breaks for her."

"I can only guess how you feel," Summer said, allowing her empathy to rise to the surface. "And I really am sorry Marianne's in pain. I'm just not able to help."

"Uhm, would it be breaching any barrier to tell me if you think Kelsey likes Marianne? As a person, I mean?"

Her instinct was to be honest and say no. But that was just cruel. "I don't really have an opinion about that. And if I did, I wouldn't express it. I really think—"

"I just wish Kelsey had been able to spend more time here. I'm not at all sure she saw her mother's best side."

"Well, it's true they didn't have a lot of time together, but I think they had the chance to clear the air. Kelsey seems to understand the facts better."

"Oh, I'm not talking about the facts. Marianne's always very precise about what happened and when. It's just that she can come across as cold. And the less she knows someone, the worse it is. Especially if it's an emotionally charged situation."

"She's Kelsey's mother. They know each other on the cellular level, don't they?"

"I'm not sure about that. In Marianne's head, Kelsey is still the child she was separated from. And Kelsey only knows a deeply conflicted mother who was trying to come to terms with her sexuality and her identity. But those people are gone, Summer. The only way they'll be able to form a relationship is to learn who the other person is now."

"I see your point. But that's got to come from Kelsey."

"I wish to hell I hadn't left them alone that first night," she said, sounding angry with herself. "When I'm there, I can help smooth Marianne's rough edges out." She was quiet for another few seconds. "That must sound odd to you, but being nervous makes her prickly. And I've never seen her as nervous as she was when Kelsey was here. I should have made her call her doctor to get...something. If she'd been her true self, I'm sure Kelsey would've been in touch by now."

"Again, I'm sorry things didn't go like you wish they had. But I think the only thing to do is give it some time. Is..." She was almost going to skip the question, but she decided to put it out there. "Has Marianne been in therapy over this?"

"Oh, no," she said quickly. "She's never been willing to do that."

"It might not be a bad idea to try to sell her on that, Kim. It can help."

"Oh, I know. I've been going for years, but Marianne won't consider it. I don't think she has the ability to open up to a stranger."

"Okay," Summer said, out of ideas to help. "I'm going to tell Kelsey about your calling. I'm not willing to keep secrets from her."

"All right," she said, sounding defeated. "I just wish..."

"Personally, I wish they could form a mature relationship," Summer said. "One where they could learn all about each other and enjoy spending time together. But I honestly have no idea if that will happen. I think we just have to watch and wait." She made sure her voice was as gentle as she could make it. "I think Marianne should be prepared for that wait to be a long one."

⊛

When Kelsey emerged from Jean's office that night, she perked up when she saw Summer leaning on her car, which was parked almost directly in front of the building.

"What lucky star brought you here tonight?" Kelsey asked. "Nice parking spot, by the way."

"It is, isn't it?" She pushed herself away from the car and took Kelsey's hand. "I know you never have time for dinner before your Monday session. I thought I'd take you out for some ice cream."

"I'm always in the mood for ice cream." She leaned over slightly and kissed her cheek. "I wish I was in the mood to go to your apartment and rip your clothes off, but ice cream's as wild as I can get right now."

"Patience," Summer said, taking her hand. "Let's hit the place just down the street. It's only about five or six blocks."

"I'm happy to go for a walk with you, even if we don't get food. Now that spring is finally here, I want to be outside every minute—preferably with you."

"That makes two of us," Summer said, squeezing her hand.

They'd only walked a block when Summer looked up and said, "Marianne's wife gave me a call this afternoon."

In less than a second, Kelsey's stomach started to do flips. "What's wrong?"

"Nothing. Well, I guess that's not technically true. Marianne's counting the minutes until you contact her. She's really anxious about it."

"Mmm. That's it?" She knew she should add a little something, but she had no idea what to say.

"Pretty much. I told her I couldn't have a backchannel relationship with her, and I wouldn't give her much of an idea of what you were thinking. We didn't talk for long."

"Thanks," Kelsey said, leaning over slightly to kiss Summer's cheek again. Then she stood up abruptly. "How did she know your number? Or your name?"

"You told her I owned a custom tile shop. She hunted me down."

"Ridiculous," Kelsey grumbled. "If she wants to make me trust her less, she's doing a great job."

"I'm sorry I had to tell you, but I'll never go behind your back."

"Thanks," Kelsey said. "Really. Giving me the space to work this out is just what I need. I *am* making progress, but it's not fast."

"And I'm making progress in finding some ice cream for you. I'm positive I'll accomplish my goal."

Summer didn't order any ice cream for herself, and she seemed pretty unenthusiastic about the bite that Kelsey offered. Actually, she hadn't seemed quite like herself since they'd met up, but Kelsey had been too involved in her own stuff to notice until now. She reached across the small, round, marble-topped table and covered Summer's hand with her own, smiling when Summer's gaze shifted to her.

"What's going on," Kelsey asked. "Something's up."

"Really?" She reached up with one hand to gather her hair, then drape it over her right shoulder. Kelsey wasn't sure if that was a delaying tactic, or a nervous tic, but she'd seen her do it countless times.

"Uh-huh. Are you preoccupied about something? You seem not quite here."

"Mmm." She leaned forward and licked a swipe of the cone. "You know, that's pretty good. I don't generally like noticeable salt in my ice cream, but salted caramel's more palatable than it sounds. I'd still never order it…"

"Are you avoiding my question?"

"No," she said, sighing heavily. "I'm avoiding having to think about the answer to your question."

"Then we'll skip it. Let's talk about the upswing in salty flavors in formerly sweet things. I love a little salt with my sweet, but even I'll admit it's getting out of hand—"

Summer reached up and patted Kelsey's cheek. "I should get my thoughts in order, and trying to ignore the issue isn't going to help." She sat up a little straighter and put both of her hands on the table. She did that whenever she was about to say something that bothered her, and Kelsey braced for hearing a lecture, even though she was pretty sure she hadn't done anything to merit one.

"My dad hit me up for money, and I'm trying to work through what I'm going to say when I turn him down."

"Oh, shit. Talk about awkward. Does he really need it?"

"Oh, sure. He always needs it. But giving him money is like feeding a feral cat. You're going to have to keep doling out more and more food, since you're enabling the cat to have extra litters of kittens."

"Ouch!" she said, kind of shocked by the harsh analogy. "I don't think I could refuse my dad if he asked for money."

Summer shook her head slowly. "It gets easier with practice, but my stomach will be in knots between now and when I turn him down. It's draining."

"Really? That surprises me." Kelsey offered Summer another bite of her cone, smiling when she popped the last two inches into her mouth and crunched noisily for a second.

"You're surprised I feel shitty about refusing my dad when I know he's in trouble? I'm not sure what that says about—"

"No," Kelsey said, grasping her hand and holding it. "No one with a heart would like to do that. But you seem so good at protecting yourself. I'd think you could be a little dispassionate about it."

Summer regarded her for a few seconds, with her gaze narrowed again. "You think it was easy to learn to protect myself? I've got the therapy bills to show you're dead wrong about that."

"I'm sorry," Kelsey said quickly. "I'm not handling this well."

Summer stood and started to shrug into her light jacket. "Ready? I need some fresh air."

"Sure." Kelsey rushed to put her own coat on, then grabbed her bag and followed Summer out. Once they were both on the sidewalk, Summer threaded her arm through Kelsey's as they started to walk.

"Um, our cars are the other direction," Kelsey said.

"I know." Summer looked up at her. "You don't mind going for a longer walk, do you?"

"Of course not. I'm always happy to spend the evening with you, even if it's just walking up and down the street."

"Good. This stuff's important, and if I haven't made it clear, I need to." She took a breath. "Maybe I haven't given you enough background on my dad."

"We're talking about your birth dad, right?"

"Yeah." She revealed a ghost of a smile. "When it's something I went to therapy for, you can assume it's my birth dad. Sorry I didn't refer to him as Matt."

"Got it," Kelsey said, pulling Summer closer for a brief hug. "I can keep up."

"Here's the backstory. When my dad was pretty young, early twenties, I'd guess, he was a commodities trader in Chicago."

"Chicago?"

"Uh-huh. That's where his family's from. If he's to be believed, his family arrived in America not long after the Civil War. They hightailed it to Chicago, where some relatives had already gotten established in the building trades. My ancestors were carpenters."

"Why would he lie about—"

"He lies about everything, Kelsey. There's no pattern. If he can boost a story, he does. Facts are very, very insignificant."

"Sorry," she said, certain she wasn't helping.

"Anyway, he and two or three other guys took a huge gamble to execute a trade they were sure would make them rich. Or would send them to jail."

"Jail? You can go to jail for making a trade?"

"You can if you 'borrow' the money from your other clients. They illegally moved money around to cover the trade. Of course, the price went down when it should have gone up, and they were faced with a several hundred thousand dollar shortage they had no possible way to cover. My dad and one of the other guys went straight to the airport the minute the market closed that day. I'm not sure where the other guy went, but my dad chose Pittsburgh."

"He chose Pittsburgh? Out of every other place in the world?"

"Uh-huh. He'd read somewhere that criminals always stick to places they know, or places where they have friends and family. He must have thought the feds were more on top of things than they really were, so he was afraid to cross any border. That left him with just the US. He'd never been to Pittsburgh, so he didn't know a soul." She held her hands up in a helpless gesture, basically saying, "What can you do?" "He found his people pretty easily, and bought a new identity from some crook." She met Kelsey's gaze. "My name should be Lindstrom."

"You're kidding," Kelsey said, staring at her. "You are, right?"

"Do I look like I'm kidding?"

"Did you always know about this? Like when you were little?"

"Nope. When the FBI broke our door down before dawn one cold, snowy morning I found out many fascinating details about my heritage." She gave Kelsey a flat, emotionless look. "You haven't lived until you've been out on the street in your pajamas, trying to calm your little brothers down while the feds rip your house apart to search for evidence. Watching your dad being dragged away in handcuffs was kind of a blast, too."

"Oh, shit, Summer. That must have been awful."

"Worse for us," she grumbled. "At least he got to sit in a big, black SUV during the search." She shivered a little. "Because he's such a stand-up guy, he sold his co-conspirators out with very little pressure, and got a reduced sentence. I'm sure that was also partly due to Robert paying for a good lawyer, a debt that I'm absolutely certain my father has never tried to settle."

"Shit! Why would Robert do that?"

She captured Kelsey's gaze and held it for a few seconds. "Because he's a wonderful guy. He didn't want me and my brothers to have our family torn apart."

"Unreal," Kelsey murmured. "So he got off?"

"No, but he served less than the other guys. Almost two years. For all I know, he's still on probation. We don't talk about it. We've *never* talked about it."

"Is that when he and Beth…"

"She filed for divorce before he even got out on bail. I begged her not to," Summer added, her voice getting soft. "But she told me she couldn't trust a man who'd been living a lie. I get that now, but I was really angry with her for a while."

"Not at your dad?" Kelsey asked tentatively.

"Not then," she admitted. "I was in the 'let bygones be bygones' portion of my youth. It wasn't until he got out of prison and wanted me to lie about some fake job if his probation officer ever called that I checked out. Since then, I've been on Beth's side whenever a dispute arises. Anyway," she said, drawing the word out, "I was already pretty screwed up from my mom's two divorces, and having my dad go through two of his own didn't help. I'd always been a people-pleaser, but it got significantly worse. I spiraled into a long, futile cycle of trying to make everyone happy. I couldn't *stand* it when someone at school didn't like me, and when I had a teacher who didn't seem thrilled by my mere existence, I went on a year-long quest to win them over. My world revolved around how people viewed me." She faced Kelsey again. "I had no accurate view of myself."

"Poor little girl," Kelsey soothed. "I know you got help, because you've got the healthiest self-esteem of anyone I know."

"Thanks," she said, her gaze shifting to the sidewalk. "It's hard-earned. I was lucky enough to have a mom, Beth, of course, who found me a good therapist, and a dad, Robert, of course, who paid for me to go." She gave Kelsey a wry smile. "I have the least evil stepparents of anyone in the world."

"You really do. I'm not sure how your birth parents wound up with such nice people, but I'm glad they did."

"As I think I've said, I wish Robert had married Beth and had all of us kids. But having them as step-parents is second best."

"So how does this connect to your current problem?"

"Oh. Simple. I'm terrified of conflict, so my instinct is to roll over. I have to talk myself down every time I get even a whiff of it." She gazed at Kelsey for a second, with her eyes taking on a steely quality. "I have to work through a mental checklist, but if I can have a minute to reflect, I can get past the terror and find my logical, self-protective instincts. That's what therapy helped me develop." She tapped at her head. "I've got a great checklist."

"I could use a good checklist. Want to share?"

"Sure. When I start to feel frightened, I step back, if possible, and think about what the conflict is and whether it's my business."

"Sometimes it's not?"

"Oh, sure. Here's a recent example. After Natalie and I broke up, I decided I was going to date anyone who asked. I'd give them a chance, but if I wasn't feeling it, I'd tell her thanks, but no thanks. A lot of women got angry with me over that, but not getting defensive let me see they were hurt more than angry."

"These were people you'd been with for a while?"

"No way," Summer said. "I'm talking about one dinner, or even a cup of coffee. Saying no in a clear way really pisses a lot of people off. But it's been great practice for me. I get better and better at it, and it's bled over to helping me at work."

"How about with your family?"

"Things are better now. Matt panics when he's in over his head, and he can lash out at me for not helping him climb out of the pit. But if I can step back and realize he's terrified that he's going to lose something important—a car, a vacation, Lauren's respect—I can usually respond in a loving way. I still refuse, but I refuse with empathy."

"Mmm. That still sucks, though."

"Oh, yeah," she said. "It sucks hard."

"Do you know why he needs money right now?"

"I wish I didn't, but I do. Poppy's Montessori School tuition. It was due in *January*," she stressed. "I'm not sure why they even let her start spring term, but they did."

"Will they kick her out?"

"No, no, but they won't let her register for next year. I feel awful for the kid, but it won't hurt her to go to a public kindergarten."

"Mmm. I don't think I'd be able to refuse," Kelsey said. "At least where Poppy's concerned."

Summer gazed at her for a minute, looking pensive. "He just bought, or leased, a very expensive SUV to replace the perfectly lovely one he'd had for two years. That lease payment would have easily covered Poppy's tuition if he'd delayed gratification and saved it for just a few months. If I dug into my savings to pay the tuition, he'd consider that a get out of jail free card. I guarantee he'd take whatever portion of the tuition payment he has and blow it on something else flashy and unnecessary. He's a bottomless pit, Kelsey, and I'm not voluntarily jumping in there with him."

"I didn't—"

"I'll pay for Poppy's therapy, which I'm certain she'll need, but that's my limit." She looked like she was going to cry when she added, "My main worry is that he'll send Lauren to beg. He's done that before, and it makes things difficult between us for months." She showed a smile tinged with sadness. "Luckily, she needs babysitting on a routine basis, so she can't shut me out even when she's humiliated herself by begging for money."

"Oh, damn. It must be particularly hard when you could easily cover something like that."

Summer looked up at her sharply. "Says who?"

"I just assumed—"

Clearly annoyed, Summer sharply said, "Do you know how much of my profit I reinvest in my business?"

"No, of course I don't—"

"Do you know that after I fund improvements for the shop, my draw is shockingly small?"

"No—"

"Do you know that I put away half of that draw to fund my vacations, since they're really important to me?"

"Of course not—"

"Do you know how hard it is to live so lean when my dad—Robert— would give me money any time I asked for it?" She gave Kelsey a poke in the chest with a finger. "Do you know I'd rather cancel a much-needed vacation than have Robert pay for it? I will never—ever—act like my dad. *Matt*," she snapped, clearly furious.

"I'm sorry, Summer. I clearly don't know what your financial picture is. I just thought—"

"You're making assumptions that aren't accurate. Of course I could delay buying the kiln I need, but where's the fairness in that? I'm telling you, if I gave my father *all* of my money, it would be gone in a week. But even though I know he's being manipulative and downright cruel when he asks, I still struggle with saying no. It's hard," she added, with her chin quivering.

"I thought it was easy for you," Kelsey said softly. "The fact that it's not makes me admire you even more." She pulled her close and they hugged tenderly for a minute.

"I've made a good life for myself, but I couldn't have done it without Robert's financial help. He paid for my therapy for *years*." She lifted her gaze to the heavens. "Thank god I finally graduated. I've got the tools to keep myself from going off the rails." She patted Kelsey's cheek when they broke apart. "Sorry I'm touchy about people making assumptions about how much money I have. People assume you're rich if you own a business, and that's been a sore spot."

"It would be for anyone who's been put into the position Matt's put you into. Sorry I poked at a tender place."

Summer put her fingers over the spot where she'd touched Kelsey a minute earlier. "Sorry I poked you back. I don't like to show my temper. Even a finger-full of it."

They turned to walk back to their cars, with Summer musing, "I wonder why my dad didn't have to give up his fake ID. Or maybe he did. He could be back to Lindstrom for all I know. Come to think of it, why am I a Hayes?"

"We could both switch. I could be Maliarova and you could be Lindstrom."

"Maybe," Summer said, finally giving Kelsey a wan smile. "I'll see how that looks on the 'Save The Date' cards."

Chapter Twenty-Eight

On a warm Wednesday afternoon, Kelsey drove over to Summer's shop. She'd spent the morning helping her mom with spring cleaning, and after she'd found a parking spot and started to walk she realized she had stripes of dust on her dark jeans. Normally she would have spent time trying to clean them off, but they might wind up on the production floor, the place where dust lived.

Entering the building, she smiled at Chelsea, who was still rocking the silver hair.

"Hi," she said. "Kelsey Maliar. Here to see the big boss."

Chelsea nodded, with a smile building. "She told me to keep an eye out for you." Her gaze slid down Kelsey's body, then she pursed her lips. "Summer said you'd be the best looking woman to come in today, but I think that's selling you short." She let out a laugh that would have made a true curmudgeon smile. "You're the best looking woman who's come in since the last time you were here." She paused for just a second. "But…we really don't get many walk-ins."

"I can see why Summer hired you," Kelsey said. "You've got her sense of humor."

Chelsea kept her gaze on Kelsey as she leaned over to press a button on her console. "I've got a hottie in the lobby," she said, winking. When she sat up straight again, she said, "We really do make each other laugh. But she'd fire me in a second if I didn't pull my weight. She's got a heart made of stone—oh, hello, boss." She turned and batted her eyes at Summer.

"Quit flirting with my girlfriend," Summer said, tucking her arm around Kelsey's waist to pull her close. "I've got to watch her like a hawk," she added, giving Chelsea a narrow-eyed glare.

"Girlfriends, huh?" Chelsea nodded. "Nice catch, boss. I was hoping she was back to see me."

"This one's mine," Summer said. "You're too young for a serious girlfriend." She cocked her head, adding, "Since when are you into women?"

"Depends on the woman," Chelsea said, giving her a flirty look.

"Well, whoever you're into, thirty should be the bare minimum before you hook up." She let out a laugh. "I mean that in the relationship sense. Hooking up for fun is fine at any age."

"Then I'll keep doing what I'm doing."

"You can start doing that right now," Summer said. "Go ahead and take off."

"I'm out of here," Chelsea said, grabbing her purse with such gusto she knocked a stack of files onto the floor. "As soon as I pick up that mess," she added.

"Great instincts," Summer said, grasping Kelsey's hand to lead her down the hall. She turned and gave her a luminous smile. "I'm glad you were able to stop by. I can't wait to show you my drawings." They were about to go into Summer's office when she stopped and said, "Want a beer?"

"You keep beer here?"

"Sure. We break out the booze on Friday afternoons at around four. We clean extra hard on Friday, and having a drink or two makes it go by in a snap. We've got the music rocking… You'll have to come by some night."

"First time I'm off on a Friday holiday you don't observe, I'll be here."

"Your schedule sucks," Summer said, taking her hand again to pull her onto the production floor.

It was near the end of the day, but no one was cleaning up yet. Nearly every head was bent, concentrating on what they were doing. But low voices filled the huge room with a pleasant hum, while the music bounced off the walls at a moderate volume.

Summer led Kelsey to the area near the loading dock and opened one of two old, beat-up refrigerators. When she opened the door, she said, "Take your pick. We try to have a wide variety."

"You sure do." Kelsey moved a few bottles around, finally reaching in to grasp a chocolate stout. "This might be heavy, but I like a good stout."

"I'll go with this kick-ass IPA. It's tremendously hoppy, but I like it."

They walked toward a worktable, with no one appearing to have noticed them. That was unlikely, but it was nice not to feel like the whole staff was staring.

"I'll show you the drawing I'm happiest with," Summer said.

The table had a drawer, and she opened it to pull out a drawing pad. After flipping it open, she turned it so Kelsey could see it right-side up. "What do you think?"

"It's beautiful," Kelsey murmured. "But so intricate. Won't it take forever to get right?" A beaver stood on its back legs, leaning into the trunk of a tree, gnawing away. Its smooth tail was arranged so you could see the whole of it, and Kelsey could see tiny dots on it, indicating texture.

"Very. It'll take me a couple of days to do just two of these. I thought I'd flip it around and mirror it, and use them at the corners of the mantle —if you love it."

"I do," Kelsey said, wishing she could lean over to give Summer a kiss. But doing that at her place of business was being too presumptuous. "I look forward to seeing our busy beavers decorate our mantle. So, that takes care of two tiles. Don't we need…a lot?"

"Sure do. But I'm not going to go to this much trouble for all of them. I think we can get away with ninety percent field tile, and just ten percent unique ones." She held up the drawing. "This represents about five percent of the ten percent. I've got my work cut out for me."

"You sure as heck do!"

"I'll get there. I'm going to blatantly copy some Batchelder designs. He's got a Celtic knot I like and one with clusters of grapes. I've got copies of them in my office. You can take a look and see if you like them as much as I do. If those work, I only need to do a couple more originals. Actually, I might use that raven you saw last time you were here. That turned out great, don't you think?"

"I loved it," Kelsey said. "But if you need to do another, why not throw a cardinal in. That's my favorite bird."

"You've got it. Favorite tree?"

"Maple."

"I love that you have one." Summer turned to face her, getting very close, and for a moment Kelsey was sure they were going to kiss. To really kiss. But she blinked a few times, then turned away and replaced her pad. "What are you in the mood for? We're still having dinner together, right?"

"Sure are. Where can I go with dusty jeans?"

"Just about anywhere. You look really good dirty." She was laughing to herself as she started to walk toward the office, with Kelsey absolutely sure she was thinking lascivious thoughts. They were going to have to get back on the path to the bedroom, or one of them was going to burst. Check that. Summer was going to burst.

CHAPTER TWENTY-NINE

SUMMER HAD BEEN SO BUSY she wasn't able to think straight. While she could normally turn off her brain fairly easily, she had so many to-do lists, with so many tasks still un-done that she wasn't getting a full night's sleep. Lying in bed scolding herself about not sleeping wasn't helping in any way, but she forced herself to stay horizontal even when her mind was whirling. Even if she wasn't sleeping, her body was resting—sort of.

They'd closed on the house the day before, but the only physical mark of that momentous event were two sets of house keys lying on the counter in the kitchen. Kelsey had found a general contractor they both liked, and they'd agreed on the broad outlines of what had to be done, but they were leaving room for changes. After they'd done the demolition they were going to reassess. Still, she longed to be in the new place right now. It just didn't seem like theirs when they couldn't move in.

That night, she left her office to find a pair of headlamps flashing at her. She was smiling when she walked over to the nondescript steel grey car. "Hey, there. Is it common for you to hang out in empty parking lots, trying to pick up women?"

"Not common, but I struck it rich tonight. How about dinner to celebrate our closing. My treat."

"Your treat?" She grasped at her chest, teasing like they often did about their habit of splitting the bill. "Do you even know *how* to pay for two people?"

"Help me take a crack at it. We can go somewhere nearby so I can run you back over here for your car."

"You're on."

They drove to the most bustling part of Lawrenceville, choosing a pizza place they both liked, where the crust was made from sourdough.

There was always a line, but it was a nice night, and they were able to sit at one of the small outdoor tables and have a beer while they waited.

After clinking their glasses together, Kelsey said, "To many stress-free years of happiness in our home. Do you have any ideas for a name for it?"

"A name?"

"Sure. They're always naming houses on the home reno shows. We should have one."

"Mmm. I'll have to think. The obvious one is Recliner Ranch, but those dumb chairs will be gone by tomorrow."

"Tomorrow? They're ready to start?"

"Tomorrow," Summer said, very pleased. "I talked to AJ, and he's sending his demo crew to start tossing everything the previous owners left, then get moving on knocking down the kitchen walls." She reached over and grasped Kelsey's hand, giving it a squeeze. "I'm so glad AJ was available. He's just the kind of person I like to work with. Reliable and accessible."

"Oh, he'll disappoint us at some point," Kelsey predicted. "But I'm confident he's honest, and he'll stand by his work. You can't ask for more than that." She touched the lip of Summer's beer bottle with her own. "You sure you don't mind being the main person he connects with? I'm willing to share the burden, but I've always found it better to have just one person doing the communication. Then the contractor can't claim they told the other person and the message didn't get relayed."

Summer smiled at her. "You've got more experience at this, but it's easier for me to be available for calls. And I know just what you mean with the 'pass the buck' tactics that people use. I'm happy to be the only contact." She took a sip of her beer, liking the way this one tickled her tastebuds, almost, but not quite hitting a sour note. "Are we ready to order our kitchen cabinets?"

"Oh, no. Definitely not. After they've knocked down the walls we can make some decisions, but I can't even measure until the room is framed in. Then we order—and wait."

"How long?"

"Six weeks minimum. Often closer to eight."

"Damn! We're going to be right up against our deadline. I thought we had all the time in the world."

"You never have all the time in the world," she said, clearly the voice of experience. "Don't forget that I can't measure for the countertops until the cabinets are installed."

Summer slapped at her face with her open hand. "We're going to be living there with no countertops."

"Or sink," Kelsey added. "Can't put that in until the countertops are installed." She reached over and held Summer's hand for a second. "My landlord's willing to let me leave in September, even though my lease isn't up until December, but he's pretty flexible. If everything isn't finished you can move in with me."

"I don't even want to think about moving in December," Summer grumbled.

"But at the end of the story, we'll have a house we love. We'll do this right. Even though I'm not going to be the contact, I'm very good at riding someone until they finish a job. AJ has seen me in action, so he's been warned."

"I want to see you in action," Summer said, then caught herself. This wasn't the time to let her flirtatious voice seep into their daily interactions. She had no idea when that would be, but it certainly wasn't now.

❧

After dinner, Summer sat in the passenger seat of Kelsey's car, enjoying the ride. It was unseasonably chilly, so she cracked her window just enough to sniff the clean scents of late spring.

When they reached Summer's car, she leaned over to give Kelsey a sisterly kiss. But a firm hand slipped behind her neck and held her in place for a few extra seconds. Just that tiny bit of heat made the somnolent nerves between Summer's legs wake up and take a look around.

Kelsey moved away, but not very far. With a hungry look, she continued to stare at Summer's lips. "Did I tell you how nice you looked tonight?" she asked, using her sexy voice.

"Nooo. But there's no statute of limitations."

Smiling, Kelsey placed a quick, but tender kiss to her lips. "You look really nice in this blouse," she said, tugging on the placket. "Green and yellow checks make me think of spring."

"Me too. I love spring."

"I love summer. But spring's a close second."

"You can love summer at my pool." She reached down to her bag and found the key card and set of keys to her apartment she'd put in there that morning. "Pool opens Memorial Day weekend, and you're welcome to use it whenever you want. No one will blink an eye if you come down in the elevator from an apartment."

"Fantastic," Kelsey said, looking about as pleased as Summer had ever seen her. She took a look at the dash and said, "Why are we in such a rush to go home? It's only ten."

Summer was usually in bed by ten thirty, but she was more than willing to stay up if Kelsey was in the mood to be closer—as the subtle messages she was sending out seemed to suggest.

"Let's go to your apartment. Then you don't have to drive home."

"But you will…"

"True. But you bought dinner. So it's my turn to do something nice."

"Deal. See you there?"

"You certainly will," Summer said. She got out and opened the door to her car, happy they'd agreed to go to Kelsey's place. Then she could leave when she got tired, saving her the uncomfortable task of having to ask Kelsey to leave. The fact that she often stayed up until one made her regard time with a more relaxed eye than Summer was ever able to. And she'd found herself almost unable to sleep if Kelsey was in the living room. She was certain that would change once they were in their new house, which just made her that much more anxious to get moving.

Sleeping together, even without sex, was something she was very much looking forward to.

⊛

Kelsey sat on her sofa, holding a glass with a small amount of Port in it. She looked very relaxed, so much more than even a couple of weeks earlier. Something was changing. Something good.

Summer sat next to her and picked up her own drink. "This is much nicer than saying goodnight in a parking lot," she said, touching her glass to Kelsey's.

"Much. I…uhm…don't want to jump the gun, but I think I'm getting back to my old self. I'm not there yet," she warned, "but I'm closer."

Summer kicked off her shoes, then poked Kelsey's leg with her foot. "I can tell. You seem lighter, for one thing. For a few months there you seemed like you were carrying weights in your pockets. Not now."

"I think that's true. Having Marianne show up really knocked me on my butt. But spending every available dollar on therapy has helped. Not my bank account, of course, but I can deal with that. I'm learning that it's much more important to have a calm brain than a hefty savings account." She smiled. "I honestly didn't know that before."

"I'm very glad you've come to see that. It'll make your life better in every way." She took Kelsey's hand and held it gently. They hadn't spoken —at all—about the process, but Kelsey seemed more open tonight. "Do you think you're making *significant* progress? You seem like you are, but…"

"Oh, yeah," she said, nodding confidently. "I've still got a lot to work on, but I've made some critical decisions. Now I just have to work on how to move forward."

Summer felt like someone had run a live wire up her spine. She sat at attention, staring at Kelsey, waiting for more. When she just gazed back placidly, Summer said, "Want to share? You've barely mentioned Marianne's name since you got back from Santa Barbara."

"I know," she said, sitting up taller to continue gazing into Summer's eyes. "I didn't have anything to say when I was working my way through everything. But now that I've made some decisions, I feel more comfortable talking about her."

"Want to start?"

"I think so." She clasped her hands and stared at them for a few seconds. "The most important thing is that Jean's confident I'm not running from my feelings any more." She gazed down at her hands and nodded soberly. "That's freed me up a lot."

"I'm thrilled for you, Kelsey. I really am."

"I'm proud of myself," she admitted. "This has been ridiculously hard for me, and it's going to continue to be tough, but I'm going to get through it."

"There's not a doubt in my mind. So? Do you have thoughts on what kind of relationship you want to have with Marianne going forward?"

"I do. I've looked at this from every viewpoint I can think of. I went through a couple of months of unrelenting anger, but I've worked my way through the worst of that. Since then, I've been trying to put myself in Marianne's shoes and see how I might have handled things if I'd been in her position."

"That's important," Summer said. "That's what I try to do with my mom. Jackie," she added. "I wouldn't make the same choices she has, but I have some empathy for why she made the ones she did."

"Yeah," she said, nodding. "I've worked at summoning all of the empathy I can, even though I'm sure I'll never truly understand how hard things were for her."

"It's probably helped that you're gay too. You understand how hard it is to come out, since you had trouble doing it twenty years after Marianne had to."

"Right. I'm sure that made this a little easier than it would have been for someone who didn't understand how tough it can be to claim your sexuality."

"So? What's your plan? Are you going to visit her again? Or will you try to get to know each other through email—"

"You're jumping to conclusions," Kelsey interrupted. "I've decided I don't want to have a relationship with her at all."

"What?" Summer stared at her, gobsmacked. "What was all of that about empathizing with her about how tough it was to come out?"

"Separate issues," she said briskly. "I feel bad for anyone who had to come out in the eighties and nineties. But that doesn't mean I can forgive her for the way she left me. She had other options, but she chose the one that was best for her—and worst for me." She faced Summer dead-on. "I can't forgive her for that. So rather than have her build up any false hopes, I've written her a letter. I haven't sent it yet," she added. "I wanted you to read it first. I might show it to my parents, too. I haven't decided about that yet."

Summer couldn't get her stomach to stop cramping. The spicy pepperoni was about halfway up her esophagus, giving her a killer case of heartburn. Thoughts swirled around in her brain, making her a little light-headed. Blindly, she stuck her hand out and gripped Kelsey's arm. She'd been sure. One hundred percent sure that Kelsey was going to find a way to forgive her mother enough to have an adult relationship with her. And now she was totally back on her heels, feeling like the woman at her side wasn't exactly who she'd thought she was.

"You look like you've seen a ghost," Kelsey said, reaching out to put a tentative hand on Summer's knee.

"No, no, that's not..." She took in a deep breath, trying to get past the surprise. "I was just sure you'd forgive her enough to have some kind of relationship. I was *certain* of that."

"Can't do it," she said firmly. "I can think of ten different scenarios that Marianne could have chosen, and each one of them would have been less harmful. But she took the one that insured she'd have basically no contact with her only child. That's not what a good mom would do, Summer. It's just not. I appreciate that she feels guilty, but it's not my job to absolve her. In my book, she's earned it."

"Oh, Kelsey," she said, unable to hold it in. Tears started to fall, and she found herself shaking, unable to stop them. "I can just picture her house—with photos of you all over it. Can't you see how her decisions have haunted her?"

"I can," she said softly, scooting over to hold Summer in her arms. "I'd feel bad for any woman who made such a terrible parenting mistake. But where's the empathy for me? Who was there to soothe me when I cried my eyes out for months on end? She kept me in limbo for the longest damn time," she grumbled. "At first I thought she was just visiting her aunt, then I got hit with the fact that she was leaving my dad and me, then she announced she was moving across the country. Nobody explained it properly. Nobody thought to get me any help. I was just supposed to suck it up and get on with my life. At six!"

"I know," Summer said, unable to stop herself from sobbing. "If I could go back in time, I'd straighten both of your parents out. But I can't," she whispered. "They both made mistakes, but you agree it worked out for the best. If Marianne had stayed in Pittsburgh, and had shared custody with your dad, I don't think you would have adjusted as well. Thinking of Kitty as your only mom might have saved you."

Coldly, she said, "Marianne didn't know Kitty's name when she left. Don't make it sound like she was doing some charitable deed by abandoning me."

"You've got to stop using that word," Summer said. "Yes, she moved away when she undoubtedly shouldn't have. But abandonment implies something voluntary, and you don't know that's true."

"When a dog bites you, do you give him another chance to take a piece out of you? No. You keep your distance. That's what I did, and I'm glad I did it." She stood up and looked down at Summer as she cleared her throat. "We had two days together, so she knows I turned out fine. I'm not a neurotic mess, so she can stop worrying about me. She's going to have to be happy with that."

Summer looked up at her as she pulled away to grab a tissue from the box on the coffee table. While she dried her eyes, she tried to remind herself that Kelsey was a generous, loving, caring, connected woman. But all she could think of was how devastated Marianne was going to be. No one could argue that she hadn't made grievous mistakes. But George had a big part in this mess, too, and Kelsey didn't seem to have a lick of animosity toward him. He'd gotten off without a black mark on his record, while Marianne had gotten the death penalty.

⊛

Kelsey sat back down when Summer went to use the bathroom. She was clearly unhappy about the decision, but that just made no sense. Whose side was she on?

Watching Summer cry like a beloved pet had run away had Kelsey puzzled and more than a little pissed off. It was none of Summer's damn business what kind of relationship she and Marianne had, and her trying to sway Kelsey's decision was really out-of-line. Kelsey had her own feelings about Summer's need to be close to all of her many parents, but she'd never expressed them. Those were Summer's relationships, and if she wanted to be close to a dad who was a total fuck-up, that was her choice. But it sucked that she felt she had the right to push for a reconciliation with Marianne. She didn't. And if she didn't back off, Kelsey was going to tell her that—clearly.

⊛

A few minutes later, Kelsey watched Summer cross the living room to sit close to her on the sofa. After tentatively taking her hand, Summer didn't say anything for a minute, staring intently as she started to trace Kelsey's fingers with one of her own. Then she looked up and gazed at her soberly. "Give me some time to catch up here, okay? You've got months of working through this under your belt, while I'm really behind."

"Uhm…sure. I guess that makes sense."

"I don't want to guilt-trip you, Kelsey. And I definitely don't want to tell you what to do. I just need to digest all of this."

"All right," she said again.

Summer put her hand on Kelsey's cheek, gently asking, "Did I let you down by what I said?"

"Yeah." She could have gone on, but thought brevity was best.

"I'm so sorry. I hate it when I'm not there for you when you need me. Just give me some time. I'm stuck on thinking about Marianne's loss, and that's not fair to you."

"No, it's not." She looked up and met Summer's eyes. "We've each got to make peace with our parents in whatever ways work for us. Let's try to stay in our lanes, okay?"

"I think that's good advice. I promise I'll try to follow it." She leaned forward and opened her arms. "Hug?"

"Sure," Kelsey said, with her feelings slightly soothed by Summer's embrace. As she smelled her hair and felt the soft fullness of her breasts pressing against her arm, she waited for the first flush of sexual desire to hit her. But it didn't come. The sparks she'd felt when they were in the car had died out. Whether that was from feeling like Summer wasn't fully on her side, or if this was just how things were going to be for some unspecified period—she hated it. A lot.

CHAPTER THIRTY

THE NEXT NIGHT, THEY PLANNED on meeting at the new house to see if it had been properly cleaned out. Summer was a little anxious about it, really hoping AJ's guys had started off on a good foot. The clean-up was a very easy task, so it didn't necessarily mean much if they did it well. But it might mean a lot if they did it poorly.

She'd had time to eat a salad, and had offered to bring one along for Kelsey, but she hadn't been interested. Summer waited by her car, knowing Kelsey would be on time. A minute later, Summer crossed the now-quiet street to kiss her cheek when she pulled up. "Did you get dinner?"

"I wasn't in the mood for anything healthy." She held up a paper bag as she got out of the car. "Snack night."

"Whatever works," Summer said. She took her hand and led the way to their new front door. The lock was a little balky, but the key eventually turned.

She blinked in surprised when Kelsey grasped her firmly, turned her, then placed a long, soft kiss to her lips. It didn't take long, maybe five seconds, for Summer to feel herself begin to heat up. She missed this kind of unexpected intimacy so much…

Kelsey let her go, but she stayed close for another few seconds. "I hope that was the first kiss we share in our new home," she said, sounding a little shaky.

"I do too," Summer agreed, hugging her tightly.

"I know it's not guaranteed at this point, but I promise things will get better—between us," Kelsey clarified. "I'm certain of that."

"I am too," Summer said, lying just a little. She was definitely hopeful, but not certain at all. They'd taken too many left turns for her to be sure of anything.

"I'm kind of nervous to look inside," Kelsey said. "You?"

"Very."

"Then let's just do it. Throw that door open and see if we've made a terrible mistake."

Summer half-closed her eyes, trying to prepare herself for having a room full of recliners. But as the door opened fully, she was thrilled to see basically nothing, and smell only dust. Maybe from drywall…

"I'm damn glad they're gone, but aren't you going to miss being able to fall into a recliner the second you get inside?" Kelsey teased. "I could plop down in one right now to eat my snack."

"I'll buy you one if you like recliners. You can keep it in your room."

"I'm going to have a room?"

Summer took her hand again, and they went into the kitchen—which had been opened up to the studs. No more appliances, no more cabinets, no more countertops. "Nice job," Summer said, smiling contentedly. "They cleaned up well, too."

"Very good first impression. But now I can't do the 'Summer Special' and climb up on the counter to eat my snack."

"Front porch?"

"I guess that'll do. It won't take me long."

They went outside, and Kelsey started to sit, but Summer stopped her. "I've got something you can sit on." She pulled a sketch book out of her tote bag and placed it on the top step. "Not the nicest chair, but you won't get dust on your slacks."

"But you will."

"Just jeans. And they're already dusty." She sat down on the step and watched Kelsey start to dig into her bag.

"I've got some snacking habits that you'll discover sooner or later, so it might as well be sooner." She pulled a jar of chunky peanut butter from the bag, then produced a massive sack of M&Ms. Waggling her eyebrows, she pulled out a spoon and started to remove the top from the peanut butter jar.

"Don't you need…something?" Summer asked. "Like a bowl?"

"Nope." She got the jar open, then bit the edge off the bag of candy. After sprinkling it liberally into the jar, she stuck her spoon in to ease out a heaping mound full of peanut butter and M&Ms. The spoon slid into her mouth, and she smiled in satisfaction.

"That's…interesting," Summer said, only slightly disgusted. Every once in a while she was reminded that she was pretty persnickety when it came to food presentation. "I'd have to say that's the first time I've ever seen anyone eat peanut butter directly out of a jar, but if you're going to do it, I guess the M&Ms make a nice addition." She pulled out her phone and took several photos of Kelsey grinning while holding the laden spoon close to her mouth.

"Years from now, I'm going to look back at all of the pictures you take of me and have to admit I'm kind of odd."

"No need to wait that long," Summer assured her. "I'll send this to you," she added, knowing Kelsey liked to share the goofier looking ones with her mom or Rob.

"Can't shame me," she insisted. "My sweet-salty snack is near and dear to my heart." She pointed her spoon at Summer. "I should admit I have two beloved snacks. I also like to take a jar of fudge and jam pretzel sticks into it." Her eyes closed halfway as she shoveled another spoonful of the candy into her mouth. "I should start putting peanut butter in with the fudge along with the pretzel sticks. That would be kind of epic…"

"Mmm. You can keep your epic snack, buddy. Neither of those sound good to me." Summer thought of something, asking, "Is this one of the things Ashley didn't like?"

"Didn't like is way too weak a descriptor. When I was in a snack-for-dinner mood I had it at work. I had to lock my goodies up so my co-workers didn't steal them, but every month or so I'd mix the whole thing up and eat it on the way home. I'm sure Ashley could smell the peanut butter on my breath, but she never asked why I didn't want dinner."

Summer laughed. "You don't have to hide things from me. I'm simply not into shaming people. Unless you do something morally wrong, of course. Sometimes public shaming is a good thing."

"I don't think I do anything that deserves public shaming, even though I'll admit I'd never eat this in front of my mom." She stuck her spoon into the jar again, looking very happy. "Hey, I've got one for you, since you like spicy food. My spicy-salty snack might be just up your alley."

"I'm afraid, but go right ahead."

Her eyes were dancing with happiness when she said, "I take a bag of hot taco chips that I break up into little pieces, then throw in some salsa, sour cream, and grated cheddar cheese. After shaking the bag, I eat it with a spoon. Delicious," she added, showing a playful grin.

"Yet another snack I'm sure you don't eat at home."

"I could, since it's my dad's creation. When he's in the mood, he'll roll up to a 7-11 and make his lunch in his truck. No fuss, no muss."

"Lots of muss! That would be a mess in a car, especially with the tiny spoons they give you."

Kelsey shrugged. "He's not too worried about cleanliness when he's hungry. He's a guy," she added, as if that explained it all.

"Glad I'm gay," she said, more certain of that every day. Men had their place, but they had some very odd habits.

"What do you like to snack on? We could keep some stuff in a bin that we leave here. We'd have to hide it so the workmen didn't eat everything, but I bet someone makes a tradesman-proof box of some sort."

Summer smiled at her. "This will not excite you, but I like to snack on a nut-heavy granola. If I'm feeling wild, I might add dates or cranberries to it."

"Amateur," she said, laughing a little as she stuck her soup spoon into the jar again, taking a bite that wouldn't have even fit into Summer's mouth. You learned things about people when you were preparing to live together. Some of those things were truly odd.

"What did you mean when you said I'd have a room?" Kelsey asked, slowing down as her blood-sugar must have spiked.

"Oh. Well, we'll use the biggest bedroom for our master, and I assumed we'd each claim one of the other bedrooms. I want to set mine up with cabinets and pull-out drawers for all of my art supplies. First time I'll have a semblance of a studio."

"No guest room?" Kelsey asked, taking another massive bite.

"Well, we could… But I really need a place for my art stuff. I've got a *lot*."

"I don't really need my own space," Kelsey said. "I thought we'd use your living room furniture, since it's nicer than mine, then stick my audio set-up on the opposite wall."

"In the living room?" Summer asked, raising an eyebrow.

"Where else?"

"I've never had a TV in my living room. I'm…not a fan."

"So I've got to give up my TV in order to have a guest room? I really think we need one, Summer. Your college friends live all over the country. Don't you want them to be able to stay with us?"

Well, that was a thoughtful way of looking at the world. Summer had to be just as generous. "Let me think about it," she said, surprising herself at how much she didn't want a big screen TV right in her line of sight when she walked into the house. In her dreams, their cute little bungalow looked much the same as it would have in 1920—well before some wise guy ruined every living room in America by having a big, black box taking up too much prime real estate.

Summer didn't usually have to work on the weekends, but having to divert her attention to the new house had left her a little short of time for some of the more mundane office tasks. So one rainy Saturday afternoon in early June, she sat at her desk, going over the numbers their bookkeeper had put together for the month of May. Her phone rang, and she was going to ignore it, but after taking a look at the area code, she picked up. "Hello?"

"Summer? Hi, it's Kim."

"Hello," she said warily. They hadn't spoken since that one call, and she waited for Kim to reveal her reason for calling.

"How's everything?"

"Good," Summer said. "You?"

"Oh, you know. Things are always changing. Um, we're in Pittsburgh. Well, Mt. Lebanon, to be exact. Can you…let Kelsey know that?"

"You're here? Now?"

"Uh-huh. You know Marianne's brother died last year, right?"

"I do. That's why she was in town."

"That's right. Well, he left his house to Marianne, and we got to talking about it and decided we'd like to keep it and spend our summers here. We both really love Pennsylvania, except in the winter. And I've got a sister and some nieces and nephews here."

"Kim?"

"Mmm-hmm?"

"Kelsey's not going to be happy about this. She hates to be pressured, and she's going to be certain you're doing this to force her into staying in touch."

"That's not true! Well, not the only thing that's true. We both love it here, Summer. We've already found tutoring jobs, so we'll be busy. But if Kelsey's willing…we're here until the end of August."

"I'll let her know," Summer said, then clicked off without even a goodbye. It took a lot to make her angry, but Marianne and Kim had managed to do it with very little effort.

An hour after Kelsey got home from work, she sat on the sofa, shoveling spoonfuls of vanilla ice cream she'd studded with broken up Reese's Peanut Butter Cups and pretzel sticks. It was an unholy mess in Summer's opinion, a concoction she didn't think she could be hungry enough to even take a bite of, but she wasn't going to tease Kelsey about it. She was clearly trying to soothe herself after finding out that her mother had chased her nearly to her doorstep.

"I'm not going to contact them," she said, every crunch of pretzel making Summer flinch. "I actually might go live in the house while it's being worked on." Summer started to speak, but Kelsey added, "I won't do anything until I talk to Jean. She can calm me down—usually." She took another crunchy bite, then gazed at Summer for a long minute. "What do you think their game is?"

Summer didn't have to think for long to answer that question. "I think Marianne's going to try to find a way to *make* you talk to her. I don't think it's any more diabolical than that. She has a goal, and she's seemingly unable to move on from it."

"Yeah, that's what I think too." She stood up and put the top back on her ice cream, then tossed it haphazardly into the freezer. "I'm going to bed so I don't have to think about it." She trudged into her bedroom, either forgetting that Summer was there, or unable to realize that walking away when you had a guest in your house wasn't the norm. The woman was seriously off her stride, and at this point, Summer truly understood why.

⊛

Summer was waiting outside of Jean's office on Monday night, certain Kelsey would need some support. But when the door opened, Kelsey stepped onto the sidewalk, looking...absolutely normal. "Hey," Summer said, surprising her.

"Whoa!" She stepped back slightly. "Good thing I don't know karate. Or whatever martial art lets you grab someone and have them on the ground in half a second."

"I'm glad you don't know it, either." Summer stood a little closer, looking into Kelsey's eyes. "Need to talk?"

"Need to eat. Have you had dinner?"

"Just a salad. Pick someplace that has a liquor license, and I'll be happy."

"There's a good place right down the street. It's kind of a bar, but they have good burgers."

337

"Then we can both be happy," Summer said, taking Kelsey's hand as she led the way.

On the walk, Summer could tell that Kelsey's session had gone well. Even though she wasn't very talkative, she didn't seem like a bottled up ball of anger or confusion. Tonight she just seemed quiet.

After they'd looked over the very short menu and ordered, Kelsey leaned back in her chair, making the front legs leave the floor. Summer had never gotten into that habit. She'd done it once when Randy was still in the house, and he'd purposefully jabbed at a front leg with his foot. When her head flew back to hit the wall, he'd said, "I just bought those chairs, and if you break a rung, I'll beat your ass with it." She was just about to recount the episode, but even after all these years she was still shaken by the casual cruelty of the one guy in her parent line-up who had never earned the term.

Their drinks were delivered, and Kelsey took a sip of her beer, looking a little lost in thought. "Remember when I said I'd written something to Marianne, but hadn't sent it?"

"Uh-huh. You were going to show it to me, but you never did."

"Right." She took another drink, but she didn't seem anxious, just thirsty. "Well, I'm going to send it. Do you have a local address for them?"

"No…"

"I can get it. No big deal."

"Uhm…do you want to talk about it?"

"Not really. Well, I guess I mean there's not much to talk about. I was holding off, thinking I might change my mind. But I'm done. I want no contact—ever." She took a bigger sip, then set her glass down firmly. "I'm not going to let her have the power here, and allowing her to think she just has to try harder is going to give her that. I'm going to make it clear —crystal clear—that she's gotten all she's going to get from me."

Summer kept her gaze on her glass of wine, certain Kelsey would see how upset she was if their eyes met.

"Nothing to say?" Kelsey asked after a few seconds.

"Not really. I'm sure you've thought this through."

"I have," she said, with her voice gentling. "I know she's going to keep pushing, and I can't have that. I need to make it clear that there's no wiggle room here." She was quiet for another moment, then said, "If she shows up at my apartment, I'm going to move out. It won't kill me to drive in from Monroeville for a few months."

"You can move in with me, Kelsey," she said, finally meeting her eyes. "There isn't a lot of room, but there's enough."

Kelsey moved her chair around so she could rest her arm on Summer's shoulders. "I appreciate that. I'd just much rather stay right here until the house is ready."

"I feel the same," Summer said, unable to get past thinking of how devastated Marianne would be when she opened that letter. What could be worse than having your child completely and permanently turn her back on you?

CHAPTER THIRTY-ONE

ON A WARM, HUMID NIGHT, Summer raced across town to meet up with the Friday night gang at a new spot in North Oakland. Pittsburgh, while a good-sized town, wasn't really huge, in Summer's opinion. But they'd been meeting for drinks for over ten years, and had yet to run out of options. When she spotted the bar, looking cool, and open, and modern, she recognized it as a dark, clubby, 60s era cocktail lounge they'd visited a few years back. The little group was obviously starting to hit up retreads, but that made a certain amount of sense. Some people loved going to the same place all of the time, but a lot of people went out only to try something new. Many businesses had to bite the dust to quench that need for novelty.

Patty was in Chicago on business, so it was just four of them tonight, with Summer bringing up the rear, as always. She stood in front of the booth, hands on her hips. "I will never understand how you guys always beat me."

"None of us are the boss," Leah said, standing up to kiss Summer and give her a tight hug. "You look cute," she added, before sitting back down and scooting over.

Summer was pretty sure she didn't look particularly cute, not having had time to change or even take her hair out of the pony tail she'd haphazardly fashioned when her hair had gotten in the way as she was helping cut tiles. But if she'd asked her sister to be specific, Leah would have quickly mentioned something, even if she had to resort to complimenting the color of her eyes.

"As do all of you," Summer said, taking a second to check her friends out. "I'd buy whatever you're selling, or settle my lawsuit in a second if any of you were on the other side of the transaction. What are we drinking?"

"Gin and tonic," Leah said. "Want a sip?"

"I'll take your word for it." She signaled the waiter and ordered another round for the table, with an extra gin and tonic. "So what's going on in the world of marketing, sales, and law?"

"We've finished the 'why my week sucked' portion of our evening," Wendy said. "We were just starting to talk about you."

"Me?"

"Uh-huh," she said, showing the little smirk that Summer was never sure was entirely benign. "I was just wondering if you and Kelsey were going to go super old-school and get married before you moved into your new house."

"Married?" Summer asked, sure her eyes had widened significantly. "We're not at that point yet."

"But you've in love, right?"

She was gazing at Summer with a fairly pointed look. Like she had information she wasn't necessarily going to reveal, but might pull out to trip her up. Instead of answering directly, Summer tried to sidestep. "Believe me, I'm not going to buy a house in joint tenancy if we're not in love, and fully committed to one another. I'm not looking for a roommate."

"Does that mean you're not committed to each other now?"

Wendy was like a dog with a bone when she had a question. You could either lie or tell the whole truth, since she'd badger you if you tried to be vague. "We're close," Summer said, hoping that was the truth.

"What's the holdup? The way you talk about her, I thought she was just about perfect."

"She is," Summer said. "But we've only known each other since November. I'm wary about doing anything permanent until we've known each other for at least a year. I'm just cautious," she added. "When your parents have four divorces between them, you get like that."

"Isn't your house supposed to be ready in a couple of months?" she asked, leaning close like a cop doing an interrogation.

"It sure is. So we're trying to spend a lot of time together. It's like speed-dating, but for home-ownership." She opened her phone and went to her photos. "Check this one out. Here's my perfect girlfriend eating M&Ms out of a jar of peanut butter. See why I'm being careful? People reveal some weird shit when they start to get comfortable with you."

For a change, Summer stayed until they'd finished their third round. She'd only had two, but was still sure she couldn't walk a straight line. Now she had to take a car service home. Drinks with the girls really added up!

Wendy and Lori had already departed, leaving Summer and Leah, neither of whom had requested a ride yet. "Why don't we grab a salad or something," Leah said. "You're hungry, aren't you?"

"A child-sized serving of nuts didn't fill you up?" Summer teased. "Whatever happened to good old-fashioned happy hour snacks?"

"People still fill the new places, even if they don't provide free food. Why offer it if it's not going to hurt you to stop?"

"Because I'm hungry!" Summer said, finding that comment really funny. Thank god for car services.

"Come on," Leah said, taking her hand. "I'll buy you a nice salad."

"I'm in." She slid her hand up to take Leah's arm, getting even closer. "I love getting to see you every week, but we've been slacking off on just the two of us. Once my house is ready, I won't have to sneak into the shop to work on tiles all weekend."

"I can wait you out," Leah said. "I know you'll give me whatever time you can spare." She tilted her chin northward. "You don't mind walking a little, do you? There's a new place six or seven blocks up Forbes. Dad told me about it."

"I don't mind a bit. If I get some food into me, and a little time for my liver to catch up, I might even be able to drive home."

"Speaking of home…" Leah gave her a smile, but Summer detected a little hesitancy. "Are you sure about putting Kelsey on the title?" She grasped Summer's hand, adding, "Tell me to butt out if I'm crossing a line."

"You're not," Summer said, even though she would have been upset if any other friend had been so blunt. But when you trusted someone to never have an agenda other than your well-being, you could lower your guard. "Umm, what's your concern?"

Making a funny little sound, Leah said, "I think it's the obvious one. Sharing a house with a woman who isn't able to have sex seems…like a roommate situation. Which is exactly what you don't want." She was gazing pointedly at Summer when she turned to face her. "You've scrimped and saved and cut back on all sorts of things to be able to live alone, even when you couldn't really afford it. You were living on ramen noddles when you first moved back, girl."

"I know, I know," she said, sighing heavily. "I prefer to live alone if I'm not in a romantic partnership. But I'm so damn hopeful about Kelsey. I really am."

"I can see that you love her, Summer, but is that enough? I hate to have you stuck in a situation it won't be easy to get out of if things don't work out. Are you sure…" She paused, and Summer could tell Leah was going to say something she thought she should keep to herself. But she took in a breath and spit it out. "Are you sure you're hanging in there for healthy reasons?"

Summer put her arm around her sister's waist while she considered her question. She and Leah were the therapy queens of the family, both of them having logged many years in therapeutic relationships. Instead of being defensive, Summer let herself really think. It took a block, but she finally thought she had a good answer. "I think Kelsey's the one for me," she said. "I'll admit we didn't have long before Marianne showed up and turned everything upside down, but I swear there wasn't a thing about Kelsey that I wasn't crazy about."

"But that was just a month…"

"I know. I really do realize that the perfect time was a lot shorter than the not-so-perfect time. But even now I love nearly every thing about her, Leah. With time, and lots more therapy, I think she'll make a lot of progress. I'm very willing to give her that time as long as I believe she's willing to keep working."

"And if she's not?"

Summer hated having someone she respected and trusted ask questions she didn't want to consider. But she had to consider it now. It took her a minute to answer, but she finally felt clear. "I'd have to break up with her."

Leah shrugged away from Summer's arm to face her, then hold her arms out. Summer snuggled into her embrace, resting her head on her sister's shoulder. "I hope she's able to keep working on this. I really do," Leah murmured. "But I worry about you getting entwined financially at this point."

Summer took in a breath, then stood up tall. After grasping Leah's hand, she started to walk again. "I've purposefully arranged this so that I have an escape hatch. So far, Kelsey hasn't contributed a cent, and that's going to continue. If we move in together, we'll come up with a plan for her to pay me back for half of everything." She breathed a little easier when she could see that Leah looked relieved. "I paid close attention to the ways my dad tried to screw Beth out of the little bit of equity they had in their house. That will never happen to me. My dad's given me a grad level course in how to avoid being left holding the bag."

By the middle of June, the new kitchen was framed in. Now it was time to make the final decisions on the cabinets. Summer went to Kelsey's office on a Saturday afternoon, just about an hour before closing. She had Kelsey's full attention, and had been confident they'd whip through their work and would be eating dinner by eight. But at seven thirty, they were still in the weeds, and it didn't look like they were getting out soon.

"I thought we were nearly finished," Summer said, watching Kelsey change a little something on her computer.

"We were," she said, seemingly willing to keep at this as long as they needed to. "Then you decided you wanted the sink on the other side of the cooktop. That messed everything up, since there's much more room on the left than the right. Getting the cutting board drawer and sheet pan drawer where I want them is taking me some time." She raised an eyebrow. "It wouldn't be so tough if you didn't want two spice drawers. I keep all of my spices in a simple rack on my counter."

"I buy things for a lot of different types of dishes. I'm not going to buy saffron or sumac and just throw them away, even though I don't use them often. I've got stuff."

"Clearly. So…" She'd been making some proposals on a sheet of paper, not bothering to put the ideas into her computer. "I've got a nine-inch pull-out drawer on each side of the cooktop, then a double pull-out spice rack to the right of this nine-incher." She tapped at the rough drawing for a second. "That leaves me six inches here on the right… Which is a problem. That's too much space for a fill-in, and not enough for anything else." She looked up at Summer. "I could put a fifteen inch cabinet here, but that would ruin the symmetry, which I'd rather not do."

"I guess I could go back to the original. I only wanted to switch the sink because of all of the stuff I read about that damn work-triangle. The distance between your sink and your cooktop seems like it *has* to be greater than four feet."

"That's just a guide," Kelsey said, looking a little dismissive. "The way we had it originally still gives you a triangle between the sink, the cooktop and the refrigerator. It's just that one leg is at the far end of the recommendation."

"That's nine feet?"

"Uh-huh." She made another sketch. "No leg is supposed to be less than four or more than nine feet. But that's assuming a single person's in the kitchen." She gave Summer a lopsided smile. "I think having that distance be a little more than nine feet is perfect if you're going to be cooking with a partner—which you are." She tapped at each element of her original drawing. "Thirty-six inch cabinet under your sink, fifteen inch trash receptacle, dishwasher, turn the corner and plunk down your spice rack, then sheet pan storage, cooktop, then cutting boards."

"Do you really need the cutting board thing?"

"I do…" She pulled out a new sheet of paper and started to draw. "Actually, I want the cutting boards closer to the sink. If I move them over to the left, we can have two double-width cabinets, one for spices and one for sheet pans and anything else that's tall and thin. And they'd be symmetrical," she said, frowning. "That would leave three inches you could fill with a spacer."

"One spice rack?"

"Two. But one will be over here," Kelsey said. "That's where you can keep sumac and saffron and the other stuff you use occasionally."

"Okay," Summer said, really liking the symmetry. "Can you plug it in so we can see how it looks?"

"Sure can." Her fingers were a blur as she entered all of the details. Then a real look of pride covered her face when she turned the screen around so Summer could see it. "I think it looks perfect. What's your vote."

"I'm getting out my credit card right now. I'm one satisfied customer."

A couple of days later, Summer was sitting at her desk, going over the past-due invoices. She hated spending her time chasing down money, but when her bookkeeper, who was a trifle meek, couldn't get anywhere, she got involved. It was always a little unpleasant, but she had her own bills to pay, and hard-luck stories from small tile stores couldn't keep her solvent.

She was about to pick up the phone to call a mom and pop store in Cleveland, asking for the three thousand bucks they owed her, when Chelsea buzzed. "Personal call, boss. Kitty Maliar."

"Thanks," she said, then hit the proper button. "Hi, Kitty. What's up?"

"I have an appointment in town this afternoon, Summer. Do you have time for a quick lunch?"

"Uhm…sure. There isn't anything good in my immediate neighborhood, but I could meet you somewhere. When are you coming in?"

"Any time," she said, further confusing Summer.

"How about one? One thirty?"

"Either's fine. Can you text me the address?"

"Sure. I'll pick some place where we'll be able to park. What side of town is your appointment?"

"Any place you pick is fine, Summer. See you later."

Summer hung up the phone, but she continued to ponder the meet-up. Kitty definitely didn't have an appointment in town. She was coming in just to talk. It didn't take a big brain to figure out what the topic would be, but where Summer fit in was truly puzzling.

Summer got to the restaurant a little early, but she didn't beat Kitty, who was standing in front of the building, looking like she was waiting to be shot. After stashing her car, Summer walked quickly, meeting Kitty's worried gaze with a wave. The concerned expression left her face, replaced by a smile that looked pretty genuine. Summer hoped she didn't have a lot of practice in looking happy when she wasn't.

"Hi, there," Summer said, accepting a hug. "I'm glad you called. I don't normally take time out to have a real meal, but I didn't bring anything today. I would have been reduced to getting a very mediocre piece of pizza from a joint just around the corner."

"I'm glad you were available. This place looks nice. I've been reading the menu."

"Let's do it," Summer said, holding the door open. She never felt taller, or stockier than when she stood by Kitty. The woman couldn't have weighed a hundred pounds.

After they'd ordered, their server left them with a basket of rolls and glasses of water. Kitty had looked at the wine list pretty thoroughly, but after Summer didn't go that way she put it aside. But the slight tremble in her hands showed she could have used a shot.

"What's on your mind?" Summer asked, leaning over so they could speak quietly in the bustling restaurant. "I can see that something is."

"Something is," she admitted, nervously biting the inside of her cheek. "Kelsey sent that letter," she began. "The…one."

"Where she told Marianne never to contact her again."

"That one," Kitty said, nodding. "I tried to talk her out of it, but I made no progress at all."

"I tried, too," Summer admitted. "But I didn't try hard. Kelsey made it clear she wasn't asking for my opinion, so I backed off."

"She didn't want mine, either, but I kept trying to make her listen." She let out a sigh, closing her eyes for a second. "She's talked about Marianne so little that I'm not at all sure what Kelsey even remembers about those early days. But I honestly feel that she might not cut off contact if she knew more. I just don't know how…"

"Which days are we talking about?"

"When Marianne first left. And the whole next year. The really bad times."

"I know hardly anything, since Kelsey never talks about it. Other than her refusal to forgive Marianne for abandoning her, I'm clueless."

"That's not the right term," Kitty said, shaking her head just a little. "At least it's not all of it."

"I'm willing to listen to anything you have to say. Anything at all."

She gave her a wary look, and Summer jumped back in. "I had to tell Kelsey about the calls Kim made, but I'm willing to keep anything we discuss between us—if you'd like me to."

"Would you?" she asked, looking very relieved.

"Sure. Do you need someone to vent to? I don't want to make assumptions, but you look like you're about to blow."

She closed her eyes again, then picked up her glass with a shaky hand and took a sip. "I can't talk to anyone about this. Even George. *Especially* George," she stressed.

"If you haven't done something blatantly illegal…" She shrugged. "Who am I kidding? I wouldn't turn you in even for a minor felony. You can trust me."

"I need advice. Just promise you'll give me your honest opinion."

"You've got it," Summer said.

"Well…when Marianne and Kim left Pittsburgh, the plan was that Kelsey would spend summers and some holidays with them. They had eight weeks off, and everyone agreed that Kelsey needed time with her mom."

"Right. But Kelsey didn't want to go."

"George and I weren't married that first year, so I wasn't as involved as I was later on, but I think everyone will agree that Kelsey did *not* want to go. She was truly miserable. But having that summer together let George and me get much closer, and within a few more months, we'd decided to marry. Once I was living in the house with them, I saw how the weekly calls were torture for Kelsey."

Summer cocked her head. "Marianne called every week?"

"She wanted to call every night, but George limited her to once a week."

"Because…"

"Because Kelsey cried before, during, and after the call. The poor child had every Sunday afternoon ruined." She let out a heavy sigh. "I saw them frequently, but I didn't know about the calls, or about how Kelsey was tortured by them. If I'd moved in sooner, I might have been able to help in some way…"

Sick to her stomach, Summer said, "How was she otherwise?"

"Good," Kitty said forcefully. "Amazingly good. She and I got along like gangbusters from the start. I'm sure Marianne was…fine," she said, damning her with very faint praise, "but she was obviously not very… playful. Kelsey was used to set meals, schedules…all of that kind of thing. She was amazed the first time I asked her what she wanted to eat for dinner. Robotically, she said it was Thursday. Apparently, that meant a tuna casserole was going to appear."

"Kelsey mentioned Marianne was a little robotic."

"She was. But that's not a *fault*," Kitty stressed. "It's just how she was. But Kelsey's playful. You see that, right?"

Summer nodded. "She was more playful when I first met her, but yes, I'd say she's naturally playful."

"Right. So, by the summer after she'd finished second grade, I knew everything that was going on. Kelsey *seemed* to be doing very well. Her nightmares had stopped, and she had plenty of friends. But every Sunday —pow! Meltdown."

"It didn't get better over time, huh?"

"Worse," Kitty said. "It got worse. We were married in May, and Kelsey was scheduled to go to California again in June. When Kelsey kept insisting she wasn't going to go, Marianne said she'd come to Pittsburgh for the summer. But when Kelsey learned that, she swore she wouldn't see her. And you know how hard it is to talk that child into something she really doesn't want to do."

"I'm learning," Summer said, smiling.

"So…what was I supposed to do? Force Kelsey to go? Force her to spend weeks away from George and me just when she was getting her feet back under herself?"

Kitty had started to look a little…insolent? That wasn't the exact word, but whatever she'd done, Summer was pretty sure she didn't regret it.

"What happened?" Summer asked when the silence went on for a minute.

"Marianne kept suggesting different ideas, but Kelsey was adamant. One day Marianne must have been at the end of her rope, and she asked me what I thought she should do. I told her Kelsey would be better off not having any contact with her at all." She stared at Summer, sticking her chin out a little. This woman did not regret her decision.

"You're…you're the one who convinced Marianne to…"

"I am," she said. "She was making Kelsey miserable. She'd be a happy little girl all week, but as soon as we got home from church on Sunday,

Kelsey shut us out. Wouldn't talk, wouldn't even answer a direct question unless you stood right in front of her and forced her to look at you."

"I'm familiar with that defense," Summer said, feeling sick at the thought of Kelsey having to develop it just to protect herself. "You know she still acts that way when she's emotionally stressed."

"I do," Kitty said, "but I keep hoping it will get better."

"I do too," Summer said. "It's like the majority of her brain shorts out. She's truly not all there."

"After a phone call, Kelsey used to say she was ready for bed, no matter the time. I watched that child climb into bed—and stay there—at three o'clock in the afternoon. I think she had to be asleep to let her emotions settle down."

"Right, right," Summer said, seeing that might have been the point.

"So I convinced Marianne to leave Kelsey alone, but I thought that would only last for a while. We both thought it was a bridge to a better relationship. But the plan didn't work at all. Kelsey wouldn't discuss her, wouldn't even acknowledge she had a birth mother. Marianne sent gifts, toys, cash for her birthday, but Kelsey would not even open the packages. To her—Marianne was dead, and if she'd had her way, they never would have spoken again." Her eyes narrowed, and she added, "I now see that would have been best. Giving Marianne Kelsey's address was the stupidest thing I've ever done."

Their food was delivered, but Summer had completely lost her appetite. Kitty certainly didn't seem hungry either, but they picked at their plates while making silly small talk. Eventually, they had their meals boxed up, and Kitty walked Summer to her car. When they got there, she put her hand on Summer's arm. "I have no idea how Kelsey will feel if she learns I convinced her mother to leave her alone. But I'll tell her, I swear I will, if you think I should."

"Me?" Summer gasped. "Why do I get to decide?"

"Because you're more impartial. I've got George and Kelsey on one side, and you know neither of them wants to give her a chance. You might not know how far this goes back, but I've been on the Marianne campaign for years now. At least since Kelsey started her job. It's not good to hold onto that hatred or fear or whatever it is that Kelsey feels toward her mother. She's an adult, and she should deal with Marianne like another adult. It would be good for both of them."

"I'm with you, Kitty, but I can't guess what the right thing to do is."

Her jaw started to quiver when she said, "If Kelsey stopped speaking to me, it would kill me. Even though I think I did the right thing for a little girl, now I feel like I have to fight for Marianne. If Kelsey knew the truth, maybe she'd be a little more understanding."

Summer put her carryout container on the roof of her car and wrapped Kitty in a hug. "Kelsey's right. She's awfully lucky to have you." She kissed her cheek, then pulled away. "I think the last thing she needs right now is more upsetting news. But if she finds out—through Marianne—she'll be very hurt."

"That's my dilemma," she grumbled. "I don't know what to do."

"Why don't you sit tight for a while? Kelsey's already sent the letter, right?"

"I think so."

"Let her sit with that decision for a while. I have a feeling she's going to soften—maybe soon."

"Do you really think that?" She looked relieved at the mere thought. "Refusing to give Marianne even an occasional hour of her time is just so unlike my girl. She's always been so generous, and…" She looked up at Summer, seeming like she was having a hard time even getting her thoughts out. "There's a hardness there that I'm having a difficult time getting my arms around. I see it in George, too, and I hate it."

"I know what you mean," Summer said, really wishing she didn't.

"Both of them are very forgiving of most slights. They're both very easy-going, for the most part. But if you hurt them in a certain way, or to a certain degree… You're done for."

Summer touched Kitty's arm again, gazing at her intently. "You're not afraid to tell George you gave Marianne a push because you think he'd —"

"Be angry with me? No," she said immediately. "I'm just afraid he'd use that as ammunition for his side. You know…why would I want Kelsey to have a relationship with Marianne now when I helped her sever ties back then." She swallowed nervously. "I'm not sure how Kelsey will feel, though. She's just starting to seem back to normal, and I don't want to make things worse for her." She closed her eyes for a moment. "And, if I'm honest, I don't want her to blame me if she does feel worse." She shook her head mournfully. "Neither George nor I knew how to help back then. Our only goal was to make Kelsey feel more secure. Moving to a new neighborhood, severing ties with George's old friends, both of us finding new jobs… We acted like we were in the witness protection program, Summer, but that's when Kelsey finally snapped out of it. Once we could guarantee that no one knew about Marianne, she was finally happy."

CHAPTER THIRTY-TWO

ON THE NIGHT BEFORE HER birthday, Summer opened the door to her apartment, surprised to find Kelsey in the kitchen, making something that smelled really good. "Whew!" she said, playfully wiping her brow. "Good thing I turned down a last-minute invitation to go over to Jackie and Robert's house for dinner, huh?"

"Ooo. That would have been kind of awful," Kelsey said. "I've spent the last four hours making your favorite meal."

"Mole poblano?" Summer asked, racing over to see what was cooking. "I couldn't tell what that fantastic aroma was, but I knew it was going to be good." She put her arm around Kelsey and gave her a hug. "What a nice surprise."

"You've made me some great dinners, so I thought I'd go all out for your birthday."

"This is *really* all out. Especially since you don't like spicy food. Will you even eat this?"

"Sure will," she said, grinning. "After this much work I'd eat it even if I hated it, which I won't. I left out the puya chilies, since the recipe said they were the spiciest." She stuck her finger in the sauce, licked it off, then smiled broadly. "We're both going to have a nice meal tonight."

⊛

It was late when they'd digested their delicious dinner, worked their way through most of a six pack of Mexican beer, and had just a touch of ice cream. Kelsey almost passed on the ice cream, which would have been a first. But she'd rallied enough to have a few spoonfuls. Now that her appetite was better, she was back to her usual two meals a day, both of them pretty hearty, and was finally feeling good.

She took a look at the clock when it was clear Summer was fading. "Mind if I crash on your sofa? I shouldn't drive after drinking so much, and I'm too cheap to pay for a car."

Summer stood, giving her a curious glance as she started for her bathroom. "I'm happy to have you sleep here. But why not share the bed?" Then she went into the bath, leaving Kelsey to think about the offer. It was an appealing one; that was undeniable. Neither of them had suggested an overnight since she'd been to Santa Barbara, and neither of them had addressed that fact. They'd just let that intimacy fade away.

Summer walked out of her bathroom, dressed in a roomy T-shirt and a pair of knit boxers. She was clearly not going for seduction, even though she looked as cute as a bug. Yawning, she got into bed, then patted the empty side. "Joining me?"

Kelsey shrugged, then went into the bath to get ready. She'd thought they would have kind of a big moment when they decided to sleep together again, but maybe it was better to low-key it. Still, her nerves were beginning to act up as she searched for a new toothbrush. When she finished brushing and flossing, she opened the door, hands shaking. But Summer was lying on her side, mouth slightly open, sound asleep.

Summer stretched and blinked her eyes open when the morning sun warmed her face, then she sat up abruptly. "It's nine o'clock!"

Kelsey was lying next to her, grinning. "I know," she said, her eyes still half-closed. "When I got into bed last night, I turned off your alarm. It should be against the law to get up at seven on your birthday."

Summer stared at her. "I'm always in the office by eight, Kelsey. Jesus," she grumbled, getting to her feet. But a hand jutted out and grasped her boxers, slowing her down.

"I talked to Chelsea a week ago. She arranged your calendar so you had nothing important going on today."

"What? Really?"

"Happy birthday," Kelsey said. "I was so pleased when I saw that the big day fell on my day off. I've been planning this for weeks."

Summer let herself drop back onto the bed. "I haven't slept in for…I don't know how long."

"Why not make it a little longer. This is my usual time to get up, so another half hour would be kind of a treat…"

"Whose birthday is it?" Summer teased, then leaned over to snuggle her face into Kelsey's neck, making her giggle. "I'll give you a half hour, but you'd better have a plan for breakfast."

"Under control," Kelsey said, flopping onto the bed as she contentedly closed her eyes.

After getting coffee, along with some awesome donuts at a place Kelsey had discovered, they went back to the apartment to spend the day poolside. It was just the two of them, making it seem like they owned a massive pool and thirty deck chairs. The temperature hovered around eighty, with a nice breeze rippling the water. But best of all was the very pretty woman doing a lazy backstroke, all alone in the crystal water. Summer took out a pad of artist's paper and started to draw, capturing an impressionistic image of Kelsey moving through the water—mostly a streak of red for her suit, and a dark head amidst the cool, blue water. Birthdays were awesome.

⊛

Summer woke with a smile on her face. Lying in the sun on a warm day, with a hat over her eyes was a very effective soporific for her. She wasn't sure how long she'd been out, but it might have been a while. Rested and content, she looked for Kelsey, then realized the crinkling sound was from a note tucked under her arm.

I had to have a snack. I'm upstairs, ready to make one for you if you ever finish your birthday nap. You really needed a day off, girl!

That was the truth. And she'd had a great one.

Summer opened the door to the apartment, seeing Kelsey sitting on the sofa, with a plate of crackers covered with cream cheese on them.

"Aren't you hungry?" she asked, flipping another cracker into her mouth.

"Not very. I could sure use a shower, though. I hate being covered with sunblock." She walked by Kelsey and tugged on her wet hair. "I see you've already cleaned up."

"You don't mind that I borrowed your robe, do you? I didn't think you'd want me to sit on your sofa bare-assed."

"You look cute in it," she said. Very beachy. I can wear my winter one."

"Make it snappy. We've got a few more things on our agenda."

"I will shake a leg," Summer promised, knowing that whatever Kelsey had planned, they'd have fun.

After scrubbing off all of the sunblock and shaving her legs, Summer finally felt clean. She wasn't in the mood to blow her hair dry yet, so she just combed it back and went to find Kelsey. She didn't have to look far. When she opened the door, she was right there, giving her the kind of racy look she'd given her when they'd first met.

"Uhm…hi," Summer said, unable to even see around Kelsey with her forearms resting on the doorframe. "Come here often?"

"Not often enough." Kelsey put a cool hand on her cheek, cupping it. "Remember when we talked about our ideal days? Early on?"

Summer blinked up at her. "How dumb am I! You've given me another perfect day." Then the rest of the items on her list snapped into focus, and she felt herself freeze.

Kelsey leaned over slightly. With her voice low and warm, she said, "There was another important part, a part that fits perfectly into our schedule." She dipped her head and placed a gentle, but meaning-filled kiss to Summer's lips. "How would you like to spend your birthday afternoon welcoming me back into your bed?"

Instinctively, Summer linked her hands behind Kelsey's neck and pulled her down so their lips touched again. It was fantastic to kiss those sultry lips and let out just a hint of the desire she'd been storing up. A fresh, clean scent filled her lungs, letting her relish images of the warm summer day, the cool pool, and a whiff of suntan lotion lingering on Kelsey's glowing skin. She looked—and felt—so fantastic that Summer's head began to swim. The thought of welcoming Kelsey back to a space where they'd shared a deep sexual connection made her slightly dizzy. But jumping into bed meant something very different now. They weren't just seeing if they clicked. Loving each other now meant just that—declaring their love. If they started being sexual again, it was time to get those "save the date" cards printed.

Summer pulled back and looked into Kelsey's clear, cool eyes, seeing so much in their depths—her intelligence, her bravery, her playfulness, her sexiness. But this was the same woman who'd cut her birth mother off without a second thought. Who'd done that despite her actual mom's entreaties. Did a woman who could do that have the capacity to forgive *Summer* when she did something painful? What was Kelsey's limit? What kinds of things could set her off? How bad did the hurt have to be to earn permanent banishment? After all of these months, Summer still didn't know.

She let her hands slide down Kelsey's arms, then took her hand and led her over to the bed. Tugging her down, Summer faced her and said, "I've got so many thoughts in my head I'm not certain I'm able to think clearly."

With a shy smile, Kelsey said, "I don't really need for you to think at all." She grasped her shoulders and pulled her close for a warm, wet, kiss; a kiss all but guaranteed to make you lose your rational mind.

But Summer's rational mind was very tenacious. And her equally tenacious mouth kept speaking. "I don't ever want to dictate to you, Kelsey. I swear I don't. But the fact that you won't even talk to Marianne scares me."

"Scares *you?*" She sat up tall and gazed at Summer like she wasn't making sense. "My not talking to my birth mother frightens you?"

"It does. It makes me worry about how likely you are to forgive me when I hurt you." She gripped her firmly and looked into her eyes. "I *will* hurt you. It's inevitable."

"You're not serious," she said flatly, looking at Summer with a fire starting to burn in those pretty eyes.

"I am. I wish I didn't have doubts, but—"

Kelsey jumped to her feet and moved all the way over by the windows. Facing Summer, she growled, "You've been stewing over this for how long? I've been working my butt off to be able to put myself out there again, while you've been thinking of all of the ways I might screw up?" Her voice gained volume, and she was nearly shouting when she said, "Do you have any idea how hard it was for me to make myself vulnerable enough to make a sexual overture?"

"I'm not refusing you," Summer insisted, getting to her feet and starting to approach. "I'm not rejecting you."

Kelsey stared at her for a moment, stopping Summer in her tracks. "That's exactly what you're doing," she said, each word quieter than the next. "I know you want me to see Marianne, but if my relationship with her was so damn critical, you owed me a conversation about that."

"I screwed up," she admitted. "It *is* important, but only because it makes me worry what I might do that would make you banish me."

"That's so unfair," she said, with her voice starting to break. Kelsey moved over to a chair and sat down heavily. "You've led me to believe you want to be my partner. That's part of my motivation for how hard I've worked at getting myself in good working order." Their eyes met, and Summer could see the tears welling up in Kelsey's. "I've never done anything harder. Never. Making myself sexually available again has been the only thing I've been working on recently. Each session's been painful and frightening. But I kept at it because I knew I could trust you," she murmured, now crying hard. "I knew you'd help me feel safe being vulnerable again."

"I will," Summer insisted, dashing over to kneel at Kelsey's feet. "I'm just...worried."

"How do I make you stop worrying? What do I have to do?"

"I'm not sure," she murmured. "I truly don't know. I'm frightened to get close again. It just feels like you'll have so much power over me..."

"Power? That's what my love feels like?"

"No, I don't..." She dropped her head and took in several deep breaths. "I'm so confused."

Kelsey put her hand on her shoulder and squeezed it. "If I got on the phone and made plans to see Marianne tomorrow, would you have sex with me now?"

She shook her head. "Not right now. I'm too upset to even consider being close. But if you'd talked to her earlier today and made plans? Yes," she admitted. "I'd feel safer."

"Even though I'd feel so, so much less safe." She squeezed a little harder. "That's how it has to be between us? I have to welcome someone I deeply distrust into my life just so you feel safer?"

"But you'd feel better once you normalized things with Marianne. I'm *sure* of it."

Kelsey got up and walked over to her tote bag. Carefully and thoughtfully, she started to pull things out. First came the key card for the pool. Then the apartment keys. Then the keys to their home. Turning to gaze at Summer with a very sober expression, she said, "If you were really ready to move forward, Marianne wouldn't enter the picture."

"Yes she would!"

"No. I'm certain she wouldn't. You're moving the bar, Summer. You're probably not even doing it on purpose, but you move the damn thing just far enough so I can't reach it." She looked like she was on the verge of tears, but her voice was calm and steady. "I don't want to do this. God damn, I don't want to do this." She gently patted the keys, then tossed off the robe and hurriedly put her shorts and shirt back on. When she got to the door, she turned and gave Summer an achingly sorrowful look. "I will miss you so much," she whispered. Then she opened the door and stepped into the hall, with Summer still on her knees, frozen.

As soon as Leah was able to get away, she raced over to Summer's, bearing two bottles of wine and two different kinds of ice cream. After setting everything on the counter, she took Summer in her arms and rocked her like she had when Summer had been a child, soothing her just as effectively as she had when Matt failed to show up for his weekly visit, or when she and Jackie had one of their frequent blowups. Leah had always been there, providing a calm, loving presence.

"I screwed up," Summer murmured, resting her head on her sister's shoulder. "I hurt her, Leah."

"I'm sure you did, but you can fix it. Go over there right now and tell her you just got freaked out. It's only been like…two hours. You can make it right."

"But that's not true. I didn't get freaked out. I honestly don't know if I can trust that Kelsey's heart is big enough to be able to forgive." She pulled away and went over to put the ice cream into the freezer, then slip the white wine into the fridge. "She was in love with a woman who moved to California for a job, and they broke up because Kelsey wasn't willing to move. But the job didn't work out, and the woman returned just a month or two later, only to have Kelsey stonewall her. That's bothered me ever since she told me about it. But it didn't send off warning signals like her not talking to Marianne has."

"So you're saying this is an extinction level event? You're willing to give her up if she doesn't form a relationship with her birth mother?"

"No, that's not it," she said, leaning against the counter while she gathered her thoughts. "She could convince me. She could honestly convince me without too much trouble. I mean, it would definitely take a little time, but she could have reassured me that I'm worrying about nothing. But she didn't have any interest in doing that. I saw the look in her eyes." She dropped her head onto the counter, unable to hold it up for another moment. "She's done with me, Leah. When she's hurt enough, she shuts the door and leaves you out in the cold."

CHAPTER THIRTY-THREE

IT TOOK KELSEY TWO DAYS TO even get out of bed. She'd called in sick on Friday and Saturday, knowing she wouldn't be able to pay attention to anyone's kitchen needs. Late on Saturday night, she finally sat down to write to Summer. It wasn't the most eloquent thing she'd ever written, but she couldn't just walk away without explaining herself. It had taken both days to figure out exactly what had caused her to bolt, but now that she had it down, she had to share it. She owed her at least that much.

> "Dear Summer,
>
> I don't want to lose you. I swear I don't. But I can't be with someone who doesn't trust me to fully commit to our relationship.
>
> I suppose we could get past this if I kept Marianne in my life to some extent. But that's not the kind of relationship I want. I'll admit to being skittish about commitment. I don't think it's possible to have your mother abandon you and not be—at least a little. But I've worked hard to make sure I was able to be with you through thick and thin. The problem is that commitment has to go both ways. And learning that you needed me to do things that don't feel right just to earn your trust made it clear that your commitment to me—as I am—wasn't strong enough.
>
> You've been an incredible friend to me through all of this. And I know that you love me—probably as much as I love you. But something's off, and I'm not willing to get more deeply involved when I don't think the level of trust I need is there.
>
> I hope that we can continue to be friends—good friends. Obviously not now, but once we've healed I think we can get

back to the things that made us a good pair. We've had a great six months without sex. There's no reason to think we can't continue down that path. One day, and I hope it's soon, I'd love to sit in your fantastic kitchen and watch you whip up some spaghetti ai limone. I'll bring dessert. I'll make it something very sweet, just like your generous heart.

I'll contact you when I feel ready to try to build a friendship. I know I don't have to remind you that I need to take the lead on that.

With love and affection,
Kelsey

On Sunday night, Kelsey sat with Rob at a surprisingly quiet, mostly gay bar in Lower Lawrenceville. It was probably quiet because it was only seven o'clock, but she couldn't stay up late. Actually, she was surprised she was up at all, not to mention out. Being upright these days was an accomplishment.

"Second thoughts?" he asked when their drinks were delivered.

"Second? How about two thousand and second? I've been looking forward to being able to talk about something other than Marianne in therapy, but I didn't expect it to be whether I've just done the dumbest thing in my whole life."

"I thought you loved her," he said, obviously trying to keep the judgment out of his voice.

"I did. I do," she corrected. "But it's like one of the first kitchens I ever designed—"

"Summer's like a kitchen? Don't ever admit to that!"

"She's not like a kitchen, but the situation reminds me of that."

"I can't even guess where this story is going to lead…"

"Then just listen. Years ago, I designed a really nice space, but my measurements were off by a little over an inch. I could go into how that wasn't really my fault, but that's not important. I had X number of inches, and the cabinets were X plus one. It was a weird run, a perfect length, needing no filler at all. First and last one of those I've ever had. So, the contractor calls me in a panic, and I go over there. The cabinets were clearly an inch too wide, but we spent an hour trying to figure out how to make them work—including redoing the wall to make it an inch wider. We *really* didn't want to have to wait another six weeks to redo one box out of like twenty."

"What did you do?"

"I got one of the more seasoned designers involved and she gave me some excellent advice. Every inch is equally important. You can't wish away an inch just because you want to. That's totally true, Rob. Summer's almost perfect, but the one inch that isn't is just as important as all of the inches that are."

"You're really sticking to this, huh? You can't overlook one flaw? It sure sounds to me like she's the type of person who'd work on it…"

"Every inch is important. I'd give anything to be able to overlook this, but she doesn't trust me, Rob. She doesn't trust my decision-making about my own life. And all of her other fantastic qualities—and there are so, so many of them—still leaves that one inch sticking out into the doorway. I can't move in with her and hope it doesn't bother me. I'd bump up against it every time I went into the kitchen. And, not to belabor the point, but I've been bruised enough. I have to protect myself —even against the people who genuinely want the best for me. And that sucks more than I can say."

On Tuesday night, Summer knocked on the door to her sister's apartment. When Leah answered, the scent of something good—maybe something spicy—hit Summer's nose.

When she entered, Leah wrapped her in a hug, and Summer let herself relax, no longer needing to act like a competent adult out in the world. "What an awful day," she sighed as they broke apart.

"Would some nachos and a beer cheer you up?"

"You made me nachos," Summer said, nearly in tears from a simple act of generosity.

"I assumed you wouldn't have time to get dinner. Have a seat and I'll get you set up."

Summer's instinct was to help, but she was bone-tired. Sleeping very little, and having bad dreams when she finally did, had begun to grind her down.

Her sister's apartment was about what you'd expect for a woman who'd had an excellent job for over twenty years, as well as a rich father—and no dependents. Summer plopped down on the pristine off-white sofa, made of some kind of textured silk fabric. It was custom made, since Leah wanted it very cushy. She'd gotten her wish. It felt like sinking into a silk cloud.

Summer looked up when Leah approached with a tray filled with nachos, a pair of beers, and tall glasses. "Shouldn't we sit at the dining room table? I don't want to drop anything onto the fabric."

"You won't," she said breezily, spoken like a woman who could afford to have a service arrive first thing in the morning to professionally clean the piece if Summer screwed up. Leah sat down and poured their beers. "Tell me all about it," she said as she handed one over.

Summer took a sip and leaned over to make sure her plate was as far from the edge as possible. "I've generally lost my appetite, but these have brought it back," she said, relishing the spicy, yet comforting food.

"Not the healthiest thing in the world, but only junk food seems to work when you're really down." She put her hand on Summer's leg. "And you're as down as I've seen you in a long, long time."

"I am." She took another drink of her beer. "Where to start… I guess the good news is that it felt good to be back on Barbara's couch. She seems really good. Still very focused. Empathic. Attuned."

"She's an excellent therapist," Leah agreed. "I've sent a lot of people her way. Very few have taken me up on it, but I keep sending them," she added, laughing a little.

"Yeah. Starting back isn't fun. I honestly thought I had the tools to fight my way out of anything. But I don't."

"Want to talk about it in any detail? It's fine it you'd rather not."

Summer nodded, even though she didn't want to talk. She didn't want to eat, either, but her sister had gone out of her way to be hospitable, so Summer forced herself to chomp on a few more chips, trying to wake her appetite up.

"Here's what I got out of my first visit." She closed her eyes, trying to recall everything Barbara had said, knowing she'd forgotten half of it. Remembering details when your feelings were in such turmoil was an exercise in futility. "Barbara implied—strongly—that I'm doing my usual —trying to make sure everyone at least acts like they're one big, happy family. The fact that Kelsey won't do that scares me. Simple, huh?"

"Nothing's simple in therapy," Leah sighed. "But...isn't that good news? Can't you talk to Kelsey and let her know you think you've identified the issue and you're going to work on fixing it? I'd be relieved to know you weren't really trying to supervise me."

"Mmm. Yes, she might be relieved to know that," Summer said, having kicked that idea around a hundred times in the last hour. "But I've been working on this for years, Leah, yet I fell right back into it the first time I got a hint that Kelsey wasn't going to play the dutiful daughter."

"Right. But you're going to work on it again. And you'll keep an eye on it, Summer. I know you."

"I know me, too—intermittently. I'd love to be able to tell Kelsey I can fix this quickly. But I'm not sure I can. And if I can't stay on my side of the aisle, I'm not ready to fall in love. Not with Kelsey or anyone else. I'm going to concentrate on myself for a while. If Kelsey's ready to move on—that's just what I get for being so fucking certain I was this super evolved person who had my shit together."

"You're being too hard on yourself," Leah soothed. "Everyone has blind spots. I'm sure Kelsey doesn't expect you to be perfect."

"No, I'm sure she doesn't. But until I can stop focusing on her problems instead of my own, I'm too far from perfect for my own peace of mind." Facing Leah, she added, "I'm afraid I'm going to have to cancel next year's trip to Poland. My vacation budget's being redirected to therapy. Even though I wish it could, leaving the country won't fix me."

CHAPTER THIRTY-FOUR

THE EXTENDED MALIAR-O'SHEA family gathered for their annual two-week vacation on the first of July. During the winter, Kelsey had secured her own cabin for the first time, so thrilled to be able to share the event with Summer, sure they'd be securely in love and very much needing some privacy. Luckily, one of her mom's cousins decided to come at the last minute, relieving Kelsey of paying for her own place. It wasn't terribly expensive, since the cabins were very rustic, and the lake was smaller than most. And having to use the communal bathhouse made them even less desirable. But her family had been coming here since the year her parents married, and the event had gotten so big that for the first time they'd bought it out. Everyone on the property was either a Maliar or an O'Shea—either by blood or marriage.

It was funny how you could look forward to something for a full year, yet not want to be there—at all. Kelsey knew it would upset her parents if she stayed home and sulked, so she went. But finding herself back in a small bedroom—alone—didn't make her feel very festive.

They'd been there for two days, both sunny and mild. On Monday, a storm had rolled across the Alleghenies, dumping enough rain to make driving difficult, and gathering outdoors impossible. So they'd stayed inside most of the day, with Kelsey reading and her parents playing gin or canasta. Her mom beat her dad handily at gin, so he always tried to switch over to canasta, where he thought he had more of a chance.

After sprawling out on the big L-shaped sofa for most of the day, Kelsey got up and sat in a chair after dinner, just for a change of pace.

Her dad emerged from his bedroom with some kind of electronic device, and he started to hook it up to the back of the big TV, an addition that had been installed just a couple of years earlier. Even in the woods, people demanded Wi-Fi and cable now.

"What's that?" Kelsey asked, looking up from her book.

"DVD player," he said, a little distracted. He finished, then stood up and stared at the set-up for a minute. "I think that'll work."

"For what?"

"Got you something," he said, going back into his room to emerge a minute later with a paper grocery bag. He put it on the table in front of the sofa, then tilted it so she could see inside.

"Are those...DVDs?"

"Yep."

Her mom walked over to stand behind him, looking a little—-tense? Her dad spoke again. "I was at the drug store not long ago and saw a sign saying they took VHS tapes and turned them into DVDs." He glanced at the bag. "I took all of the old tapes we had and converted them. Thought you might want them."

Puzzled, Kelsey opened the bag, pulling out a handful of jewel cases. "How many did you have?"

"A lot more than I thought. I didn't add them up before I handed them over, so I didn't know how much it would cost. If you like 'em, you can consider them part of your birthday present."

After putting her hand into the bag again, she pulled out stacks of photos held together with ribbon. "Where did you have all of these?"

"Around," he said, shrugging. "There were a lot of photos hanging up, but you made me put them away. The rest of these were just here and there."

"I kept everything in my closet," Kitty said. "One time you stumbled upon a photo of you and Marianne, and when I saw your face when you ripped it up..." She pursed her lips. "I made sure you never had to see another one."

"Why give them to me now?" Kelsey asked, still not having truly taken a look. "Have I given you any indication I want to see any of this?"

Her dad shrugged. "I got a kick out of looking at everything, and I thought you might, too. If I was wrong, leave 'em right there."

"They're yours," Kelsey said, unbending. "You don't have to buy me a birthday gift to replace them, either."

"I'll never forgive her for leaving," he said, with her mom now holding his arm as she gazed up at him. "But she was a damn fine mother until…you know." He paused for a second, then said, "What was the name of that cat you brought home?"

"Dippy?"

"Yeah. The black one with the tail that looked like it had fallen into a can of white paint. Remember when she had a litter of kittens?"

"Of course," Kelsey said. "How could I forget having a mostly feral cat in the house?" She looked at her mom. "Dad let me do anything I wanted for a while after Marianne left. He didn't even complain when I came home from school with a cat I'd found on the playground. A day later she gave birth to a litter of kittens on the kitchen floor."

Her father let out a laugh. "I had to clean up the kitchen while explaining the birds and the bees to this one," he said. "That was a fun afternoon."

Even though touching the photos filled her with dread, Kelsey couldn't help herself. She pulled the bag over to peer at the ones that rested on the top, seeing herself as a small baby. Even though she didn't want to think about that time, finding a batch of photos of yourself you'd never seen was kind of compelling. "Why did you mention Dippy? I haven't thought of her in decades."

"I thought of her when I looked at the pictures," he said, growing sober. "Marianne was like that. Totally devoted to you when you were a baby."

"She was like a cat?"

"Yeah," he said, clearly having thought this through. "She wasn't very maternal at first, but she figured it out well enough. That woman spent every minute of every day making sure you were safe and happy. If she'd made minimum wage for every hour she doted on you, she could have bought a luxury car."

"She did?" Kelsey asked, looking up at him and seeing how serious he looked.

"No kidding, Kels. And when you were a little older, she taught you everything you could teach a kid." Even in the dim light Kelsey could see his eyes darken. "Then…bang! Just like that damn cat, she thought she was finished. Once we gave those kittens away, that cat was glad they were gone. Took off the first time I cracked the door open."

"I think it might have been a little more complicated than that," Kitty said softly.

"You didn't know her," George said. "Marianne was working on instinct of some kind. At least at first. She had a hard time being close to anyone, but you can't say she didn't try."

Everyone was quiet for a minute or two. Then Kelsey said, "I just broke up with a woman I loved because she was pressuring me to see Marianne, Dad. I don't want to have to break up with you, too."

"Me?" He looked stunned. "If I never hear her name again it'll be too soon. She doesn't deserve another chance to hurt you. But she was a very big part of your life, and I don't think you know that. Your mom thinks you should." He nudged her mom with his shoulder. "Go on. This was all your idea."

Kitty walked over to Kelsey and sat on the nearby footstool. "I know how you feel about Marianne. I really believe I do. And if you decide to never speak to her again, I will stay out of it, honey. Promise. But when I saw some of these old tapes I felt like I knew her a little better." She took Kelsey's chilled hand and added, "You talk about her like all she ever did was leave you. But there was much more to your relationship than that. She wanted you, sweetheart. I know it seems like she didn't, but I swear she did. Can I show you just one of the tapes?"

"Do you have to?" Kelsey asked tiredly, so sick of everyone in her life trying to get her to acknowledge a relationship that never existed.

"Just one." Her mom jumped up and put a DVD in, then hit "play." In a couple of seconds, her dad's voice came on as the camera fought to focus on a very pretty, very young Marianne, sitting up in bed while holding a tiny baby. Marianne was smiling, but she looked absolutely wiped-out.

"Can you move the blanket?" George asked. "I need to see that beautiful little face."

"Hold on," she said, wincing when she tried to move the baby into a better spot. "How's that?"

"Perfect," he said, getting closer.

A tiny face came into view, making Kelsey gasp. "I'm a wrinkled mess," she said, but she found herself gazing at the images like they held the secrets of the universe. "I've got a nice head of hair, though. Did you comb it?"

"Marianne always wanted you to look neat," her father said, chuckling. "I think she used a cat comb." Kitty move the footstool to sit beside Kelsey, then took her hand. "You'll never convince me you weren't wanted," she whispered.

The camera bobbed and swayed, and Kelsey was able to hear her dad say, "Introduce her to the world, honey."

Marianne looked down upon her, with her chin beginning to quiver. "I want the whole world to meet Kelsey Maliar, the prettiest little baby I've ever seen." Her voice broke when she added, "I want every good thing in the world for her." She looked up at George. "Am I asking for too much if I pray she never has a bad day?"

"Yeah, I think so," he said, not seeming to even take the question seriously. "Let me hold her now. You know how to work the camera, right?"

"I think so," Marianne said. "Give me a second."

Kelsey was about to throw up from the camera careening around, but it finally settled on her dad, looking like the happiest man in the world, with his full head of dark hair and his firm jawline. He looked into Kelsey's eyes and spoke to her. "Hi there, baby. I'm your daddy. That's right," he whispered, clearly tearing up. "I'm gonna take care of you for your whole life." He grasped something from out of the camera's range, then his voice went up and down in a sing-song fashion when he held it in front of the camera. "My little girl's first Steelers jersey," he sang, displaying a black onesie with gold trim. "Steelers Nation has a new member as of today."

"Oh, George, I'll feel silly taking her out in that."

"I won't," he said, still grinning. "Besides, I'm going to be the one carrying her most of the time." He touched Kelsey's little chin with his finger, which looked huge next to her diminutive features. "I've got a new best friend," he said. "And her name is Kelsey."

Kelsey gripped her mom's hand firmly when she heard her sniffling, realizing she was doing the same. "You seemed happy," she said, looking at her dad, who was also wiping at his eyes with one of his meaty fists.

"We were," he admitted. "It didn't last, but you had two parents who loved you very much, Kels. That's nothing to sneeze at, right?"

Her mom was crying so hard she was hard to understand, but Kelsey thought she caught the whole sentence. "Things went off the rails much too soon, but you started off with a good foundation."

"Maybe I did," she sighed. She dumped the bag out and sorted through the DVDs, putting them in date order. "We don't have much else to do. Let's take a look at some of these. I'd like to see ones where I look like a human."

"Thank you," her mom said, gripping her arm.

"You went to a lot of trouble to do this." Their eyes met, and she added in a shaky voice, "And to raise me. If you want me to see this stuff, it's the least I can do."

"You owe me nothing," her mom said. "But I'd love to watch these with you. I want to see the years I missed out on."

As Kelsey stacked the DVDs up, she mused, "I guess it's *possible* that Marianne was a decent starting pitcher. But you definitely had to come in to do a bang-up job in long-relief."

"I think that might be true," her mom said. "That's baseball, right?"

Kelsey returned to Pittsburgh in mid-July, just in time for a heat wave to settle onto the city like a wool shirt. She was meeting Rob at a pizza place they liked, and as she strolled down the sidewalk she saw him sitting at a tiny table behind a flimsy sidewalk enclosure. As she walked by, she slipped her hand over his head, mussing his hair.

He tilted his head to give her a long look as she sat opposite him. "Every once in a while I notice how pretty you are. Like tonight," he said, grinning. "You know people aren't supposed to tan any more, right? Skin cancer's not sexy."

"I put sunblock on every day, but I still tan when I'm in the sun as much as I was. It just happens."

"Uh-huh," he said, clearly dubious. "And wearing a white sleeveless blouse wasn't a way to look even darker? Everyone knows that's a trick to show off a tan, Kels."

"Let's be honest. It's a waste to look this good and cover myself up." She leaned over to kiss him. "Did you miss me?"

"Of course." Soberly, he added, "I was worried about you. I thought you might not be able to enjoy yourself."

"No, it was good to get away. New surroundings, new perspective." She ordered a drink when a server passed by, then took a couple of pretzels from a tiny bowl and popped them into her mouth. "It was a weird trip, buddy. I learned a lot—most of it stuff I didn't want to know."

"Like…?"

"Big one," she said, nodding when someone placed a beer in front of her. "Found out that my mom told Marianne to stop calling me. Back when I was a kid, that is. That means that Marianne didn't *exactly* abandon me."

"The fuck she didn't," he snapped, no fan of her birth mother's. "She moved two thousand miles away from you. That's abandonment by any definition."

"Yeah, yeah, you're right. But she didn't want to lose contact. My mom convinced her to." She took a sip of her beer. "My mom's been worried about telling me that ever since, but I was glad to learn she stood up for me then. I was a mess when I had to talk to or see Marianne, and my mom didn't think it was going to get any better."

"I'm glad, too. She's always had your back."

"Right. And now she wants me to at least talk to Marianne. She claims she'll stop bugging me if I do." She laughed a little. "I think she's lying, but I trust that she'll try."

"And you're seriously considering it?"

"I…think I am," she admitted. "My mom thinks I'm being cruel, and that clearly disappoints her. She's always thought I was nicer, and smarter, and prettier than I really am."

"You look damn good now," he said, giving her another assessment. "And when I look at a woman, it's an event."

"I'll start going to a tanning parlor," she promised. "So? What do you think? I could see Marianne—easily. She's supposed to be in town until the end of August."

"Mmm. I'd shut her out," he said thoughtfully. "But if my mom was as crazy about me as Kitty is about you, I'd do whatever she asked. Does that help?"

"I think it does. I always say I'd do anything to make my mom happy. I guess it's time to put up or shut up."

CHAPTER THIRTY-FIVE

KELSEY DELAYED FOR A FULL DAY, torn between calling Marianne and writing to her. She finally got off her duff on her day off and sat on the deck of an above-ground pool one of their family friends had in his backyard. Her mom had been with her, but she'd run home to make sandwiches for lunch. Taking the opportunity, Kelsey took out her phone and tried to construct a rough draft.

> Dear Marianne,
> I've given my earlier letter some thought, and have decided I was too harsh. If you're willing, I'd like to see you while you're still in town.
> I can't promise we'll get anywhere, but I'm willing to try. If you're interested, call me on my cell.

She finished up by giving her number, something she couldn't have imagined doing even a few weeks ago. She hated to admit it, but having both her mom and Summer nudging at her had made a difference. Whether that turned out to be a good thing was still up in the air, of course. But at least she wouldn't run the risk of having her mom think she was heartless. Summer already did, but having her mom think the same might break her.

❀

Marianne must have gotten the mail at ten, because Kelsey's phone rang at 10:01 on Monday. Then again at 10:05. And 10:10. She finally reached into her bag and turned off the ringer, then finished with her customer. When she was free, she took a mid-morning break, going into the Italian-style kitchen to make herself a cappuccino. They didn't have a true break room, but there was a conference room that wasn't in use, and she went in there to listen to her messages. Each one said basically the same thing—that Marianne would meet her any place, any time, any where. The sooner the better. You certainly couldn't say the woman was averse to groveling.

Kelsey dialed her number, feeling only a small amount of the fear and anxiety she'd felt when she'd been in contact with her during the spring. Doing this mostly for her mom changed everything.

"Kelsey?" Marianne asked, her voice shaking when she answered.

"It's me."

"You're really willing to see me?"

"I am. When's good?"

"Now," she said, with Kelsey almost certain she was crying.

"I'm at work right now, and I've got therapy tonight—"

"I'll meet you there. Just give me the address. Please?" she asked, with her voice breaking.

"All right," Kelsey said, feeling like an ogre. "You get texts, right?'

"Of course I do. I'm certainly not afraid of technology."

"Good. I'll text you the address. I finish a little before eight."

"I'll be there," Marianne said. "Early."

⬧

Kelsey had plenty to talk about in therapy, and as she walked down the staircase after her session, she decided it had been a very good idea to schedule the meeting with Marianne directly after speaking with Jean. Now that every session wasn't torture, she often felt a little inoculated from emotional scenes. Unless they were talking about Summer, of course. You knew things were bad when she enjoyed talking about Marianne more than the woman she was sure she was in love with.

As Kelsey opened the door, Marianne was right there, gazing at her with all of the poise of a startled cat.

"I'm glad you could come," Kelsey said, kind of unnerved by Marianne's anxious gaze. "Uhm…how about some ice cream? My treat."

"All right," she said, looking like she was glad Kelsey hadn't taken a swing at her.

"There's a place I like that's about five blocks away."

Marianne turned in the proper direction, and waited for Kelsey to start. They'd gone for about a block before Kelsey realized she wasn't going to talk. That was odd, but she'd learned in California that her birth mother didn't have the slightest idea how to make small talk. Surprisingly, Kelsey didn't feel the need to carry the conversational load. She thought of some of the questions Jean had asked her over the last few months, landing on the one about any interactions Kelsey could recall from childhood. It had taken her a while to come up with anything at all, but her brain had finally allowed a few memories in. All of them were of learning something. Arithmetic, reading, all kinds of educational games. Oddly, she didn't have one memory of just chatting for no purpose, or any songs they sang together. They definitely spoke, but there was always a purpose behind their conversations.

As they walked down the street, Kelsey decided that Marianne viewed speech only as a means to inform. If she wasn't telling you something of some significance, she kept her mouth shut.

The weather had cleared while she was in the office, with the mild storm of the early evening having blown away. They went inside the ice cream shop, and Marianne spent a moment checking out the flavors carefully. "Salted caramel's what I always pick," she said. "Kim tells me I'm too predictable."

"That's what I usually get," Kelsey said. "Funny, huh?"

Marianne nodded, but she didn't seem to get the point. They went outside with their cones, finding themselves alone out there, even though the night had turned very, very nice. The other ice cream eaters probably didn't trust that the rain would stay away, or that the benches were dry. That wasn't a problem for Marianne. She carried a bright yellow poncho in a small bag, and she unfolded it and draped it across a bench. "Problem solved," she said, even though she hadn't given voice to there being a problem in the first place.

"Nice," Kelsey said, taking a seat. "I'd always rather sit outside."

"Carry a poncho," she said. "You can use it for rain, warmth, a seat in the park..."

"Maybe I will," Kelsey said, certain she wouldn't. She was less practical than Marianne was, more concerned with looking good than being dry.

"So," Marianne said, clearing her throat. "I've got something to say."

Kelsey took a look at the cone in her hand. "Your ice cream's about to drip onto your slacks."

"Oh!" Hurriedly, she ate the cone in record time, then wiped her hands on a blue bandana she carried. She'd used that one in Santa Barbara, suggesting it was smart to carry one to clean your glasses, wipe your hands after eating messy food, and no doubt a hundred other uses.

"All right," she said, clearing her throat as she placed her hands on the top of the picnic table, as though she expected it to fly away after she'd been charged with holding onto it. "I thought I'd apologized to you," she said, not yet making eye contact.

"You did," Kelsey said. "Lots of times."

"No, I really haven't. My therapist—"

"Your therapist? You're seeing a therapist?"

"Actually, the proper term is counselor. I don't think she has a license to practice therapy. Kim found her for me."

"Why did you want someone who isn't licensed—"

"I didn't. Not really. But it's been helpful. I tell her what I want to accomplish, and she tells me how to achieve it."

"Hmm... That's not how therapy is for me."

"Well, I didn't have time to get into all of the things they want you to do in therapy. Kim's been, you know. She's gone for years." She made a face. "The last thing I wanted was to talk about my mothe—"

Kelsey jumped in to save her from having to finish that sentence. "So...you tell this person your goals, and you get advice, right? She's more of a life coach?"

"That sounds right. I told her I wanted to figure out how to have a relationship with you, and she asked me if I'd apologized properly. It turns out I hadn't," she said firmly. "I hadn't done even half of the steps."

"Steps? There are multiple steps?"

"Seven," she said, meeting Kelsey's eyes. "Only four are pertinent to us. The other three are for when you're apologizing for something you can fix."

"Something you can fix...?"

"Like if your job around the house was to mow the lawn, you'd apologize when I told you I was angry that you hadn't done it. But that wouldn't fix things. You'd have to start mowing the lawn if you were sincere about your apology."

"Ahh. And that's not something we have to worry about."

"No," she said solemnly. "I can only abandon you once, and I can't make up for that. Ever."

"That's the word *you* use?" Kelsey asked, astounded. "You agree that you abandoned me?"

"That's the right word," she said, looking down again. "Here's the apology." She took a breath and met Kelsey's gaze. "I'm truly sorry for all of the pain I caused you. It was wrong of me to leave you, and it was even more wrong to not come back when I could have."

"Thank you—"

"It was wrong of me to stop calling."

"Kitty told me she'd convinced you to—"

"It was wrong of me not to force your father to take you to therapy after I left. You needed it desperately."

"That's also true, but—"

"No excuses," she said, blinking her eyes slowly. "I was your mother, and my job was to protect you from harm. I didn't do that, and I couldn't regret my actions more."

Kelsey looked into her eyes, clearly able to see the regret that filled them. "Thank you," she said, fighting the urge to cry. "That means a lot."

"I wasn't apologizing before," she said, sounding so earnest it was almost funny. "I was explaining why I did what I did, but that's not important."

"Yes, it is," Kelsey said, even though she was certain it wasn't the *most* important thing. "I have a better understanding of why you did what you did."

"But you weren't able to forgive me. When I think of our time together in Santa Barbara, I don't blame you a bit for not being able to. I didn't even ask for forgiveness! I wanted you to ignore your hurt because of the pain *I've* been in."

Kelsey nodded briefly. "Yeah. That's how it felt. I haven't put it in those terms, but that's it. You didn't seem to have any idea of what you'd done to me."

"But I *did*," she insisted. "I simply thought you'd gotten over it. I thought that you'd gone on to have a good life, while I'd been stuck in my grief for all of these years."

"I have had a good life," Kelsey said quietly. "*And* I've had a lot of trauma. Both of those things are true."

"I'm starting to see that." Their eyes met again. "I really am."

Kelsey was sure she was treading into dangerous territory, but she had to know. "If you had to do it over again, what would you do?"

Marianne looked stricken, with her mouth dropping open for a few seconds. Then she closed her eyes and seemed to think for a while. "I don't know," she finally said. "But if I knew then everything I know now? I'd change jobs, change my phone number, and never speak to Kim again. I would have missed her with all of my heart, but I might have made it through."

"I'm glad you admitted you don't have an easy answer," Kelsey said softly. "It wasn't an easy situation."

"No, it wasn't. But making my little girl suffer so I could be free wasn't the right choice." She gave Kelsey such a sad look that she almost started crying. "I love Kim. I hope that's clear. But it would have been better to stay married to your father. The guilt has sucked so much of the joy from my life."

That didn't sound like a great idea, either. "Do you honestly think dad would have wanted to be married to a woman who didn't want to be married to him?"

"No," she said quickly. "But if I could have had a therapist or a counselor or someone to talk to, I might have been able to limp along…"

"How about facing who you were, telling Dad, then trying to figure out how to stay in town? I know you would have lost your job, but there were other jobs…"

"There were," she said quietly. "I probably couldn't have gotten a job teaching, but I could have done something for a store, or a bank." She kept her head down for a moment, then said, "The truth is that I ran. I was terrified, and I ran. Your father hated me, my own parents hated me, you wouldn't even look at me… I took the only option that seemed like I'd have some peace… But I didn't. Not really."

Kelsey held out her hand, smiling when Marianne tentatively took it. "We can't change the past, but we can try to have a better future, right?"

"You'll try?" she asked, with her chin quivering hard.

"I'll try. I know someone with three moms," she said, with a knot lodging in her throat every time she thought of Summer. "The original, the greatly improved replacement, and the peer. There's no reason I can't have two."

"Kitty will always be the greatly improved replacement for you. She's earned that title."

"She has. But it's not so bad to be the original, is it? I'm going to start telling people," she said, nodding to herself when she heard how right that sounded.

"Telling people…about me?"

"Uh-huh. I've never told my friends from high school, or college, or work."

Marianne let out a heavy sigh. "I didn't know that."

"I couldn't," Kelsey said. "But now that I'm not so angry, I can tell the story and not feel like I'll explode." She reached over and took Marianne's hand again. "You had to really hang in there to get this far, but I'm glad you did."

"I'm glad I did too," she said, offering up a watery smile. "Would you mind if I bought myself another ice cream cone? I was so nervous I didn't even taste the one I had."

Kelsey put her hand on her shoulder as she got up, elated that her hand didn't burn from repressed anger when she touched her. "It's on me."

⊛

Thinking the sticky heat that she'd suffered through at work that day had gotten to her, Summer stared at her therapist for a good minute, her burst of insight having knocked her off her pins. "Could it really be this simple? Is my perspective so damaged that I was convinced Kelsey couldn't possibly want to stay with me?"

"That's not a simple concern," Barbara said, gazing at her soberly.

"Oh, I know that. And in my case it goes both ways. I don't trust anyone to commit to me, and I don't trust myself to fully commit to anyone else."

"I don't think that's an accurate perception, Summer. You were with Natalie for a very long time, and you were completely faithful to her."

"But I wouldn't marry her, and I wouldn't buy a house with her. I needed an escape hatch. Always."

"Ahh. You're talking about making a permanent commitment."

"That's what I keep saying I want, but I'm terrified of making one! I've seen each of my birth parents enter into three marriages. Three times they've promised to love another person until death parts them. I've watched Beth have her heart broken so badly she hasn't even tried to find another man. I watched my mom's second husband create a baby with her, then take off just months later, never to return. I've had awful modeling," she insisted. "It's hard to think I'll be the one person in my family to honor my commitments."

Barbara maintained eye contact until Summer felt her anxiety wind down. Gently, she said, "Aren't you the only person in that group to try to figure out why you do things?"

"I suppose," she admitted. That was, of course, the truth. Her dad was a very genial narcissist, absolutely full of self-regard no matter how often he screwed up, and her mom made *other* people run to therapy. Neither of them had given any deep thought as to why they did what they did.

"I have every confidence you can be happy and fulfilled in a marriage, Summer. We'll simply shine a bright light on your fears, and you'll work through them. Just like you always have."

"But I wanted this to be *Kelsey's* issue," she sighed. "It was so much easier when I thought I could fix her."

"I'm sure that's true, but we both know the only person we have any chance at changing is ourselves."

"That's what you *tell* me," she said, unable to keep herself from joking, even during the most serious situations. "Maybe I just haven't tried hard enough. If I found someone more malleable…"

Barbara gave her a fond smile. "You've tried that. This time, why don't you face the truth. You can only change yourself."

CHAPTER THIRTY-SIX

KELSEY WAS NOW ABLE TO socialize—a little. She was back to bowling with her friends in Monroeville, and continued to have dinner with her parents every week. She also saw Rob pretty frequently. And she was able to work fairly productively. But she wasn't bouncing back like she'd hoped she would.

Jean had assured her that it would take a while, but that she'd eventually work through Summer's loss. But she had her doubts. Big ones. She was acting like Marianne a little bit, only instead of having pictures of Summer all over her house, she had them on her phone. There wasn't a day that went by that she didn't look at a few of them, and on bad days she could spend an hour examining them, trying to recall where they'd been and how she'd felt when they'd snapped the photo. Every single time she did that, she felt worse. But she couldn't stop herself. The pictures reminded her of how magical most of their days together had been, which only caused her to go into a spiral of rumination about what had happened, and why. But despite talking about it twice a week, and thinking about it ten times a day, she still didn't know what had broken what she'd thought was a damned strong connection.

If only she could go into some form of hibernation. Being in a state of suspended animation for a few months would be awfully nice. Then she'd wake up with the pain of the breakup mostly behind her. But she was just a human woman, and she had to suffer through it.

When her first girlfriend had broken up with her, she'd thought she'd gotten the raw end of the deal. Being dumped was truly awful. But it was no day-at-the-beach to be the one who'd made the decision. She felt not just the sting of loss, but the guilt at having acted. That was a dreadful combination, one that made her have many thoughts of living the rest of her life without the entanglement of a relationship. Was the pain of loss even worth the trouble?

Her phone rang, and it took her a few seconds to place the ring. She'd obviously compelled her brain to forget the tone she'd assigned to Summer, but when it connected to her emotions, she felt like her heart might burst.

She'd specifically told Summer not to contact her, and her anger flared in a nanosecond at the violation. Picking up the phone from her bedside, she glared at the photo, the one she'd taken of Summer after the first time they'd had sex. What a stupid fucking picture to have linked to Summer's contact info. Kelsey looked so damned happy. Maybe happier than she had since that night. The phone stopped ringing as she snuggled down into the covers and closed her eyes. Then the voicemail sound rang out. She growled and reached blindly for the device, then searched for the voicemail button in the muted light.

"Hi," Summer said, her voice small and tentative. "I hate to do this, but we've got a problem. The cabinets were delivered today and there's a screwup. A huge one. I was tempted to call your office, but I was sure you'd want to check this out before anyone else got involved. I'm sorry, Kelsey. I know you don't want to hear from me, but this is business. If you want to come over, I'll be here. If not, I'll call your office and see if someone else can help. Thank you," she said quietly, before switching off.

"Fuck, fuck, fuck, and fuck again," Kelsey cried, throwing off the covers and going into the bathroom to shower. "I've got one day to rest up and baby myself, and I have to spend part of it with Summer." She turned on the water, still steaming. "I'm sure that damned order was perfect. I bet the installers screwed up and are trying to shift the blame onto me." She got into the enclosure and let the hot water hit her right on the head. She normally conserved water very carefully, but she was going to stay in the spray until she could be civil. She dreaded having to see Summer, and she very much wasn't in the mood to argue with the installers. The only thing worse was getting her boss or her coworkers involved if she *had* screwed up. She'd made one mistake that had cost the firm money, and that was only to redo one box. She prayed this wasn't the day she found out she'd made her second.

☙

It took almost an hour for her to grab some juice and a bagel and drive over to Summer's. The street in front of the house was empty, with not a single truck parked nearby. That was odd. After she got out, she walked along the side of the house, assuming someone would be parked in the back yard. Nothing. She stood on the side stoop and knocked, and in a few seconds Summer's image appeared through the screen.

Damn. She looked fantastic. Her hair was down, and moved with her as she walked, those golden strands glimmering in the rays of colored light that shone through the leaded glass in the dining room. A sleeveless, pale blue cotton shirt topped khaki shorts, along with flip flops —something no one should ever wear near a construction site.

Kelsey had been so taken by her look that she hadn't peered inside to see the cartons, but when Summer flung the door open, she stepped in to see a perfectly orderly cabinet installation, just waiting for the countertops to be measured. "What…?" Kelsey turned around in a circle. "What's the problem?"

"My office," she said. "They did the kitchen first, then ran into problems there."

"Shit," she grumbled. "Was it the upper corner? There was so little room to get that in. Did it overlap with the window frame? If so, they can redo the molding if someone's really good with a coping saw. I know it's a pain, but—"

"Don't you want to take a look at your handiwork?" she asked, with a hesitant smile curling her lips. "You did a great job, Kelsey. Even the installers were impressed."

She was embarrassed to admit that appealing to her vanity worked, but getting cabinets to fit perfectly in a hundred-year-old bungalow took some skill. She folded her arms in front of herself as she looked around. "Great choice on the color," she said, nodding. "I was afraid that having the lowers darker than the uppers might be too much, but you were right. It's perfect."

"Look at how well the island turned out." Summer touched the properly installed boxes, still waiting for a countertop. "I'm so glad you talked me into installing one. There's room for a nine inch overlap, which will provide plenty of room for four stools." Standing by the wall that abutted the dining room, she said, "And your idea to turn this into a half-wall will prevent people from seeing into a dirty kitchen. The carpenter added this oak cap. Turned out great, didn't it?"

"Like it was here originally," Kelsey said, so pleased that AJ's subs were pulling their weight. In her head, she started to think about the perfect countertop for the room. Quartz was probably best, but using hardwood on the island would be nice... Then it hit her that she was in Summer's house, not some random client's. How could she feel so comfortable with her after less than three minutes?

"Let's take a look at your problem," she said, trying to get back into business mode.

They had to go through the dining room that was now partially open to the kitchen, then the living room. Summer didn't say anything, but Kelsey planted herself right in front of the fireplace, unable to continue. At either end of a new mahogany mantle was a beautiful tile representation of a proud red cardinal on one side, his fawn-colored mate on the other. The male had bent to pick something up from the ground, his tail fanned out. The female stood proud and tall, just a few degrees off from facing straight out. Even though she was less colorful, she was simply stunning.

"They're so beautiful," Kelsey said, recalling the day Summer had asked her what bird she favored. Her hand went to the tile, able to feel the bony yellow legs on the male, as if he might jump onto her hand.

"I got a little carried away at the base," she said, revealing her gorgeous grin. "You said the maple is your favorite tree, so I added an inset on the beaver tile we'd talked about."

Kelsey couldn't help herself. She dropped to her knees and traced her fingers over the beaver, who was happily gnawing on a thick trunk. Amazed, she was just about to ask for details when Summer said, "The background is a maple in the fall. That tiny pop of red really made it sing didn't it? The same tree's shown when it's newly leafed-out in the spring on the other side. I didn't want to belabor the busy beaver theme, so I have him standing up in that one. In my mind, he's been spooked, and is just about to take off."

"Amazing," Kelsey murmured. "Truly amazing."

"They're some of my best work," she said, clearly proud of herself. "If I'd made them for a client, I can't even guess what I'd have to charge." She lifted her hand above her head as she rolled her eyes.

"I'm so touched," Kelsey said, standing to take another look at her birds. *The* birds. "I'm surprised you didn't have a hawk eating the cardinal…"

"I wasn't angry," Summer said, with the warmth of her voice making chills race down Kelsey's spine. "Well, maybe at first. But it didn't take me long to see that you were simply protecting yourself. That's nothing to be ashamed of."

"It's a lot of work to protect yourself," she admitted. "Painful work."

"That's the kind that pays the biggest dividends," Summer said, acting so normal Kelsey couldn't quite get her mind around it. Had she really slipped into "friend" mode so easily?

"Come on," Summer urged. "Almost there." The doors to the first two bedrooms were shut, and when they entered Summer's office, Kelsey walked directly to the corner where she thought the problem would be. But she was unable to see any error. Every cabinet was exactly where it belonged, very professionally lined up, square with the window.

"Where's the problem?"

"There isn't one," she said. "I lied to get you to come over."

"Are you kidding me?" she demanded, flinching at the power of her own voice as she turned to glare at Summer. "I believed there was a major fuck up!"

"There was." She put her cool hand on Kelsey's bare arm and held it gently. "I fucked up. In a major way."

"*You* fucked up?" She'd been breathing heavily, with her heart pounding in her chest. "Is this about your office?"

"No." Summer looked her right in the eye and said, "On my birthday, I got scared when you made it clear you were ready to take the leap. I tried to convince both of us that I couldn't go along because you had a problem. But that wasn't true, and I'm so sorry for trying to shift the blame."

She stuck her hands in her pockets, shoving them into her shorts so forcefully they almost slid off her hips. She couldn't speak, couldn't even guess at what to say. She'd been waiting for Summer to fix this, but now that she was clearly trying to, Kelsey was stunned into silence.

The hand she'd come to treasure lightly touched between her shoulder blades, then trailed down to rest on her hip. Summer moved closer. Kelsey could feel her heat as she stood right next to her. "I'm so sorry I let my knee-jerk reaction prevent me from pulling you right into my bed and proposing to you."

Letting out a sigh, Kelsey turned to fully face her. Summer's skin was always beautiful, but it was particularly luminous this morning. She'd been outside a lot, and had tanned a little. That gave her a healthy glow that made her eyes look green, Kelsey's favorite shade of Summer's ever-changing eyes. "It hasn't been very long. How could you possibly have banished your fears? Revelations take time. I know that now that I've had to work through a few."

"They do. But I've been seeing Barbara for so long that I'm in AP therapy," she said, with an impish smile. "I'm able to move quicker than I used to." Both of her hands were now on Kelsey's arms, and she had so many tingles running through her she almost dissolved into a puddle.

"What exactly are you saying?"

She tilted her chin up, and closed her eyes. "On my birthday, I got frightened when I had to acknowledge that we were past the point of just having sex. It was time to make a firm, lasting commitment to each other. But I had so little faith in my ability to do that. Or to trust you to."

"How has that changed? In a matter of weeks," she said, reminding Summer of the brevity of the interval.

"Barbara reminded me that I'm not like Matt or Jackie. Actually, she thinks I take after Robert when it comes to love. If she's right about that, we've got nothing to worry about."

"So...you're honestly not upset about my refusal to have a relationship with Marianne?"

"No," she said, shaking her head slowly. "I was just looking for things to put on you so I didn't have to see the problem inside myself."

The words had registered, but they hadn't connected to her feelings. Kelsey couldn't just accept them as fact. "I can't have you telling me how to feel, Summer. I just can't."

"I won't," she said quietly. "I've got enough parents to worry about. What you do with your own is none of my business."

"And you're not going to get frightened again? If we get back together, you're not going to leave me at the altar?"

"I might get frightened," she admitted. "But I'll deal with it. That's why I'm going to stay in therapy for a while. Actually, I'm going to stay until Barbara kicks me out. Checking in when things are going down is mandatory when there's something so precious at stake." She put her hand over Kelsey's heart, undoubtedly able to feel it hammering away. "You're the most precious thing in the world to me, and I'm furious with myself for not checking in with Barbara when things started getting dicey. That was a grievous mistake. One I'll never make again."

When Summer reached out to pull her into a hug, Kelsey found herself willingly sliding into the embrace. It felt so damn good to be in her arms again. Like she'd found the key to happiness, right in that simple hug.

"Will you kiss me?" Summer murmured gently as she tilted her head back.

"Now *I'm* afraid," Kelsey said, realizing she was shaking. "I couldn't take you pulling the rug out from under me again. I swear I couldn't take it," she whispered fervently.

"I promise that I'll work hard to trust you. To cherish you," she added softly. "I do cherish you."

Kelsey wasn't able to stop her body from responding. She didn't *want* to stop her body from responding. This was dangerous. Horribly dangerous. But she was going to jump right in. "How about that kiss?"

Summer didn't respond with words, but her head tilted back as her eyes closed. Kelsey wished she could get her phone out to capture the beautiful look on her face, but she knew she'd keep this image in her heart, the one storage device that would never be obsolete.

Her arms tightened around Summer, then she dipped her head and kissed her, allowing her body to savor every sensation. The firm breasts that fit just under her own, the scent of her hair, freshly washed, the softness of her skin when Kelsey cradled her face in her hands. And, most of all, the incredibly soft, pliable lips that fit so well against her own.

"Perfect," Summer whispered when Kelsey lifted her head slightly. "I need a million more."

"I do too, but we'll get tired standing here for the hours and hours that's going to take."

"Walk this way…"

Now that Kelsey had her wits about her, she saw that Summer hadn't made any changes to the hallway, but when she opened the door to the larger of the guest rooms, the one that was supposed to be hers, Kelsey's mouth dropped open.

"Holy…"

"You wanted a woman-cave. You got a woman-cave."

Kelsey walked into the room, amazed to find a gigantic TV hanging from the wall, cords magically hidden. A nice wooden cabinet held some components, red and blue lights glowing from them. Across from the TV was a comfy looking sofa, with a sleek leather recliner fitting alongside nicely. "I can't believe—"

"I want you to be happy," Summer said. "I ordered all of this the day after you told me you wanted it." She smiled, looking a little abashed. "But if you'd refused to come over today, I was going to return everything. The boxes are all out in the garage." She shrugged, with a tiny grin making her look mischievous. "I'm too practical for my own good sometimes."

"You can officially recycle them. I'm going to shoot off an email to my landlord tonight. If you want me to, that is."

"I do," she whispered. "More than anything. I'm going to buy a big container of vanilla ice cream, a case of Reece's Peanut Butter Cups, and a crate of pretzel sticks. You can create an unholy mess to snack on while we sit in here and watch whatever ridiculous sport you're into."

"Just the Steelers," she said, holding up her hand in a pledge. "If I want to watch the Penguins, I'll go to my dad's."

Summer wrapped her arms around Kelsey tightly and whispered, "I love you so much, I don't mind if you watch sports for ten hours a night."

"I love you too," Kelsey murmured, her voice choked with tears. "I've been so sad…"

Summer took her hand and led her to the sofa. It really was as comfy as it looked, but Kelsey's thoughts were so jumbled it was hard to concentrate. Her untrammeled joy was still just an overlay to the pain that had wracked her for weeks.

"I've been sad, too," Summer said, her composed features making that clear. "Sadder than I've ever been." She took Kelsey's hands in her own and kissed each of them. "I wanted to contact you. *So* many times," she murmured. "But I knew that doing that after you'd asked me not to would be a breach of trust. And I never want to do that to you." She grasped her hands more firmly and held them to her chest. "I always want to respect the boundaries you've set." She lifted Kelsey's hand and kissed it gently. "I waited until I was one hundred percent sure I could be a good partner to contact you. I hope that's…"

"I'm so glad you did," Kelsey sighed, close to tears. "I never should have told you to leave me alone. I…" She let out a breath. "Jean thinks I did that so you couldn't disappoint me. Kind of a 'you can't fire me, I quit,' kind of thing."

"Makes perfect sense." Summer released her fervid grip, but kept hold of one hand, placing it on her lap. "You're always going to have that instinct. You can't suffer the kind of trauma you did and ever automatically believe that anyone's going to stay. But you'll figure out ways to calm yourself. I'll help if I can."

"Can I help you with anything?" Kelsey asked, not as all sure she had the skills, but she certainly had the will.

"Absolutely. You can remind me that you're not Matt or Jackie. You're honest, and loyal, and thrifty, which doesn't seem like a sexy attribute, but when you grow up with the repo men kicking the door down, it's highly prized."

"No repo men," Kelsey promised, smiling at Summer's earnest expression. "Everything will be secure. Our home, our love, our commitment to one another." She took in a deep breath, with the tightness that had hampered her breathing now easing. "We're going to be happy. There isn't a doubt in my mind."

Summer leaned over and squeezed her tightly. "We'll be happy today, and tomorrow, and the day after, and the day after that. At the end of our lives, we'll feel like we've been together—very happily together—forever."

"We will?" Kelsey asked, thinking it beyond cute that Summer had been planning not only for the future, but of how they'd think of it. "How do you know that?"

"My grandma told me," she said, eyes shining. "She and my grandfather were together for fifty-one years, and she swears she doesn't even remember her life before him. She just has snippets of her youth that don't leave a big impression. It's him she remembers." She kissed Kelsey gently, then looked into her eyes. "It'll be just like that for me. A little static, then us."

"I feel like we should do something to celebrate," Kelsey said, unable to stop what she knew was a silly grin from showing. "Can you think of anything?"

"I've got a couple of ideas. Want to see?" she asked, scooting closer. "Can't wait."

Summer had been so intent on creating a ruse for getting Kelsey into the house that she hadn't given a lot of thought to what she'd do with her once she had her. But she definitely had her now, and Kelsey was definitely giving her a very hungry look. Luckily, Kelsey didn't seem as unsure of herself as Summer did at that moment.

Warm arms slid around her body, holding her tenderly for a minute. "This feels so good. So right," Kelsey murmured. She moved her head slowly, allowing their cheeks to brush against one another. "Every part of my life fell apart when I walked out of your apartment. Literally nothing felt right."

"For me either," Summer said. "I don't know how I would have coped if I couldn't at least have been your friend." She tilted her head so their eyes met. "You're such a part of my life. The very best part."

"My lips are getting mad at me," Kelsey said, showing the wry grin that always made Summer smile. "They're tired of talking."

"What would they rather do?"

"They'd really prefer kissing. I've tried to reason with them, but they've made up their minds."

Summer let her finger glide across the deep pink lips, addressing them as though they were sentient. "I never want to disappoint you two. I love you both."

"I think I missed your playfulness most of all," Kelsey said, with a flash of pain crossing her face. "I thought I'd forgotten how to smile."

"I haven't had a lick of fun since you walked out of my apartment," Summer said, leading her toward the sofa. "Let's make up for that."

Kelsey sat and guided her by the hips to pull her onto her lap, with Summer facing her, knees astride.

"Mmm. I love being on top."

As Kelsey's hands slipped across her shoulders to lace behind her neck, she pulled her close until they were face-to-face. "Don't get used to it," she growled, tugging gently until their lips touched. In seconds, it was impossible to tell who was leading and who was following. Their mouths merged so seamlessly that they seemed as if they'd been designed to touch. All Summer knew was that she'd never felt so whole, so much more *herself*—while simultaneously feeling like a part of Kelsey. It made her head swim, and the relentless rain of kisses didn't make it any easier to think clearly. Kelsey didn't seem like she was thinking much, either, which was perfect. They'd spent far too long overthinking how they felt about each other. Now it was time to let their bodies take over.

Just when she'd settled down for a long exploration of Kelsey's mouth, she stiffened slightly, then started to pat her leg. Summer sat up to gaze at her quizzically.

"You took a selfie of our first kiss," Kelsey said. "I thought we needed one of our first...whatever we call this." She produced her phone, looking very proud of herself.

"Really? That's what's on your mind right now?"

"Partly." She stuck her arm out and framed the shot, then put her hand on the back of Summer's head and guided her down for a sweet, gentle kiss. The camera clicked a few times, then Summer sat up and tried to take the phone from her hand.

"Not so fast," Kelsey said. "I've got to make a call."

"A call?" Summer stared at her, astounded.

"I'll do a text. That's faster."

"Kelsey!"

"Just give me one second, then I can focus." She finished, then looked up at Summer. "My mom, and, to a lesser extent, my dad, have been *very* worried about me. I have to let them know I'm all better."

Summer waited for her to finish, then pulled the phone from her hand and turned it off. Then she took her own out, turned it around and took a photo of herself giving Kelsey a narrow-eyed glare. "I want to always remember that you're a very thoughtful woman who really cares about the people she loves—even when she has to drive me crazy to do it."

"You've got me pegged," she said, clearly not bothered by the characterization.

"No more phones." She pointedly turned her own off, and put both of them on the table. Placing her hands on Kelsey's shoulders, she gazed into her eyes. "Do I have your attention now? Your full attention?"

Her head nodded solemnly. "It's just taking me a few minutes to go from having a broken heart to knowing you love me. Big jump."

"Did you really doubt that I loved you?" The mere thought of that felt like a blow.

"No," she admitted quietly. "I was confident you *wanted* to love me, but not as confident that you'd let yourself. I…I wanted to believe in us, but it was very hard going." Her gaze slid down to hover somewhere around Summer's belly. "I thought you'd follow me home that afternoon and convince me you just needed a minute to get your thoughts in order. But when I didn't hear from you…" Her gaze moved up to land on Summer's face. "I thought we were done. That's when I wrote to you. I needed to feel like I was in control, even though I've never felt so out-of-control."

"I would have come after you, but I was so friggin' confused. Once I got back into therapy, I *knew* I had no idea of what was going on. I swore I wouldn't try again until I was certain I was able to commit." She could feel a little smile tug at her lips. "Once I was talking to Barbara again my confidence grew quickly. I never again let myself think we wouldn't reunite. Every time someone told me you wouldn't necessarily be waiting for me, I tried not to listen." She placed her hands on Kelsey's cheeks to tilt her head up slightly, now able to look directly into her eyes. "I couldn't imagine not being with you, and it was just as unbelievable that you'd run off and pair up with the first woman you met."

"I'd pretty much decided I was going to stay single," she admitted. "If we couldn't make it, I clearly didn't know what love was."

"You do," Summer whispered, tilting her head to be able to reach those sweet, trembling lips. For long minutes they slowly lowered the barriers they'd put up in the last weeks, both of them tentative as they adjusted to the kind of intimacy they'd so easily rushed into when they'd first met. Kelsey's body was nearly rigid, but as the heat of their kisses increased, she started to move more freely, with her hands eventually joining in to glide across Summer's back.

"I'm so happy," Kelsey murmured when they broke apart for a moment.

"Unless my skills have atrophied, I predict you've just scratched the surface of today's happiness capacity."

"Oh, I don't have any doubts about your skills. You know how to touch my heart." She grasped Summer's hand and placed it on her chest. "Feel that? The more you kiss me, the faster it beats."

"Let's see." She tucked her arms around Kelsey's shoulders and held her tightly, already feeling her own heartbeat increase just from holding her close. "I love you," she whispered before lavishing a burst of kisses to her lips that had them both breathing hard in seconds.

When Summer pulled away to lean over and rest her ear against Kelsey's chest, she tapped the beat on her leg, the rapid thump making her smile. Sitting up, she kissed her again, pressing her against the back of the sofa as her need continued to grow.

It took a second to even notice that Kelsey's hand had slid up her shirt, but as Summer's skin began to pebble from the sensation, she diverted some of her attention from Kelsey's luscious mouth to her own body.

"Your hands feel so good," she murmured, diving back in, hungry for kisses.

"I need…" Kelsey sighed as their kisses grew even deeper, with Summer's tongue probing her mouth until she began to groan.

Kelsey pulled away, panting. "I have to feel your skin. All of it."

Her cheeks were so flushed she looked feverish, and Summer raised up on her knees, as she lifted her arms. "All yours."

Hurriedly, Kelsey unbuttoned her shirt, then eased it off. Her eyes were nearly glassy when her hands settled onto Summer's breasts, with her thumbs rubbing her hardening nipples through her bra.

"I think you were planning on seducing me," Kelsey said, with a wry grin covering her mouth. "I don't remember you wearing sexy undies before."

"Special occasion." Summer closed her eyes and concentrated on the gentle, but determined touch. "But I'll wear them every day if you like them. I'll do anything to make you happy."

"I like a little flash," Kelsey said, her voice having grown lower and sexier. "But I sure don't need it." She cupped Summer's breasts gently in her hands. "You can't improve on perfection."

Summer opened her eyes to see that Kelsey looked a little stunned. She lowered her voice and purred, "Want me to take it off?"

Her head nodded slowly, making her look completely vacant. Sometimes not saying a word was a very generous compliment. Summer put her hands behind her back to undo the clasp, and as she slid the straps down she shook her shoulders, smiling when Kelsey made some kind of animal-like sound. "Open up," she whispered, guiding her breast into Kelsey's mouth as they both moaned softly.

There were very few things that felt better than having your lover's warm mouth envelop your flesh, and Summer soon found herself pressing her body into Kelsey's mouth as she sucked greedily.

Unable to get enough sensation, Summer grasped her head to pull her closer, with Kelsey now nearly frantic as she moved from one breast to the other, treating each of them as if they were giving her life-sustaining nourishment.

"Oh!" Summer yelped when Kelsey got a little too enthusiastic.

"Sorry," she whispered, pulling away to merely stare as she ran her fingernails over the pink flesh, her eyes glassy as she watched the nipples somehow harden even more. "You were right," she said, her gaze shifting up to meet Summer's. "I'm getting happier by the minute."

"I'm so happy I'm squirming like a puppy," Summer said, chuckling.

Kelsey looked up at her, eyes burning with desire. She took a finger and slid it down Summer's body, pausing at her waistband. "I've love to take these off."

Immediately, Summer slid off her lap and stood. "Give me your hand," she said. She pulled Kelsey to her feet. "We need some room to move."

After walking to their bedroom, Summer opened the door, revealing a new king-sized bed. "When I saw there was room for a king, I decided to splurge. Everything's for us alone. Sheets, pillows, comforter. A new bed for our new start." She did a quick twirl. "You may undress me."

Kelsey looked completely content when she quickly unzipped Summer's shorts and let them drop to the floor. "Matching undies," she said, grinning. "You definitely had a plan."

"Still do." Summer grasped the hem of Kelsey's polo shirt and tugged it off. "Mmm-mmm. When I look at your breasts, my brain gets flooded with all sorts of messages saying, 'You're a lesbian!'" Kelsey started to laugh, but she stopped when Summer immediately slipped her hands around her to remove her bra. "Happy, happy, happy," she purred, gazing at Kelsey's chest, her breasts appealing to her on a visceral level. "I think I'd be rabidly attracted to you even if you were a surly grouch."

"That's only funny because it couldn't be further from the truth," Kelsey said, touching Summer's jaw to urge her head up. Their eyes met for a few long seconds, then Kelsey said, "There's nothing shallow about you."

"Thanks." She could feel her cheeks begin to color, touched by how sincere Kelsey was being. "I'm joking only because I'm on the verge of crying. I'm so happy to have you back." She hugged her tightly, soothed immediately by the warmth and softness of her skin. "I love you, Kelsey. So much it takes my breath away."

"Me too. It's scary, but in a really good way."

Summer looked up at her. "A really good way."

"You know what else would be good?"

"I can guess. You're excellent at getting me back on track." She reached for her waistband and unbuttoned her jeans.

"That's exactly what I was going to suggest. You take subtle hints very well."

"You're just obvious." Summer met her gaze as she lowered her zipper, grasped the fabric and slid it down her legs. "Can you kick off your shoes?"

"Done."

Kelsey stepped out of her jeans, then Summer held her in a tender hug. After a minute, she ran her hands all over her bikinis. "You get extra credit for having taken a shower and put on nice undies even when you were just coming over to argue about my cabinets."

"My mom taught me to be prepared for anything."

"Bet your mom didn't include this in her plans," Summer said as she hugged Kelsey tightly and tumbled them to the bed.

"Whoa! My mom also warned me against rough-housing. You don't want to spend the day in the ER, do you?"

"The sun's shining on us today," Summer said, certain of that fact. "We're impervious to harm."

"God, I hope so," Kelsey said, suddenly serious. "I want to hold onto you for a very, very long time."

"I couldn't agree more. Actually, I want to do a lot of things for a very long time. Mind if I get a head start?" She slipped her hand into Kelsey's undies, grinning when her fingers encountered smooth, warm flesh. "I like it here."

A devilish smile lit Kelsey's face. "I've been told that's my best asset."

"Whoever told you that wasn't lying, but I haven't seen anything that's not perfect. All of your body parts might be in a tie for the best one."

"I've got a couple of favorites," Kelsey said. "This is definitely one of them." She slipped her hand into Summer's undies and filled it with the flesh, squeezing it firmly.

"I love it when you're forceful like that," Summer said, purring softly. "I tease about wanting to be in charge, but I like to feel a little overwhelmed."

Kelsey shifted so she was lying on top, her eyes glittering as she looked down at Summer. "When I say I like to be in charge, I'm not teasing."

"I'm versatile, but it's so much easier when you can go with your natural instincts."

"Instincts are firmly in charge," Kelsey said, with just a hint of danger making Summer's nipples harden.

Kelsey wrapped her arms around her waist, then flipped them over so Summer was on top. Then warm, gentle hands slipped into her bikinis, urging them down as Kelsey tucked just one arm around her and flipped her over again. Lying on her back, looking up at Kelsey, Summer gripped her biceps. "You're stronger than you look."

"I know," she said, waggling her eyebrows. "I've got a lot of hidden traits." Before Summer could blink, Kelsey had braced some of her weight on her forearms, giving her the perfect angle to press onto Summer's shoulders and begin to kiss her again.

Her kisses were no longer soft, gentle and exploratory. Now she knew where she was going, and had every intention of getting there quickly. When her tongue slid into Summer's mouth, it did so possessively, making Summer squirm under her. Nothing felt better than having your lover touch you like she absolutely had to have you.

Kelsey's touch was sure, and purposeful, and her body started to give off some heat as she pressed Summer firmly into the mattress, her hands never stilling.

Summer gripped her around the waist and let the kisses rain down on her. When she couldn't remain still any more, she wrapped her legs around Kelsey with the pressure of her body hitting her right where she needed it. "Jesus," she murmured, feeling like she was racing to climax while simultaneously trying to slow down.

Kelsey took the hint and lightened up on her ravenous touch. For a minute or two, they kissed gently, letting their tender feelings take over as they caught their breath. Then Kelsey started to kiss her way down Summer's body, and the anticipation started to build again.

Their eyes met when Kelsey settled between her legs, and they stayed connected as she confidently opened Summer with her fingers, then dipped her head and tasted her.

"Whoa," Summer moaned, feeling the electricity spark. "You couldn't make that feel better if you tried." Her voice hardly sounded like her own, but it didn't matter. She couldn't have spoken again if she'd wanted to. All she could do was lie there, open to anything Kelsey wanted, needing her touch to stay grounded.

"God, I love you," Kelsey sighed, looking up with tears in her eyes. "I'm right where I belong. When we're together, we're home."

Summer gave her a watery smile, unable to think of a single thing to say. Kelsey had said it all. She put her hand on her head and gently stroked her face as Kelsey kissed and nibbled and probed Summer's flesh with her tongue. The minutes passed in a state of sensual bliss, with Summer trying to make it last. She could feel how into it Kelsey was, thrilling to her little sounds of pleasure. But when fingers slid inside and started to pump, she knew the end was near. Gripping Kelsey's shoulders with her hands, she held on and tried to squeeze the last bits of pleasure out before she went over the edge. Her mouth opened, but a sound didn't come out. She was crashing over the cliff, panting for air, barely aware of anything but an inch or two of her body that pulsed rhythmically until she couldn't stand the slightest pressure. "No more," she choked out, her dry throat making her cough.

Kelsey's soft chuckle reached her ears. Then her head popped up, with her eyes bright. "I had a feeling that would push you over. Sorry if it snuck up on you."

"Do you honestly think I'm going to complain about you turning me on so much I couldn't stop myself from climaxing? Get up here," she said, tugging on her arm. "Show off." She kissed Kelsey's cheek, seeing how sated she looked. "I think you liked that as much as I did, and I've got to tell you, I liked it a whole, whole lot."

An earnest expression covered Kelsey's face. "It's important to me that you're satisfied."

"I am so satisfied you don't have to make love to me again for another half hour or so."

Kelsey grinned, looking so happy it almost made Summer tear up. "I need about thirty seconds of your time, then we can focus on you again."

Summer ran her hand down Kelsey's thigh, feeling the muscle beneath her soft skin. "I'm going to spend much more than thirty seconds on you. I can hardly wait."

"I just need a little attention here or there…" She grasped Summer's hand and placed it firmly on her upper thigh. "Mostly here. You've gotten me so turned on I could combust."

"There's no place I'd rather be." Summer lay on her side and started to touch Kelsey's smooth skin, trailing over her with the tips of her fingers, smiling when the skin started to pebble. "Is it cold in here?" she teased.

"No. You just give me chills."

"Aww… I love being able to touch you and watch how you react. I don't think I'll ever get tired of this. You're more fun than TV."

"You barely watch TV. Now if you'd said I was more fun than drawing…"

"You are," Summer pledged, pulling her close to kiss her gently. "Touching you is the most fun I ever hope to have. You're endlessly fascinating."

"That's because you love me," Kelsey said, smiling so tenderly that Summer felt herself tear up again.

"I'm so glad you know that." She gazed at her for a moment, then said, "One of the things I was worried about was whether you'd be able to believe I loved you. I thought that losing your mom might have made you feel…a little unlovable."

"That definitely could have happened, but a complete stranger made me feel like I was the coolest kid she'd ever met. That's all it takes," she added soberly. "A kid just has to feel special."

"Do I make you feel special? I really want to," Summer whispered, putting her lips against Kelsey's ear.

"You always have."

"That's because you are. You're very special, boo."

"Boo? Where did that come from?"

Summer laughed. "I have no idea. It just tumbled out of my mouth. You felt like my boo right then."

A sober look came over Kelsey's face, then she said, "Marianne used to call me Bitsy-Boo. I haven't thought of that since I was a kid."

"Ooo. I'll stop," Summer said quickly.

"I like it," she said, her smile appearing a little sad. "I must just look like a boo. Why fight it?"

"You think about it. I don't want to bring up any painful memories."

"That's not a painful one. Thinking about Marianne calling me a pet name reminds me that she did care for me. You don't do that to a kid you *want* to run away from."

"No, you don't," she agreed. "I still don't think she wanted to leave, but I might be giving her too much credit—"

"I don't think so," Kelsey said. "I'm actually beginning to believe that. Here," she said, patting the skin over her heart. She gazed at Summer for a moment, and her voice got quiet when she spoke. "When I was out there, she told me why she picked my name."

"Really?" Summer wasn't sure why this was important, but the look on Kelsey's face signaled it was.

"Yeah. I think she knew she didn't have great instincts. I think she…I think she struggles to fit in. She probably always has."

"That's…probably true."

"Right. So she was in school getting her masters when she was pregnant with me. There was a woman in one of her classes who Marianne admired. She said she was clever and very sharp, but what Marianne seemed to fix on was how happy the woman seemed. She had a little girl named Kelsey, and she used to pass around photos of her. Apparently, the kid was always giggling or laughing, and somehow Marianne thought the name might have had something to do with that. So she decided to name me Kelsey so I might be happy." She stared at

Summer for a few long seconds. "She was flying blind. Grasping for straws at how to be a good mom."

"Oh, Kelsey, that's heartbreaking," she said, feeling like she could cry.

"Yeah," she agreed, dropping her head for a moment. When she looked up again, she said, "We've met up a couple of times."

Summer stared at her, amazed. "You have?"

"Uh-huh. When you, my mom, and my therapist all think I should do something, it's just being insolent not to try."

"I didn't push you too hard, did I?"

"Yes," she said, with a slight smile showing. "You definitely did. But that's not why I reached out to her. It took me a while, but I finally decided she deserved another chance." She kissed Summer gently. "We'll see how it goes."

"You have a loving heart," Summer whispered, so pleased at her absolute certainty of that. She gave her a slow, tender kiss. "I see it all of the time, and that makes my feelings for you grow and grow."

"I can't wait," Kelsey sighed. "Of course, that's not the only thing I can't wait for." She tilted her head, looking pointedly down at her body.

"You're so demanding!" Summer grasped her and they wrestled playfully for a minute, until she had Kelsey pinned to the bed. "Tossing around blocks of clay all day's prepared me to take you down, girl."

"Now that you've got me here, why don't you do something with me?"

"With pleasure." She started at her ear, knowing it was ultra-sensitive. Then she worked her way down, visiting every part of her sexy body, spending extra time whenever Kelsey's moans and purrs indicated she'd hit a hot spot. It was like investigating a sacred site, being careful not to harm any of the precious artifacts, while pouring your attention into the smallest details.

"I feel so loved," Kelsey sighed, stretching out with her hands above her head.

"Ooo. Your breasts look awesome when you do that." She took a lick of a firm nipple. "I've thought about them so many times I'm sure I could have drawn them from memory." She sat up, bracing herself on her arm. "Could I? Draw you?"

"Um, sure. I might be self-conscious, but…sure."

"We'll do it when we're planning on spending the day in bed together. We'll take a break and I'll sketch you."

"Pencil me in for Labor Day. That's the next time we both have the day off."

"Look at the bright side. We won't get sick of each other," she said, chuckling.

"Like that's possible." She grasped Summer's head and pulled it toward her breast. "I can't even get you to make love to me, and it's already time for your second round."

"I'm so wired! I've got so many things flying around in my head it's like bees buzzing."

"I know," Kelsey soothed. "If I'd already had an orgasm, my mind would probably wander too. Of course, I haven't…"

"I'm on it," Summer said, letting out a laugh. "At least you can't say I rush you."

"No, you certainly can't say that." She tucked her arm around Summer and held her close for a few seconds. "I hope you know I'm teasing. I could be perfectly happy just lying here and smelling your hair."

"You can do that tonight, when we're getting ready to sleep. Right now, I'm on a mission."

She normally would have worked to bring Kelsey back up to a slow boil, but she was certain she was painfully aroused, and she had every intention of settling down later to explore her at length. With a burst of strength, she got her onto her back, then slid down to nuzzle against her for a few moments. "I love how you smell," she murmured. "Like sex."

"Mmm," she sighed, pushing herself against Summer, clearly trying to get some pressure where she needed it.

"I'm going to slow down and play with you until you can't stand it."

"I can hardly stand it now." Her words made it sound like she was in a hurry, but her body was moving slowly and sensually, making Summer certain she liked being teased.

Opening her with her fingers, she smiled when she took her in—pink and wet, with her skin glistening in the sun. Summer was going to find a way to paint her, even though she was certain that would be a big ask. But Kelsey was so perfectly formed, her body just begged to be memorialized.

She closed her eyes when she tasted her, quickly lost in the sensation. It was like being enveloped by Kelsey's body, with her scent, the heat of her flesh, the softness of her delicate skin all combining to fill Summer like a sensual feast.

Kelsey's body was endlessly fascinating, and as Summer probed her with her tongue, she kept veering away every time her breathing picked up or she shivered roughly. She wanted to draw this out for as long as possible, to make Kelsey remember their lovemaking for the rest of her life.

She couldn't have guessed how long she'd been exploring her, but she finally couldn't resist the urge. She understood exactly what Kelsey meant when she said she loved exploring inside. There was something so primal about having a part of your body inside your partner's that it called to her in ways she couldn't refuse.

"That's so good," Kelsey whispered, having been almost silent for the longest time. Her body spoke volumes, but she was very quiet when she was being touched, seeming like she needed to concentrate to enjoy herself to the fullest.

"Tell me what you need," Summer murmured. "Guide my hand."

Her wrist was gripped in a second, then Kelsey urged her to go very, very slowly. She pressed her body against Summer's fingers, taking over in just a few moments. "Press down a little. Actually, move your fingers to different spots and put some pressure there. Surprise me," she said, chuckling.

"I'd love to surprise you." She tried to do just what Kelsey asked, moving her fingers around like the hands of a clock, touching and gently pressing as she moved.

"Fantastic," she got out, whimpering a little. "I can't hold on much long—" She let out a burst of air, thrusting her hips against Summer so forcefully that if she hadn't moved slightly she might have chipped a tooth! "Oh, Jesus," Kelsey sighed. Then her legs stretched out and she lay there like she'd been knocked unconscious.

Summer stroked her thigh, watching her flesh pulse for the longest time. Finally, Kelsey laughed. "Well, that was certainly worth waiting for. Why don't you come up here and kiss me."

She shimmied into place, taking Kelsey's still mostly limp body in her arms. "I love you so much," she sighed. "This has been the best morning of my life."

Lazily, Kelsey moved her arm so she could see her watch. "And it's barely time for lunch. By nightfall, you're going to wish you had a spare body, because I'm going to wear this one out."

"I dare you," Summer said, chuckling, knowing Kelsey was competitive enough that she'd accept the challenge and rise to the occasion. It was going to be a very good, very long day. The first of what she hoped was thousands upon thousands of them on their life's journey.

EPILOGUE

A WEEK LATER, KELSEY LAY ON their cloud-like bed, waiting for Summer to join her. They'd been fully moved in for just a day, now only waiting for countertops, a sink, and a few items on the punch list. Those last details would probably take as long as the rest of the entire project had, but Kelsey had never been involved with a renovation that didn't leave a few things unfinished for an annoyingly long time.

Summer finally emerged from the attached bath, running a brush through her hair. She didn't brush it for long, but she always gave it a little care before bed. Summer moved over to stand by the window and throw it open. Then she closed her eyes and breathed in so deeply Kelsey could see her ribs expand. "Have I mentioned how much I love my buddleia davidii?"

"A time or two—every hour," Kelsey said, reaching out to take her hand and tug her toward the bed. "The guy at the nursery promised they'd maintain their blooms if I planted them properly and watered the heck out of them. Let's hope he's right." She ran her hand up and down Summer's thigh, watching the skin pebble. "If it's sunny this weekend, I want you to sit out there for a while and capture the butterflies going to town. I'd be a very happy camper if I came home to a watercolor of our butterfly bushes."

"Watercolor? I think that's a good idea. But maybe pastels... We'll have to see."

"Speaking of having to see, I keep forgetting that we have to organize an outing to see the Bucs before Marianne and Kim go back home. Are you interested?"

Summer gazed at her with a question in her eyes. "The Bucs? We have a team called the Bucs?"

"Uh-huh. That's a nickname for the Pirates."

Summer gave her a look that suggested Kelsey was screwing with her. "Isn't the Pirates a nickname?"

"You make a good point. But whatever they're called, I'd like to go to a game."

"Got it. Given that it's summer, they must be the baseball team, right?"

"Oh, boy," Kelsey sighed. "This is going to be a long night."

They didn't purchase tickets early, mostly because the Bucs weren't doing well, and there were plenty available. Just before they were going to leave the house, Lauren called, and Kelsey could see Summer's expression grow concerned. "Do you think it's serious?" she asked.

Kelsey stood right next to her, hoping to hear what was going on. Summer tilted the phone, making Lauren's voice come through clearly. "No, I don't think it is. Probably a UTI. She's been sick to her stomach, and she's got all of the usual signs of infection—chills, body aches. She definitely doesn't want to go to the ER, so I'm going to take her to an urgent care place."

"And…you don't want to take Poppy with you," Summer said, rolling her eyes. "Not that I blame you."

"Your dad's out," Lauren said, usually vague about where he was and what he was doing. Kelsey knew that some of the casinos he went to had terrible cell reception. Lauren likely had no way to reach him when he was gambling, which was often. "I'm kind of stuck, Summer, and I hate to think of my mom sitting there by herself…"

"We're going to a baseball game, but if Poppy doesn't mind…" She looked up at Kelsey, clearly resolved, but not seeming happy about it.

"Oh, she'd love it," Lauren said, even though Kelsey was sure Poppy loved baseball as much as Summer did—not at all.

Kelsey gave her a thumb's up. Even though she and Marianne were getting along much better, having the Popster along would provide some liveliness—which was sometimes decidedly lacking.

At eight thirty, Kelsey, Summer, Poppy, Kim and Marianne sat up in the nosebleed section of the stadium she still called Three Rivers, watching the Pirates kick the Phillies all over the field. At least Kelsey thought that's what was happening. When you watched a game with a child, not many minutes went by that weren't interrupted.

Kim sat on the far end, with Marianne next to her. Poppy wound up next to Marianne, which wouldn't have been the way Kelsey would have arranged the group. But Summer had urged the child into the row, then sat next to her. That left Kelsey on the aisle, a spot she found she was pretty fond of. That placement let her do something social with her birth mother, while not being too close. It was still early days.

To Kelsey's surprise, Marianne not only took an interest in Poppy, Poppy was seemingly fascinated by both her and Kim. It made sense with Kim, since she taught at the primary school level, and was naturally warm and effervescent. But Marianne seemed much more like a person you'd sit next to if you wanted to work on some math theorems, or had a tricky physics problem that was vexing you.

The game was in the bottom of the third, and the Phillies had already called on the services of the bullpen. Giving up five runs in the first had called for heroic measures. Kelsey looked down the row, seeing Poppy point at her. "What?" she asked, leaning over.

"You have two moms, too?" the child said, giving her a narrow-eyed glance.

"I do," Kelsey said, still very much getting used to admitting to that. "Marianne gave birth to me, but another woman raised me."

"Why?" Poppy stared at her, demanding an answer.

"I guess I should let Marianne answer that," she said, knowing she was cheating. "I was a little older than you are now when she had to move away, so I don't really know all the details." She put on a smile that she knew looked forced. "Even though she gave birth to me, Marianne and I haven't seen each other very much since I was a little girl."

"Why?" Poppy asked again, her big brown eyes boring a hole in Kelsey.

"Um…"

Summer gave her a glance that silently indicated she'd take over, but Kelsey tried to rally. "When I was a little girl," she said, swallowing the feelings that formed a lump in her throat, "my dad married a lady I really liked. She liked me too. A lot," she emphasized. "She became my mom, and I didn't…" She nodded, closing her eyes. "I didn't want two moms."

Now Summer stepped in. She gave Marianne, who looked stricken, a smile and said, "Sometimes your feelings change as you grow up. Having two moms confused Kelsey when she was little, but she and Marianne are working on being friends now."

"You have two moms," Poppy reminded Summer. "You're friends, right?"

"We are," Summer said. "Your daddy married Beth when I was about your age. I liked her a lot, just like Kelsey did with her new mom. But I still lived with Jackie, and I never stopped thinking of her as my mom." She held her hands up, indicating that she couldn't explain the situation any better. "Families are different for different people. Sometimes they change. They can get bigger and they can get smaller."

"I only have one mom," Poppy said, her high voice carrying over the noise of the crowd. "I think that's all I want." She looked up at Summer. "If I want two later, can I have you?"

"I'd take you on in a minute," she said, hugging her. "But your mom is perfect for you. I think one fits you just right."

Kelsey couldn't hear what Marianne had to say, but she spoke to the little girl for quite a while. Poppy sat very still, gazing at her carefully, clearly interested.

Furtively watching their interaction, Kelsey tried to step back and look at them as people she didn't know. They didn't interact like a grandparent and grandchild, but it wasn't far from that. Marianne was the soul of patience with the kid, and Kelsey smiled when their little confab ended and she showed Poppy her scorecard. The kid was kneeling on her seat, leaning into Marianne's shoulder, avidly watching her make a notation on the card. A very old memory hit her, of Marianne doing the same thing with her. She could almost see it. They watched the Bucs on TV often, and always played a game where Kelsey would guess what to write in the little box after a play ended. She still recalled how thrilled she was when she got it right, as well as the effusive praise Marianne heaped on her.

She vaguely recalled that her mom loved baseball much more than her dad, but until that minute she'd had no memory of going to a game together. But they had to have. Her memory of sitting in the stands was so sharp! It all seemed to come back in a rush, and when the next batter hit a fly ball to the left fielder, Kelsey quietly said, "F7. Second out."

Marianne turned to face her, with their eyes locking for the first time that night. A sad smile filled her face, then she hurriedly looked back to her scorecard and filled it in. Without excusing herself, Kelsey jumped up and started to go up to the concourse just to get a moment alone. Then she remembered her manners, and doubled back to say, "I've got to hit the restroom."

"Take me!" Poppy yelped, scrambling over Summer to slap her hand into Kelsey's. She looked up at her with a smile on her angelic face. "Where we going?" Total trust. She knew, with scant evidence, that Kelsey would take care of her.

Kelsey had to stuff down tears, but she managed to speak. "We're just going to the rest room."

"Okay." They started to climb the stairs, and Kelsey heard the kid say quietly, "I bet there's a gift shop up there, too."

※

They stayed for the whole game, which seemed like fanaticism to Summer. When the score was nine to one, and everyone around you had left, couldn't you hit the road too?

Poppy was sound asleep on her lap, the cap Kelsey had bought her still on her head, but severely cockeyed. Even though Summer knew she only weighed about forty pounds, she grew heavier by the minute. Finally, some guy did something, and Marianne stood and let out a cheer, looking kind of thrilled. Kelsey also stood up and applauded for a long time, acting like she really cared. But that was weird, since she'd never watched a game in Summer's presence, and she'd never mentioned baseball. She clearly liked the Steelers, but nearly everyone did, so that made sense. But this was a surprising affinity.

Kelsey looked down and said, "Need some help getting up?"

"Love some. Can you pick her up? When she's out like this, she's dead weight."

"Pick her up? Like...how."

Before Summer could reply, Marianne stood and scooped the child up, cradling her in the approved fashion for lugging a dead-weight kid around. As she removed the cap, she put her face near Poppy's hair and gave it a sniff, smiling at Summer. "One of my favorite memories of parenting."

Kelsey watched her, stunned into silence. She had a memory—a crystal clear one—of lying against the rear door of a car. It was nighttime, and she'd been asleep. But she'd woken partially when they'd hit the driveway. She was in that liminal space, floating between wakefulness and sleep, and she chose to act like she was totally out. That had been a *choice*. She was sure of it.

Kelsey could hear her mom come to her door and quietly open it, then unfasten her seat belt. Without much trouble, she squatted down and lifted Kelsey from the car to carry her up to the house. The *Munhall* house. The small bungalow she had only snatches of memories of. Kelsey was too old to be carried, and she knew it. She must have been...six? Could that have been possible?

The memory was so strong, so precise, that it must have been real. She recalled cuddling up against her, wishing she was still a baby. Someone who was carried all of the time. Someone too little to possibly leave alone. When they reached the door, Marianne knocked. In just a moment, her dad was there, acting like he was accepting a package from a delivery service he had nothing but antipathy for. Kelsey had no memory of what he said, but she could feel her mom hold onto her a little more tightly. When her dad took over, she flopped into his arms, but that was only to keep up the ruse. She'd wanted to stay with her mom. She was sure of it. Absolutely sure of it. She'd *loved* her...

She realized she'd been staring when she felt Summer's arm wrap around her waist. "Okay?" she asked quietly.

"Yeah. Just having a memory." She turned her head slightly to meet Summer's concerned gaze. "A good one."

She stood aside, and Summer exited the row, with Marianne following behind her. Kelsey couldn't trust her voice, but she spoke anyway. "I know we watched baseball at home, but did you ever take me to a game? Just the two of us?"

"Given how you loved baseball?" she said, pressing her lips together. "I had some math activity books, and when you'd finished five of them, I'd take you to a game as a reward. You'd work on them so hard I could barely afford to keep up."

Nodding, Kelsey said, "I think I wanted to do something with you that dad wasn't into. That made me feel like we had something special." She was so glad Poppy was asleep. Kelsey truly didn't want to have to answer fifty questions about why she and the lady with the scorecard were both crying. "I think we did," she added, with her voice shaking roughly. Summer's arm was around her again, easily able to provide the comfort and security Kelsey needed. "We're getting somewhere," Kelsey said, feeling more confident than she'd ever been about this fragile relationship. "It might take a while, but I can be patient."

Summer pulled Kelsey toward her and kissed her cheek. "I can't be. That was the longest two and a half hours of my life. Who wants to buy me an ice cream cone as a reward for not falling asleep?"

"I do," Kelsey said, so pleased that Summer could inject a little lightness into nearly every situation. "Salted caramel for Marianne and me. The rest of you can pick whatever inferior flavors you like." She lightly put her hand on Marianne's back as they started down the stairs, offering just a little support. Being able to touch her casually freed Kelsey up in ways that continued to amaze her. They definitely had a long road to travel, but they'd made a damn fine start.

The End

By Susan X Meagher

Novels

Arbor Vitae
All That Matters
Cherry Grove
Girl Meets Girl
The Lies That Bind
The Legacy
Doublecrossed
Smooth Sailing
How To Wrangle a Woman
Almost Heaven
The Crush
The Reunion
Inside Out
Out of Whack
Homecoming
The Right Time
Summer of Love
Chef's Special
Fame
Vacationland
Wait For Me
The Keeper's Daughter
Friday Night Flights
Mosaic

Short Story Collection

Girl Meets Girl

Serial Novel

I Found My Heart In San Francisco

Awakenings: Book One
Beginnings: Book Two
Coalescence: Book Three
Disclosures: Book Four
Entwined: Book Five
Fidelity: Book Six
Getaway: Book Seven
Honesty: Book Eight
Intentions: Book Nine
Journeys: Book Ten
Karma: Book Eleven
Lifeline: Book Twelve
Monogamy: Book Thirteen
Nurture: Book Fourteen
Osmosis: Book Fifteen
Paradigm: Book Sixteen
Quandary: Book Seventeen
Renewal: Book Eighteen
Synchronicity: Book Nineteen
Trust: Book Twenty
United: Book Twenty-One
Vengeance: Book Twenty-Two
Wonder: Book Twenty-Three

Anthologies

Undercover Tales
Outsiders

You can contact Susan at Susan@briskpress.com

Information about all of Susan's books can be found at
www.susanxmeagher.com or www.briskpress.com

To receive notification of new titles, send an email to
newsletters@briskpress.com

facebook.com/susanxmeagher

twitter.com/susanx